Praise,

Highland Press Books!

THE CRYSTAL HEART *(by Katherine Deauxville) brims with ribald humor and authentic historical detail. Enjoy!*
~ *Virginia Henley*

* * *

THE SENSE OF HONOR by Ashley Kath-Bilsky has written an historical romance of the highest caliber. This reviewer was fesseled to the pages, fell in love with the hero and was cheering for the heroine all the way through. The plot is exciting and moves along at a good pace. The characters are multi-dimensional and the secondary characters bring life to the story. Sexual tension rages through this story and Ms. Kath-Bilsky gives her readers a breath-taking romance. The love scenes are sensual and very romantic. This reviewer was very pleased with how the author handled all the secrets. Sometimes it can be very frustrating for the reader when secrets keep tearing the main characters apart, but in this case, those secrets seem to bring them more together and both characters reacted very maturely when the secrets finally came to light. This reviewer is hoping that this very talented author will have another book out very soon.
~ *Valerie, Love Romances*

* * *

FAERY SPECIAL ROMANCES - Brilliantly magical! Ms. Rogers' special brand of humor and imagination will have you believing in faeries from page one. Absolutely enchanting!
- *Dawn Thompson, Author of The Ravencliff Bride*

* * *

REBEL HEART by Jannine Corti-Petska - Ms. Petska does an excellent job of all aspects of sharing this book with us. Ms. Petska used a myriad of emotions to tell this story and the reader (me) quickly becomes entranced in the ways Courtney's stubborn attitude works to her advantage in surviving this disastrous beginning to her new life. Ms. Petska's writings demand attention; she draws the reader to quickly become involved in this passionate story. This is a wonderful rendition of a different type which is a welcome addition to the historical romance genre. I believe that you will enjoy this story; I know I did!
~ *Brenda Talley, The Romance Studio*

* * *

IN SUNSHINE OR IN SHADOW by Cynthia Owens - If you adore the stormy heroes of 'Wuthering Heights' and 'Jane Eyre' (and who doesn't?) you'll be entranced by Owens' passionate story of Ireland after the Great Famine, and David Burke - a man from America with a hidden past and a secret name. Only one woman, the fiery, luscious Siobhan, can unlock the bonds that imprison him. Highly recommended for those who love classic romance and an action-packed story.

~ *Best Selling Author, Maggie Davis,*
AKA Katherine Deauxville

* * *

INTO THE WOODS by R.R. Smythe - This Young Adult Fantasy will send chills down your spine. I, as the reader, followed Callum and witnessed everything he and his friends went through as they attempted to decipher the messages. At the same time, I watched Callum's mother, Ellsbeth, as she walked through the Netherwood. Each time Callum deciphered one of the four messages, some villagers awakened. Through the eyes of Ellsbeth, I saw the other sleepers wander, make mistakes, and be released from the Netherwood, leaving Ellsbeth alone. There is one thread left dangling, but do not fret. This IS a stand alone book. But that thread gives me hope that another book about the Netherwoods may someday come to pass. Excellent reading for any age of fantasy fans!

~ *Detra Fitch, Huntress Reviews*

* * *

ALMOST TAKEN by Isabel Mere is a very passionate historical romance that takes the reader on an exciting adventure. The compelling characters of Deran Morissey, the Earl of Atherton, and Ava Fychon, a young woman from Wales, find themselves drawn together as they search for her missing siblings.

Readers will watch in interest as they fall in love and overcome obstacles. They will thrill in the passion and hope that they find happiness together. This is a very sensual romance that wins the heart of the readers. This is a creative and fast moving storyline that will enthrall readers. The character's personalities will fascinate readers and win their concern. Ava, who is highly spirited and stubborn, will win the respect of the readers for her courage and determination. Deran, who is rumored in the beginning to be an ice king, not caring about anyone, will prove how wrong people's perceptions can be. ***Almost Taken*** by Isabel Mere is an emotionally moving historical romance that I highly recommend to the readers.

~ *Anita, The Romance Studio*

* * *

PRETEND I'M YOURS by Phyllis Campbell is an exceptional masterpiece. This lovely story is so rich in detail and personalities that it just leaps out and grabs hold of the reader. From the moment I started reading about Mercedes and Katherine, I was spellbound. Ms. Campbell carries the reader into a mirage of mystery with deceit, betrayal of the worst kind, and a passionate love revolving around the sisters, that makes this a whirlwind page-turner. Mercedes and William are astonishing characters that ignite the pages and allows the reader to experience all their deepening sensations. There were moments I could share in with their breathtaking romance, almost feeling the butterflies of love they emitted. This extraordinary read had me mesmerized with its ambiance, its characters and its remarkable twists and turns, making it one recommended read in my book.

~ *Linda L., Fallen Angel Reviews*

* * *

RECIPE FOR LOVE - I don't think the reader will find a better compilation of mouth watering short romantic love stories than in RECIPE FOR LOVE! This is a highly recommended volume –
perfect for beaches, doctor's offices, or anywhere you've a few minutes to read.

~ *Marilyn Rondeau, Reviewers International Organization*

* * *

Christmas is a magical time and twelve talented authors answer the question of what happens when ***CHRISTMAS WISHES*** come true in this incredible anthology.

Christmas Wishes shows just how phenomenal a themed anthology can be. Each of these highly skilled authors brings a slightly different perspective to the Christmas theme to create a book that is sure to leave readers satisfied. What a joy to read such splendid stories! This reviewer looks forward to more anthologies by Highland Press as the quality is simply astonishing.

~ *Debbie, CK2S Kwips and Kritiques*

(*One story in this anthology was nominated for the Gayle Wilson Award of Excellence*)

* * *

HOLIDAY IN THE HEART - Twelve stories that would put even Scrooge into the Christmas spirit. It does not matter what *type* of romance genre you prefer. This book has a little bit of everything. The stories are set in the U.S.A. and Europe. Some take place in the past, some in the present, and one story takes place in both! I strongly suggest that you put on something comfortable, brew up something hot (tea, coffee or cocoa will do), light up a fire, settle down somewhere quiet and begin reading this anthology.

~ *Detra Fitch, Huntress Reviews*

* * *

BLUE MOON MAGIC is an enchanting collection of short stories. Each author wrote with the same theme in mind but each story has its own uniqueness. You should have no problem finding a tale to suit your mood. *BLUE MOON MAGIC* offers historicals, contemporaries, time travel, paranormal, and futuristic narratives to tempt your heart.

Legend says that if you wish with all your heart upon the rare blue moon, your wishes were sure to come true. Each of the heroines discovers this magical fact. True love is out there if you just believe in it. In some of the stories, love happens in the most unusual ways. Angels may help, ancient spells may be broken, anything can happen. Even vampires will find their perfect mate with the power of the blue moon. Not every heroine believes they are wishing for love, some are just looking for answers to their problems or nagging questions. Fate seems to think the solution is finding the one who makes their heart sing.

BLUE MOON MAGIC is a perfect read for late at night or even during your commute to work. The short yet sweet stories are a wonderful way to spend a few minutes. If you do not have the time to finish a full-length novel, but hate stopping in the middle of a loving tale, I highly recommend grabbing this book.

~ *Kim Swiderski, Writers Unlimited Reviewer*

* * *

Legend has it that a blue moon is enchanted. What happens when fifteen talented authors utilize this theme to create enthralling stories of love?

BLUE MOON ENCHANTMENT is a wonderful, themed anthology filled with phenomenal stories by fifteen extraordinarily talented authors. Readers will find a wide variety of time periods and styles showcased in this superb anthology. *BLUE MOON ENCHANTMENT* is sure to offer a little bit of something for everyone!
~ *Debbie, CK²S Kwips and Kritiques*

* * *

NO LAW AGAINST LOVE - If you have ever found yourself rolling your eyes at some of the more stupid laws, then you are going to adore this novel. Over twenty-five stories fill up this anthology, each one dealing with at least one stupid or outdated law. Let me give you an example: In Florida, USA, there is a law that states "If an elephant is left tied to a parking meter, the parking fee has to be paid just as it would for a vehicle." In Great Britain, "A license is required to keep a lunatic." Yes, you read those correctly. No matter how many times you go back and reread them, the words will remain the same. Those two laws are still legal. The tales vary in time and place. Some take place in the present, in the past, in the USA, in England... in other words, there is something for everyone! Best yet, profits from the sales of this novel go to breast cancer prevention.

A stellar anthology that had me laughing, sighing in pleasure, believing in magic, and left me begging for more! Will there be a second anthology someday? I sure hope so! This is one novel that will go directly to my 'Keeper' shelf, to be read over and over again. Very highly recommended!
~ *Detra Fitch, Huntress Reviews*

Cat O'Nine Tales

Deborah MacGillivray

Highland Press Publishing

A Wee Dram Imprint

Cat O'Nine Tales

For information, please contact
Highland Press Publishing,
PO Box 2292, High Springs, FL 32655.
www.highlandpress.org

ISBN: 9780978713904

PUBLISHED BY HIGHLAND PRESS PUBLISHING

A Wee Dram Book

Dedicated to the 'herd' of my heart:
Stuff, Gydney, Clloydd,
Pokey, D.C., Bigger, Biff (Lacey),
Sweetums, Alfie, Ian-Michael,
Seymour, Jeep, Auggie Moggie,
MsShane, Spike, Harry Orwell,
Mickey, Laurel, Scout, and Mary Jane

and especially...
Foutchie

also, to all the homeless babies...may
you find a place in someone's heart

and

Monika and Ballou (the doggie!)
Dober, Kelly and Brandy
Leanne and Tigger
Dawn and Mizz Fuzz

Table of Contents

Bad Cat

RIO Award of Excellence Winner 2006 –
Best Short Story from an Anthology

• *Destin, Florida — Any dog or cat, which attacks and bites a person or another animal without provocation, shall be deemed a 'bad dog' or 'bad cat' and the owner or custodian of such animal shall pay a civil penalty of one hundred dollars...*

Present Day

"That is *not* a cat. That's a pit bull with fur!"

Ian St. Giles stood nose-to-nose with the sexy redhead, both of them leaning over the smiling cat. He never knew cats smiled. Actually, it wasn't a smile—the bloody beast *smirked*.

Ian enjoyed cats, but this one he could really grow to *hate*. Unfortunately, Katlyn Mackenzie adored the ridiculous creature, which was one-quarter Scottish Wildcat. Likely the only person on God's green earth—in this case Destin, Florida—who did. This *pony-sized* menace turned over trashcans, knocked-up half the female pussycats in a ten block radius, chased people down the sidewalk as they passed Katlyn's house and terrorized the town's dogs. From day one, after Katlyn moved into her great aunt's beachfront property, Destin hadn't been safe.

Just last week, Auggie Moggie shredded the ear of Molly Mays' toy poodle. Granted, he hated that dog even more, so he sniggered when the annoying poodle ran into Freddy Krueger in a fur coat...hmm...Katlyn's *darling*.

"There's a city ordinance against *bad* cats. You can be fined, you know," Ian warned.

Eyes flashing, the sexy woman in the black lycra bathing suit fired back, "Is there an ordinance against grouchy neighbors?"

Ian pointed at The Cat Auggie. "That beast is a menace. I've been over here every day this week to complain about his antics."

As he stared at the longhaired, grey-striped tabby, with the half-white face, it finally hit him—Katlyn wore a swimsuit. It left *nothing* to his imagination. Evidently, she'd been tanning in the backyard before he interrupted with his latest complaint. She was sun-kissed pink and a sheen of perspiration coated her silken skin.

The black suit had a deep scooped-neck front and high, French-cut legs that went *all the way up* to her hipbones. He hadn't seen the back view yet, but figured it was barely there, close to a thong. The stretchy material may as well be spray-painted on!

His mouth watered and his groin achingly throbbed to life. A state he'd found himself in with increasing frequency since she'd moved into the house next door to his. Worse, it played seven kinds of havoc with his writing.

Her magnificent auburn mane hung in a braid over one shoulder and down to her waist. Hair like that sent a man into overdrive. Ian imagined it spread on a pillow as he drove his body into hers. Nearly groaning, he pressed back the urge rising within him to play caveman, snatch that long hair and haul her off to his cave—er, house.

Ian had been delighted to meet his new neighbor when he stopped by to act as *Welcome Wagon* three weeks ago. It was nice to hear another British accent in the midst of these Floridians. Gave them the first thread of commonality. Quite delightfully, the air crackled with sexual tension whenever they were near. The impact she had on his senses was electric, magic.

He'd rented the beach property for the summer to get a feel for the setting of his latest crime novel, an eye on his looming deadline. Only, every day that bloody beast sneaked into his house and stole something, dragging him away from his work. Today, the wee monster from Hell slipped inside while Ian carried in groceries. Auggie helped himself to a New York Strip steak and scampered off with it like a bandit.

How the hell was he to meet his deadline with the distraction of mouth-watering Katlyn Mackenzie and her demon pussycat creating mayhem for his mind and libido?

While he *really* craved to lure Katlyn into his bed, this feline varmint saw Kat and he remained at loggerheads over Auggie's behavior. *Or lack of it.*

"Bad neighbor? How about turning that pony with fangs and claws loose on this poor, unsuspecting town? He just ate seven bucks worth of prime New York Strip. I think feeding the cat my supper goes beyond the call of being a good neighbor."

"Auggie," she put her hands on her hips, looking down at the cat with a frown, "did you steal the man's steak?"

The cat blinked up at her with an innocent face.

Ian expected a halo and wings to materialize any second. "Oh yeah, the little demon's going to admit his criminal ways. Look at him. He's *not* a cat. He should be playing Nose Guard for the *Chicago Bears.*"

Katlyn sniffed disdain—*at him.* "Obviously, Mr. St. Giles, you're *not* a cat person."

"Auggie's *not* a cat," he repeated. "I don't care what he's told you. Will Smith and Tommy Lee Jones are looking for him."

"Well, follow me." She sighed, then turned on her heels.

The blasted cat sniggered at him. Ian balled up his fist and held it to the cat in silent threat, going into a Jackie Gleason imitation. "*Pow...zooooom*, Alice!"

"Auggie, ignore the bad man!" she called over her shoulder.

Ian had trouble drawing air as he caught the full view of that next-to-nothing swimsuit as Auggie and he trailed after Katlyn. With feline sensual grace, Kat crossed the yard and climbed the steps of the deck, heading to the backdoor. Auggie bounded behind her as if his legs were pogo sticks. Rather amazing considering his *tonnage*, but Ian spared little attention for the comical sight. His eyes were glued on the inch-wide strap that followed her spine and the itsy-bitsy, teeny-weenie, black triangle dead center on those two glorious orbs.

What an arse! His hands *itched* to grab it. He wondered what she'd do if he broke into a wolf howl. She'd certainly have divine tan lines—ones he'd loved to explore with his tongue.

So intent on watching those magnificent curves, he tripped on Auggie. The cat squalled as if Ian smooshed him flat. *Deliberately.*

"Oh, poor Auggie Moggie. Did the bad man hurt you?" she crooned, bending down to pet the feline on his head. The cat flashed Ian a look that said, *nanabooboo.*

Ian suspected Auggie tossed himself under his feet just to

make sure he came across as *Snidely Whiplash* in Kat's eyes.

As he stared at her bent over at the waist, he just wanted to grab hold of those rounded hips and take her from that position. Blood left his brain in a whoosh, heading south. He rubbed his forehead in pain. "Aspirins," the dazed word came from his mouth.

Kat raised up and gazed at him with concern. "You have an ache?"

"Hmmm, yeah...I've got...*an ache,*" he mumbled disjointedly.

Long, black lashes batted over the huge brown eyes, then they traced over his body and returned to his face. "Maybe too much sun? I wanted to tan, but the sun was making me woozy." She opened the refrigerator and took out a pitcher of lemonade. "This should do the trick."

She handed him a tumbler, then ambled down the hall. It afforded Ian another chance to view that perfect derrière as it moved with a dancer's grace and sensuality.

He leaned back against the counter afraid his legs wouldn't hold him. "Mercy."

Returning with her purse, she held out her hand. Like an idiot, he just stared. Her front view was as devastating. Oh, boy, how he wanted to yank down the top of that swimsuit and fondle those full breasts until she writhed and keened with a raspy need.

He realized she held something out to him. Opening his hand, she dropped two aspirins in his palm. Figuring they couldn't hurt, he popped them in his mouth and washed them down with the tart lemon drink.

Katlyn opened her purse and removed a five and two-ones. "Here. Auggie shouldn't have filched the steak. Auggie, tell the man you're sorry."

Auggie rubbed against his leg, almost contritely, then his tail vibrated as if he was going to spray. "Don't even think about it, you menace from Mars."

"You really don't like cats, do you?"

Her tone said, *such a shame, for otherwise I'd find you attractive.* Instantly, the urge possessed Ian to grab Auggie up and do nose rubs. "I like cats. Auggie isn't remotely like a cat."

She waved the bills under his nose. "Take them."

"What for?" Ian blinked blankly, drowning in her hypnotic eyes. He wondered what she'd do if he grabbed her and kissed her—*long and hard.*

"The steak."

"I don't want your money," he growled. *I want you.*

"Auggie stole your meat. If you won't let me repay you, permit me to cook for you."

Both his head and Auggie's snapped back. "You're offering to fix me supper?"

Her witchy eyes flashed. "Seems fair. I have a couple steaks." She wagged her finger at the feline. "And Auggie, Bad Cat, doesn't get a bite."

"When?"

"Tonight? Seven o'clock?" she queried, with a come-hither smile.

Ian nodded. "Done." He felt like sticking out his tongue and going *nanabooboo* at Auggie.

She put the bills back into her purse. "See you then."

Sensing dismissal, he sat down the glass. "Thanks for aspirins and the lemon squash."

His hand was on the doorknob when she called. "Bloody shame you hate cats."

"I don't hate them, just have...a *personality conflict* with that *thing* you call a pussycat." His eyes danced over her sexy body as she stood, leisurely unbraiding her long hair. "Why would it be a shame if I hated cats?"

With a mysterious smile, she shrugged her elegant shoulders. "Love me, love my pussy...cat."

Ian missed the step down onto the deck and nearly broke his ankle.

The woman was a bloody menace! *Mind out of the gutter, St. Giles. You've only been away from the British Isles three months. You haven't forgotten a pussy is a cat in Britain, not the other connotation Yanks used.* Since she was from Scotland, she used it in the Brit mien, though he judged she was perfectly aware of the American usage and did it just to push his buttons.

Well, they say pets take after their masters. *Bad Kat.* He struggled to hide the pole-axed expression as he slowly stalked to her. Invading her space, he let her feel his heat. And, oh brother, was he hot! The little witch had no one to blame but herself for playing with fire. Standing in that next to nothing swimsuit, unwinding that bewitching mane, she'd deliberately provoked him. The predator within him growled.

Realizing she pushed one button too many, she backed up.

Until she hit the refrigerator.

Putting a hand on either side of her shoulders, he grinned, pinning her. Playing Big Bad Wolf was entertaining. She sucked in a deep breath and held, shrinking back from him. That just lifted those perfect, grapefruit-sized breasts up closer to his face. It required all his remaining willpower not to gobble her up in three bites.

"Oh yeah, I figured if a man loved you, he'd just adore your pussy...cat." He leaned his body toward hers, yet not touching. His every muscle clenched as her tongue swiped her dry lips. "What's wrong? Cat got your tongue? Pity that, lass. Tongues...can...be...so...*useful*."

He saw the pulse in her graceful throat throb, pounding out arousal. Wanted to feast on that vibrancy. As she stared, hypnotized by his scent, his closeness, he saw the skittishness shift. Deep hunger flared in her golden-brown eyes.

"Hmm...maybe we could...*discuss* that over supper."

Ian arched a brow. "Can we lock the tubby tabby terror outside? I'm sure he'll entertain himself menacing the Hood. After all, he's already eaten din-din."

"Oh, Auggie Moggie vets my dates. Weeds out the short-hitters." Her laughter was musical, something you'd expect to hear from a faery.

Ian chuckled. "Bet he does. Also weeds out the dog population and maybe small farm animals, too. Remember, if he bites me it's a hundred dollar fine."

She snaked her arms around his neck and nipped his lower lip. "And what if this Kat bites you?"

"Name your price, woman, I'll pay." His hands grabbed her waist and pulled her hard against him, relishing the perfection of how their bodies fit. Just as he lowered his head to kiss her senseless, the alarm on his Rolex sounded. With a groan, he bonked his forehead against hers. "We'll have to discuss *price* later. Sorry, lass, I have a conference call with my publisher and agent in five minutes. Gotta dash, luv."

He made it to the door, then jogged back, grabbed her and kissed Kat hard and quick. "To whet your appetite. I'd like my steak medium-rare and my woman as intoxicating as Highland Single-Malt Whisky."

Kat watched the sexy man dash across their yards to his house. She couldn't contain her sigh. Ian St. Giles was everything a woman could want. Precisely, what *she* wanted.

Not too tall—a shade under six-foot—he wasn't the bulky muscle of a jock that often lacked real strength behind it.

Lean hard bodies really pack the power. Elegant men were deceptive, as people didn't notice just how strong they were. Ian St. Giles may be a writer, spending long hours at the keyboard, but there wasn't an ounce of flab on him. From her bedroom window, she'd often watched the black-haired man doing laps in the pool in his backyard. Those beautiful arms sliced through the water as if he could keep up that pace for hours.

Arms she kept seeing in her mind curved over her head as he pistoned his body into hers—as though he could keep up that pace for hours, too. Each day brought them closer to that reality.

Thanks to Auggie.

She sniggered, wondering when Ian would twig Auggie was horribly bright and fetched on command. A cautious lass, she didn't want Ian for a night, a week or a month—she wanted to bewitch him, sex him, drive him wild until they were old and grey.

"I think he likes us, Auggie. I like him. Oh, do I like him." She watched as Ian entered his house and the door closed. "Think we can make him love us?"

Ian sat listening to the two women nattering over the speakerphone. *That's what I get for having a female editor and agent.* After seventeen bestsellers, both these harridans wanted his hard-boiled, Sam Spade-style character to get *warm and fuzzy.* He listened to them reciting statistics, how sixty-five percent of all books sold were geared for the women's market. They had it in their mercenary little brains that he needed to buck the trend, and in a field dominated by women writers, pen his current crime drama with a heavy dose of romance and erotica.

"Ian, it's called *Romantica...*" Maggie Caldwell, his agent explained.

In a conference call with the two women, he was redundant.

"Leave it to women to muck up erotica with romance," he muttered to the fat cat, dancing in place on his desk and purring louder than a diesel engine. He swiveled in the chair to make sure he'd closed the door. Still shut. He wondered how the Moggie Monster slipped in again.

"Ian, you have asthma?" Jess Black, his editor, queried.

Ian frowned at the cat. "No, just a big furball."

"Furball?" both women echoed puzzlement.

"Never mind." He reached to pet the cat. The stupid thing tried to bite him. He shook a finger at Auggie and earned two more snaps. "Your mistress may bite me all she wants, Cat. You sink fangs into me, you're charbroiled pussycat."

He groaned, *pussycat* summoning images of his near brush at sex with Kat in the kitchen. He adjusted his aroused male anatomy, his black jeans suddenly too tight for comfort.

"Ian, do you have company? Are you listening to us?" Maggie demanded.

"I'm listening. You want me to change the book so it'll pick up women readers. You want hot sex, laced with romance," he repeated, glaring at Auggie who now gnawed on the mouse cord. He snatched the mouse away from him. "It's not a real one, Buster."

Jess asked suspiciously, "Who are you talking to, Ian?"

"A cat named Auggie."

"Oh, Ian, a cat! How delightful you got a pet. Now *that's* what we're talking about with your character. Tanner Descoin needs to stretch emotionally. He's been this freelance investigator for years. While the stories are sharp, Tanner's stagnant. He needs to grow."

"Did Archie and Nero *grow*?" Ian grumbled. "*I think not.*"

"Today, Ian, the big money's waiting for the man who delivers what women want. If you deliver a hot romance, from a man's point of view, we could push you into this new market. Double your sales practically overnight. Jackson's ready to shoot the cover. *Check & Mate* is the title—"

Ian snorted a small laugh. "Thanks for telling me the name of *my* book."

She went on as if he hadn't commented, outlining plans with the full-steam ahead of a runaway locomotive. "Descoin is in half-shadow, a sexy long-haired blonde just behind him, her arm around him, her long red nails stroking his chest. Descoin meets his match and tumbles hard."

"Redhead," Ian growled.

"What?" both women chimed.

"I said make her a redhead," he insisted.

"Okay, redhead. The cat is an interesting touch, too. Perhaps you can work a kitty into the plotline. Let Tanner mature. Find love, fall in love. Maybe she can help him on his cases, be an equal. You've got to have lots of steamy sex, Ian."

"Amen to that, sister." Ian chuckled.

Maggie's question carried a note of doubt. "Think you can do that, Ian? This is a new direction. Are the prose in you?"

Ian's eyes flicked to the computer screen. Auggie was on top of the monitor with an arm hanging over, batting at Ian as he leaned forward. His eyes scanned the words on the page.

> *...he trembled as he went down on his knees before her, an acolyte ready to worship at the altar of her body. Instead of the reverence that humbled him before her, he reached out and took, rolling her distended nipples until she moaned. Her head lolled back, the mass of auburn hair cascading down to her hips...*

Ian cleared his throat and shifted before his arousal had a zipper impression on it. "Um...well...so happens I started this little project. Perhaps the two can be... uh...*merged*."

"Marvelous!"

"Wonderful!"

The two women carried on their discussion about marketing, release date, dare they advertise in *Romance Writers of America* magazine? Their chattering faded into the background as he dodged Auggie's fat leg waving to swat at him.

The power of his words held him.

He couldn't sleep last night. Tossing and turning, two cold showers, and yet he still throbbed with the driving urge to mate with Katlyn. Obsession full blown. He'd stared at her bedroom window, willing her to come to it. When that failed, he ambled to the keyboard thinking to work. He couldn't write about Tanner. He could only see Katlyn before him. Him making love to her in every fashion imaginable. His fingers started typing and the words poured from his soul-deep hunger.

As he'd written the words, he understood he wanted more from this woman than just a hot affair for the next month while he stayed in Florida finishing his book. When he left come August, he wanted Kat to go back to England with him.

"Can you make these changes and still hit the target deadline?"

Jess intruded on his daydreams of Kat being in his bed, her body moving over him in a pagan rhythm. That mass of hair curtaining her shoulders and back, tickling him. He groaned as he realized with the length of her hair, it'd fan across his thighs, brushing in whispery, silken caresses as she rode him hard.

He choked on his parched throat. "Um...deadline...yeah... it's doable." He needed to shower and shave. Glancing at his watch—just enough time if he hustled.

"You'll get a couple of the love scenes roughed out and fax them to us next week so we can see if you're hitting target?" Jess suggested.

"Um...certainly." His eyes caught the light come on in Katlyn's upstairs bathroom.

"Super!" Maggie and Jess chimed like magpies.

Ian wondered if Kat knew her bloody bathroom was about 50% visible from his bathroom. *Time to move location, St Giles. Showtime.* "Uh...maybe make that...two weeks."

Kat appeared dead center of the window and peeled out of that black suit. The witch did a striptease for him. *Someone shoot me quick and put me out of my misery!*

"This is...a new direction...I'll need time...get in tune with ...*things*. Catch you two later. Don't do anything I wouldn't do."

Which left everything under the sun. He smiled at the cat. "I'm a man with plans, Auggie."

Ian and Auggie pulled up in the midnight blue Jaguar XJ to find the Destin police parked in Katlyn's drive. Ian and the cat looked at each other, silently asking what the other knew about this development.

After Ian had hurriedly showered, he grabbed his keys to the Jag, knowing he could reach the florist before they closed. Auggie had trailed right behind him. He nearly knocked Ian's legs out from under him as he bounded into the car, clearly going with him. Ignoring the command to decamp, Auggie sat in the passenger's seat as if he rode in cars all the time. "You claw my leather bucket seats, I'll hogtie you and let Mrs. Mays' poodle chew on your ear."

Ian had reached the flower shop as it closed and pur- chased a gorgeous bouquet of two dozen yellow long-stem roses. Stopping at the liquor store, he intended to buy a bottle of blush Chablis. Instead, he spotted a three-hundred-dollar bottle of Glenlivet Scotch. Anyone could bring wine. He figured the straight path to his Scots lass' heart would be with a wee dram of Scotland's finest. Confident his choices would please Kat, he rushed back, arriving fifteen minutes early.

"Auggie, appears this is one of those occasions where being early won't ruffle the hostess." The cat sat innocently.

"What say, pal, you stay safely in the car while I suss out what's up with Destin's finest..."

Auggie dashed across his lap as he opened the door and beelined for Katlyn on the deck. Ian saw Kat waving her arms at the policemen, her expression riled. One of the uniformed men swiped at Auggie as if to grab him. "Uh oh, *not* good," Ian muttered, as Katlyn stepped between the feline and the officer.

Ian approached in cool fashion, though he was anything but. Katlyn stood shaking and wore the expression of a mother lioness defending her cub.

"Evening, Officers. Anything I can do for you?" Ian moved to stand beside Katlyn, hoping she'd calm now that he was here.

"We came about the cat—" one started.

"Ian, they want to take Auggie with them. He'd be terrified. They can't have him." She trembled worse.

"Auggie's not going anywhere." Ian fixed both men with a level stare, silently telling them he *meant* what he said. "What seems to be the problem?"

"Mrs. Mays filed a complaint. Said that cat," the taller man pointed at Auggie who'd gone into his cherub-with-halo-and-wings routine, "bit her."

"Unless Miz Mackenzie can produce proof the cat had rabies shots he'll have to be quarantined," the man's partner clarified.

"Auggie doesn't have rabies," Ian stated, daring either man to contradict him.

"We need papers proving that. Auggie has been deemed a *bad* cat."

Kat swiped away a tear. "I don't have papers. I misplaced them in the move. If they call the vet's office, he'll confirm Auggie has all his shots. It's just until morn."

"I'm sorry, Miz Mackenzie, but a complaint has been lodged."

"When did Auggie *bite* Mrs. Mays—the lady with the poodle that *attacked* Auggie last week, I presume?" Ian challenged.

The two exchanged glances. "Yeah, she has a toy poodle."

"Irritating thing," the shorter one chimed.

"Something we can agree on, Officer. I believe if you check the ordinance you'll note it says, '*Any dog or cat, which attacks and bites a person or another animal without provocation, shall be deemed a bad dog or bad cat and the owner or custodian of such animal shall pay a civil penalty of one hundred dollars.'* I judge that stupid poodle gnawing on Auggie's hind leg would fall under *provocation.*"

Ian put his hand on Kat's back and gently rubbed, hoping to soothe her fears. Auggie twined against the back of Ian's legs, peeking around his left calf. Silly feline knew Ian stood as his champion, ready to do battle for him.

"So when did Auggie bite the biddy?" he pressed. "Maybe we should take Auggie to the vet and have him examined. Might make him sick."

The shorter one sniggered, only to fall silent at the glare from his by-the-book partner. When the other man quieted, he answered Ian. "About forty-five minutes ago. Said she was walking the toy dog near the end of the block when Auggie jumped out and bit her."

"Did you see the bite marks?" Ian disputed.

There was a hesitation. "Well, no...but her hand is bandaged."

"I'd go back and demand to see her hand. Then I'd inform her it's against the law to file false charges. Auggie was with me for the last four hours. He was here with us until four p.m. Then I went home to take a conference call from my agent and editor. They can attest to the cat making noises and purring in the background. After that, I showered. He rested on the bathroom floor and shredded a box of Kleenex. When I drove into town, Auggie rode with me. We stopped at the florist's before six. The florist will recall. She commented on Auggie following me about. About a half hour later we stopped at the liquor store. Jake Wilson laughed at Auggie in the car window waving his paw. Pray tell, how was Auggie supposed to bite some dried up troublemaker when he was in the car with me the whole time?"

Auggie wiggled as if he knew he was off the hook. He'd abandoned his angel mode for his *nanabooboo* face.

"Officers, if that's all...Kat, Auggie and I are grilling out this evening. Sorry, you had a trip out here for nothing."

The two officers nodded and started to turn.

"I believe you meant to say you're sorry for upsetting, Miss Mackenzie," Ian prodded.

Both mumbled an apology, then shuffled off. Auggie started pogo-ing around the deck sideways and hissing at the officers. Ian reached down and grabbed him by the scruff of his neck. "Don't push it, Auggie-nator."

Katlyn threw her arms around his neck and planted a

noisy kiss on his lips. Giving a small hop, she wrapped her legs around his waist and proceeded to kiss him senseless. Dropping Auggie, Ian put one hand at the small of her back and one on that sexy derrière and shifted, so she didn't pull them off balance.

With one foot, he pushed Auggie into the house, then swung Kat and himself inside and kicked the door shut.

He'd wanted to give her yellow roses and share a toast of Glenlivet under the moonlight. He planned to make the night special, then he'd let Kat lead him inside and welcome him into her bed, her life.

Scratch plan A. They'd *never* make it to midnight, doubted they'd make it to the bloody bed. Kat already lost the playful euphoria, and downshifted into rabid arousal with the force of lightning striking. Spiraling pheromones now blinded them with need.

With his remaining vestige of sanity, his poor beleaguered, bloodless, male brain searched *desperately* for the nearest safe spot to land. Kat yanked at his shirt, breathing as hard as he. Buttons popped and ricocheted against the walls as she tugged it from his slacks. Kat's legs loosened. She slid slowly down him, ending with her long nails raking over his painful erection and then along his thighs.

*So much for looking for a convenient spot—*his last sane thought as she pressed her face against his thigh, rubbing like a cat. He barely undid the slide hook on his black pants before she had the zipper down, raking her long nails down the turgid length of his flesh.

He about lost it—then and there.

Damn woman! She was out to torture him. Ian's blood thundered through his body as he fought to keep from passing out. "Yes...damn..." he panted. "Oh Kat...my Kat...my *bad* Kat."

Shaking, he grabbed her arms and pulled her up, as he went down, unable to stand. On his knees—and still mostly in his pants—he slid his hands up those smooth thighs, then under the skirt to those globes of her firm arse. He smiled wickedly as he felt she wore thongs. *"Bad Kat."*

He spread her legs, pulling her to straddle him as he rolled to his back. Shifting the panties aside, he smoothed his fingers over her sensitized opening, drenched with her body's arousal. She was so wet. The scent clouded his brain. Shifting the thong aside, he yanked her down hard on his aroused flesh, filled her with one, hard stroke. Damn she was tight, fisting around him with a power that blew his mind.

He shifted her so her knees straddled his hips, but that movement sent her to shuddering. Kat came apart with a force that saw her internal ripples vice around him, the shudders snaking down his flesh in waves.

Unable to hold back, Ian shattered in a thousand red-hot pieces.

Head spinning, he tried to focus. Shaking, he rolled them over and pulled her to spoon against him. "Well, bugger. Sorry, lass, don't think I've ever been so out of control. I bought yellow roses and thirty-year-old Glenlivet. Wanted tonight to be special."

"It *is* special." She turned and kissed him softly. "You rescued Auggie. My hero."

He laughed, full of joy. "Well, this promises to be a happy life. My agent and editor want me to write Romantica, though they feel I need help with my *research*."

She rubbed her head in the curve of his shoulder. "Um...I can *help* with *research*."

"Since Auggie is continually in one bother or another, I guess I'll be playing hero on a regular basis."

"And I'll be *rewarding* you regularly."

She rolled and planted a kiss to his chest. "Ian..."

"Hmmm."

"I have a confession. Auggie is a very bright cat. Brighter than any cat I've ever seen. Watch." She raised up on one elbow to see Auggie sitting on the chair. "Auggie, fetch."

When Auggie just looked at her, Ian laughed. "Teach you."

"He's being Auggie." She snapped her fingers. "Auggie, go get my car keys."

He sat, unmoving for a minute, then scampered off. Bouncing on his pogo-stick legs, he returned, the keys jangling from his mouth. He dropped them on the center of Ian's chest.

"Auggie, fetch my hair brush," Katlyn commanded.

Again, the cat dashed off. After a small wait, he came in with a brush, dropping it next to the keys. He sat and pushed out his chest, proud of his accomplishments.

Kat leaned over Ian to give Auggie a pat. "Good Auggie."

Ian caught the wrist of her arm and towed her across his body. "You're telling me when Auggie stole things he wasn't being a general pain in the arse, he was on a mission?"

"Sorry. In a way Auggie has been playing cupid for me."

"So you just *happened* to be in that sexy swimsuit after Auggie stole my steak."

"I have to admit what Auggie stole each time was his selection. I didn't say steal your steak."

"What did you say?"

She leaned forward and nipped his chin. "I said, *Auggie fetch Ian.*"

He shifted, rolling her under him and pinning her arms over her head as he drove himself into her slick, welcoming warmth. "Hmmmm, *Bad Kat.*"

She arched up, meeting his every thrust, sending him out of control. His body splintered from a force he'd never experienced. He smiled ferally as he figured this was the first of many new experiences with this woman. Gasping, he tried to keep his heaviness from pressing Kat into the hardwood floor, but she snaked her arms about his chest and pulled him against her, obviously relishing his weight.

"You're not angry with Auggie and me?"

Panting, he laughed. "What can I say?" He reached up and patted Auggie who danced just above Kat's head. "I love you, love your pussy...cat—and will for the rest of my life."

Auggie meowed, seconding that.

Getting It In The End

• *York, England - Excluding Sundays, it's perfectly legal to shoot a Scotsman with a bow and arrow*

Present day, York

"Why don't you shoot me? It'd be more humane!"

James Douglas Kinloch heard those words echo in his brain the past two weeks, though most writers would insist a brain couldn't echo. Still ticked, he was prepared to argue the point of creative license. He'd meant those words when he tossed them at his boss Murray, editor-in-chief for *Money & Trends* magazine, after he'd been assigned to cover a Writers' Renfaire in York, England.

As he surveyed the pandemonium around him, he saw *no* reason to retract them.

These were writers, he should feel at home with them. He penned a monthly column on books and contributed to *M & T's* reviews section. Nevertheless, in this case misery did *not* love company.

These were Romance writers. *Another breed of wordsmith entirely,* he'd learnt.

Amazingly, women were responsible for sixty-five percent of books sold in the world, virtually financing publishing houses to stay afloat on their efforts alone. He understood why *Money & Trends* sent someone to cover the gathering. *Only why him?*

Accepting there was no reversing his boss' edict, he'd done his homework and learned a lot about the power these females wielded, how often the male bastions of fiction writers—jealous of the higher incomes—mocked them. He'd come prepared to have a male ego adjustment and accept these women for the dynamos they were, give them their professional dues. Having sampled dozens of the genre since taking up *M & T's* bookbeat, he admitted they were as talented in their craft as their male counterparts. Maybe more so. He approached the forthcoming article, planning to portray them in the professional light they fully earned.

Then he landed in the middle of this weeklong madness.

First Annual York Historical Romance Writers Renaissance Faire.

He glared at the huge banner strung across the fairway entrance, then sighed. "What a mouthful."

These mothers, wives and lovers—even grandmothers— seized the chance to kick loose and let down their hair. *Oh, mama, did they ever let down their hair!*

His tush was tender from the grab-arsing going on. Any good-looking male became a target for their *turnabout's-fair-play.* Male models, historians, re-enactors and servers were ogled, teased, tormented—and pinched—as the ladies fair let it rip. They were having a high time and it was only the first day!

This week was going to be a *long* one. He considered putting in for hazardous duty pay.

Getting into the spirit of things, most wore period dress. Queens, scullery maids, Scottish lasses and even female warriors flooded the grounds of the two-thousand-acre *Majestic Park Hotel.* Once, William Wallace had laid siege to York. While he wasn't a descendant from Wallace, James began to feel he now paid for all Scottish transgressions against the ancient city.

The faire was a chance for the women to meet their fans, but it was also an opportunity to do hands-on research. They could learn to buckle their swashes, try a hand at jousting, handling a claymore or give the English Longbow a go to strengthen their writing.

So far, the only *hands-on* he'd experienced was on his arse!

Gaggles of giggles alerted him to the approach of marauding females, so he darted around a huge tent to dodge another gauntlet of bum-pinching.

Peeking around the edge of the canvas pavilion, intent on hiding from the bawdy wenches, James backed up as their voices neared. Focused on saving his tender backside, he failed to pay attention where he was going. Turning another tent corner, he crashed into a body.

Putting hands out to stop his fall, one closed over a full,

round breast, the other on a curvy hip. *Female.* As he attempted to prevent himself from crashing to the ground, their feet caught on the pegs of the tent. Spinning around the taught lines, they went down in a tangle of arms, legs and a mass of honey-coloured hair.

He landed on his arse—hard—with her on top of him, air whooshing from his lungs. That sweet curve of her pelvis rode perfectly over his groin as she straddled him, a white-jeaned knee on either side of his hips. He'd enjoy the position if he hadn't been nearly writhing in agony.

Vision spun as he fought the urge to puke. With her planted on top of him, he couldn't raise up. Blawing wasn't an option! He'd end up drowning in his own vomit. His mind could see the headlines in the papers now—*Man dies in hurling accident.* And they wouldn't mean in the game *Hurling* either!

His assailant wiggled her derrière against his thighs, then tried to flip that mass of hair from out of her face.

"Bugger," the sexy voice muttered.

The sort of voice that made James think of fine Highland whisky, silk sheets and late nights. Only right now, he *really* didn't want such images intruding on his *pain.*

She tossed her hair over her shoulders. As the ache receded, James saw a red leather strap was around her wrist and there was a strain on it. Small wonder the collision went out of control. A *beast* was on the end of the lead.

"Cat...you'll be the death of me yet!"

James turned his head to eye the feline on the end of the leather tether. "Bloody hell—that's a Scottish wildcat! What idiot runs around with a wildcat on a leash? And one wearing an eye patch?"

"Half-wildcat," she corrected defensively.

She ceased trying to unwind the cat as her eyes locked with his. She stared at him, transfixed, wonder in her voice. "You have lavender eyes."

James was ready to throttle her and she worried about his eye shade? "I have grey eyes," he snapped gruffly.

She sniffed. "Males. Most are colourblind. They're not blue or grey. They're lavender. Liz Taylor eyes. Oh, man, you're not wearing contacts, are you?"

"No, I only wear reading glasses." James stopped and felt for his eyeglasses in his shirt pocket. His *flattened* glasses. "Or used to."

"Oh, you broke your glasses?"

"No, *you* broke them...and *other things*...I think."

She wiggled again and turned to look at his legs, as if they were the part of his anatomy he referred to. Then she leaned forward to run her hands over his arms.

Finally able to focus, he stared up into a pair of witchy eyes. Dark amber with streaks of jade, they appeared green one moment, then transmuted to the color of whisky the next. All about him receded. He stared bound by them, unable to see anything else.

Part of his body proved it hadn't been damaged in the collision and pulsed to life under her shifting. "Scratch *other things* being broke," he muttered.

"I'm sorry. My beastie is hard to control."

His erection throbbed, insistent. James moaned, then chuckled. "Yeah, I know the feeling."

Shocked, she realized she sat on his aroused groin. "Oh!" Hazel eyes wide, she looked from side-to-side, searching for the best way to get up. "Sorry...really I am."

Witchy Eyes started to rise, but couldn't gain balance. James saw what would happen—she'd come down sitting on his face! He put his hands up to her thighs to stop the descent, but didn't count on her weight pushing downward to where his thumbs ended on her crotch.

Well, this is smart. She sits on my groin and I grab her— James groaned. He couldn't jerk his hands away or she'd tumble. Bloody hell, they didn't even know each other's names. What an introduction!

With a squeak, she grabbed the guide wire and straightened her knees, allowing him to scoot from under her. James sat up carefully so he didn't end up with him burying his face where his thumbs were.

She reeled in the long leash to a controllable length, then offered her other hand to help him to his feet. "I apologize— especially the glasses. Send me the bill. I'll replace them."

He rose to his six-foot height, glad she was tall, about five-seven, but not too tall. As Goldilocks would say, *just right* for him. She was pretty, no doubt, but something unique, a quality feline, drew him as he stared into those hazel eyes.

"Perhaps we should introduce ourselves?" He laughed as the huge cat rubbed against his leg like any ordinary house-cat. "I'm James Douglas Kinloch."

She gazed at him, enrapt. "You have the most beautiful eyes."

He was about to suggest she'd enjoy staring at his beauty-

ful eyes over supper, when enrapture morphed into shock—
and maybe something *worse*.

"*James...Douglas...Kinloch?*" she repeated with loathing.

Bloody hell, the way she spoke his name you'd think she'd
said Osama Bin Laden. "Yes." What else could he say?

"*James...Douglas...bloody Kinloch...*reviewer for *Money
& Trends?*" she growled. "I'd like to know I have the right
James Douglas Kinloch. But of course, you are. There could
only be one despicable, *loathsome worm* by that name. The
world couldn't stand two."

"Have we met?" James glanced to the side, hoping someone spotted them. While he'd truly love to jump her bones
after all the bumping and grinding they'd just done, he began
to fear he faced a crazed woman—with a one-eyed, Scottish
wildcat, all three stone of him.

Her teeth flashed, but not in a grin. It was feral, what a
cat wore just before pouncing on prey. "Met? Not face-to-
face." Her countenance shifted to a magazine smile. "I'm a
follower of your writing. You've quite the *penchant* with
words. Ever considered fiction? You'd excel in it."

She moved so fast, male instinct to protect himself
couldn't engage. Her knee connected with the part of a man
that could fell the mightiest of modern day warriors. James
crumpled to his knees, clutching his groin, trying not to puke.
Down on knee level, he saw her feet and the cat's stalk off,
only to hear her steps return behind him. He should've
expected it, but occupied with writhing in agony, he failed to
anticipate the kick to his arse.

"*James Douglas bloody Kinloch,*" she snarled.

This time her steps stomped off down the fairgrounds.
The cat with the eye patch came pussyfooting back, dragging
the red leash. Putting his feet on James' thigh, he stretched
up and gave his chin a tongue bath. James managed to push
him away, only to have the purring cat bump its forehead
against his chin.

"Puss, this is going to be a *long* week."

Catlynne Falconer's cheeks burned with anger. "The nerve
of the bloody man to have such beautiful eyes."

She'd envisioned James Douglas Kinloch—the man who
trashed every one of her Scottish Romance novels over the
past five years—pictured him as a dried up old Scotsman, with
an expression like he sucked lemons! Never once had she
imagined such a sexy, elegant man. Younger than her furious

mind had conjured, Kinloch had blue-black hair that lay in wild waves. And those eyes. Wow! Never had she seen such *lavender* eyes! Most are too blue or grey. His were truly lilac. He was strong, lean, hard...yep...very *hard*.

Oh, why did James Douglas Kinloch have to be as sexy as his name? This man summoned visions of a tartan blanket over silk sheets, maybe a set of lavender ones matching those to die for eyes. He'd hit her senses with the power of a run-away locomotive, provoked her to want to kiss all his booboos and make them better. She wanted those beautiful hands on her, stroking her, squeezing...

"Bugger. I'm going to have an orgasm daydreaming about him and those eyes," she commented to the cat. Then she looked down and saw the silly beast wasn't with her. "Fu...dge."

She'd been so bloody turned on by the man, then hit with the bucket of ice water that he was that flaming reviewer from *Money & Trends,* she'd forgotten her cat.

"Well, nothing to do but find the pussycat before he eats Virginia Keller's teacup terrier. Blast."

The feline may be half-wildcat and sported a ridiculous black, pirate's patch, but he obviously was tame. After they had a *meeting of the minds,* James rather liked having the beast on the leash. Women kept their distance. He strolled down the fairway, checking out tents and booths with no fear of being ravished by Queen Victoria or a Lady Pirate.

Finding a vendor serving bangers and beer, he and the cat shared lunch. Lifting his mug for a drink, he spotted Witchy Eyes storming toward him. Dark auburn hair swirled about her shoulders, seeing her stand out in the crowd. A Pict warrior-princess out for blood.

Breaking off a chunk of the banger, he fed it to the fat cat. "I like watching her walk, Cat. She has world-class breasts. Very athletic legs, though I'd prefer she not use them to kick me. It's hard on a man's...*ego.* You have any idea why she hates me?"

The cat finished the num-num and meowed for another bite.

As she stalked up, James pretended not to notice her, but fed the beast his last bit of the sandwich. He stared at the jean-covered thighs, the lush hips and envisioned them wrapped around his waist as he drove his body into hers.

"Kinloch, you're one sick puppy," he muttered under his

breath. Of all the women chasing him, ready to jump his bones, he'd developed a case of severe lust for the one who kneed him in the groin.

With a huff, she put her hands on her hips. "What are you feeding my cat?"

"My lunch. It's debatable if this critter is a cat. Personally, I think he's a small pony in a cat costume."

Snagging the red leash, she tugged. "Come, Jack."

"Jack? As in One-Eyed-Jack?" James suppressed his smile as Jack sat staring at him, ignoring her yanking on the red tether. "Mind telling me why you're dragging Jack around the Renfaire, Miss..."

Her body rocked with another huff, as amber eyes flashed daggers at him. "You may ask. Come, Jack." She pulled again on the strap, but the pussycat wouldn't move.

"Had lunch? Want a banger?" Kinloch signaled the waitress. "Jack and I want another, eh, lad?"

She blinked in shock, then composed her face. "Oh, yeah, it's a big hotdog."

"You're not Yank with that accent," he observed.

"Scot born, but I lived a big part of my life in the US until the last three years."

"Where do you live now?"

"Colchester."

James paused to give the order to the waitress. "Sit. Jack isn't finished yet. Isn't that right, Jack?"

The cat turned his head and meowed at her. Pursing her lips—delectable lips—she flopped down on the end of the bench. Witchy Eyes glared at him as the waitress returned with food, but said nothing until the woman left with the empty tray.

James broke off the excess and put it before Jack. "Mind telling me why you want to end my family tree? Often I affect women strongly, but I've never had one physically attack me, especially when I don't know her name."

He took a bite of the banger and was about to swallow when she spoke.

"You want my name, Mr. James Douglas Kinloch? Fine. My name—Catlynne Falconer."

James simultaneously choked on the hotdog and almost spit it out. Rising, she slapped him on the back—with a bit more strength than called for, James feared.

Small wonder. *Catlynne Falconer.* Surely, there was only one.

"Yes, Mr. James Douglas Kinloch, I'm the writer whose books you've shredded with glee. You've called me a sophomoric writer who must still wear Maryjane patent leather shoes, one whose stories are 'so cute it's painful.' Two of the kinder comments you've penned when reviewing my works. Every time sales of my books soar, you take great pleasure in posting your reviews—not only in *Money & Trends*, but on Amazon.com and Amazon.co.uk. My sales go down the tubes. After eleven books, I could sue you for loss of income."

James reached for his ale to dislodge the stuck bit of banger. With a forced swallow, the lump moved down his throat.

Catlynne Falconer. This vivacious lass with the flashing amber eyes and breasts he'd a hard time keeping his eyes off of was *Miz Hearts & Flowers?* She pens a rather original series about a pirate reincarnated as a huge cat. The beast went around solving murder mysteries and playing cupid to mismatched couples.

Bloody hell. Why hadn't he made the connection?

He stared at the mangy wildcat—her inspiration obviously. Explained why she had him here at the Renfaire. He recalled seeing her name on the program as one of the guest speakers, giving a talk on animals as characters in Romance writing. She'd dragged Jack along for *show and tell.*

What did one say to an author you'd taken great pleasure in harpooning? She was such a sensual writer. Her sex scenes had caused him to take more than one cold shower. Only she persisted in having mismatched lovers falling head-over-heels into happily ever after. When he reached the end of her books he felt he needed a shot of insulin to counter the overdose of *sweet.*

Well, best defense was an offence. He stared into her kissable face, raked his eyes down her made-for-sin body, reveling in every delicious curve, then slowly traveled back to lock eyes with her. "Pity. I guess the chances of me getting you into bed tonight just dropped by half."

She jerked up to her feet, acting as if he just asked her to go down on her knees before him and do the *wild thang.* The lass had a temper. Went with that auburn hair. Why did he find that so...ah...stimulating?

Catlynne shifted her stance, as if balancing her weight to one leg, prelude to delivering a stiff kick. James held up his hands, flattened palms to her. "First kick was getting acquainted. Kick me again and I'm going to turn you over my knee, Catlynne. Hmm, Cat," he growled. "Your mum named you well."

All sorts of images sprang to mind. *Here, kitty kitty.* He wondered if she'd purr when he stroked the curve of her spine with his tongue. Would she hiss and flex those claws when he'd enter her body with a sure thrust?

"Your mum named you after one of Scotland's greatest heroes. How did she muff it so?" she snapped.

"So, that means you won't sleep with me tonight?" James suppressed the grin fighting to escape. He wasn't usually a jerk, but he enjoyed teasing Ms. Catlynne Falconer. "I promise to make you purr, lass."

She drew back her hand to slap him, but he was quicker. He caught her wrist and yanked her forward, pulling her into his lap. Cat let out a strangled yelp. Before she closed her mouth, he kissed her.

Oh, man, did he kiss Miss Catlynne Falconer! Not a gentle first kiss, but with full pleasure and passion that erupted within him. Her lips tasted of tart lemonade. She wiggled, so he leaned her back, cradling her neck in his hand, the other on the small of her spine. His mouth molded hers, tilting for a better angle.

He couldn't ever recall enjoying a kiss as much. Catlynne stopped the squirming, her hands clutched his waist, hanging on. Her responses ran the gamut from resistance to acquiescence, then surprise, ending with her kissing him back.

James lost sense of where he was, until applause broke out around them. Recalling they were on the picnic grounds with about two hundred female writers, he reluctantly pulled back.

Dazed, Catlynne blinked several times, then grew aware of the hooting, whistling and clapping. Turning five shades of red, her eyes narrowed on him as she clearly considered slapping him again. She was furious. Even so, he saw the flash of desire threaded with confusion at the back of those whisky eyes. She nibbled on the corner of her kiss-swollen lips.

He leaned his head to hers and threatened, "Don't do it. Each time you do me bodily harm, I shall extract vengeance by kissing you senseless—no matter where we are."

"You...you..." she spluttered, at a loss for words.

He flashed a smile guaranteed to dazzle the ladies, then rose to his feet and executed a bow.

Catlynne dashed away from the area where the picnic tables were cordoned off.

James scratched Jack's head. "She left you again, beast. I think she does that just to have an excuse to come back and fetch you."

James tossed down a tip for the waitress, picked up the leash and started down the fairway with Jack. He began whistling an old *Blondie* tune, *One Way or Another*. "Yeah, I'm gonna get ya', get ya', get ya', get ya'."

Suddenly things were looking up.

Catlynne finished blow-drying her hair, then wound up the cord. Going back into the bedroom, she replaced it in her travel bag. She noticed the red blinking light on the phone indicating she had a message and had an idea from whom. Kinloch. He had Jack and wasn't answering her pages to return him.

Putting her fingers to her lips, she recalled how James Douglas Kinloch tasted. Her body started that low burning thrum that reminded he was an excellent kisser.

She was a little concerned. Jack didn't like men. And considering the scathing reviews Kinloch did for her books, she figured the man didn't like cats either. *This character—a cat mind you—is more annoying than a dozen Garfields rolled into one.* So she was uneasy about the beast of *Money & Trends* and her beastie paling together.

Going to the phone, she listened to the message. She'd called him seven times and demanded he return her cat.

The clipped Scot accent came across the recorded message. "Your cat? Mine now. Finders keepers, losers weepers." Then a click.

She imagined the self-satisfied smirk beneath the flashing lavender eyes. Knees feeling weak, she sat on the bed with a thump. A man like that was a heartbreaker. Worse, he was a bloody book reviewer.

Why suddenly were things looking so down?

Catlynne marched to the desk of the elegant, gold-tone foyer of the *Majestic Park Hotel* and addressed the desk porter behind the reception counter. "May I have the room number of Mr. James Kinloch?"

The young man sniggered. "Hotel policy doesn't permit giving out room numbers. You may leave him a message or I can ring a call through to him."

She gritted her teeth. Accepting the note pad, she scrawled, *return my cat or I shall have you arrested for cat-*

napping. Folding the paper, she pushed it at the man.

He lifted an eyebrow. "What? Not going to bribe me with a hundred-pound note? All the ladies wanting to get a message to Kinloch have funded my daughter's coming wedding."

"Much happiness on your daughter's nuptials, but I wouldn't spend one shilling on James Douglas Kinloch."

Spinning on her heels, she headed toward the ballroom. From behind her, she heard the porter say, "Methinks the lady doth protest too much."

"Would you look at that?" someone halfway down the row of tables gasped.

The cacophony of wolf-whistles and chuckles caused Catlynne's head to snap up from autographing her books.

Leanne Burroughs, award-winning author of *Her Highland Rogue* and owner of Highland Press Publishing, sat to Catlynne's right. Pausing, she leaned to Catlynne and pointed with the end of the pen. "I believe that's your cat, isn't it?"

Catlynne glanced down the crowded isle. Women stood in lines before authors to get their books signed. Suddenly, the interest wasn't in the tables where the books were displayed or authors busy autographing them, but at a ruckus behind them. The crowd parted so all could observe the man coming her way.

James Kinloch wore a black turtleneck sweater, stunning with that blue-black hair. What caused women to go on pheromone overload—he wore a black tartan kilt with purple in the plaid. Those pale eyes spotted her, then flashed with smug arrogance. Catlynne burned to slap the expression off his much too beautiful face. Torn, she watched as Jack bounced along, keeping pace with the man better than any dog could. Though she itched to bring the reviewer down a peg, her heart couldn't help but be touched by how man and cat had bonded.

"I found my Highlander hero for my next book." Leanne chuckled. "I'd take him home, but my Tom might not approve."

Catlynne repressed the urge to growl. "Trust me, you don't want him."

"Easy—I'm not going to arm-wrestle you for him."

Reaching for another book to sign, Catlynne had to tug the book from the fan's hand, as the woman was transfixed on the sexy man in the kilt. "Not what I meant. He's James

Douglas Kinloch—a book critic."

"Ah, sigh. Just as well I have Tom, then. He's very supportive of my writing." Leanne watched the man draw near. "He does favor what I always imagined Good Sir James Douglas looking like. Can't you see him at The Bruce's side, claymore in his hands, fighting to free Scotland?"

Kinloch came directly to her table, scooped up Jack and set him on the tabletop. He winked at the three ladies standing in line, then turned back to Catlynne. "Sorry, we're late. Jack couldn't decide what to wear and insisted on my bow tie."

Sure enough, Jack sported a tartan tie the same plaid as James' kilt. He looked adorable, but Catlynne was too gub-slapped to speak. The man was stunning, and yes, he did appear as if Good Sir James had come to life. As she stared into those pale lilac eyes, she felt lost to all around her.

"Awww...kitty does look like a reincarnated pirate," a Scottish lady waiting to have her books signed commented, petting Jack. "He's so huge. He must've been a braw and bonnie pirate in his other life."

James handed Catlynne the leash—a black one, then moved to set the boxes of books on the floor so he could use the chair. He pushed it to sit just to her right and a little behind her. "Did I miss much?"

Leanne cleared her throat loudly, holding out her hand. "Hello, I'm Leanne Burroughs. I write Scottish historical romances and I'm owner of Highland Press Publishing."

"Smart lass. I've heard good things about your quality books and the direction your small press is moving. Very positive for Romance Writers." James flashed a killer smile. Instead of shaking her hand, he kissed it in courtly fashion. "Please set aside copies of all Highland Press books for me so I can review them."

"*You'll be sorry,*" Catlynne muttered in singsong, so the words carried only to James and Leanne. "Trust me. I've been *blessed* with a Kinloch review for every book I've written. It's something every writer could live without."

"She thinks *moi*—a humble reviewer—hurt her sales," he confided with a wink.

Damn his charming rogue hide. Women had a hard time resisting melt down around a sexy man in a kilt with a burr in his voice. Add wavy black hair and lavender eyes and it was a lethal combination.

"I've come to make amends." He arched an eyebrow at the

women suddenly lining up to get Catlynne's books.

Jack stretched out on the corner of the table enjoying the pets and adoration. Fixing on the leash, Catlynne asked, "What happened to his red one?"

James shrugged. "Red doesn't go with my plaid. We stopped by the pet centre they have here. This hotel is a small city. I purchased a new leash and some treats. Also, he found a catnip mouse he *really* wanted. Do you know they even have babysitting service for pets or the super kennel where you can park them for a spell, say like later when we go dancing in the nightclub?"

"Dream on, Kinloch." Her reply was defensive, trying to keep him at arms' length.

Oh, but her heart, and Leanne's all-knowing stare, branded her a fool.

She was a coward. As the book signing broke up, the women mobbed the sexy man in a kilt. Catlynne used the confusion to slip away from him.

Hadn't mattered. James Kinloch would prove damn hard to avoid. Especially since he ended up with Jack again.

Early the next morn, before anyone was up and about, she slipped downstairs to relax by doing a few laps in the pool. When she came up for air, she spotted Jack laying on a chaise lounge smiling at her.

James dove into the pool with a backwash of water, then surfaced in front of her. She opened her mouth to berate him for causing the big splash, but the fool man kissed her. Kissed her until her toes curled and the water in the pool rose to boiling. She nearly forgot they were in the glassed-in pool and the dining room looked into it—until she heard a rap on the glass and glanced up to see Leanne Burroughs and Diane D. White waving at them.

That became the pattern for the next three days. Now, she was so confused she wanted to cry. She was falling for James Kinloch—hard. Yet, she had no idea how the arrogant man felt about her. Sure, he chased her like mad, but was he merely passing time at the convention, an affair he'd forget once he was back in Scotland? Until her next book came out and he had to write another review, that is.

Catlynne tried to push the fears from her mind as she stood in the nightclub with Leanne and Diane discussing new projects for Highland Press. A hush fell across the room as the first chords of a guitar and piano floated in the air. As it registered what the tune was, her eyes jerked up to see James standing across the room. Al Stewart's poetic *Year of the Cat* filled the air. Her gaze locked with James' and all about her receded to black.

Drawn to him, she walked away from Leanne and Diane without a word. He stood waiting for her to come to him, assured she would. A warlock conjuring her with a power she couldn't resist.

She didn't want to resist.

As she neared, she saw satisfaction in his lavender eyes. He opened his arms and she stepped into them. It felt like coming home.

That *terrified* her.

They swayed, not really dancing, just caught up in the magic of the moment. Al Stewart's beautiful song wrapped around them, cocooning them. Heat rolled off his body, the hint of cedar and bergamot of his cologne intoxicating. But the scent of the man underneath was even more lethal.

"Stay with me tonight," he whispered as he nuzzled her ear.

She looked up into the lilac eyes and nodded.

It was just that simple.

It was just that complicated. She'd taken the coward's way out.

At dawn, he finally fell asleep after making love to her all night. Drowning in those sensual images, peace eluded her. She leaned against his back, her hand stroking his beautiful arm.

She was in love with James Douglas Kinloch.

Fearing pain loving him could bring, she quickly dressed and slipped out of his room. Unable to face him, she hadn't even shown up for breakfast.

Thinking to distract the inner demons tormenting her, she'd joined Leanne and Diane in the crossbow demonstration.

Her mind not on the task, Catlynne struggled, trying to load the crossbow. Blasted thing wasn't easy to manipulate. There were several types, and naturally she ended up with one hard on her wrist. The crank that wrenched the bow into place required her to push with the power of her wrist.

"Ladies, the crossbow was an important development in weaponry during the Medieval period. First hand-held weapon which could be used by an untrained man to injure or kill a knight in plate armour. The most powerful crossbows could penetrate armour and kill at two-hundred yards. The unassailability of the knight was at risk for the first time, taking the advantage from his hands." The instructor walked slowly along the line of women armed with replicas of the ancient weapons. "A crossbow contains a bowstring, which is held in place by a nut when the bolt is loaded and the crossbow is engaged. This is referred to as at *full cock.*"

This drew chuckles and baudy comments from the ladies participating in the class. One on the far end proclaimed, "Now *that's* what I'd call full cock."

"Hush, Marigold," Diane D. White, author of the successful *Tartan Cowboy* series, chided. She turned back to the others. "Ignore her, she's an erotica writer."

Catlynne knew without looking who had drawn the comment. Swivling her head, she saw James coming in their direction, that traitor Jack with him. For a cat that hated men, Jack sure bonded with Kinloch. Palies.

She'd fix him...*somehow.*

"You ladies have four types of crossbows. Pull-Lever, Push-Lever, Rachet," he nodded to Catlynne struggling with hers, "and Windlass." Taking pity on Catlynne, he paused and traded, giving her a 'baby version' about one-third the size. "Here, Miss, try the smaller one?"

She chuckled, trading with him. "My wrist thanks you."

"Careful. It's hair trigger. This smaller copy was an assassin's weapon. Easily hidden from view. Pope Urban II banned the use of crossbows against Christians in 1097, and the Second Lateran Council did the same for arbalests in 1139. The crossbow was seen as unchivalrous, a threat to social order. Ladies, aim at the target and gently release the trigger."

Just then, Virginia Keller's teacup terrier crawled out of her purse where she'd set it down to handle the crossbow. Yapping, it dashed in front of Jack. Big mistake. With a feral grin, Jack leapt, right on the mutt's trail. Jack's weight yanked the leash from James' hand, as the dog and the feline dashed onto the range just as the ladies were firing the weapons. James lunged in front of Catlynne, trying to snatch the leash to haul Jack back.

Virginia screamed, "My baby!"

She tried to go after the doggie, but the heel on her high heel snapped off, causing her to crash into Catlynne. The jarring caused the small crossbow to release its bolt.

Catlynne stared in horror. James had rescued Jack, but he now stood with a stunned expression—as a small crossbow bolt stuck out the right cheek of his arse.

"Bloody hell." James reached around and with gritted teeth yanked the small arrow out. Blood immediately soaked his pants. "I think someone better drive me to hospital so I can get stitches."

Taking the leash, Catlynne handed it to Diane. "Please, take Jack inside and tell the desk porter to have the sitter take him to my room."

Diane looked as if the Loch Ness Monster was on the end of the leash. "Me? You know I don't get along with kitties. He'd better not bite me."

Leanne laughed as she accepted the leash. "I love cats. Don't worry. Jack will be fine. Go with James."

James teased, "I think she shot me just to get even for all those bad reviews.

"I want her arrested," James demanded from his position on his stomach, where they just finished stitching him up.

Catlynne made a small gasp, staring at him with those huge hazel eyes. "I didn't do it deliberately, James."

The North Yorkshire Police Officer tried to maintain a stoic face. "There seems to be a question about whether Miss Falconer broke a law or not. There's a law still on the books which states it's legal to shoot a Scotsman with a bow and arrow every day of the week—except Sunday. Repercussions from William Wallace attacking York. Seeing as it's Saturday, by the letter of the law she didn't actually commit a crime."

"Why the bloody hell is that archaic law still on the books?" James demanded.

"It was an accident," Catlynne repeated, tears filling her eyes. "You cannot believe I did it on purpose."

"Accident or not, it's still not a crime. If she shot you on Sunday, then you'd have grounds to demand her arrest."

James shook his finger. "Ah ha! It's legal to shoot a Scot with a *bow and arrow*. She shot me with a crossbow. That's not an arrow, that's a bolt. Arrest her."

"I need to check with the station to get a ruling on this." The officer scratched his head, clearly humbugged by the distinction. Shrugging, he left the emergency room.

Catlynne stood on shaky legs, coming to the end of the operating table. "James, why do you want me arrested? It was a series of dreadful mistakes, an accident. I didn't shoot you on purpose."

"Yes, you did." He reached out, took her hand and placed it to the centre of his chest. "Shot me straight through the heart and I shall never recover. You keep dashing about, have avoided me for the last three days. I hoped to have you arrested so I could post bond and get the judge to remand you to my custody. Then you, me and Jack could go home tomorrow."

"Home?"

"Aye, lass. Home."

"Oh, James!" Catlynne gasped and hugged him, smothering him with kisses.

"Easy lass, time enough to smooch once we get out of here." He kissed her slowly, deeply. "That's an aye to my proposal?"

"Oh, aye. I've always wanted my very own personal Scotsman."

He laughed. "It just struck me. How Jack brought us together. Like a plot from one of your books."

"Proper justice for all those horrid reviews. You fell in love just like a hero in one of my stories." Doubt shadowed her eyes. "You *are* in love, James, aren't you?"

"Ridiculously, deliriously, ecstatically, madly."

"Good, because I love you, too. Will you marry me in the kilt?"

James wiggled his eyebrows. "Aye, we'll have a Highland wedding. After, I'll even show you what a Scotsman wears under his kilt."

Gathering the green sheet around his hips, he sat up so he could kiss her properly.

"See, my books told you how wonderful love can be."

He pulled her against his chest holding her tightly. "I might've taken a little time for the *point* to be driven home. But let's say, my love, I got it in the end."

Double, Double, Toil & Trouble

P.E.A.R.L. Award Winner 2006 –
Best Short Story from an Anthology

• *Scotland- Trespassing on someone else's
land is legal.*

"Now she's done it!" Cian Mackinnon glared at the chain across the road, furious it prevented him from driving to the castle the back way. He considered putting the vehicle in low, rev the engine until it reached high torque, then smash through the chain. His luck—it'd only mess up the front of his *Range Rover*. "The witch has no bloody right to stop me from using the driveway."

Aye, he could use the front entrance to Castle Dunnascaul. It'd mean backtracking several kilometers. Add to the fact, the road leading to the front door wasn't really drivable—needed grading and filling in with gravel—his mood was *not* cheerful. A gale loomed on the horizon. A sensible lad, he wanted no part of getting caught on the old cliff road when high winds howled like *The Bansidhe*.

Gillian Grant played the bitch simply because she bought into the centuries old feud between her family and his. Didn't matter she spent half her life in the States. Nor did the fact neither of them had been raised in the castle have bearing on *The Troubles*. He was a Mackinnon and she was...hmm...*a bitch.*

A damn sexy bitch, he admitted, but a pain in the arse when it came to the castle. What did he expect? She was a Grant. Their motto surely was *Stubborn to the End*. Living up to her name, she'd upped the ante by placing a chain over the back drive to prevent him from taking it.

The Mackinnon-Grant War was about to heat up.

Disgusted, he climbed out of the Rover and stomped down the winding driveway to her quaint, thatch cottage. As he neared the whitewashed, two-story structure, he saw the picture window curtain flutter. She'd been watching, expecting the confrontation when he discovered the chain.

The front door squeaked open and she stepped onto the stoop, arms crossed, a glower upon her face. If she ever stopped frowning, she'd be a damn fine woman. Neatly braided, her dark blonde hair snaked over her shoulder, around her full breast and past her hip. Always in the prim braid, he'd never seen that mass of hair loose. If just once she'd let down her hair—literally and figuratively—he feared she held the power to bewitch him until he didn't ken down from up.

From the day they'd sat in the solicitor's office and heard the will, relations between them had been anything but cordial.

The bone of contention—a five-hundred-year-old castle.

Castle Dunnascaul once belonged to Gillian's family. *Once* being the key here. When Bonnie Prince Charlie pulled his stunt in 1745, trying to claim the throne of Scotland for his father, Clan Grant remained Royalists. Supporting the lost cause, Gillian's branch blithely marched to their doom. Oddly, though most Mackinnons were *out* for Charlie—showing no better sense than the Grants—his particular sept of the Mackinnnons refused to rally to the Stuart's standard. After Culloden, Dunnascaul had been confiscated and given as a reward to Malcolm Mackinnon, his great-grandfather, thirteen odd generations back. Despite the Grants being attainted, they held tight to the burning hope one day they'd regain the castle.

Tempers cooled over the past century. Controversy again flared when Gillian's grandmother, Anne Grant, began an affair with his grandfather, David Mackinnon. Cian didn't know the story, why if they were so in love they didn't each divorce and marry, ending the feud. But no. They'd scandalized both clans, indulging in a lifelong affair. Tongues wagged for decades.

The castle's ownership became a rub once more when Anne died of pneumonia. Supposedly, David promised Anne on her deathbed Dunnascaul would return to her family on his demise. Several witnesses swore he'd vowed this. For years, the Grants waited for David *to stick a spoon in the wall* so the ancient castle could revert to its *rightful* owners.

Last month, when they met at the solicitor's for the will's reading, Gillian anticipated Dunnascaul would be hers. Shock came when they learnt it passed to Cian. Only the thatched cottage on the southern boundary was left to Anne's grand-daughter. Not uttering a word of protest, and with a defiant tilt of the chin, she accepted the keys and took possession of the thatch. Since then, she'd plagued him at every turn.

"You trespass, Mackinnon." She tugged the shawl around her shoulders.

"Aye, I am. I wouldn't be troubling you, Gillian Grant, but someone foolishly put a chain across the driveway."

"It stops trespassers. You have a drive to Dunnascaul."

Cian ran his eyes over her. She was an eyeful, not some skinny model-type, but a woman with flesh shaped to please a man. Shame she looked like she'd sucked lemons. "You know what you need, Gillian Grant?"

That stubborn chin jutted higher. "Save your chauvinistic patter, Mackinnon."

"Chauvinistic, she says." He huffed. "You thought I'd say you needed a good shagging—and I won't deny that might be the source of your sourpuss moods. What I was going to say, Gillian Grant, is you need turning over my knee and given a good paddling."

She snapped, "You and what man's army?"

"I don't need assistance, lass." He stepped up on the concrete porch, invading her space. "A pleasure it'd be to demonstrate it. If you'd rather, I could help in the shagging department...just to improve your disposition."

Gillian took a step backward, caught herself, clearly not about to let his taller frame intimidate her. Composing her face, she glared at him with regal bearing. "Shouldn't you hie yourself off. You've a wee bit of a drive back to Dunnascaul and a storm's coming."

Since it neared Winter Solstice, *night* came in the middle of the afternoon. It would be pitch-black before he reached the castle if he took the front drive. With the storm coming, he had *no* intention of navigating that kidney-busting drive-way.

"You cannot close access to the road. You may have been raised as a Yank, but surely you know simple trespassing isn't a crime in Scotland."

"Only if the trespass doesn't—"

"Destroy crops, inhibit the property's regular use or

invade privacy. Since I do none of those things, you cannot prevent me from using the drive."

"The driveway's mine. Your grandfather—liar that he was —left the cottage and ten acres surrounding to me. Freehold."

"I care less if the Pope blessed your Freehold. You can't stop me from using it."

She smirked. "I just did."

"Och, you shouldn't have said that, lass." He winked, then spun on his heels to head down the drive.

Over his shoulder, he saw her watching him. The smug expression fell off her face. Calling after him, she moved to the edge of the small porch. "What are you doing, Mackinnon?"

He swung around, walking backwards. "Guess you'll have to watch, lass."

"Mackinnon!" She raised her voice to carry over the rising wind.

He shrugged. "Can't hear you!" Jauntily, he jogged to his truck.

She didn't leave the stoop. She must be getting chilled, but stayed observing as he reversed the Rover until the tail backed up against the chain.

Getting out, he snagged a rope from the back and uncoiled it. Wrapping it around the chain, he then secured it about the boat hitch. Whistling, he scooted behind the wheel and shifted the Rover into gear. Watching the rope play out in the rearview mirror, he saw Gillian on the stoop, hands on her hips, furious as it grew clear he planned to yank the chain and the posts out.

Precisely what he did. Completing a U-turn, he sped down the drive to park. Hopping out, he untied her chain, then dropped it clanking at her feet. "Yours, I believe?"

"OOOooo, bloody Mackinnon!" She seethed. "I'm calling the constable."

"Go ahead, ring up Hamish Abercrombie. While you're at it, lass, tell him you limited the access. You'll end up fined."

"OOOooo, beast," she growled.

He shot back, "Vixen."

"Ogre."

He laughed. "Witch."

Her brown eyes blinked. "Did you call me a bitch?"

"No, I called you *witch*."

"Why would you call me witch?"

"You must be one."

"Why would you assume that?"

"Because all I can think of doing is this." Tossing good sense to the wind, he grabbed hold of her shoulders and yanked her to him, taking her mouth with his in a bruising, no-holds-barred, mother-loving, knock-your-socks-off kiss.

He must've lost his mind! Or maybe felt surge in his blood what his grandfather felt for Gillian's grandmother all those many years.

To his surprise, Gillian kissed him back! She leaned into him, her mouth softly opening under his, as though she couldn't get close enough. Inside his skin wouldn't be close enough!

She tasted of lemon drops and rain.

Rain? It registered the sky had opened up while they stood kissing, as if neither of them wanted to stop.

His sane side said he was nuts to kiss her, even more of a fruitcake for standing in the rain when they could take a few steps into the coziness of her thatched cottage. Only, instinct warned the instant he broke the kiss, her presence of mind would return and she'd probably deck him. It'd be worth it.

Gillian stepped back, blinking tear-filled eyes. "Wh-why did you do that?"

"Seemed the thing to do." Reaching out, his thumb gently stroked the curve of her cheek. Crippled by grinding hunger, his eyes traced over her face, memorizing every line, mesmerized to the point he couldn't speak. Shrugging, he pulled his hand back to massage the centre of his chest where a tightness lodged. Off kilter, he was unsure what possessed him, other than he dreamt of kissing her for the last month—of doing a lot *more* than kissing her.

Gillian put the back of her hand to her well-kissed lips, her eyes accusing. "You think since my grandmother was easy for your grandfather, that I'm easy, too? That history can repeat itself?" She pushed the door open, glaring as if he were akin to a snake. "Think again!"

She slammed the door so hard the glass of the picture window rippled with vibrations.

"There's likely one thing my grandfather and I agree on—a Grant woman is *never* easy." Sighing, he shook his head and returned to the Rover.

Gillian followed the taillights bouncing across the burn and up the steep hill to Dunnascaul. Absent-mindedly, she ran her thumb over her mouth, tasting *him* on her lips. A hint of cinnamon overlaid upon Cian Mackinnon's own unique flavour. Her mouth tingled from his possession. Wow, he just didn't kiss—*he kissed*. A slow burn licked at her body.

Never had she been willing to forget everything. Not once had she wanted a man to the point you could only see *him*, everything about him blurred to grey.

In spite of all, she *so wanted* Cian Mackinnon.

Too bad the Mackinnon men were heartbreakers. Oh, they vowed fancy promises, but weren't there when it counted, never one to keep their word. She mustn't forget that. Hadn't her mother drummed it into her brain how David Mackinnon disappointed her grandmother time and again? Hadn't he even broken his deathbed oath to Anne, leaving the castle to Cian instead of willing it to her granddaughter?

Curse fickle Fate! Oh, why had they met in a solicitor's office instead of some romantic setting— moonlight, tropical breezes and slow dancing on a shadowy balcony? They'd sway to the soft music, their bodies so close, luxuriating in the heat that rose between them. She closed her eyes, savoring the power of the vision.

"Instead, I'm trapped by this blasted feud. His grandfather pledged to my grandmother on her deathbed. He broke it. I gave one to my mum on hers. I keep my word—unlike bloody Mackinnons. Mum said it's left to me to see the castle was back in the family...my duty." Sighing, Gillian frowned at the cat lying by the fireplace. "Don't know why I talk to you. You might as well be a stuffed toy, Basil."

The brown and grey tabby snapped his tail, as if that was all the recognition she deserved. *Nothing* stirred Basil. The laziest cat in the world, if he more than twitched his tail three times in a day she needed to mark it on the calendar.

"Oh, Gran, I wish I could talk with you, learn why you loved David Mackinnon with such a passion you'd trust the lying, conniving..." Feeling futility, she shrugged and headed to the bedroom to change into dry clothes.

It was spooky, living in the small thatched cottage where Anne and David carried on their lifelong, torrid affair. Their love *permeated* the house, lending her imagination flights of fancy at times, as if she heard bubbly laughter in another room. Sounds lovers might make.

After taking possession of the fairytale cottage, vivid erotic fantasies plagued her. At first, she passed them off as *residual memories* of Anne and David, seeing her grandmother at the age she was now. One night, after a particularly gripping fantasy of a man making love to her before the fireplace, she'd awoken in shock. The woman in the images was she, and the man was David Mackinnon's arrogant grandson, Cian. Ever since, she'd worked to keep a shield between them.

Her mother, Maeve, had resented David Mackinnon, and for more than the centuries old Grant-Mackinnon feud. She'd abhorred Anne never loved Maeve's father, blamed David for ruining Anne's marriage. Gillian shivered. Her mother had been a bitter person, and in that dark coil tried to control Gillian's every thought. In ways, Gillian supposed Maeve succeeded. Why else couldn't she let go Dunnascaul hadn't been returned to the Grants?

In her heart, she feared there's a part of her too much like Anne, waiting to rise to the surface. Cian Mackinnon got to her on too many levels. Made her want to forget the past, all the old hatreds...*and just love him.*

If only he didn't plan to ruin the castle. For a price, Blue-haired Go-Ins would queue up for twice-weekly tours, and May through August he'd throw open the doors to paying guests. A ruddy hotel! No respect for the history, the heritage! Dunnascaul should be loved, reverenced, not exploited.

Buttoning her jumper, she sat in the chair by the fire. Basil yawned and shifted closer to the flames. "You're right, you silly feline, the heat feels good."

Gillian placed her feet on the ottoman and pulled the soft plaide over her legs. Maybe dreams wouldn't come if she slept in a chair.

Gillian rested peacefully, but Basil lazily lifted his head and yawned a meow to the shadowy figures of the two people standing by the chair. The woman raised a finger to her lips in shush, warning the cat not to awaken the slumbering woman. Anne gently stroked the dark blonde hair, so like her own when she was the same age.

Sins of the fathers...how many generations must this silly feud go on?

"Gillian favours me, does she no'?" she asked the *distinguished man at her side.*

"Aye, almost as bonnie as you were..."—he cleared his throat—"are."

"Och, you're eyes fail, David Mackinnon. She's prettier than I was at that age." Anne once more touched her *granddaughter with such love, with pride.*

"Got bigger knockers, too." He winked when Anne pulled

a face and punched his arm. "Cian is a lucky lad. If he just wakes up and smells the roses."

"I dinnae recall you complaining I lacked." She huffed playfully.

"Now, lass, I dinnae say you were lacking, just she has a wee bit more than you. Males notice these things. I may be dead...but I'm no' blind."

David Mackinnon saw, indeed, Anne's grandchild was a comely woman—perfect lass for his braw grandson. Only, no one was lovelier than his Annie—never was, never would be—even though grey threaded the golden hair and lines crinkled the corner of her eyes. Smile lines. Well, he'd given Anne plenty to smile about over the years. Heart heavy, he acknowledged he'd brought her ample sorrow, too. Still, he loved her with a passion that defied time. Loved her as the years placed its stamp upon her elegant countenance. No one was more beautiful than his Anne.

"She's a lovely lass, a bonnie match for my Cian."

"You're a sly one, David. You promised Gillian would get the castle. She loves it, will care for it, protect it."

He patted her on the shoulder. "Trust me. It shall work out."

Hope sparkled in her eye as tears welled. "Do you really think—?"

"Trust me, Annie, everything shall come out right. Our love will see the dream come true."

"The woman's barmy." Fergus gestured wildly with his hands. "No bloody reasoning with her. None of us can budge her."

"What did you expect? She's a Grant," Cian pointed out, climbing into the Rover while Fergus shoved himself into the passenger's side.

Curious, Cian wasn't sure what to anticipate. After dragging down the chain, he knew Gillian would one-up him in some manner. Bloody witch wasted no time pulling an end run.

He shifted into low gear as the Rover splashed through Dunnascaul Burn, then he pulled off the side of the drive. He noticed vehicles parked on the carriageway, emergency blinkers flashing. The crew of men milled about at the mouth of the drive, clearly keeping their distance from the crazy woman.

At first, he didn't see Gillian. Then he spotted her. Aye,

she was barmy. "Only a bloody Grant would pull such a stunt," he growled, climbing out of the driver's seat and slamming the door.

Wearing a determined expression, Gillian lay across the drive. A claymore clutched in her hands! He wondered how she missed indulging in the theatrical touch of painting her face with blue woad.

"Coward," she hissed at Fergus. "Figured the worm ran to the bloody Laird of Dunnascaul to whine about me."

"Gillian, you'll catch a cold laying in that muck." Cian hid his smile. The lass had spunk.

A fat cat slowly waddled up, licked Gillian's cheek, then with an exhausted sigh, slid down to lean against her shoulder.

"That's the most moth-eaten, overweight pussycat I've ever seen." Cian snorted a laugh.

"Don't insult Basil," she snapped.

Cian knelt down to scratch the kitty's chin. "Aye, he looks insulted. Basil, tell your mistress she's cold lying on the damp ground. Why her teeth chatter." As he pulled his hand back, the cat stretched to maintain contact. He leaned so far, then sort of went *thump*—face down to the ground. "Gor, is he dead?"

Her cheeks jerked in suppressed laughter. "No, that's Basil. Any exertion takes a toll on him, poor dear."

Rubbing the cat's chest showed Basil rumbled in a deep purr. "Like your silly mistress, you don't have any more sense than to lie in the middle of the muddy drive."

"We're committed," she huffed.

"No, but you *should* be." Cian glanced to the men he'd hired to put in the new patio. "She won't use the sword on you. She's a Grant. It's all bluff."

"Bluff?" she spluttered.

Fergus the foreman shrugged. "She threatened to charge us with gang rape."

"She's a *bloody* Grant." Cian shook his head. Reaching down, he picked up the limp cat. "Someone take the pussy and put him in the house."

"He ain't goin' to bite me, iz he?" Fergus accepted the seemingly boneless animal.

"Look at him...he probably doesn't have any teeth left," Cian assured.

"Eh, watch the beastie, Fergus, he might gum ye to death," one worker called, sending the others into gales of laughter.

Standing up, Cian loomed over Gillian. Snapping his fingers he ordered, "Give me the ruddy claymore. No one believes you'll run them through."

Gillian unsteadily waved it at him, hard for a woman to control the long sword from that prone location. He wrapped his hand around the pommel and jerked her to a sitting position. Ridiculously, she tried to yank it out of his grasp. While she struggled with the sword, he leaned forward and scooped her up around the waist, then deposited her on her stomach upon his left shoulder.

"Mackinnon, you horrid beast! Put me down!" When she wiggled and almost toppled off, she changed her tune. "Don't drop me!"

The crew applauded. He considered taking a bow, but figured that would push Gillian too far. "Gentlemen, start your engines."

Cian put a balancing hand on Gillian's derrière and started toward the house. Workers sped by in their vehicles, followed by the flatbed truck loaded with creek rock. He met Fergus coming out of the thatched house as he was going in.

"I put kitty by the fire. You sure he's all right, lass? Never saw a cat that limp before," he worried.

Pushing on Cian's back, she raised up so she could see Fergus. "Oh, that's Basil. He tends not to bestir himself unless necessary."

Cian set her on her feet, spun her around, and with a swat on her muddy covered arse, pushed her toward the bedroom.

Bedroom. He moaned. Last night another of those damn erotic dreams visited him. They began after he'd met Gillian and continued nightly. Shaking with need, he'd awoken, his head pounding, covered in sweat. Unable to stay in bed, he jumped up and paced like a caged tiger, pausing to stare down the hill at the thatched cottage, willing Gillian to come to him. So the *last* thing his libido needed was to couple *Gillian* and *bedroom* in the same sentence.

"Get out of those muddy clothes, lass."

"Who gave you leave to order me about, Cian Mackinnon?" Gillian swung around, her chin tilted in a to-the-manor-born style.

Cian smiled and slowly walked to her. "Lass, you get that perfect arse into your room and out of those damp clothes or—"

"Or what?" Eyes flashing, she glared.

The corner of his mouth tugged into an arrogant smile. He could feel it. "Or I'll strip you buck naked and—"

Gillian shot into her room like a bullet. She hesitated, staring at him with big brown eyes, before slamming and locking the door.

With a chuckle, he walked to the fireplace, knelt and added peat bricks. Life around Gillian was never dull, he admitted.

Nudging the pussy with his foot to make certain the fuzzy thing still lived earned him a tail snap. "Basil, you're the most worthless feline I've ever seen."

Basil yawned.

Once the fire's warmth spread, he ambled into the kitchen and washed the mud from his hand where he'd swatted Gillian. Finding several blends of *Brodies*, he selected the silver tin of Edinburgh tea mix and then set the kettle boiling.

As he laid out shortbreads, Gillian came in. Wearing a wary expression, she watched him pouring tea. He got the impression she wanted to say something, but hesitated. Fine, he could break the tension.

He sat the cup and saucer before her. "What did you hope to accomplish, lying in the drive so my workmen couldn't get to the castle?"

Glaring at it, she finally pulled the chair out and flopped down. "Guess I didn't think it through."

"What's wrong with me repairing the castle?" he asked, stirring his tea.

"Fixing the castle is marvelous. Making it a tourist trap is so..."—she gestured with her hands—"mercenary. Dunnascaul is part of my heritage, part of *your* heritage."

"Allowing Go-Ins twice a weak for a tour and tea or putting up a few tourists during the summer won't ruin it," Cian countered.

"Have you seen what they've done to Urquhart Castle? It's disgusting." Gillian shuddered.

Cian nodded. "I'm not doing anything like that. I'm merely trying to repair the place before it falls down around my ears. I hope to restore it, with my money, blood, sweat and likely a few tears."

"Why turn it into a hotel?"

"It's a monster of a castle, Gillian. I've tried counting the rooms and lose track. Over seventy-five rooms, twenty-three bedrooms. There's enough to have two wings for guests and still keep the rest as a private residence. Neither of us was raised there, but we both hold a deep love for Dunnascaul, want what's best for it, to see it survive."

"Restore it, Cian, but drop plans for the hotel," she pleaded.

He glared into the tea as if the answer might be found floating there. "If you dropped the Grant-Mackinnon feud, you'd understand. The hotel is the only option left—"

"You'll ruin it, being greedy—"

Cian's anger flared. "Damn it, Gillian. Don't you think I want the castle repaired and not put up with a bunch of Yank tourists poking about?"

"Then why?"

"Use your mind, lass. The same reason my grandfather didn't leave you the castle, despite promising your gran— money. *The lack of it.* You've done nothing but huff and glower since you learnt the castle wouldn't be returned to the Grants—"

"He promised—"

"Aye, he did. He also comprehended you wouldn't have enough money for taxes. Then what? You'd sit in the castle while the roof leaks like a sieve? I've money. Not enough to see the castle saved. Am I to sit in that bloody monster while it crumbles around my head?"

Her face brightened. "What about the treasure?"

"Och, you buy that cock 'n bull story?"

"No story. They couldn't take it with them. Cumber-land's men would've gone through their belongings and stolen anything of value. They *had* to hide it in the castle."

"I've heard the legend. We all have. Why my back pasture is full of holes. Why vandals and potholers broke in, ripping out walls and floorboards in Dunnascaul, searching for treasure. You stubborn Grants wanted a last laugh on the Mackinnons. They started nonsense about a fortune in gold and gems hidden inside Dunnascaul. For centuries they've sat on their arses and laughed while Mackinnons ran themselves ragged, trying to find that blasted gold."

Gillian put down the teacup. "If you'd only believe, I bet we'd find it."

"We?" he prodded, with an arched brow.

"Yes, we."

Cian eyed her from behind hooded lids so Gillian couldn't tell what he thought. She had to focus on the argument, not get lost in those beautiful pale eyes that were neither green nor blue, but aquamarine, shade of the water around the Isle of Lewis on a bright sunny day.

"You, me and that dilapidated excuse of a feline?" He chuckled as Basil waddled in.

Gillian touched his hand, then yanked hers back as a blush tinged her cheeks. "If we applied ourselves we'd figure out the riddle."

Cian's long lashes flicked over those mesmerizing eyes as he stared at the hand she used to touch him. "The riddle says none shall see the gold until the castle once more is in possession of a Grant."

"Why your grandfather should've left Dunnascaul to me. I'm the last Grant from the attainted Dunnascaul line."

He nodded. "I'm the last of the Mackinnons that Dunnascaul was given to after Culloden." Though he placed no value in it, he knew the riddle by heart.

> *Until a Grant comes home to Dunnascaul, Secrets remain unearthed. Some search far afield. Some smarter look closer to hearth.*
>
> *Clever is the lad or lass who can wisely riddle, to see something others cannot...right in the middle.*

Gillian leaned forward to close the distance between them, putting a hand on his thigh for balance. "Surely, it cannot be that hard."

A lowly male, blood rushed from his brain and went south at the touch of her fingers on his leg. He struggled to focus, wanting to reply, *yes, it could be that hard*. With effort, he dragged his mind from below his belt. "Who says the Grants haven't found the treasure centuries ago?"

She laughed. "We might not have told the Mackinnons, but you can bet if a Grant discovered the treasure, they'd have bragged to other Grants. The treasure waits for us to discover it."

As he stared into her brown eyes, he felt like a warrior of old, ready to slay dragons and to topple kingdoms just to win his lady's smile. Hell, if she was underfoot, rummaging through his castle, it'd give him time to build a bridge over the centuries of hatred that lay between them.

He exhaled resignation, feeling this lass just slipped a ring through his nose. "When do we start?"

With a small squeal of glee, Gillian wrapped her arms around his neck and kissed him. Not a peck, but a big thank you smooch. Seizing the moment, he wasn't letting her go. He wrapped an arm about her waist and dragged her across his lap. Cradling her, he savored the taste of tea and lemon, nibbling her soft lips, using his tongue to outline their seam until she opened for him. Images of sending the tea and biscuits crashing across the room while he took her on the oak table flooded his mind.

Hell, they wouldn't disturb Basil!

Her perfume was a hint of jasmine and heather. It did nothing to mask the scent of the intoxicating woman underneath. Man had lost many animal instincts, depending too much on sight as a primary input to his brain. Only, as he held Gillian, something dark and primeval rose within his blood, of a man wanting to claim his mate.

Pulling back, he stared into the amber eyes, caught in the wonder of Gillian. He was lost. No hope for rescue.

As he drank in the image of her silken hair, he wanted to see it loose. Reverently, he slipped off the elastic band and untwined the coil of the honey-coloured braid.

Cian admitted being pole-axed. Shifting his fingers through the golden mass, mesmerized, he figured this was the *real* treasure of the Grants.

Exhausted, Cian dropped to the sofa before the massive fireplace. For a week, Gillian and he searched Dunnascaul from top to bottom. He still lacked an accurate room count. This time he blamed Gillian. Somewhere around forty-to-fifty, he became lost, watching her body move, the way her braid brushed against her derrière as she rapped on walls, how her eyes often were upon him as much as searching out a hiding spot for treasure.

Gillian came in, an on-the-rocks glass in each hand. She handed him one and gently clinked her lead-crystal tumbler against his. "Cheers, Mackinnon."

"Sorry, lass, I warned there's no gold." He wasn't saying I-told-you-so as much as admitting defeat.

He never believed in the treasure. It would've been nice to find the cache. He could undertake a total restoration of Dunnascaul instead of piecemeal efforts he planned over the next few years. What irritated, he felt he'd let Gillian down by not finding the hidden fortune for her—old warrior's instinct to slay dragons for his lady.

"Sorry, I put you through all this searching." She leaned against him, staring into the fire. Slowly, her eyes roved about the huge library. "I love this room. The heart of the castle. I like how the platform runs around the second level, leaving the room open. What a beautiful place this will be decorated for Christmas."

The vision shimmered before his eyes, of evergreen and holly with Mackinnon and Grant tartan ribbons lining rail of the upper level. Over where the stairs turned ninety-degrees, the tallest tree imaginable would be tucked up in the curve. More importantly, he saw Gillian, mistress of Dunnascaul, hosting an open house Christmas tea for the Blue-haired Go-Ins, wrapping gifts for under the tree, or tying a tartan bow on Basil.

Making love with him before the fireplace.

"So, you're back to Blue-hairs trooping through the castle twice weekly," she grumped.

He wrapped an arm about her, shifting so they stretched out on the soft sofa. Leaning his head against hers, he kissed her temple. "Would that be such a hard life, lass? Sharing the history, the wonder of Dunnascaul for a few hours. Rest of the time it'd belong to us."

Her hand holding the glass trembled. "Us?"

Basil waddled over and tried to hop onto the sofa. So fat, he landed on his belly, hind legs kicking in the air. Cian leaned over and grabbed him. "Yes, us. You, me and this worthless furball."

"Are you—?" Gillian paled.

"I am." He took the glass from her hand and set it on the coffee table next to his.

She jumped on him. He laughed, liking how her body felt draped over his. Wrapping her arms around his neck she kissed him hard. He kissed her back. She tasted of the Malt Whisky, tasted of Gillian.

"Two ways this can go, lass, fast and wild or slow and torturous." He nibbled along the curve of her neck. "I'm thinking slow..."

She sighed. "I'm up for suggestions."

"*Up* for suggestions? Hmm...so am I, lass." He smiled, but then yelped.

Gillian frowned. "Cian?

He shifted to pull the fat cat out from under him. "We're squishing this moth-eaten excuse for a pussycat. Why didn't he fuss before?"

"That's Basil. Only imminent suffocation could make him stir."

Dropping the fat feline on the floor, Cian took hold of Gillian and rolled so she was under him. "Ah, have you where I want you, lass, wanted for the past five weeks. Five weeks gives a man a powerful hunger. One that could take a lifetime to satisfy. Is that a yes, *cushla mo fuil?*"

"*Pulse of my blood...*" Gillian echoed the translation in wonder. "Oh, aye. You know—"

"Right now there's not enough blood in my brain to know much of anything, lass." His grin felt wicked. "My hand is up under your sweater and I'm heading to *first base* fast. You should ken better than to expect a lad to think at times like that. Shush, and kiss me. You just said yes to a marriage proposal."

Basil twined around the legs of the man. Leaning his arms on the balustrade, running around the second level of the library, her David watched the couple sleeping on the sofa below. Anne's eyes lit as she studied the man and animal. Fondly, she recalled owning a dilapidated pussycat just like this one, recalled when the pet died and how she cried. David had been there, holding her, rocking her through the night.

She smiled to think much of her still lived on in her granddaughter. As David lived on in Cian. The love she saw growing between these two bode well for the Mackinnons and Grants. Peace between the two Dunnascaul clans would reign, first time in over two centuries. Cian would give her Gillian beautiful babes. The castle would ring with laughter and love.

When she linked arms with David, he asked, "Where did you disappear to, mo gràdh?"

She leaned her head against his. "My love? Do you ken that never stops making my heart flutter? After all these many years?"

"Same as when you tell me you love me forever." He rubbed his shoulder against hers. "Told you the lad would see the real treasure of the Grants, that Gillian would get the castle. I promised."

"Aye, you just didn't tell me she'd get Dunnascaul—and Cian."

"They're the best of you and me, lass. They were destined to come together. With Maeve carrying her off to the States

to spite you, I needed to play cupid in my fashion." His eyes roved over her face. "You dinnae answer, lass, where did you go?

Anne smiled, but a glint of sadness flickered over her countenance. "I needed a moment alone."

He sighed and slid his arm around her. "Out with it, Annie, it's too late in our sojourn to keep secrets."

"It's just..." She exhaled a sigh of regret.

"What, my bonnie lass?"

"I envy them. They have it all before them..." A tear sparkled in her eye. "They'll have each other in a way we never did."

"We loved each other, Annie Grant, don't be forgetting that. We had responsibilities we couldn't walk away from. No matter what life threw at us, we always had our love." His chide faltered. "Oh, Annie, we have so much more than many people ever have. I would've loved for you to be my wife. You wouldn't leave John Grant and I couldnae leave poor Janet. The cancer destroyed her over time, but by then you decided it wasn't right to take Maeve from her father. Life wasn't fair with us. Seldom is life fair."

"It comes full circle."

He gave her a squeeze. "Aye, with a Grant in Dunnascaul, part of the riddle's fulfilled. Maybe they'll find that ruddy treasure."

Anne pushed away her sadness. "Do you think there's really a treasure?"

"I believe Cian agrees with me—the real treasure of the Grants is their women."

Gillian woke, the chill of the library touching her as she shifted.

Mrs. Cian Mackinnon. Hundreds of Grants must be rolling in their graves. Divinely happy, she wiggled her toes, then scooted her body against Cian. Oh, think of waking up every morn wrapped in those beautiful arms! Who needed a fireplace blazing when she could cuddle to this sexy bod?

The lids lifted over those sea-green eyes, a lazy half-smile spreading across Cian's sensual mouth. Cian pulled her under him, his weight pressing her down in the soft sofa. His hot mouth nibbled along her collarbone, and up the column of her neck, sending prickles of sexual anticipation snaking over her skin. As he latched onto her earlobe and sucked, she about melted.

Tilting her head to the side to give him better access, her unfocused vision half-saw the portrait of the braw Highlander in a kilt over the fireplace. Cian's ancestor two-hundred-years ago. Breeding ran true, for Cian could've posed for the painting. Beautiful Mackinnon men.

Something attracted notice at the edge of her peripheral vision. With Cian's hands moving on her body, it was hard to pinpoint what bothered her. It would be too easy to surrender to the power he wove around her. She finally pinpointed it.

The scroll of the stone fireplaces. There were seven saucer-sized discs across the face of the mantle. Each depicted a scene of Highland life, all related to harvest themes. The one in the centre showed men drinking. Underneath, was the word *Meadhoney*. Mead was made of honey, so it struck her as odd to have it said in that fashion. Wouldn't it be two words?

"Cian?"

"Hmmm," he murmured as he slid down her body, chaining kisses across her stomach.

"Why would they paint mead and honey together as one word?"

"What?" He raised his head. "You're asking a man with his tongue in your bellybutton to hold a reasonable conversation?"

"Put your randy thoughts on hold, Mackinnon, I'm on to something." She tried to sit up, but he pinned her to the sofa with his weight.

The sexy man flashed a killer smile. "No, I am *on* to something." He slid his hand around her breast, cupping it. "Something I find absolutely amazing."

She slapped his hand. "It thinks you're amazing, too. But I need your mind in gear and not on shagging me."

Cian sighed and sat up as she slithered out from under him. Pulling a grumpy face, he ran his hand through his hair as Basil tried to drag his tonnage onto the couch. Holding his palm up to his mouth he blew into it, then made a face. "Think it was the dragon breath, Basil?"

"Basil's not much of a conversationalist." Feeling the chill since she wore only Cian's T-shirt, she dropped a couple peat bricks on the fire and poked it. Then she rose to examine the tableau. Just a carved scene of men drinking from horns. "Why *meadhoney*?"

Lifting Basil on the sofa, Cian patted the kitty. "Woman's gone barmy on me again. Mead is made from honey. What's the deal?"

"Why *one* word?"

Shrugging, he came to stand beside her. "Lass, you in nothing but my T-shirt is more than my poor beleaguered brain can handle. Besides, I don't think about anything until I've had my tea."

"Cian, this is important. Think. What is middle in the Gaelic?"

"Basil, now she wants me to converse in the language of warrior kings." He chuckled as Basil laboriously rubbed against his leg.

"Cian!" she growled. "*Some smarter look closer to hearth. Clever is the lad or lass who can wisely riddle, to see something others cannot...*right in the middle."

"Gor, she's henpecking me already and I haven't gotten the ring on her finger. *Mead...*"—he paused as the reality hit him—"*...hon.*"

"Precisely. It was there all the time. Right before their eyes. It was soooo simple. *Meadhon* means *middle.* This is the centre tableau. The room is the centre of the castle." She leaned over examining the bottom rim. "Cian, look. There's a tiny groove here. You have a flat-headed screwdriver we can use to pry?"

Sliding into his shirt, he tossed her slacks to her. "Hide that tush if you want me to concentrate on treasure hunts. Don't get your hopes up lass," he cautioned, not wanting to see disappointment in her brown eyes.

"I'm not, but this is the only one with the groove. They told us *right in the middle of the hearth.* So simple. Everyone expected a difficult puzzle to solve. Told you I was good at riddles!" She shimmied into her black trousers, excitement nearly more than she could contain. "See, Basil, these hard-headed Mackinnon men needed a Grant lass in possession to figure it out."

Gillian shook her head as Basil keeled over in one of his death-faints. Pushing him aside with her foot, she examined the plate-size carved, green marble. There were no grooves on the other six and they appeared mortared in place.

Cian returned, shirt still not buttoned. If he thought she was distracting in just his T-shirt, she found it near impossible to concentrate on ancient riddles when flashes of that wonderfully sculpted chest tantalized her with visions of giving him a tongue bath. She buttoned the two lower ones, earning a kiss. Well, she left three undone. It'd be a sin to hide that chest completely.

"Sorry, lass, no having your wicked way with me. I think you solved the Grant's Riddle." He held up a foot-long screwdriver. "I think this'll do."

Gillian chuckled. "That thing's obscene."

"Stand back, Gillie, I'm very good with my *tool*." Scooting the limp cat to the side so he had room to work, he frowned. "I see pussycat's playing dead again."

"The excitement's too much for Basil."

"Breathing's too much for Basil." He inserted the screwdriver and used it as a lever. "I feel it give, but it's not coming out. Damn, I thought we were on to something."

"Ye of little faith. Let a Grant at it. It was under your Mackinnon noses and none figured it out." She saw it wiggle in place, but it wouldn't let go. She'd hoped they'd pry the face off and out would pop the treasure. "It jiggles."

"So does that sweet arse of yours, but it doesn't detach either." Sitting on the arm of the sofa, he watched her. His brow furrowed as he considered the problem. "Maybe it doesn't come out."

"Then why wiggle?"

Coming to the mantle he examined it. "Okay, right or left, lass?"

She shrugged, "Deasil."

He rotated it to the right until he felt the groove settle into a slot. "By damn...watch."

He gradually pushed the whole disk inward, recessing into the mantle. They heard a scraping sound, but couldn't tell where it came from. Cian looked at Gillian to see if she pinpointed the source of the noise. She shrugged. The disk stopped, didn't sink any farther into the marble mantle.

"Now what?" she asked.

Cian stepped back to look at the fireplace to see what he was missing. "You're the great unriddler."

Putting her hand on his bicep for balance, she leaned over to look up at the underside of the deep hood of the mantle. "It sounded like maybe from inside here. Look...isn't that a crack? Give me the screwdriver."

"Mitts off my *tool*, lass," he joked, kneeling down until he was beneath the mantel. Inserting the flat of the blade into the crack, he pried. "It's moving—"

There was a pop, and instantly, gold coins rained from the mantle.

"Bloody hell." Cian yanked her back as the fireplace

spewed hundreds of large gold coins like a berserk slot machine.

Gillian jumped up and down and hugged him, thrilled they'd found it. "Cian, we did it! We found the Grant's treasure!"

"No Blue-haired Go-Ins?" He picked up a coin, examining it front and back.

Gillian chuckled. "Actually, after spending this past week exploring the castle, I decided opening part to guests isn't such a bad idea. Dunnascaul is something rare, magic. Wouldn't hurt to share that for a few hours."

Cian glared at the coin. "Might be good you feel like that."

"Why? What's wrong? We found the treasure. No telling how old those coins are. Their weight in gold is worth a fortune, but old coins should go to auction for collectors. No telling their value."

He held a gold coin between his fingers flipping it. "We found a treasure, but not the Grant's cache. The date on the gold Louis is 1740."

"I don't understand."

Cian reached up in the hidey-hole dislodging more coins. "Your Yank raising is showing its head, lass. The French sent £4000 in gold Louis coins to the Bloody Bonnie Prince. Only when they arrived on the shores of Loch nan Uamh to deliver the four chests, they couldn't find anyone to give it to. Supposedly, they just left the gold on the beach. You think the Mackinnons and Grants hunted for the Grant's fortune. All of Scotland has hunted for centuries for Charlie's gold. The government will snatch this up. We'll get a finders fee. Certainly will give the Go-Ins something to natter about."

"Cian, the finders fee won't be small change. Can help with repairs—"

"I found something else." Cian pulled his lower arm from the hole, his hand holding a small chest. He rubbed his thumb across the dusty metal crest that adorned the top. "'ello, 'ello, I think this is the Grant's booty. Your family's crest."

"Maybe the Grants hid their treasure with Charlie's."

With a playful grin he held up the screwdriver. "We're about to find out."

"Down, *Toolman*. Let's try this before you destroy a piece of our history."

She removed the delicate chain from around her neck, then carefully pried apart the heart-shaped locket. Inside was a small key. Holding it up, she fit it into the lock on the box.

Her hand shook as it finally gave in the lock and the key turned. "Gran gave me the locket, when I was seventeen. Passed down through the Grant women. Said it'd hold the key to my heart's desire."

Moving to the table, Cian spilled out the contents. Large gems of every colour twinkled in the light. Basil tried to hoist himself up to the table to see what was going on, but only succeeded in looking as if he did chin-ups. Cian laughed, picked him up and put him on the table. Immediately the cat seized the idea the pretty toys were there for his enjoyment and batted a large yellow stone like a hockey puck.

"Careful, Basil. You're due to keel over any second," Cian teased.

Gillian snatched the stone away from the cat at the instant he sent it sailing off the tabletop. "Watch it there, Puss. Oh, Cian, they're...beautiful. Prepare for a little I-told-you-sos."

"They're beautiful lass. But basically worthless. These are garnets of various shades, citrine, beryls. Semi-precious stones. They were likely worth a lot to them, but not much today." Cian's eyes reflected his fear she was disappointed.

Gillian leaned to his kiss. "Oh, don't know about being not worth much. I think this citrine Basil used as a hockey puck would make the most beautiful engagement ring, and this green garnet would be a gorgeous pendant. Cian, we found not just the Grant's treasure, but Charlie's treasure. Our Blue-hairs will be so excited. Think what a great PR tag it will make when we advertise our vacation package."

"Lass, as long as I have you by my side I can face a whole herd of Blue-haired Go-Ins."

He leaned to kiss her, but there was a loud thump on the table.

"Basil," they said in unison, then slid their arms about each other.

The cat lay sprawled in the middle of dozens of semi-precious stones, purring.

The library was dim, lit only by firelight. Its orangish cast lent a magical glow to the room, fading into deep shadows. Anne patted the snoring kitty, still resting on the table in the midst of gold coins and the glittering gems.

"You're a silly beastie, Basil," she said in a whisper. Her eyes took in the couple drowsing on the sofa. Oh, but David's Cian was a braw and bonnie lad. Perfect for her beautiful, valiant Gillian.

David approached, just behind her shoulder and placed a hand on her back. "Mo gràdh, why do you fash? I thought you'd be happy. Cian and Gillian will marry soon. The castle shall fare well in their care. People will come from all over the world to see where Bonnie Prince Charlie's treasure was found. All is settled and well, isn't it. Did I no' promise you, lass?"

"Oh, aye. It's all so perfect. Dunnascaul is in their safe-keeping. Gillian and Cian are a beautiful couple, their love grows stronger every day. He'll give her beautiful bairns..."

"And?"

She forced a smile, her hand still rubbing the purring body of the silly pussycat. "You were never one for letting me hide from realities, David Mackinnon. That can be damned annoying at times."

"Stop avoiding the answer."

"He'll give her beautiful bairns, but we won't be here to see them."

"Och, Annie, where do you think we'd go?" He lovingly took her into his arms, cradling her head to his shoulder.

"But you said once our duty was finished we'd—" Anne looked up into the face she loved, willing to follow him into the fires of Hell.

His chest vibrated with the soft chuckle. "Annie, lass, you and Glennascaul are Heaven."

Rider in the Storm

P.E.A.R.L. Award Nominee 2006 –
Best Short Story from an Anthology

Pressing her foot down on the gas pedal, Ciara MacIain braced for the series of sharp S-curves up ahead. She was driving too fast on the dark, rain-slick road. Didn't give a damn. Hadn't given a bloody damn since that stormy, autumn evening seven years ago.

Her eyes glanced to the clock on the dash. Strange, she hadn't planned it, but she would reach the exact spot...*almost precisely to the minute.* A shiver shuddered up her spine as she half expected to see Rod Serling step from the shadows.

Portrait of a woman who thinks she has nothing to lose. Driving home too fast on a lonely, country lane one rainy night, she's about to find out she just took a turn onto a road ...that leads straight to The Twilight Zone.

Life bizarrely had come full circle. Did that mean something would *finally* happen to break the pall that held her in suspension? She'd read that every cell in your body is replaced within the passing of seven years, that you're really a new person at the end of the cycle. If only that were the case.

She thought back on the folly, which brought her to this point in time.

Blue Moon Madness. Had she really hoped a simple, heartfelt wish on a moon would work magic? Folklore said a rare enchantment could happen on the night of a Blue Moon. Too bad, she stopped believing in faerytales seven years ago this night.

The night Derek died.

She fought back the black depression that always came with the anniversary of his death. Friends assured her time healed, she'd let go of her grief and move on. Part of that was true. The raw ache, the crying jags, hysterical laughter edging toward madness—all that had faded, leaving a deadness inside. For years, she embraced that numbness, preferable to the pain. She just did her best to get through one day at a time.

The nights were the hardest. When she was alone—except for her cat, Sinnjinn. In the long hours of darkness, she'd cradled his huge, dark grey body to her chest, a purring, fur-covered life preserver, and simply endured until another sunrise came.

Now, she sensed the time had come to live again. She wanted a life, a home, a family. Only Derek's memory wouldn't let her go. She couldn't conjure that shimmering vision and not see Derek's beautiful face as a part of that future.

This morn she'd awoken to the pain of being thirty-seven, the years passing her by. Time to break the chains of the past. She'd hoped to shatter that hold, the suspension of her life by visiting his grave.

What an eegit she'd been.

On impulse, she'd gathered the bottle of champagne and come out to the cemetery, intent on wishing Derek a final farewell. Harebrained idea. Instead of a goodbye toast, she'd foolishly railed at the injustice of life, so furious Derek still haunted her...*that she hadn't followed him into the grave.* An utter dolt for dashing the bottle against the headstone when none of it—tears, pain, frustration—would change anything.

The warm autumn sun had filtered through the tall oak trees as she sat beside the grave and toasted their lost love, the beautiful life they would've had...the child they'd never create from that love. She ended up drinking the whole ruddy bottle, then hurled it against the gravestone in anger. Unable to stop herself, she'd flung her body across the grave and cried until she slipped into a stupor.

Coming to, she'd been cold. Small wonder. How stupid could you get? She'd fallen asleep on a grave in a cemetery. No, not a grave—*Derek's grave.* Fearful, she'd glanced around, but no one was about.

Just the Blue Moon overhead.

She couldn't have slept long. Maybe an hour or two. Deep dusk had settled over the silent landscape, but with the full moon up early there was enough light. Her eyes had taken in the shards of the broken *Moet* bottle, where she'd smashed it against the marble headstone, then to the oozing blood on the inside of her left arm. Evidently she'd cut herself on the glass. And bled. The blood upon the grave appeared black in the moonlight.

She looked at the huge blue orb in the sky. Gathering storm clouds worked to shroud it from view as the first droplets of rain hit her face. If only one could wish on a moon, to turn back the clock to that point in time where her life had been shattered...just like the wine bottle.

"I wish..." The words died in her throat.

What did she expect? There was no wish that could mend her life, her heart. No Faery Godmother. No putting Humpty-Dumpty back together again. Just her and the Blue Moon... and the body of the man she had loved more than life.

Blinking against the tears, she stared at the marble headstone bearing Derek's name. "Goodbye, my love." Choking back a sob, she'd run to her car.

The deluge hit, pounding on the metal roof. Outside, the tires made a soothing, whooshing sound as the car sped down the winding narrow road. The sound was hypnotic, lulling. It'd be so easy to close her eyes and let Fate take control of her life...*or death.*

Not a coward, Ciara fought to stay focused instead of letting the memories suck her into the past. Eschewing the break, her left foot shoved in on the clutch while her right increased the pressure on the gas. She downshifted and roared into the S-curves, losing no speed as she took the hairpin turns. Two more winding bends were up ahead, then the final one—the hardest of all to face.

Named the *Devil's Spiral,* the locals had laughingly called it *Dead Man's Curve,* after the old *Jan & Dean* song of the '60s. Her stomach did a small roll. They were right on that account. It was, indeed, a dead man's curve.

The spot where Derek had died.

Suddenly, that night was alive in her mind. The police calling...there had been a wreck—her fiancé, Derek Adams, was pinned in his shiny red Jaguar X-J sedan. A drunk driver had rear-ended Derek's Jag, slamming him into the path of an oncoming cement truck. The engine of the sports car was driven back, causing the steering wheel to pin him. They were using the Jaws of Life to get him out, but it would take time. An ambulance was already on the scene to transport him.

The female voice had been so kind, so solicitous. The words she'd spoken sounded like she was talking under water. As gently as possible, the officer suggested Ciara might wish to be at the hospital waiting. It chilled her blood.

Since the accident scene was closer, she'd raced there instead. The lights were the first thing she'd seen—the blue and red of the police cars, blocking off traffic. Their glare and flashing seemed to lash out and fill the rainy autumn dusk. Trembling, edging toward shock, she'd pulled off the pavement and jumped from her vintage Triumph. The officer had caught her about the waist as she ran toward Derek's car.

A scream tore from her throat when she saw the horrible wreckage. The red Jag looked like some bizarre accordion; the long, sleek sports car was neither long nor sleek.

"Miss...miss..." The officer's steel embrace dragged her back. "There's nothing you can do, Miss. He's gone. His femoral artery was sliced by a shard of metal. He bled to death before we could get to him. I'm sorry...so sorry."

She saw them pulling Derek from the wreckage, an IV attached to his neck. "But they're giving him fluids."

The EMT glanced up as they hoisted the stretcher to the back of the ambulance. "He's an organ donor, Miss. So sorry."

She nearly lost it. She recalled how laughing, beautiful Derek had signed his driver's license, designating in the event of his death his organs should be donated to help another to live. *I want my passing to count for something, my love.*

Blackness had claimed her, though the words echoed in her brain. *So sorry...so sorry...so sorry...*

Oh, how utterly obscene.

The memory never left her. Awake or dreams, it was always there. Odd. To this day, she couldn't recall the face of the man who uttered the words that had destroyed her world.

So sorry.

Like a robot, she heedlessly sped into the steep S-turns, downshifting and increasing the rev of the engine. Her foot never touched the break pedal. The velocity pulled the car out of the curves.

Ciara blinked again, shocked. A sense of unreality filled her as if she *had* taken the turnoff into *The Twilight Zone.* Just ahead was a flash of brilliant red, off to the side of the road. Her heart jumped into her throat, pushing her to slow the speed of the Triumph. She made out it was a car—a *red* car. She might puke. A vivid red Ferrari was off the pavement and nearly to the creek.

Right in the spot where Derek had died.

The engine whined a protest as she downshifted and stomped on the brakes, fishtailing on the wet road.

Ciara could barely see as the rain poured in sheets, cascading down the window screen and preventing the wipers from keeping it clear. She hesitated. Too far from the relay tower, the cell phone was useless. Common sense warned getting out and checking wasn't a good idea on this lonely road, yet she couldn't just pass and not ascertain if someone needed help.

She batted her eyes to blot away tears, straining to see through the rain lashing against the car. There was movement in front of the other vehicle, as if someone tried to push it from where it was mired in the mud. Suddenly, a figure—a man—straightened and came jogging toward her TR-6, waving for her to roll down the window.

He wore a black parka, the hood pulled up over his head. She couldn't make out the features of his face as he put his forearm on the roof and leaned down. "May I use your cell phone?"

He almost had to shout over the thunder that boomed the instant he'd opened his mouth. Droplets of rain hit her lashes as she stared up at his darkened countenance, wondering what he was doing out here. In a red car. At this precise instant.

Her heart thudded, slow, but it wasn't fear...precisely.

Ciara shook her head. "No good around here. The hills are too high."

"Bloody hell. Look, I know it's not smart to pick up a stranger..."—he hesitated, frowning and then glancing back toward his car—"but I really need to get somewhere to fetch a tow truck. I'm stuck. There's no getting that baby out of this mire."

Ciara liked the sound of his voice, a deep, sexy British accent that had an underlying hint of Irish brogue. A shiver crawled over her damp skin in reaction. It wasn't fear. Her fae sense whispered this man would do her no harm.

He was a total stranger, yet she found herself saying, "Come on, I'll give you a lift."

White teeth flashed, almost boyishly. "Thanks. Let me shut the 'rari off and lock up."

He trotted toward the low-slung sports car, the vivid red almost obscene in her car's high beams. Swinging open the driver's door, he leaned inside and cut the lights. When he pulled back, his hand held a black leather duffle. He locked the Ferrari, then pocketed the keys into his black slacks. Playfully male and about to be parted from *his baby*, he patted the car's roof, sighed and then jogged back.

Jagged lightning flashed, washing everything in brilliant blue-white.

Ciara's breath caught. Couldn't expel it. Bathed in the luminous glow, the long legs, the general shape of his torso evoked the memory of Derek. Then darkness fell and he was just a shadow moving in the rainy night.

He opened the passenger door and started to get in. "Tight fit," he complained, using the lever to scoot the seat all the way back. The long legs pushed in, his body followed, then he chuckled, "Very tight fit."

Her heart slowed at the seductive cant of the British accent. She forced words from her mouth, lest he think her an eegit. "*I* don't have a problem."

He leaned toward her, so he could stuff the duffle in the back. "That's because you have shorter legs."

She swallowed hard. Derek had always said the same thing when forced to ride in her vintage TR-6. "Why...why would you say that?"

The beguiling scent of male hit her full force, clouded her brain. Her heart jolted and beat fast, irregular. She tried not to breathe, to inhale his heady scent. Not a cologne, just a faint hint of soap and pure unadulterated sexy man. Heat rolled off his body and buffeted her senses.

Shifting, he reached up to tug back the hood. He sounded as if he wasn't sure. "Actually...it just popped into my head. I guess you being female, you're shorter than me, so..."

Feeling silly, she shrugged and reached to put the car into gear, but he dropped the hood and turned to smile.

Ciara flinched. His hair was blue-black, thick and wavy, not the white blond lion's mane of Derek. Derek had a lean hungry look, where this man's jaw was squarer, stubborn. But there was...*something about him*...a faint resemblance in the bone structure that evoked the poignant image of Derek in her mind.

"Roarke..."

Finally registering he'd spoken, she strained to focus. "Pardon?"

"I said my name is Roarke. Roarke Devlin." Full sensual lips crooked into a faint smile as he put out his hand to shake. He frowned, perplexed. "Are you all right?"

Ciara nodded, trying to force all thoughts back into their proper shoeboxes. She glanced to the beautiful hand, long, deft, the type found on a magician or a pianist, almost afraid to take it. Steeling herself, she slid her hand into his, then jerked when his warm fingers closed around hers. He held tight, not letting go.

"Jittery?" he asked.

Ciara shook her head, striving to dismiss her reaction. "Just static electricity and a little lightheaded—unnerved by... the storm."

Lightning flashed, flooding the car's interior. His smile froze as he turned her arm to examine the inside. "Small wonder. Do you realize you're bleeding?"

She felt like she'd been slowly bleeding to death for seven years. What did it matter it was now literally? She shrugged. "It's stopped...mostly."

"Maybe you should let me drive," he suggested gently. "You look pale, like you've seen a ghost."

Lightning flashed again and she stared into the very beautiful face of a stranger...*and yet...*

"A ghost? I think I might welcome something as simple as a ghost." She tried to grasp the fragile threads of reality. "Your name's Roarke?"

"Yes, Roarke Fraser Devlin. And you are—?"

"Ciara McIain."

"Ciara." Her name rolled off his lips with a hint of a brogue, spoken in awe as if it was magic. "Lovely name. Sounds Irish. With a name like Roarke Devlin, I should know." He grinned.

She struggled to make small talk. "Saint Ciara was an Irish nun who established a monastery at Kilkeary in the 7th century."

"But you're Scottish, aren't you? I hear the hint of the Highland burr in the odd word."

Ciara finally dragged her stare from him, pulled her hand back and put the car in gear. "Aye, I was born there, lived there with my grandfather part of each year. My mother just loved the name. Her mother was half-Irish."

"Whatever the motivation, it's beautiful."

"You're not from around here. I hear England in your voice, despite the Irish name and the faint brogue. Maybe around Colchester?" she guessed.

He shifted sideways in the bucket seat to observe her. "Very good. I was born outside of Colchester. Irish father, English mother. I'm from around here now. I bought one-hundred acres across the river and just finished putting up a log cabin style lodge."

"So you're the one."

"One what?"

"You erect a beautiful home out in the middle of nowhere,

you have to expect to be gossip fodder for miles around. Odd an Englishman would settle on the Kentucky River. The Palisades are awe-inspiring, but a little far out for jetsetter types. What made you choose to build way out here?"

He shifted in the seat once more and looked straight ahead. From the corner of her eye, she noticed a small tic at the edge of his mouth, as if he suppressed a smile. "You might say I followed my heart."

"Your heart?"

"Aye, I traveled the past few years, a lost soul, seeking... something. No place spoke to me, said this was where I belonged. I was in New York, walking down the street and saw this painting in an art gallery window, advertising a coming show. I stood there for the longest time, mesmerized by it. The painting was entitled, *The Palisades.* I went back and spoke to the artist when they held the show. He told me the painting was done one autumn while he was in Kentucky. I bought it, hangs over the fireplace in my home now. It was odd. I had never been to Kentucky, not even for the Derby—" He paused as if some stray thought distracted him. "Well, I was here for a spell, though I don't recall much of my stay."

Ciara echoed, "Don't recall?"

"Long story." He shrugged in dismissal. "As I stared at that painting, I knew in my heart this was where I was meant to be. So here I am."

Ciara swallowed hard. *Where his heart wanted to be.* In some ways she understood that. She could've moved far away, even considered it several times, knew it would likely be best to go somewhere new, then memories of Derek wouldn't pop up around every corner. At first she stayed to be near him, wrapping herself in the cocoon of what had been. He didn't feel so distant if she kept to the place where they had lived together, loved together. As she gradually returned to life, she contemplated selling the cottage and going back to Scotland, even took steps of listing it with the local realtor. In the end she couldn't go through with it.

Something kept her here. Her heart.

The turn off for Camp Robson was just up ahead. There wasn't much left of the old Civil War Camp since the state built the highway bypass forty years ago. Just the motel, the restaurant, gas station, small Post Office, the souvenir shop/ general store—that hadn't sold a souvenir in the last four decades—and J.C. Penny, a lawyer-realtor. Poor man could have avoided all the teasing by using John Calhoun Penny, but he seemed to enjoy the ribbing.

"Do you want me to stop in at Camp Robson or drive you to your home?" She flinched as lightning cracked overhead, the immediate sound of the thunder deafening. "It's the river. It attracts the storms."

"Stop at the garage. I hate leaving the 'rari out there. I fear coming back and finding it stripped or stolen."

She slowed and took the turn, following the steep winding road down the hillside. The tiny village appeared closed for the night. J.C.'s offices were dark and the restaurant was shut tight. Her TR-6 hummed its low-throttle noise as she swung into the semi-circular parking lot. In the lights' sweep she saw a white paper taped to the inside of the door and scrawled in a shaky hand: *Me and J.C.'s gone fishing until Monday—Mac.*

Roarke chuckled. "Scratch Plan A. If you don't mind, could you please take me home? I'll thank you by giving you a tour of my lodge and make you a cup of hot chocolate."

She shifted the Triumph into gear and rolled past the long motel that bore a striking resemblance to the one in the movie *Psycho*. Two cars were out front, but they belong to Mac. She couldn't recall anyone ever staying there, except for Anita Johnston's and Talbot Manning's Wednesday after lunch 'meeting'.

Once, this had been the main highway, with traffic so heavy it'd been dangerous to walk alongside it. As she stared at *Maude's Souvenir and Things*, the closed restaurant and motel that no one ever used, it struck Ciara how this place seemed suspended in time. All the buildings were well maintained, picture perfect. Only no one ever came anymore. The sleepy river village was caught in a bubble in time.

Just like the last seven years of her life.

As they started up the steep hill, the winds grew wilder. Trees swayed and bowed as jagged streaks of lights popped and sizzled about them. As the car came around the curve at the top of the hill, a bolt of lightning slammed into the huge water maple tree, splitting it in half in a shower of sparks that rained down on the hood of the car. Half of the centuries old tree crashed down across the road blocking it.

"Close call." Roarke laughed, stating the obvious.

Ciara sat shaking. "One way to put it."

He glanced back at the tiny village behind them. "Hmm, I guess we can break into the restaurant—or the Bates Motel."

"Twelve cabins—" she started, only to have him finish.

"—twelve vacancies." He looked at the antebellum house

on the far hill. Please tell me Mac and J.C don't have a Mother Penny stashed away in the root cellar."

"She died back in the '60s."

He chuckled. "Mrs. Bates wasn't exactly kicking, if you know what I mean."

She sighed, the hand of Fate on her shoulder. "There's another option."

"Oh?"

She pointed to the narrow road, which led up the other side of the hill. "You can come home with me."

Ciara was silent as she turned into her drive and followed it to the small cottage. What made her suggest to Roarke Devlin that he come home with her? A complete stranger. Was she mad? Maybe the rays of the Blue Moon had done something to her brain as she'd slept on the grave. Yes, the only logical alternative. However, logic had gone out the window the first time she looked into his pale green eyes.

"I could've walked home, you know." Roarke's words broke her mental ruminations, almost reading her second thoughts.

Lightning crackled again and the rain, that couldn't possibly come down any heavier, did just that. She glanced up at the roof, listening to the hammering. "Oh yeah, nine miles in this?"

He nodded acceptance, then leaned close to reach between the seats to get his duffle. Pulling back, his expression held awareness of her reaction to him. A seriousness flooded the luminous eyes. "I would never hurt you, Ciara MacIain."

The rain seemed to pause as they stared at each other. Maybe the world stopped turning. Spellbound by Roarke Devlin, Ciara forgot to breathe as her heart thudded in an almost forgotten rhythm.

His hand opened the car door, the sound snapping the spell. "We better run for it while this torrent is slowing. Thunder's off in the distance, saying another cell is headed our way."

Watching him push out of the seat, she sat for a moment to relish the lingering heat from his very male body. She mechanically pulled the keys from the ignition and gathered her purse to follow him.

Lightning flashed before they reached the porch, and in the white-blue brilliance, she stopped dead in her tracks, feeling as if someone had a hold of her heart and was squeezing it. Her senses were thrown for a loop. Ignoring the black hair, from the neck down his shape, how his muscles moved, was like watching Derek. *Deja Vu* slammed into her, every nerve screaming as desire crested, a wall of fire in her blood.

Not good. This was Roarke Devlin, not her lost love. Still, her mind cast back to the Blue Moon and her half-spoken wish. A wish to live again. How Roarke had been at the exact spot where Derek died—nearly to the minute—and in a shiny red sports car. Her heart nearly pulled a Charlie-horse as she watched his broad shoulders, the lithe torso, buns of steel moving in the faded jeans in a gait that had her feeling she saw in stereo—the memory of Derek, clouding and now mixing with Roarke.

Roarke.

He turned and waited as she shakily mounted the five stairs. Her footsteps sounded hollow on the plank porch and her hand trembled as she tried to separate the house key from the others on the ring. Blocking the images crowding her mind, she concentrated on getting that blasted key in the lock.

Roarke leaned near, his hand closing over hers to halt the quaking. She sucked in a sharp breath, as his heat, his scent rolled over her, through her. It awakened a hunger deep in the pit of her belly that was frightening.

His crooked finger slid under her chin and lifted it, forcing her to meet those haunting eyes. "If you're scared of me, I can leave. Are you scared of me, Ciara MacIain?"

"No...yes...it's just...an odd night. There's a Blue Moon tonight, you know. Folklore says if you wish on a Blue Moon, the wish will come true." She closed her eyes feeling an utter dope for rattling on about a ridiculous belief. "Silly, huh?"

"Perhaps. Perchance the Blue Moon was what called me. I was out driving, then suddenly I *had* to take Old Post Road. Don't even know how I ended up that far out." He paused, frowning out into the darkness. "There's a cemetery out there ...isn't there?"

She nodded, tears clogging her voice.

"I can't explain. I just knew I had to go there." He shrugged. "Not sure what I expected to find waiting. Destiny, I suppose. I just followed my heart. Silver lining, eh? We finally met."

Finally? She wanted to ask what he meant, but Roarke inclined toward her, so close his breath caressed her face.

Ciara fought the compulsion to lean into his body, to fling herself against him. Embrace that radiant heat that could warm her soul seven years cold.

Awe reflected in the crystalline depths, the green eyes slowly traced her countenance. His free hand seemed to lift of its own volition, the trembling fingers gently cupped the side of her face as his thumb stroked the curve of her cheek.

Emotions rose in her, so strong they swamped her mind, her soul. Swallowing the knot in her throat, she closed her eyes against tears threatening to spill.

The Venetian blinds covering the glass door rattled as a cat pushed up under them and waved his paw, meowing loudly.

The magical, precious bond, that breathless instant in time, was shattered.

Roarke's hand dropped as he chuckled. "Someone wants to be fed, if I know cats." He tapped on the glass as he worked the lock. "Hey, puss, puss..."

"You have a cat?"

"No, actually I never had one."

Ciara found the statement odd, contradictory. The train of thought was lost as she reached just inside to flip on the lights. The switch clicked in the stillness. Nothing happened. "Oh, bugger."

Roarke sniggered at her outburst, but followed her inside the silent house, bumping into her when she stopped abruptly.

"Um, maybe you should stay put. I'm not the neatest person. My tennis shoes are around...somewhere. I wouldn't want you to trip. I'll fetch you some dry clothes so you can change out of your wet ones. I forgot to get batteries for the torch last week, so I'll light a candle."

"Candlelight is more romantic." Roarke's deep voice sent a chill up her spine.

She whipped around. In the darkness, he was nothing more than a shadow. A frisson racked her body as she stared at him. The timbre of his softly spoken words...it almost sounded like Derek. Ciara gave herself a mental shake, once more wondering if she really hadn't wandered into a *Twilight Zone* episode.

"Stay here," she croaked inanely.

Kicking out of her shoes, she padded barefoot through the dark house, heading to her bedroom. Candles were kept in the nightstand, used to losing power as the river often drew the storms. Making her way to the cherry table, she slid the drawer open and pulled out the long taper. Flicking the lighter, she set the flame to the wick, its pale yellow glow instantly holding at bay the long shadows. Sticking it in the small brass holder, she went to the walk-in closet. At the back, she pulled out the bottom drawer and paused.

Derek's things.

She'd kept some items, not able to bring herself to give away all his belongings. A lot she'd donated to Goodwill, knowing he'd like his clothing helped someone less fortunate. Only she couldn't give away everything. It would've been letting go completely. She set aside a couple pair of jeans, shirts and sweaters, almost as if...she swallowed the sadness... almost as if he'd come back for them one day.

Her hand hesitated as she pulled out the black jeans and black oxford shirt. They'd fit Roarke. Their builds were too much alike not to go on like a glove. Sucking in resolve, she lifted the clothing from the deep drawer, picked up the candlestick and headed back down the hall into the living room.

A warm glow filled the room as Roarke knelt before the creekstone fireplace, feeding the catching fire twigs. They popped and crackled as the flames hungrily licked at the dry wood.

He was so handsome. Droplets of rain clung to the blue-black curls as firelight caressed the strong jaw, the sensual mouth. Ireland was stamped on his countenance. A warrior poet from ages past conjured by a wish on a Blue Moon.

Ciara watched as the fuzzy grey cat bumped against Roarke's thigh, purring so loud she heard it half a room away. Silly beast had never loved anyone but Derek. He disdainfully tolerated her because she fed him, let her blubber tears against his shaggy fur because he wanted to sleep under the duvet with her. At best, Sinnjinn treated her like a child he took care of, bossing her around, telling her when it was time to go to bed, time to awaken, and reminding they needed to be fed.

Oh, he had loved Derek. The critter had been mad for him and had licked his skin like the man tasted as good as catnip. Since Derek's death he refused to have anything to do with any human that came to the house. He would run and hide under the bed until company was gone. Now, he rubbed against Roarke like a long lost friend.

Roarke replaced the spark guard, then chuckled as the

mangy cat started slurping his wrist. Ciara's heart pounded. She fought vertigo as she watched the long beautiful fingers scratch the kitty's chin.

He smiled at the cat's antics, then stroked his head. "Hey, Sinnjinn, careful with that rough tongue. You're about to lick my skin off."

The room swayed about Ciara as she took two steps toward the man and cat. "You...you called him Sinnjinn." The words sounded like an accusation. Well, wasn't it? How did he know the cat's name?

Green eyes locked with hers, wielding a power that ripped into her soul, yet she couldn't read his emotions. Long black lashes swept downward, veiling his thoughts as his fingers searched the thick hair around the cat's neck until he uncovered the silver collar. Rotating it a half turn, he showed the metal plate with Sinnjinn's name.

She stood stunned—and not believing him. The collar had been hidden deep in the fuzzy cat's fur. He had to root it out. He couldn't have seen the cat's name by chance. Only there was no other way for him to know. She observed as the cat went back to washing Roarke's wrist.

Rising, he reached out his hand. "For me?"

She nodded and released the clothes, her eyes scrutinizing him with a wariness she couldn't quite fathom.

"Your husband's?"

A normal question under the circumstances. Only why did she have the feeling he already knew the answer? He was going through some pantomime. A shiver ran up her spine.

"No. My fiancé. He died seven years ago." *Tonight, almost to the minute when I picked you up*, she wanted to add, but left the words unsaid. Not wanting to say anything else, she suggested, "You can change down the hall. Then I'll toss your clothes into the dryer."

The pale eyes scrutinized her with an intensity almost feline. "Fate moves in mysterious ways, eh, Ciara MacIain?"

He headed down the hall, Sinnjinn capering at his heels. Her eyes followed Roarke in the dimness, once again struck by how much he evoked nuances of Derek. Halfway down the passage, without pause he turned to the left and closed the door on the bathroom.

"I'm losing it," she muttered.

Going back to her bedroom closet, Ciara stepped out of her damp denims and then shimmied into a pair of worn jeans, fastening them. Before closing the drawer, she snagged a soft, teal sweater.

The hairs stood up on the back of her neck, alerting her she wasn't alone. Turning, she was rattled to see Roarke leaning with his shoulder against the doorframe, Sinnjinn weaving around his legs. Relaxed, as if he belonged here.

She stared at one drop-dead, sexy man. The jeans lovingly encased his strong thighs, and the black shirt, buttoned just once, was a slight shade tighter across the shoulders and chest. It was almost reassuring to see it didn't fit him to perfection.

That small comfort was quickly replaced with something more disturbing—a stirring of her libido. She hadn't made love with a man since Derek's death. That part of her died with him on that wet, lonely road—she'd thought.

Now, she was awakening to life and she wanted this man with every fiber in her pores, craved him with a force she found crippling. Her breasts grew heavy, tightening, pushing against the dampness of her bra. She attempted to swallow the knot in her throat. It didn't budge.

He came to her and took her wrist, then tugged the sweater from her grasp. Rooted to the floor, Ciara told herself to breathe as she fought against the waves of his intoxicating heat, his haunting scent. Images flashed through her. His hands grabbing hold of her derrière and lifting her, her legs wrapping around those strong, lean hips. Of his mouth feasting on her neck, taking her lips in a no-holds-barred kiss that'd fry her mind

And she'd let him. Encourage him. There wasn't a bone in her body that would offer resistance. All she had to do was take one little step toward him. Supercharged by his potent male pheromones, singed by how he turned her on, Roarke made her feel alive for the first time in years.

Just...one...little...step.

Using her wrist, he towed her toward him. Her blood jumped, turning to molten lava. He was taking the choice from her, making it easier. She didn't have to decide.

Just as she almost arched to his strong body to accept that first kiss, he turned, nabbed up the candle and gently pulled her from the enclosed space.

Oh bugger, embarrassment flooded her cheeks. How pathetic, how easy she must have appeared to him. She wanted to shove him out of the closet and yank the door closed behind him.

What a silly fool she was—wishing on a Blue Moon and

wanting kisses from a stranger.

Like an obedient child, she followed him into the bathroom. The hooded eyes assessed her as he set the candleholder down on the sink so the mirror reflected the light, permitting him to work. With deft, sure movements he opened the medicine chest and selected items. Turning on the tap to fill the sink with warm water, he tugged a plastic cup from the wall dispenser.

"Hold your arm over the water," he instructed calmly.

Damn him. Her heart knocked painfully, still in overdrive due to his virile sensuality. While the basin's level rose, he cuffed and rolled the sleeves on Derek's black shirt. Ciara couldn't take her eyes off the beautiful lower arms, the sure hands. Large hands, yet they worked with a deftness, a precision of an artist or a magician.

She shuddered. If he ever laid them upon her cool flesh, she feared he would truly be the Magic Man. That conjured the old song by Heart...*seemed like he knew me...he looked right through me*...that was the sense she got off Roarke—he knew her.

He kept pouring water on the jagged cut to be sure there weren't tiny shards of glass left in the wound. Finally confident it was cleansed, he poured iodine on it.

"Ooowwww..." Ciara sucked in her breath and tried to jerk her arm back, but his grip held firm.

"You would've let me kiss you, wouldn't you?" he asked carefully, blotting the wound, then rolling the gauze around it.

Being in the bathroom with Roarke was too close. He sucked all the air from the enclosed space...filled it with the heat from his body, his burly fragrance, which conjured whispers of cool sheets and hot sex.

She could deny the truth. A silly game not worth the time. They both knew the answer; he merely forced her to admit it.

Ciara watched his gentle hands wind the gauze around her arm, mesmerized by the dexterity of a magician's fingers, envisioning them on her face, her neck...her breasts. He took her hand and placed her index finger on the gauze while he ripped tape from the roll to secure it in place.

"Thank you." When she started to turn away, he caught her wrist.

"Want to tell me what you were doing bleeding in a cemetery at night?" His voice had a note of humor, but there was also a thread of real concern.

"Not really."

One side of his mouth tugged upward. "Then answer my other question. You would've let me kiss you, wouldn't you?"

Lowering her gaze, Ciara gave a faint nod.

"Lady, you live dangerously." His laugh was soft, magical. It sent Goosebumps up her spine.

Lifting her eyes, she met those haunting, pale ones. "No, you're wrong. I don't live a'tall anymore."

Fearing she revealed way too much of the torment within her, she swung around. He pulled her back where he still gripped her wrist. "He wouldn't want you to die for him."

She closed her eyes, anguish roiling within as if he'd physically slapped her. "What could you know about it?" she choked out.

His reply stopped her cold. "I know what my heart tells me."

She blinked away tears, trying to control the black despair. "Your heart seems to do a lot of talking to you."

"These days it's quite insistent."

Needing distance from his potent enchantment, she turned her back to him and hurriedly slid on the sweater. "Come on. I'm hungry. I'll fix something to eat."

She didn't wait for him to answer, just left him to follow.

To distance herself from Roarke, she'd used the excuse she was hungry, a means to break the lethargy in which he'd held her. Yet, she now realized it was true. Most days she ate simply because she felt bad when she skipped a meal, not because of an appetite. Oddly enough, she was ravenous. Damn. First time in years she really wanted food and the electricity was off, so they'd be relegated to bologna and pork 'n beans. She stopped short and both the man and cat collided into her back.

Roarke put a hand on her shoulder, then one on her stomach to stop her from falling. Then didn't release her. "Watch it. You already have a gash on your arm. Wouldn't want to add a sprain to that."

She closed her eyelids against the wave of desire that exploded in her blood. Her spine remained ramrod stiff, lest she'd step back so that hard male body pressed against her curves. His long fingers flexed on her stomach as she sent out a telepathic plea for that hand to move up, to cup her breast, squeeze it...or lower, to snake between her legs.

Forcing her thoughts past the violent yearning, she forced out, "I'm not sure about this...I never tried it, but I have a grill that's meant to work on the fireplace. I could fix a steak and a salad."

"A delightful idea. Embracing the unknown is often quite enlightening. I find I'm suddenly ravenous."

Her head snapped around to assess his handsome face, his words echoing her very thoughts. She had the fae suspicion Roarke Devlin had read her mind.

Ciara leaned back, her stomach aching from eating every bite of the strip steak and the garden salad. Using oven mitts, Roarke removed the fireplace grill so it wouldn't smoke up the living room. He dashed to the kitchen with it, dumped it in the sink, then came back. Sinnjinn dogged his every step, frolicking around his heels.

She hadn't seen the cat this happy since Derek died. In the first few weeks, she feared the cat might actually grieve to death. He would sit for hours on end in the picture window, watching, waiting, sure Derek would return home. Slowly, he finally accepted Derek wasn't coming back.

Almost tripping due to the feline, Roarke leaned over with a laugh and scooped up the fuzzy cat. One hand holding Sinnjinn's front legs, the other the back ones, he draped the pussycat around his neck as if the cat was a fur collar.

She'd been smiling, but suddenly it was a challenge to breathe normally. Derek used to do that with Sinnjinn. The huge kitty would curl around his neck loving their 'game'.

Roarke sat on the floor with his back against the sofa. He released the cat, but the fuzzy beast stayed, purring his heart out. "You look sad, Ciara. What summons your melancholy."

She hesitated to bring Derek up, yet his spectre seemed so close. Only she wasn't sure what to say, how to start.

"You think of your Derek," he answered for her. "Remember him, the precious love you shared, Ciara. No one likes to think they die and are then forgotten, their presence little recalled. So Derek would appreciate you keeping his memory, honoring him in your heart. What he wouldn't want is for you to permit that love to cripple your life."

She reeled from the impact of his words—his truth. Angry, hurt, she resented him speaking so. How dare he? A stranger shouldn't be able to see so much, like her soul was stripped naked. It left her exposed, incensed.

"You haven't moved on with your life, have you, Ciara—as he would've wanted you to?" he pressed, giving her no measure. "He died seven years ago and you've spent every day drowning in your grief, haven't you?"

Unable to speak, Ciara steeled herself against the pain. It couldn't hurt any more if he'd slapped her. She started to rise, but he caught her arm and yanked her back to the floor. The penetrating eyes held hers, bore into her mind. So startling in their paleness. Nothing like Derek's hazel ones, yet...for a brief instant she felt she stared into Derek's eyes. *A trick of shadow and flame,* she told herself.

Anguish flooded his face. He closed his eyes and leaned his head back as if to ward off the intensity of what he'd seen within her. Swallowing hard, he licked his lips, striving to regain control of his emotions. Slowly the lids lifted and the green eyes fixed her with a power that made her shudder. "You've considered suicide. Haven't you?"

"Damn you, you have *no* right!" Ciara tugged against the hand holding her upper arm, willing him to release her.

"Truth or dare, Ciara." Determination rang clear in his voice

Her heart nearly stalled, then jumped, slamming against her ribs. She sucked in a breath. "How?" Once more, how could he know? Derek always used that taunt when she tried to hide from answering him. "Did you know Derek? Were you friends?"

"Friends? I suppose I consider him a friend...in a strange sort of way, but no, we never met. I think I'd have liked him. Surely, he was a man to be admired if he made you love him so strongly. You have thought of killing yourself. Truth or Dare."

Her trembling hand reached out and rubbed the nose of the cat. The silly critter's hind legs had slid off Roarke's left shoulder, but he remained draped over the right and was half-sleeping, content. "Once, I saw no reason to go on. The doctor had given me a tranquilizer and that brought a fuzziness to where I didn't care. I thought how easy it would be to take the whole bottle. Then the question of caring, pain, of being alone...wouldn't matter."

"What stopped you?" His grip eased now he saw she'd stay and answer the truths she'd rather not face.

Her voice was barely a whisper. "Sinnjinn knocked the bottle from my hand."

"Remind me to order him a case of caviar tomorrow." The corner of his mouth twitched in a half-smile as his head inclined to the cat's and rubbed against his. "You said once?"

She leaned back against the couch and looked to the

ceiling. She hadn't realized she said once. Damn man was too astute. Once...meaning she considered it again.

"Tonight? Why you were out at the cemetery visiting him?" He lifted her arm and frowned. "Did you try to kill yourself tonight, Ciara?"

She shook her head. "No."

"No?" It was clear he didn't believe her.

"I think I went there to die tonight. Not in the fashion you think. I'm not sure how to explain. I went to say goodbye. To toast our love. I need to live again...or just give up. I drank the whole stupid bottle—and I'm not a drinker—ended up crying and smashed it against the headstone. I'm not sure how I cut my arm."

"Life is precious, Ciara MacIain. Every morning of the last seven years I'd awaken and welcome the sunrise. Each is beautiful, special, because I'm alive to see it. You asked what I know about your pain, about losing something very special. You see I almost did...my life. It made me cherish those sunrises, made me reach out for every day with both hands, never to waste a moment."

He brushed his lips across hers, faintly, then increasing the contact. Finally settling fully. Ciara, cold for so long, suddenly felt warm down to her toes. She leaned into the kiss hungry for more, to absorb his passion for facing sunrises, make it her own.

Just as he shifted to pull her against him, the lights came on. At the same instant the alarm on his gold watch sounded. Pulling back, he blinked at the brightness, then checked the wristwatch and shut it off. "Ah, saved by the bell. If you will excuse me."

With no explanation, he rose in a fluid movement, picked up the black duffle from the sofa and headed to the kitchen. Curious, Ciara tracked him through the open arched door. He went to the cupboard, where the tumblers were kept, and took one down. Next, he reached into the fridge for the ice water. His actions were sure, as if this were his home and not the home of a stranger. Sinnjinn curled around his ankles, murring to him.

Logic said the actions were intuitive, he'd likely seen her getting the glasses before...surely most people kept water or juice refrigerated.

Only when Sinnjinn whined, begging for goodies, and Roarke—without pause—opened the bottom cabinet and reached in for the bottle of Pounce, did that nagging fear travel up her spine in prickles. The cat danced on his paws until Roarke put a few in his bowl by the stove.

She could no longer wrap herself in logic and excuse Roarke's actions.

Rising, she slowly entered the kitchen. Hearing her, he turned his back to what he'd been taking from the duffel. Blocked her as if he'd rather she didn't see. His eyes studied her as she reached past him. With a resigned shrug he stepped aside, permitting her access. There was half a dozen bottle of pills. She picked up one after another, not getting any quick answers...*Cyclosporin, Tracolimus, Prednisone, Azathioprine, Methotrexate*...immunosuppressants and steroids.

Trembling, she set down the last amber bottle. Her throat nearly closed around the forming words, the enormity more than she could absorb. Cold, she fought the edge of shock, a rising despair threatening to claim her.

"You're ill?" She hardly believed it. He looked so very healthy.

"No."

She sucked in a deep breath trying to steady herself. "Oh, you take steroids and immunosuppressants for the fun of it?"

"I'm not ill. In fact, they say I'm quite the picture of health ...now." He began opening the caps and popping the pills into his mouth, washing them down with the chilled water.

"Now?"

"Yes, now. Seven years ago I contracted a rare virus, some sort of super strep and it damaged my heart. I thought I just had a really bad case of the flu. On a business trip to Chicago, I realized how ill I was. I collapsed in a meeting. They moved me to Louisville, because of the advanced heart transplant program there." He laughed, but it wasn't mirthful. "Thirty-nine-years old and suddenly they told me my only hope to live was a new heart. I don't recall much of that period or maybe I would've been more terrified. They flew me into Standiford Field in Louisville on a stretcher, too weak to make the trip otherwise. No sooner than they settled me for the night, they woke and prepped me for surgery. To make a long story short, a miracle happened—I'd barely been on the recipient list two days when they found a heart. A perfect match. I have a rare blood type—"

Faint, Ciara clutched at the cabinet to steady herself. "AB Negative?"

He nodded, keeping several paces away from her as if he

feared she wouldn't want him closer.

A mournful wail rose up within her, a wounded animal sound. She shook her head, fighting what she knew was to come. "Nooooooooo!"

I want my passing to count for something, my love.

Legs rubbery, she backed up, leaning against the sink's counter for support. She stared at Roarke, feeling so many conflicting things that nearly overwhelmed her.

"Fate's a bitch sometimes, Ciara." He unbuttoned the single button on the black shirt, exposing his gorgeous chest. A chest marred by a long scar, running down the center. "Don't hate me because I lived and he died."

"You...*knew*...who I was...that you..." It hurt too much for her to form the words.

His beautiful throat worked to swallow as he observed her reaction.

"How...long have you known?"

"Known?" His body jerked as he tried to laugh but failed. "You wouldn't believe me if I told you. *I don't believe it. Sometimes...ah, hell...I don't know anymore.*"

He moved toward her. Ciara put out her hand to stop him from getting closer. She didn't want all those supercharged male pheromones confusing her brain. Instead of accepting she limited access to her space, he invaded, walked up to her until her hand touched his chest.

Sure that her panic showed in her eyes, she was transfixed by her hand nearly fused to the spot where, so warm, so alive, the heart thudded. So strong.

Maybe too strong? Concerned, her eyes jerked up to collide with his. "Are you all right?"

Lips pulled in a self-deprecating smile. "No, I'm a man and a very sexy, warm, sensual woman is touching my flesh. A male's never *all right* in such circumstances."

"But your...heart is racing." Ciara swallowed the pain clogging her throat, pushing past her pain, to embrace the concern for Roarke.

I want my passing to count for something, my love.

It had. Roarke Fraser Devlin lived because Derek's heart now beat for him. Derek died. Nothing could change that. She could resent Roarke was alive while Derek's life ended that night seven years ago. Silly skewed logic. Derek died because Fate decreed his time had come. It was as simple as that.

It wasn't Roarke's fault. He didn't take something away from Derek. In his passing, he'd given her one last gift—he'd saved this beautiful man's life.

She tried to smile through the tears, all of it hurting like a knife in her chest.

As a tear trickled down his cheek, Roarke returned her smile. "You're upsetting me on two levels. I react to your physical stimuli to my male system, and I'm concerned about how you are taking the news that a part of Derek lives within me. Why I stayed away from you these past months since I came to Kentucky. I'm worried, yes. The racing seems exaggerated to you because this heart beats faster for me than it did for him. During the operation, they had to cut the nerves to the heart, so the transplant beats faster—not sure why, it just does—about 100 to 110 beats per minute."

"But you are healed? You're not in any danger?"

"The doctors call me their miracle patient. My body has accepted his heart better than any transplant they have ever seen. The tissue match was so perfect. I was healthy up to the virus attacking. I take very good care of the gift given me. My cardiologist said he feared without the transplant I wouldn't have lived through the night. I would've died—seven years ago this night. Derek Adams gave me a second chance. I take all my meds to see my body continues to accept his heart. I watch my diet, take lots of vitamins and exercise daily. Thousands of transplants are done every year. Many people do very well with them. I've lived seven years with it. I just had my yearly check up last week. My doctor is very pleased how I'm doing. A lot of the statistics on longevity is misleading. Some continue with bad habits that endangered their own heart in the first place. They continue to drink and smoke, eat foods heavy with fat, don't take vitamins. They abuse the second chance they were given. Also, most were in very bad health for years before the transplant. I was a very healthy male before the virus hit." He paused, the tone of his words lowered, "I'm a very healthy male, Ciara *mo anam cara.*"

She braced herself against hearing the Gaelic. *Mo anam cara.* My soulmate. "*How?* How can you know these things? You didn't see Sinnjinn's name on his collar. Derek called me that—Ciara *mo anam cara.* But you know that. You speak his words—"

"I told you—my heart speaks to me."

"I don't understand." she whispered, in disbelief, in a shard of hope.

He spun away, then dragged his hands through his hair

nearly pulling at it. Stopping, he closed his eyes and breathed slowly, inhaling and exhaling to almost a count of ten—lowering his heartbeat, she realized.

Lightning cracked overhead, causing the lights to flicker. In some ways she could almost believe Roarke summoned the bolts. So easily she could see him as a warlock drawing down nature's power, envision him walking across the darkened land with jagged streaks of lights cracking from his fingertips. She sighed at her imagination. Well, it was no more bizarre than this man knowing Derek's thoughts because of the heart beating in his chest.

"How? I don't know. It started when I awakened after surgery. I was heavily sedated, tied up to every monitor imaginable. At first, I had trouble recalling who I was. Then as images came to me, I expected you to be there holding my hand. You were so clear in my mind. Later, I asked where you were and the nurses seemed puzzled, had no idea who Ciara was.

"As I healed, pieces of my life came back. Still, I have big blanks of the past that's gone, like my memory was wiped clean. The doctors explained that there's a time when the heart is stopped, as the old one was removed and the new one took over. It causes a memory loss. Memory loss I could accept; there wasn't anything special in my life. I was a workaholic. The job was everything. It was all the other..."

"Other?"

"Memories gained. They dismissed me, chalked up what I saw in my mind as dreams. I stopped trying to tell them after awhile because they looked at me strangely. They said once I was on my feet and back to my life these things would fade." He shook his head. "They didn't. They increased. There was no going back to my life. I stopped caring about my business. I sold it. Colchester was no longer home. I didn't belong there anymore. I went to Scotland. It called to me. I even bought a place there. Only..." His eyes roved over her, hungry. "Only a part of me was missing. I came back to the States, wandering lost, not knowing where I needed to start to put my life together again. One day walking aimlessly, I stopped before an art gallery and saw the painting of The Palisades...knew as I stared into it, I had to come here, the answer was at the end of that trail. Same as I knew when I saw the land across the river."

"Knew what?"

"Knew I had lived here before. As I began building the

house, I hired a private detective. They don't like to give out donor information. Fearful of a lot of mental problems on both sides. Even so, it wasn't hard for him to piece the puzzle together. Then I had to accept I had not only Derek's heart, but his thoughts."

He moved to the back door, looking out in the night as thunder shook the whole house to the foundation. With the last rumble, the lights snapped out.

"If you knew about Derek...about me...why did you wait?" She moved to relight the candle on the oak table.

As its glow filled the room, she saw him lift his hand to the glass of the door, very slowly placing his fingertips to his ghostly reflection. "I've watched you, kept my distance. It's my problem, I wasn't sure I had the right to drag you into it. If someone came up to you with a story of having not only Derek's heart, but his memories, would you not think him a lunatic? I cannot explain, Ciara. I just *know* things. The Egyptians used to remove all the organs from a body before they mummified it. But not the heart. The heart was left with the body because they believed that was where the soul lived, where your memories were housed."

Ciara walked to him, seeing his pale eyes reflected in the glass of the door, where his hand was pressed to the pane. She understood the gesture. He touched the reflection, the ghost in the glass—Derek.

Those haunting eyes tracked her, using the panes like a mirror. He was so still as if afraid of her reaction to all he'd told her. Afraid she would hate him. Maybe afraid she'd *accept* him because of his connection to Derek.

The pain, the depression was suddenly released within her. She loved Derek, always would. Would always feel pain at his tragic death, his life being cut short. But Roarke was right. Derek would be angry that she'd given up on life. He would never want that from her.

Maybe in some bizarre way this was her Blue Moon wish answered. Derek's final gift to her—he gave her Roarke.

The heaviness in her heart that lived there for the last seven years was released, left her just like a fist opening and releasing its hold. Peace flowed through her, an acceptance that wishes did come true, that there was magic in the world, a reason to go on.

She lifted her hand to stroke his jaw, but pulled back.

"Don't touch me casually, Ciara." The warning was soft, almost a whisper.

She managed a smile. "Casual? I don't think I could touch you casually. I have been inundated by images of your hands caressing me—"

"My hands?" The challenge was there.

"Yes, your hands." Very carefully, she placed her left hand over the back of his where his fingertips were pressed to the glass, touching him as he touched the ghost in the glass. "Seven years ago I lost Derek. He was a very special man and I loved him. He used to tell me he signed his organ donor card so his passing would count, that another could live. He gifted you with life that night. I know he would have liked that. Now I think he is gifting me with a miracle, giving *me* life again."

"I'm not Derek, Ciara."

She nodded. "I know. You are Roarke Fraser Devlin."

"A part of him lives in me. I accept that. Can you?"

"Yes, I think I can." There was a strange tranquility in her, an inevitability. Fate. Of things wished for on a Blue Moon that were granted.

Lightning tore jaggedly through the night, punching into a large oak tree in the back yard, sending sparks flying and a huge limb crashing to the earth. Ciara jumped in fright. Roarke caught her. Like a terrified child, she clung to him, wrapping her arms about his ribcage and holding him tight. Her head nestled in the curve of his neck, relishing the shelter of his embrace. He was so warm, so alive. His heart thudded strong, causing hers to match its cadence. His heat poured into her blood.

It felt like coming home.

"Oh, Ciara, lass, I've watched you for so long...burned to come to you." He squeezed her tightly to his chest.

Snuffing her stuffed nose, she let tears fall. "Why didn't you?"

"I didn't think it was fair to you...fair to me. I had just about made up my mind to leave Kentucky. I was going for one last drive when I knew I had to take Old Post Road. I felt an urgency pushing, compelling me. I followed it." He paused, his mind obviously casting around to explain. "I had to go out there...to the cemetery. As I started those series of curves I felt oddly like a watcher in my own body, as if there was another presence inside of me."

"How did you get off the road?"

"The closer I got to that point, the less I felt like me. I'm not one to believe in ghosts, but I think I relived Derek's last moments...the accident was real in my mind, the car crashing in the back of mine slamming me headlong into the cement truck. Only at the last instant did I seem to awaken and cut the wheel, spinning off the road."

He was silent for a moment. The only sounds were the rain lashing at the door and the pounding of his heart.

"I guess you think I am crazy...sometimes I do."

Ciara shook her head. "No, I believe you. There are things in life that often defy the normal boundaries of our understanding." She placed her hand on the heart that now beat for him. "Miracles do happen."

"His last thoughts were of you, Ciara. How he loved you, sorry he'd been driving too fast, was careless with something precious...his life, your love. His last wish was he wanted you to be happy."

I want my passing to count for something, my love.

Ciara raised on her toes and brushed her lips against his cool ones. They were soft. He tasted of the wine they'd shared. He tasted of Roarke.

She yearned for more. As she leaned into him, pressing her body to his, she felt his muscles tense.

"Don't play with fire, Ciara. Don't give me the promise of something you cannot keep."

She sighed and exhaled deeply. "I've been cold for too long. I could use a little fire in my life." Reaching up she used her thumb to trace the sensual mouth, the fullness of the lower lip.

Suddenly, Roarke lifted her into his arms—his very strong arms—and cradled her with ease against his chest. His forehead dropped to hers as he started to kiss her.

Her shaking hand pressed to his mouth. "I don't mean to..."

"What, Ciara?"

"Should you—"

"Ciara, I'm more than capable of making love to you. Don't make an invalid of me."

She laughed softly, "No, I was worried about you lifting me."

He leaned his face against hers. "I can lift you. I can make love to you. Right now, I just want to hold you through the night and keep you warm. Just that. Anything else is too soon."

Ciara cuddled against the curve of his strong neck as he carried her into the living room and then down the darkened hall to her bedroom. She loved the scent of his skin, better than any expensive cologne. It was pure Roarke. Intoxicating.

Carefully placing her on the soft bed, he sat and slid off his shirt. Rolling on his hips, he snagged the duvet and pulled it over them. Roarke shifted, curling almost protectively against her.

"Close your eyes and rest, Ciara *mo anam cara*. We have plenty of tomorrows to come."

Filtered sunlight touched her face. Opening her eyes, she was covered with the fluffy duvet. She smiled and stretched. Pausing, she reflected this was the first time since...since Derek died she'd awakened and felt like smiling.

Roarke.

He'd held her all night, his arms cradling her tightly. Later, she'd drowsily shifted and found herself spooned against his chest. His heart thudded strongly against her back. She'd slept so peaceful.

Maybe Blue Moons did grant wishes.

Suddenly, the scary sense that it'd been nothing but a Blue Moon dream filled her with panic. Her eyes searched around for some sign that Roarke had been real, he'd been with her all through the night, kept the coldness at bay. Frightened, she rushed down the hall and into the living room. Her rising fear only slowed as she saw the black leather case sitting on the kitchen counter. Relieved, she put a hand to her heart until the pounding stilled.

Finally making her way to the front door, she opened it.

Sinnjinn sat in the middle of the porch swing, his purrs causing it to rock. She could swear the cat was smiling.

Roarke stood, his bare back to her. His beautiful back. His left arm propped high against the column, he stared out into the mist hovering over the river, lost in thought.

Was he regretting things said under the Blue Moon? Had the bright light of day brought back simple realities? Realities he lived because of Derek. Did he doubt her?

Her stomach fluttered with butterflies of nervousness. She took a step backward in disappointment, in fear. Only, shafts of morning sun poked through the morning fog and the sun reflected off the glass across the river. Roarke's home.

She bounced two steps to him, wrapping her arms around his chest and hugging him.

"Morning, Roarke Fraser Devlin."

Turning in her embrace, he wrapped his arms around her and hugged her to his chest.

"Morning, Ciara *mo anam cara*." He leaned to brush his lips across hers. Pulling back, his green eyes searched her face. "I cannot promise forever."

"Neither could Derek." Ciara nipped his chin. "Me and Sinnjinn will settle for today, and tomorrow...and next week... and next month...then we will worry about tomorrows."

Devil in Spurs

P.E.A.R.L. Award Nominee 2006 –
Best Short Story from an Anthology

The road was a ribbon of moonlight,
over the purple moor,
And the highwayman came riding –
Riding –
~ Alfred Noyes

Desdein Deshaunt's spurs dug into the horse's side, goading the animal onward. *Faster. Faster.* Devil take him, he abhorred running fine-blooded horseflesh until foam lathered its neck. Grimacing, he swallowed the crumbs of conscience. Warrior's Heart was a mount worthy of royalty, only fate left him no choice. This night he must push his steed to the very limit.

His brother's life depended upon it.

He leaned forward in the saddle, willing the magnificent black stallion to sprout wings and fly through the pitch-black night. With rising dread, he glanced up at the moon, his heart slamming against his ribs when he saw how high it sat in the sky.

A Blue Moon.

Folklore said if one wished upon a *Blue Moon* an enchantment would be granted. He stopped believing in hocus-pocus parlor-magic back before he left Eaton and went to live with *grand-mère* in France. Even so, circumstances warranted desperate measures.

When man needed help, he called upon God. When no answer came, he turned to the Devil. Desdein knew his soul was black as the stallion he rode, that he cared little about anything in life these past years. But he did care for Jeremy. He'd see him set free – or die trying. If he could just rescue his brother, there was a ship setting sail at dawn, bound for the

Americas.

He'd give his life's blood to see Jeremy safely onboard.

Make a wish? If he had one wish, he prayed to catch the coach up ahead before it reached Kildorne Manor.

If he'd ridden hard on the heels of Lady Ashlyn Findlater, this night's work would have been a simple matter. Forced to hide his real identity, he played the *ton* buffoon, so all eyes had been upon him at the small country ball. His quick departure would've raised eyebrows.

Quite absurdly, he was in great demand these days. His rapier wit, droll humor and deadly lampooning of those about him saw Desdein at the top of all invitation lists for fêtes of the nobility. One didn't dare give the *cut direct* to the Marquis de Fournier. Though the title was real, it was worthless, coming through his *grand-mère,* who never had any blunt. Less since they escaped the *Reign of Terror.* Being a *ton* fop was just another mask he used to move through life these days.

By day, he was a gentleman horse breeder, but each night he donned the plumed apparel of a *ton* peacock and became the rapier-wit Marquis de Fournier at the most lavish balls of English nobility. Men feared him. Women wanted him. There wasn't a female—married or virgin—who'd deny him—except for Ashlyn Findlater.

Her image shimmered in his mind, the dark blonde hair, the huge grey eyes that always seemed to hold a sadness few bothered to notice. He dismissed the vision, though those eyes lingered, haunting him. They had drifted into his dreams more than once these past weeks.

The *Mad Marquis* they called him. What no one knew, under the moon's pale rays he was a highwayman. They whispered in dread he was the *Devil in Spurs* and the sobriquet stuck.

He hadn't taken to the roads for enjoyment or gain. His path was one of vengeance, pure and simple. Twenty years ago, the Earl Whitmore and Viscount Kildorne had robbed his father of nearly all in a game of Whist—*so they said*—then killed him in a duel to make certain no claims of malfeasance could be lodged. Desdein swore upon his father's grave that one day he'd crush the bastards. After Father's death, Mother slipped into decline, gave up on living until she, too, lay in the cold grave. At sixteen, Desdein had been left with a worthless French title and much younger brother to see into manhood.

Since their return from France, everything had been

rubbing along nicely. He robbed from the rich—men who stole from and killed his father. Gave to the poor—the very poor—he and his brother. That is until Jeremy—drunk as a lord and too cocky by half—decided to take a hand in poking Kildorne. The lackwit rashly followed the viscount home last night and stopped his carriage, pretending he was the *Devil in Spurs*. Unaware there were men in the coach with Kildorne, he suddenly found himself arrested for misdeeds his older brother had committed.

Kildorne, now the magistrate for the area, pledged he'd send Jeremy to Newgate come morn to be hanged. He swore it was because of the robberies, but Desdein feared the viscount somehow had discovered Jeremy was John Deshaunt's son. Desdein's only hope was to save Jeremy, by hook or by crook, and get him on the ship by dawn. Then he'd deal with Whitmore and Kildorne. In his own time and on a ground of his choosing.

Masquerading as the Marquis de Fournier, neither man had any idea he was Desdein Deshaunt, the son of the man they'd murdered nearly twenty years ago. A man set upon revenge.

The key to stopping Kildorne rode ahead in an elegant black coach with gold trim. Nothing but the best for the daughter of Edward Findlater, Viscount Kildorne. He grimaced as his mount failed to overtake the swift vehicle.

Lady Ashlyn Findlater was a riddle. He'd spotted her lurking around the edge of ballrooms, watching him these past weeks. The sly country mouse unnerved him, made him think she saw through his foppish mask. Her witchy grey eyes seemed to see past the façade he conjured. It was demme unfashionable for a woman—especially one firmly on the shelf and never had a season—to show she had a mind. Clearly, Lady Ashlyn needed a husband to take her in hand, keep her fat with babes and living in the country away from this nest of noble vipers.

A strange knot formed in his belly at the image of Ashlyn Findlater carrying a child. Another man's child. His groin bucked, saying the harridan had appeal. That startled him. He'd never warmed for a *healthy* lass before. Oddly, his blood buzzed from this unexpected bit of nonsense. Gritting his jaw, he dismissed her image from his mind.

The horse's neck inched forward as he spotted the coach up ahead through the trees, the light of the moon shining down upon it. He smiled. He doubted the *Blue Moon* could grant wishes, but it sure made hunting his prey easier. Reining up, he decided to cut through the wood and come out ahead of the Findlater party before they crossed Ravens Creek Bridge.

Perfect spot to stop them.

He matched the speed of the carriage, then finally pulled just ahead. Warrior's Heart vaulted the ancient stone wall, then clattered across the creek and emerged at the middle of the road, blocking the bridge's entrance.

He reined the stallion in the centre, turned and walked him slowly forward. His free hand skimmed over his pistols, at ready, but figured there would be little call for them. He noticed as Lady Ashlyn and her aunt decamped the Clevengers' route that there were no outriders for protection, just the spindly old coachman. Damn fool Kildorne obviously didn't take good care of his beautiful daughter.

It only made his night's work easier. He cocked his pistol and leveled it at the balding driver as the coach rattled around the bend.

Ashlyn leaned out the coach window, ignoring Aunt Dora tugging on her gown, trying to haul her back inside. Words on the proper deportment for a lady of her station went in one ear and out the other.

"You hang out the window like some Irish boghopper," Dora railed, giving the gown another stiff yank. "Damn your father, leaving your entry into society until this late date."

"Do stop, Auntie," she chided playfully. "You are Irish. You should not insult the land of your birth or its people."

"Aye, sure Irish, I am. And a boghopper, too. So I know perfectly well how they act. Like you are now."

Ashlyn smiled. "There is a *Blue Moon* out tonight and it's beautiful."

Her aunt sat back on the cushion with a resigned thud. "I despair. You shall never learn the value of proper deport-ment."

Ashlyn didn't want to hurt her aunt's feelings. Aunt Dora tried hard to help her fit in. Only, she was so *tired* of being told what was proper—and especially what was *not*. Life was *dreadfully dull*. She hadn't been welcomed by the *ton's* cliques. Hated corsets. Refused to play their frivolous games or hide her intelligence, however unfashionable that might be.

She cringed. Her father clearly had her on the marriage mart, 'for sale' to the highest bidder. It was beyond understanding why they didn't just line up the eligible females and trot them around the room, let men check their teeth like they did horses at *Tattersalls*. Ashlyn felt out-of-step. At twenty-six, she was too old for a season. Father insisted he was trying to make things up to her. She didn't believe him. Once he got it through his maggoty brain she wasn't what men wanted for a titled wife, she figured he'd ship her back to Chattam Lane Hall. Well, she wouldn't mind. She was good at managing, making do on damn little—money or emotions. She accepted she was a bluestocking, not the proper rave, not an *incomparable*. Not even an *original*.

She was poor Ashlyn. No one ever wanted her.

Father had schooled her tonight on whom to favor, which titled sons would be a suitable match. Stuff and nonsense. The jugheaded man actually talked of the Duke of Devonfield as being a good catch. She didn't want a Duke for a husband. Nor an Earl or a Marquis. Father deemed the Marquis de Fournier his choice above all others. Her sire was impressed with the power the man wielded, the connections that would come with having him for a son-in-law.

Haunting lavender eyes flashed before her mind. Especially not a *Mad Marquis*. He'd never want her. Even if he did, she'd shoot him before the week was out. The supercilious sop. She'd seen him look down his nose at her as if he sniffed something odious. She wasn't sure why that hurt. She laughed at the *ton* and their foolish airs, but for some reason, the *King of the Buffoons'* disdain pierced her self-worth as none other. At odd instances, when those pale lilac eyes met hers, she felt a bond, a connection, like he, too, harbored scorn for the shallow people around them. Then he'd arch a brow, lift his quizzing glass haughtily and look down that aristocratic nose at her. It was all she could do to keep from kicking him in the seat of his satin-clad arse!

Oh, what she wouldn't give for a dashing warrior to sweep her off her feet. Maybe ravish her, too, though she wasn't entirely sure what ravishing involved. She knew Aunt Dora fanned herself with her hanky when the word was spoken, so surely it couldn't be all bad.

"Whatever is happening?" Dora's curiosity was aroused as why they'd slowed to a crawl.

"I cannot see. I popped out the wrong side."

She started to scootch back in, but the *Blue Moon* peeked out from the clouds, capturing her enrapt attention. It was huge! And it was beautiful and blue. Most *Blue Moons* were really white, but this one was a true blue. Her maid said on the night of a *Blue Moon* charms could be cast and enchantments woven. The huge, luminous ball surely called faeries out to dance.

"Oh, I wish something wonderful would happen to me. If not something wonderful, may I please be ravished just once before I am too old to enjoy it!"

"Ashlyn, you shameless hussy!" her aunt hissed.

The carriage rolled to a standstill, but she couldn't see anything other than the back of the driver's bald head. She heard John Coachman—whose real name was Horace—talking to someone, but the words were low, murmured. Curiosity biting, she pushed inside, intent on finding out what was occurring, when the opposite door swung open and a man leaned in.

He motioned with his gun. "You, Lady Ashlyn, come with me."

"Ashlyn is my charge. I guard her with my life," Aunt Dora declared in thespian fashion. Her mouth formed an O as the muzzle of a pistol pressed to her nose. Almost going cross-eyed, she tried to stare down the barrel.

"I take it you see my point, Madam."

Dora blinked in umbrage. "No, I see your gun, sir. This is nothing short of rude."

Ashlyn wondered if all *Blue Moon* wishes were granted so promptly. Could one make more than one wish?

Patting her aunt's arm to reassure her, Ashlyn took measure of the man on the other end of the gun. She had only the moonlight to distinguish by, just enough to make her think she wanted to see more.

His hair was dark, midnight under the moon's glow. A swatch of black material covered his eyes and nose, holes cut for them, and was fastened at the back of his head. Dressed in black and in the heavy black cape, he was little more than a phantom.

A phantom with a sensual voice that sent a shiver up Ashlyn's spine.

"I have no coinage, no valuables, you despicable varmint. I shan't give you my wedding ring. 'Tis all I have left of my poor George." Dora sniffed, then waved her kerchief in dismissal. "So off with you. We have nothing for your likes."

Ashlyn rolled her eyes. 'Uncle George' only existed in her aunt's imagination. She hated being an *old maid* and thought it better to have a dashing husband who died fighting for

Wellington in Spain. In true widowly fashion, she spent her time *pining away,* for no man would ever measure up to her saintly George.

"Madam, I sorrow for your *loss,* but I am not here to rob you, especially not of anything as *cherished* as your wedding ring."

An odd note of humor in his deep voice gave Ashlyn pause. She tilted her head to study him. He sounded if he knew George Fitzgerald only existed in Dora's pretend world. Squinting, she tried to see the eyes behind the mask. She *knew* that voice. It haunted her. Something about it made her think of...

Dora fell back on the cushion, fanning herself. "Oh, mercy! My niece is a virgin. You shall ruin her. The Marquis de Fournier shan't offer for Ashlyn's hand if she has been spoiled."

"Thank God." Ashlyn turned her face aside. "Not that he'd ever want me."

The masked man's head snapped around. "Pardon?"

Their eyes locked, their minds meeting. She *knew* those eyes. It was almost *there,* shimmering out of reach, precisely where she recognized him from. In the eerie light of the *Blue Moon* they appeared a light grey. They were bedeviling, holding her until she felt air swell in her chest, unable to expel it. Incisive thoughts flickered in those ghostly depths, but she couldn't read the emotions or understand why they held such hypnotic sway over her. Why they caused her heart to slam against her ribs.

"If you must have your wicked ways with a female, then I sacrifice myself," Dora proclaimed in histrionics.

The highwayman trained the gun on Dora once more. "Keep your distance, Madam. The only sacrifice would be mine."

Ashlyn giggled discreetly as Dora spluttered in outrage. "Well, I never—"

"On that I have little doubt." With a wicked smile, he grabbed Ashlyn's upper arm and pulled. "As I said, you come with me."

Ashlyn grabbed the edge of the door and stiffened her elbow to stop him dragging her from the carriage. "Wait!"

"Resign yourself, you *are* coming with me." Resolve threaded his statement.

Ashlyn nearly growled through gritted teeth. He was strong. Very strong. And determined. "I realize you are a highwayman and all, but must you be so precipitous? I merely ask that you wait."

"Do not force me to shoot your aunt," he threatened, renewing his effort to haul her out.

Ashlyn used her foot to brace against the inside of the coach. "You...shall...not... shoot...anyone—"

"Shall I gun down your coachman to prove I mean what I say?"

"Oh, gor!" Horace fell on his bony knees, hands steepled in supplication. "Please, Mr. Devil in Spurs, do not murder me." He groveled at the highwayman's boots.

"Get up, man. Have some pride." The poor man looked quite exasperated.

Horace kept repeating his plea, inching closer. The highwayman gave one strong tug and dragged Ashlyn out the carriage door as two things happened in the same breath. The spindly coachman, in the guise of begging for his life, wrapped his arms around the robber's knee and held on, and Dora latched onto the arm he used to control Ashlyn. Her aunt fell forward and began to gnaw at the man's wrist to break his hold.

"Damnation, woman, you want me to club you down?" He shoulder butted Dora to get her to remove her teeth from his flesh while shaking his leg to force Horace to let go. "Bloody hell!"

He lifted the pistol with his left hand and discharged it into the air. Instantly, both Dora and Horace fell back, mouths agape, eyes wide.

Ashlyn frowned as he released his hold on her. She was quite willing to go with him and be ravished—maybe more than once if she liked it—but she wasn't going anywhere without her basket.

He waved the weapon at Horace. "Over there by the horses, they are spooked. Calm them or you and *this mastiff*..."—he leveled the pistol at her aunt—"shall walk back to Kildorne. And you—as I said before—Lady Ashlyn, are coming with me."

"No." She leapt toward the carriage. "I am not going without Cyril."

"Who the *bloody hell* is Cyril?" He dragged her back, swinging her in a circle to face him. "Lady, you are not worth the effort."

Ashlyn couldn't move. Pain spread through her until she

couldn't hurt any worse than if he'd doubled up his fist and slammed it into her stomach. Her mouth quivered as she tried to find a witty retort to show him his words held no sway over her. Extraordinarily, they did. She wasn't sure why a stranger wielded such power to cut her so deeply.

But was he a stranger? Again, a sense he was familiar brushed against her mind.

"Not worth the effort? Most likely. I have been told the same thing, many times before, so your words hold little sting." She sucked in a deep breath to steady herself. "I merely wanted Cyril."

She leaned into the carriage and snagged the basket's handle. He snatched it from her and stepped the coach light to see inside. "Is it alive?"

Ashlyn jerked the basket back. "Of course he is."

He tilted his head as if he doubted her. "*That*, I presume, is Cyril."

Ashlyn lifted the old cat from the basket and cradled him to her chest. "If I am to go with you...Cyril comes, too."

"That is the most pathetic excuse for a moggie I have ever seen."

She tilted her chin in defiance, ruining the stance by trembling. Scared for the first time since he'd stopped the vehicle, she shuddered, clutching the tabby cat to her. "He comes."

He frowned at her in dismissal, then motioned with a second pistol for Horace to mount the coach. "You, woman, inside the carriage before I shoot you where you stand."

"Sire, your deportment is horribly lacking." Aunt Dora huffed, then stepped before Ashlyn. "Ashlyn is my charge. I shall not abandon her."

He pointed the weapon at her aunt's chest. "Fine. I have no time to argue."

Ashlyn kissed the kitty's head. "Auntie, do run along. Cyril and I shall be fine."

His smile flashed winningly in the moonlight. "Yes, Auntie, do run along—and take Cyril with you."

"Cyril goes with me." Ashlyn stomped her foot.

He cocked his head at her show of temper as if assessing her, surprised by her spirit. "I shall shoot him, but I am not taking him with us."

"Over my dead body."

At the break in her voice, his tone softened. "We have a hard ride ahead. Your kitty would not be happy. Leave him where he will be comfortable and cared for."

Tears welled in her throat. She clutched the precious cat tighter. Her only friend, at times. "Then go ahead and shoot us both. He shan't be cared for. If I am not there, *my father* will see he starves or order him drowned. I'd rather you kill us both now."

The cat in her arms purred reassuringly, as if to remind Ashlyn they'd been through a lot worse. What did it matter if the most exciting thing to happen in her life was to be shot down like a dog in the middle of the road by a highwayman? There were worse ways to die...like loneliness

He exhaled his irritation. "Can you hold him? Or does he have to be in the basket."

"I can hold him," Ashlyn assured, the tightness in her chest easing.

The man remained motionless as if making up his mind. He gave a faint nod.

"Where are you taking Ashlyn?" her aunt demanded as he slammed the carriage door.

He took aim at Horace. "Drive...drive like the Devil is after you."

"Mr. *Devil in Spurs*..." Horace hesitated. "You ain't gonna hurt Lady Ashlyn? She's a good 'un, not like the rest of you nobility."

The highwayman cocked the trigger. "What do you know of my heritage?"

"Quality speaks. Lady Ashlyn is the only one in neigh on fifty years who ever bothered to learn my name was Horace instead of John Coachman."

"Drive on, Horace Coachman."

"Only if you give your word of honor you shan't harm the lass. She has had enough sorrow heaped upon her young shoulders."

White teeth flashed. "You accept the word of a highway-man?"

"The word of the *Devil in Spurs,* aye. A modern day Robin Hood, they say he is."

"I am no Robin of Loxley. Off with you, man." He slapped the flank of one of the horses; the coach lurched, then settled to a swift pace.

Ashlyn clutched Cyril to her chest, needing the warmth from his small body. The night was cool, but she figured the trembling was from fear. Not from standing before a devil in spurs, but the unknown.

What did he want from her? No one had ever sought her for anything before. Her father had only taken interest in her of late because he decided to use her, sell her to the highest bidder. So what could this man expect in plucking her from the carriage?

Blue moonlight broke through the passing clouds, almost shining down upon him in a halo. Stirred by the rising breeze, his mantle pulled back slightly on his shoulders, rippling and swaying with a sentient force. Her eyes traveled down to the black jackboots, which lovingly hugged his muscular thighs, to the gold spurs gleaming, then slowly up the strong, virile frame. His inky hair lay in stubborn waves, so thick she itched to touch them, discover if the curls were that soft.

Even with the mask covering part of his face and dressed all in black, he made Ashlyn's breath catch, stirring to life something in her that left her lightheaded. It wasn't quite alarm. This emotion was a drug that stilled rising apprehension within. Bathed in the sweet rays of the moonlight, he was surely conjured from her darkest heart, all that her whispered words to a *Blue Moon* could summon.

A fire started at the pit of her belly and spread downward, the radiant heat taking off the edge of the night chill. She wanted to touch this strong man, make sure he was warm, that his heart beat in his chest. Reassure herself he was man and not phantom.

He slowly came toward her, sliding the pistols under his belt. "Give me the cat." He held out his beautiful hand.

Jolted from the bit of moonlight reverie, she stepped back from him. "No. You'll hurt him. If you kill him, then shoot me, too."

"You are mad." He laughed derisively.

She tilted her chin. "Cyril is my friend."

His sensual mouth pursed as he seemed to silently count to ten. "Stop trembling. I promise not to shoot you or your kitty. You need your hands free to mount." He whistled shrilly, then his black stallion pranced up, shaking its head. "Give me...*Cyril*...while you get on."

"What a beautiful horse." Ashlyn looked at the finely arched neck and the broad back of the animal. "I've never ridden a horse. I am not sure how..."

"Damn *rouleaux*," he muttered about the trim on the hem of her gown limiting her movements. "You have to ride side saddle."

Grasping her about the waist, he easily swung her up to

sit crosswise on the horse, still clutching Cyril to her chest. He rearranged her cloak so it was tucked under her legs. Lightening shot through her blood, as she'd never been touched by a man before.

Actually, no one touched her, outside of Cook when she was growing up. Mum had been too weak, bedridden most of Ashlyn's early life. She rarely saw Father in the years after Mother's death. The servants—what few Father maintained at Chattam Lane—took care of her, but none ever hugged or touched her.

His hand remained on her thigh for an instant before he looked up. In the blue luminosity, his pale eyes stared into hers with thoughts she couldn't fathom.

Then with a swirl of his heavy mantle, he swung into the saddle behind her. His strong hands took her waist and settled her securely across his thighs, enfolding the heavy cape around her. Instantly, warmth from his body rolled over her, spread through her, banishing the night's chill.

Ashlyn sat shivering, hardly able to breathe. The highwayman had his arm about her. She couldn't see it, since Cyril rested against her chest, but his hand was firmly on her waist. Each exhale pushed against his palm.

She'd often wondered what it would feel like to have a man touch her. And while it wasn't a caress of a lover, it still made her feel strange inside. Scared. Yet, not precisely panic or fear.

He urged her closer. Nervous, she tried to keep her spine stiff, but his radiance lured her. Never had she felt such body heat. Her shoulder rested against his chest. Melting slowly against him, she basked in his fire. Her eyelids slowly lowered. She was tired. So tired.

Father had played cards late last night. On nights he had men in the house and they gambled and drank, she dared not sleep, fearful one would try to slip into her room. She'd sat holding Cyril until dawn, clutching a loaded pistol.

So tired, she sighed...*so very tired.*

Scatty female had gone to sleep. She and that moth-eaten cat seemed quite content wrapped in his cape. Had they no sense a'tall? A masked man kidnaps her—and her kitty—and the two of them sleep like babes in his arms.

Jacob rushed out as he neared the cottage. His valet started to take the reins, but hesitated when he saw the sleeping woman and the cat. "Well, if that ain't trusting, your lordship."

"If you value your life, say no more." Desdein shifted, trying to figure how to dismount without waking her. "Take the cat."

Jacob's brow lowered. "Do I have to? Pretty decrepit looking."

Cyril is my friend. Why did he hear her words and think she really meant to say Cyril is my *only* friend. One she was willing to die for.

He wondered if anyone ever cared for him like that. Jeremy adored him, but he figured if pushed to the limit his brother wouldn't make that choice. Had Mother or Father cared for their eldest son that strongly? He doubted it. Oh, Father had been proud of his first-born, but Desdein was unsure if he *loved* him. Mother had lived only for her husband.

Suddenly, Desdein felt very alone in the world and envied that damn cat. He'd do what he must to set things right for Jeremy, but then he needed to take a harsh look at his life. If he survived the dawning. He wasn't a young man any more. At thirty-six, he should have a wife and sons of his own. Longing suddenly wracked his body. He *wanted* a son. Wanted that child to grow up knowing he was loved.

Jacob shook his head. "She ain't letting go of the cat."

"Hold the horse steady." He turned so he could land on two feet, still cradling her and the stupid cat.

He carried her inside the cozy hunting box and gently placed her on the bed in the darkened room. The cat let out with a raspy meow, stretched and then cuddled back down against his mistress.

Desdein pulled off her shoes and unfolded the blanket over her. He noticed the shadows tingeing under her eyes. Reaching out, he lightly brushed the back of his hand against her cheek. A pressure built in his chest, regret he had to use Ashlyn in this manner. Inhaling to exorcise shards of scruples, he went to the outer quarters.

Putting a chunk of wood into the fireplace, Jacob looked up at Desdein in question.

Desdein glared at him as he removed his cape. Why did he have to have a valet determined to play his conscience? "Stop looking at me in that manner or I shall turn you out."

"We go back too far, you and I."

"Yes, we do. That's why you shall do my bidding without question."

"Take off that bloody mask. You'll give her a fright."

"Best I keep it on until she is ransomed."

He crossed to the table and took up the quill, scratching out a note to send to Ashlyn's father. He looked at the ring on his index finger. His father's seal. Taking up the taper, he dripped it on the flap to close it, then pressed the ring into the black wax. The time had come to let Kildorne know a ghost had arisen to haunt him.

"Take this to your contact." He tossed him a gold coin. "See he delivers it this night. I shall return the Lady Ashlyn unharmed to her adoring father as soon as Jeremy is set free. If he tarries past sunrise, I will return her *well used.* If he still has not met my terms by sunset, I shall kill her and leave her body on his doorstep."

Jacob looked down at the missive in his hand, then into Desdein's eyes. "You ain't going to really do those things to the lass, are you?"

Desdein didn't hesitate. "I shall do what it takes to see this matter at end. Now go. Time wastes."

Jacob nodded sadly and shuffled out the door.

Desdein stood staring into the fire, contemplating his actions. He felt a presence, then glanced down at his feet. That mangy cat curled around his ankle, rubbing. Irritated, for reasons he couldn't enumerate, he did his best to pretend the cat wasn't scratching his chin against his boot.

Cyril didn't take a hint.

Exhaling disgust, he leaned over to pet the cat. The beast began a raspy noise, which he took to be purring. "Worthless puss."

As he looked up, his eyes were drawn to the dim bedroom. Ashlyn lay on her side and was wide awake. From the unblinking stare, he knew she'd heard him say he'd kill her if Jeremy wasn't released.

Those grey eyes always seemed to have the ability to strip away the mask he wore, to reach into him. Why he'd kept his distance from her at the balls. Somehow, he'd always felt her stare and would look up to find Ashlyn watching him with hungry eyes. Those times, when their eyes locked, he'd found it hard to look away.

Once again, she held him spellbound with their witch's power. He couldn't even draw air.

The cat jumped up on his hind legs, trying to gain Desdein's attention. Silly thing nearly fell over he was so wobbly. Giving his head a shake, he picked up the feline and laid him across his arm. Running his other hand down the kitty's spine, he strode into the room.

"I believe this is yours," he said, but didn't return the cat to her arms, just stood stroking him as he studied her.

She sat up, pulling the blanket around her like a ruana as if cold. "I am sorry."

Perplexed, his brow lifted. "For what, *demoiselle*?"

"You think to ransom me for someone called Jeremy?" At length, she smiled sadly. "It shan't work. I hold little value for my father."

Desdein's breathing slowed as a mix of emotions hit him. He assumed she lied, most people would under the circumstances. Her eyes said otherwise. A predator's stillness spread through him. Fear unfurled as he worried he'd miscalculated. Deeply. A blunder that could cost Jeremy his life.

What father wouldn't go to any lengths to protect his precious daughter? He wouldn't have thought even Kildorne could be that low. He was getting a sense that Lady Ashlyn was a sad lass and not aware of her true value.

"My father married my mother under mistaken impressions. He thought she had a lot of money, would gain him entry into the *ton*. Oh, she had the bloodlines, ancient ones, and Chattam Lane Hall was impressive—if one didn't look too closely. Mother was frail, a country lass. When she fell ill, Father grew distant. Drank a lot. Often, he would go away for long spells. She died when I was eleven. This spring, I presume he decided I might be of use on the marriage mart. My reputation shall be in tatters once word of the kidnapping becomes *on dit*. I shall have no value. So your ploy of using me to get something from him shan't gain you anything."

She looked down at the blanket, her finger tracing the lines of the tartan. Desdein's heart tightened at the sight. Ashlyn seemed so lost, so alone. Legs weak, he leaned his shoulder against the door for support.

"If...if..." The long lashes lifted over fearful eyes. "I...I ask a boon. I know you owe me naught, and possibly resent me since I cannot aid your quest...if...when you kill me..." She stopped and went back to tracing the lines of the *plaide*. Finally on a heave of her chest, she continued. "Will you care for Cyril? If you will not do that, please...kill him when you kill me."

Desdein wasn't sure what to make of this strange woman. "You are going to sit there and let me kill you? Are you a coward?"

She tilted her chin up at the insult, swallowing hard. "I am no coward, Sir, but adept at facing facts. I have no weapon to fight you. You are stronger than I, faster, so I cannot outrun you. If you want me dead, there will be little I can do to stop you. I merely wish to make sure Cyril shan't suffer. I would not like my last thought to be of him cold...hungry."

He sat on the edge of the bed, tired, in need of a few hours sleep, but this gentle soul's acceptance of her death troubled him. She was no coward. She'd fought him with amazing strength when she struggled to get the cat. She wasn't stupid, but there was a childlike innocence within her the *ton* hadn't spoiled yet. So why this acceptance of death?

"Why would," he stopped stroking the cat and lifted her chin with his crooked index finger, "a lovely young woman such as yourself accept death? I saw spirit in you tonight. You fought to keep this worthless feline with you. I have no doubt if I said I was going to shoot him right now, you would likely claw my eyes out. Why fight for this bag of bones, but not for yourself?"

She shrugged, tried to smile but failed. "I am tired. My life has been such a struggle. Making do. No one there to care. Still, I was happy with Cyril. Then my father decided I could be turned into the proper lady a rich titled husband could want. Several nights a week his friends come. They drink and play cards until the wee hours of the morning. I sit with a gun in my lap, fearful of falling asleep. Several made crude suggestions so I knew what they would do if given the chance. Should you send me back, what would my life be like? Father will have no use for me. His *friends* will view me as prey. I am soiled goods now, even if you do not ravish me...Desdein de Fournier."

"Desdein Deshaunt," he corrected, dropping his hand. "De Fournier was *grand-mère's* name. I lived with her in France after...my parents died."

Ashlyn observed the violet eyes, enchanted by their power, as he put down Cyril and untied the mask. She'd never seen the *Mad Marquis* up this close. "You are beautiful."

There was a slightly mocking glint to his eyes, as a crooked half-smile curved the well-formed lips. Ashlyn blinked, trying to fight the spell. Despite, she couldn't help but wonder how it would feel to be kissed by those lips. Silly wish, perhaps spurred by the *Blue Moon*.

"Beautiful? Women are beautiful. Men merely handsome."

She shook her head. "You are beautiful." She nearly jerked when she caught herself leaning into him, almost tasting that kiss.

The *Mad Marquis* would never want to kiss *her.* She turned away to hide the pain that surely showed upon her face. She was so tired of being alone, tired of living with disappointment and fear.

"What is it?" he asked.

"I am weary. Not much rest last night. May Cyril and I sleep before you kill us?"

"Oh, for godsake, sleep. We shall talk about me committing murder on you two later."

Ashlyn cuddled Cyril to her stomach and huddled under the blanket, shaking. She was scared, despite what she'd told him. No one accepted death, but she was limited in what she could do in life. Women didn't have choices. A woman of her station, the best she could hope for was a good marriage. She had no control of her small inheritance, no money, no place to go. Now, the chance of an offer for a decent man was moot.

Her wants weren't many—a safe, warm place for Cyril and her to live. In the odd moment, she secretly wished for a man to care about her. One to make her feel safe, even loved.

His weight shifted on the bed, causing her to jerk. Peeking over her shoulder, she saw he slid behind her. With a quick flick of the blanket, he scooted his body against hers. Her heart jumped, slamming with strong thuds against her ribs.

"What...what are you doing?"

He lay on his back, staring up at the ceiling. "You, I and that pathetic excuse for a cat are napping until dawn."

Ashlyn had never slept with anyone but Cyril. "With me?"

Desdein raised up on his elbow and glared. "Oh, that's not proper, eh? Since I am going to ravish you and kill you, and other such horrendous things, what does it matter if we both close our eyes until light?" Yawning he laid back. "It is much easier to murder when there is light to see by."

Ashlyn feared he laughed at her, but then the *Mad Marquis* had, more than once, looked down that aristocratic nose as if she'd crawled out from under a rock.

"I never said you would ravish me." She swallowed the tightness in her throat.

"I know the Marquis de Fournier deems me unworthy enough to polish your jackboots."

His brow furrowed in perplexity. "Since I am weary, mayhap this makes no sense to me. Only, it sounds like you are disappointed because you assume I shan't ravish you."

"Don't be silly," she huffed.

He chuckled. "You believe I will kill you—and that cat. Such deeds are in keeping with your expectations of me, yet you have no fear I would *ravish* you?"

Her chin quivered. She felt it. Tilting it up, she shrugged indifference, though she felt anything but that inside. His aloof dismissal of her as not worthy of the *ton's* acceptance had hurt. Somehow, in that setting his disdain had been hard enough to swallow. However, this very approachable version of Desdein de Fournier—Deshaunt—left the rejection all the more piercing.

"I would never presume such self-value to think the Marquis de Fournier would ever lower himself to ravish one he obviously finds distaste with. So, yes, you might kill me, but no, I would expect only your disdain at the idea of anything else."

He shifted so quickly it startled her. One moment he was quiet behind her, the next he was over her, pinning her to the bed with his hard body. Shocked, she started to ask what he was doing, when his mouth closed over hers. Then she knew! The *Mad Marquis* was kissing her!

So many things came at her all at once. His taste, the warmth of his lips. The heaviness of his body pressing down on hers. His heat seared through her, warming her to the tips of her toes. She tried to breathe, but that only filled her mind with hints of male sweat, leather and the soap he'd used, leaving her dizzy.

He lifted his head, watching her face. "You have never been kissed?"

Ashlyn faintly shook her head.

A strangled cry came from against her side. "Oh, Cyril. You crush him!"

He moved his leg so the cat could crawl out from under the blanket. "So sorry, Cyril."

The cat staggered a few steps, then crumpled. Desdein leaned toward the feline, checking to see if he breathed. He said, in his most droll fashion, "I think he's dead. If he croaked, I am chucking him out. I shall share my bed with a live cat, but I draw the line at sharing it with a dead one."

She sat up and cradled the limp creature to her breasts. Nice breasts, too, he noted; he rather envied the ruddy beast.

"He just wore himself out. Poor dear tires easily days."

He carefully lifted the tail, so limp he really questioned her assessment of Cyril's ability to breathe. "Poor thing is about to stick his spoon in the wall." Desdein was sorry he mentioned the stupid cat dying, for she clutched him all the tighter.

Rubbing her cheek to the furry head, she sneaked a tearful glance at him. "There is no need to be cruel. I know I shan't have him for much longer."

Desdein sighed, feeling like a knave. "How long has Cyril been your friend?"

"I was eight when I found him. It was deep winter and I kept hearing a kitten crying. At first it sounded like it came from within the wall. Then I figured out he was under the house. I went out and found him, hiding in a break in the foundation. Hungry, thirsty and scared to death. There were no other kittens about, no mum kitty, so I don't know where he came from. You might say he was my Christmas present. Never had one before."

"You were not allowed a cat before?"

Her grey eyes reflected sorrow. They held his with a power that seemed to reach into him, affect him, change him. With such love and tenderness, she rubbed her cheek against the cat. "No...never had a Christmas present before."

Desdien's head snapped back, shocked by her statement. "Why ever not?"

She swallowed, then shrugged as if it didn't matter. "Mother was sick, bedridden for most of my childhood. Some days she barely knew what day it was. Father was often in his cups or off in London gambling for weeks at a time. Christmas came and went. More important things to spend money upon. Food, medicines for Mother."

So Cyril had been her friend for eighteen years. A pressure welled in his throat and the muscles tightened as he considered Ashlyn's friend's days were few. Who would be her companion then? "Let me fetch him something to eat. He is likely hungry."

"I would appreciate it. It gets harder and harder to keep his weight up."

He bit back commenting on Cyril's numbered days and scooted off the bed, wishing he'd never kidnapped Ashlyn Findlater.

Wishing he'd done it years ago instead.

Ashlyn curled on her side, staring into the flames, as she stroked the cat. After a meal of milk, oatmeal—and whisky— he was quite content. The oatmeal had been Ashlyn's suggestion since he needed to keep from getting any more decrepit than he already was.

As Desdein stood mixing it to a good consistency, he chuckled to himself. The *Mad Marquis* making gruel for a cat. The *ton* would have a hearty laugh if they ever learned about that. Then he noticed the bottle of Highland Whisky. Maybe the silly beast had aches and pains from being old, so he slipped a wee dram into it and didn't mention it to Ashlyn. She seemed surprised Cyril cleaned his plate. The moggie rested on the bed, enjoying the pets, and actually looked content, eyes bright.

From across the room, Desdein sat in the chair, watching her, wishing she'd run those strong hands over his body. Heat crawled over his skin and licked at the base of his brain, then spiraled downward to his groin with a pulsing hunger he found hard to dismiss. In order to ignore the rising compulsion to stalk over and cover her, taking her with smooth and sure strokes, he sought distraction in provoking her.

"Have you a last wish?" His teeth gnashed at his foolish prodding for her eyes widened in alarm. He wasn't really a cruel bastard, but it gnawed at his mind this woman was dispirited. His intuition said she wouldn't accept death as peacefully as she presumed. There was a banked fire in this lady, just waiting for the embers to be stirred. "No, I am not plotting to murder you—*just now*. I merely thought to get the preliminaries out of the way."

She glared at him. "You are different without the affectations of the *Mad Marquis*, yet you find it hard to drop the mask, do you not?"

Putting his hands on his hips, he slowly stood. "Meaning precisely, little mouse?"

She frowned at the sobriquet, but let it pass. "You belittle people, make them feel small, worthless."

"The *ton* must have its amusements." He gave a mock bow as if a performer. He sat on the edge of the bed and regarded her. How could she make him feel shallow, empty with so few words? "I was never cruel to you."

She glanced at the cat, then buried her face against his neck.

Had he hurt her? Too often, he felt the many masks he wore beginning to take over, to where it was harder to recall who Desdein Deshaunt was. He reached out and lifted her chin, forcing her to look him in the eyes. "Was I?"

A tear glittered in her eyes. "You kissed me."

"And that is cruel?" His thumb stroked the corner of her mouth, watching her lip quiver. "Such sadness in those eyes. Why would you think a kiss was my way of hurting you?"

"Why did you kiss me?"

"It seemed logical at that moment. That still doesn't explain why you assumed I meant it as cruelty."

"Had you kissed me because you wanted to, it would have been nice. But you only kissed me to prove a point."

"*Nice?*" Desdein growled the word. "You arrogant little mouse."

"Mouse!"

He pointed a finger at her. "See you even squeak like one."

"I am not a mouse!"

"The mouse insists she is no mouse. Shall we find out just what you are?" The spurs had set in his mind. There was no pulling back.

He leaned to her, his mouth closing over hers, slowly teaching her the way to kiss. She was quickly swept up in the building sensations. He felt her release the cat, then grasp his upper arms as if she needed to hold on to steady herself.

His body burned, fire slithered under his skin, spread down his spine and slammed into his groin with a power he'd never felt. Gently he placed his hand on her waist urging her closer. Her taste sped through his system and hit his brain with the effect of whisky, making him dizzy with the need to take her. That fine edge of losing control rose within his mind, so he forced himself to pull back. Nearly his undoing, she leaned into him, following.

The side of his mouth tugged up into a smile. "Eager little mouse." He slowly ran his thumb over her lower lip as his eyes studied Ashlyn. "Now that you have had your kiss, I shall stop being cruel to you and you can go to sleep. I fear it's going to be a long night."

"Will you lie down with Cyril and me again?" came the soft question, as she slid down under the blanket. "You were so warm. It felt...nice."

"I forbid you to ever use the word *nice* again." He tried to sound threatening, but feared it wasn't reflected in his face or tone.

She shifted, covering both her and the cat with the blanket, then peeked out. "If I say nice again what will do you? You are already going to murder me, so that does limit your threats."

"I could beat you."

She took a couple of breaths, the grey eyes stripping his soul. "You could. You are very strong. Only, I do not think you would ever raise a hand to a woman in anger. Why I think you won't kill Cyril or me."

He frowned, wondering what else she saw within his black heart. Uncomfortable with her directness, he snapped, "Go to sleep, little mouse, before I think of other means of torture for you. Your constant prattle gives me a megrim."

"To torture something is to be cruel, is it not?" A glint flashed in those eyes, showing a mischievous spirit that had been missing before. "Will you kiss me again?"

"Methinks you are too interested in kisses for a virginal miss." He leaned forward, but pulled back when he realized he'd placed his hand upon her hip. Glancing toward it, he noticed the roundness, wondering how it would feel to have his palm on her warm flesh instead of the rough tartan blanket.

She propped her head upon her hand. "I asked, but you never answered. Why did you kiss me?"

Cyril's head popped from under the blanket, evidently requiring a great effort, for he promptly rolled over in a drunken faint.

"Is he strangling?"

"He's purring."

"It sounds like he's gasping for air. I think I should shoot him. Put him out of his misery."

"Stop threatening to shoot Cyril. You do that just to tweak me. You play at being perverse, Desdein Deshaunt. You wear the mask of a highwayman, but methinks it's not for gaining of coin or jewels. And the *Mad Marquis* is yet another of your pantomimes. Who kissed me? The Devil in Spurs, the Mad Marquis or Desdein Deshaunt?"

"Very well, I shan't murder you—or that pathetic creature you call a cat." He swatted her hip, causing her to yelp. "That does not mean I cannot beat you. Go to sleep, Ashlyn Findlater, or..." He nearly flinched. Why had he added the *or* on the end?

"Threatening me, Desdein?"

She smiled. The bloody wench smiled! One of those virginal come-hither smiles that sent a man's blood to boiling, asking things from him she shouldn't. He'd never spent time chasing virgins, they were so bloody boring, but he had a feeling Ashlyn would never bore him.

Like a crack of lightning, Desdein knew this was the woman he could spend his life with. She could give him fine, strong sons, maybe a daughter with her eyes. They could be happy together. Desdein saw tomorrow, and all the tomorrows thereafter in those grey eyes.

He also knew it was naught but mist under a *Blue Moon*. He wasn't sure if he truly believed in fate. Deep inside he knew one thing—come morn, Jeremy would be free and on that ship or by damn, he'd die trying. Might die in any case. Nothing mattered but his brother's safety. He'd promised Mother on her deathbed that he'd always take care of Jeremy. Comprehending this, he had nothing to offer this gentle lass, no dreams of maybes, if onlys or castles in the air to conjure.

His heart had a strange pressure, like a cramp seized it and it couldn't beat properly.

Now he faced a new problem with Ashlyn. He'd ruined her reputation. No gentleman would want a wife who'd been carried off by the *Devil in Spurs*. Poor lass would be sent to the country, once more to live a solitary life, soon not even to have Cyril. No man would look at her and see the fine intelligence, the quality breeding, the pure soul. A heart aching for love.

Unable to bear looking at her lovely face, he started to turn away, but she caught his sleeve.

"Who, Desdein?"

The mask slipped back into place—too easily. The condescending tone of the supercilious fop answered for him. "Who kissed you? Why the *Mad Marquis*, of course.

"He will have something to recant to all the *ton*. That he kissed a country mouse, and the silly goose called it torture."

Her smile faded. Her full lip quivered. "No...I called you cruel. I was right."

Jaw setting, he glared at her with icy arrogance. "Yes, I live for it."

Desdein turned and strode back into the other room to the fire to warm the chill spreading in his body. He didn't look back, knew if he did it'd be a mistake. Not even when he heard her quiet sob. Should he turn back he'd have kissed every tear he'd brought to those solemn eyes. Then he would, indeed, be cruel.

Not to her. To himself.

For touching a dream that could never be.

Ashlyn awoke with a sense of unease. Immediately she feared it was Cyril. Often she broke her slumber, fearful her small friend had drawn his last breath without her getting to hold him one last time or tell him how much she loved him and would miss his gentle company.

She reached out and felt the warmth of his body, then tension eased in her somewhat. Still, there was disquiet within her. Something was wrong.

She slid off the bed, her eyes went to the other room, seeking Desdein, saw he was in a chair before the fire.

He was slumped in the chair, a half-empty decanter on the floor within reach. His arm hung over the chair arm, the long fingers gripping a single piece of paper. As she neared, she thought he was asleep, but when her body blocked the fire from his face, he looked up.

Weary, the dark of his beard showing, he looked very rumpled, very accessible. For once the masks were down. His long legs, sprawled wide, were still encased in the tight riding breeches, the jackboots, fitting like a glove to mid-thigh.

Being a bold, sinful lass, she knelt between his knees and put her hands on the leather covered thighs. He watched her, the lavender eyes bloodshot from lack of sleep and the drink. She wanted to ask him what was wrong, but could only stare at the beautiful face of Desdein Deshaunt. She'd always thought him handsome at the few parties they'd both attended. He was a graceful, elegant man who played at being a fop. But she'd noticed how his clothes fit his body, how there was solid muscle under the silks and velvets.

There was a throb in her body, like a heartbeat, but slower, stronger, moving through her, driving her. As she watched him, the inner plaint strengthened.

"Desdein, what is wrong?"

His lower arm lifted, holding the piece of paper. "Your father's reply."

She shivered with a chill though the fire burned brightly, warmed her back. There was no need to read it. She knew what her father's response would be, had warned Desdein her sire would never trade her for his brother.

"What shall you do?" she whispered.

He leaned forward so they were almost touching foreheads. "Do you wish to know what it says?"

She swallowed. There was a hard edge to Desdein's

measured words. His mood was dangerous and she'd be stupid not to recognize it. His feral stillness set her heart to slamming against her ribs, as she stared at the sensual lips she so wanted to kiss again. And again.

"I told you I had no value to him. I am sorry. I wish I could make it up to you."

"How would you make it up to me, Ashlyn? What would you do?"

"Whatever you want." She tried to smile, but the words hurt. "I told you I am not worth much to anyone."

Releasing the letter, it fluttered to the floor. "Do you know what you offer me?"

"No. I know volumes about ancient history, or how to do accounts for an estate. I did not have a tutor. Could not afford one. I learned what I know by reading."

"Then let me be your tutor."

He took her mouth with a roughness that was startling. It shocked her, but she quickly accepted the wildness within him. His arms pulled her against his body, her breasts pressing to his chest. She felt like a leaf caught in a storm, unable to do anything but let the wind carry her along into the maelstrom.

He reached down, then rose, sweeping her into his strong arms, cradling her. She stared into the lavender eyes, realizing they had a bluish tint up close.

Just like her Blue Moon wish.

Desdein was her *Blue Moon* wish come true.

He should have never touched her. There was too much frustration, anger, blind rage boiling within him. Too many things to consider. He had to save Jeremy, but he couldn't use Ashlyn in this manner. He owed her that. There was only one thing left to trade—himself.

He looked at the paper on the floor, barely making out Kildorne's words, shakily scrawled across the cream-colored velum.

> *For God sake, please don't harm her. I shall do anything you want. Name it.*

He'd been selfish not to show Ashlyn that she'd more value to her father than she knew. But he'd wanted Ashlyn. Wanted to carry her sweet memory with him when he faced Kildorne. Maybe carry it to the grave.

Desdein sighed, then thought of the second missive he'd sent to Kildorne, telling him to protect his daughter, bring Jeremy to Hallowden Hill at dawnbreak and he would trade the Devil in Spurs for his brother. The reply came, agreeing. He'd hold Kildorne until Jeremy could be sped upon his way. Then damn his soul, Kildorne and he could die together.

Only what to do about Ashlyn? He had sat before the fire trying to drown his fury in the Scotch. She'd be ruined in the *ton's* eyes, even though he'd done naught more than kiss her. They'd brand her fallen. He recalled her speaking of being tired, from sitting up at night with a pistol to protect her honor. His kidnapping her had sentenced her to endless nights of such terror.

His hand had clenched around the paper that held Kildorne's reply to his second offer and tossed it into the fire.

No matter. He'd know he left her unsullied, the one pure, honest thing he'd ever touched in his life. He would've spared her innocence, though he burned with every fiber of his being, wanting her as he'd never wanted anything in his whole life. In Ashlyn's arms was Salvation, the power to heal his troubled soul. But for once, he was going to do what was honorable.

Maybe on nights of the *Blue Moon* she would gaze out her window and think of him, of her first kiss from a man known as the *Devil in Spurs*.

Only, she came to him, put those strong, beautiful hands upon his thighs and said she'd do anything. Sealing her fate.

He'd die come dawn, so he wanted these last few hours with her. He wanted her burned into his memory.

Pausing by the bed, Desdein kissed her, softly, sweetly, reverently at first. As he broke it, intending to put her down, Ashlyn's raspy sigh of hunger let loose the demons within him. His mouth took hers, letting her feel the power of his need, almost fearing he'd shock her. Being a virgin, Ashlyn deserved tenderness, but he wanted her with a force that rocked him. It empowered him, yet in the same breath left him helpless against the driving energy, pushing him to take. Claim. Brand.

Setting her on her feet, he trembled—not from holding her weight, from reining in the frantic craving that twisted his guts. As he unfastened the back of her gown with the care of a lady's maid, he suffered the need to bury himself in her body.

Make them one. Ashlyn held no comprehension how much it cost him not to rip the clothing from her lush body.

He left her the chemise, so thin, so sheer it inflamed his desire more than protected her from his gaze. Utterly dumbfounded, he paused to stare at her beauty, the rounded hips, the full breasts. Unable to stand not touching her, he fell to his knees before Ashlyn, intent on worshipping her. His hand seized her waist, yanking her to arch to him so his mouth could latch upon one breast through the gauzy material. Her hands clutched his upper arms, her fingers biting the muscles. He drew hard on the soft breast, sucking with a rhythm that brought mewls to her throat. He kept it up, pushing her higher and higher, her hips pressing against his stomach in age old mating instincts. Her open responses made it harder for him to keep control.

"Oh, Desdein, is this ravishing?"

His mouth released the hold oh her nipple to reply. He lifted her onto the bed, as he began to undress. "It is indeed."

"Can a man ravish a woman more than once in a night?" she asked in seriousness.

His smile was predatory. "He can...should he enjoy it."

"Will you...*enjoy* ravishing me, Desdein?"

As he pulled off his shirt, the sly minx leaned to him and her mouth latched onto his hard male nipple, her actions mimicking his. He sucked in a sharp breath to steady himself as his groin nearly exploded with the wildfire she set off in him. "Enjoy? Hmm, ah...yes...I think that is a distinct possibility. Enough! I cannot think with you doing that."

He pushed her back on the bed, dancing on one foot then the other as he pulled off the jackboots. Ashlyn laughed and lay back on the bed, watching him with hungry eyes until he finally was naked. Putting a knee on the bed, he slid over her, careful to keep his weight on his elbows.

"Why are you laughing, you scatty woman?" He slid one of his legs between hers, pushing them apart, smiling at her lack of resistance.

She loosely wrapped her arms about his neck. "I think Aunt Dora's comments on ravishment to be grossly misconstrued."

"Shall I teach you the right of it, my pet?"

Her radiant countenance, bathed in shadow and firelight, turned solemn. Her grey eyes stared into his, so open, so needing him. "Teach me, Desdein."

"For you, lass, I would slay dragons and duel wizards." He liked the sheer material of the chemise, gossamer, as if it was made of faeries wings, so he left it on. As if feasting, he took her other breast in his mouth, using his tongue, his teeth, drawing on it until she writhed and keened in need.

She came apart in his arms, barely understanding her body's responses to him.

Barely felt the virgin's pain as he entered her.

Ashlyn jerked awake and tried to focus. Sore in places she didn't know a woman could be sore, she smiled, recalling her night with Desdein. If Aunt Dora knew how much she enjoyed being *ravished*, poor dear would faint and need smelling salts.

Blindly, she yawned and stretched, looking for Desdein. She wanted to touch him, run her hands over his strong body. Her lover. Those two words had a special, secret ring to them.

Cyril sat on the end of the bed, his tail snapping, unhappy for some reason.

Apprehension crept up her spine as she felt the bed was cold where Desdein had lain beside her. She looked about for her dress, then spied Desdein's black breeches and shirt, and quickly dressed in them. They were much warmer, and it felt rather free wearing men's clothing. Easier to put on, requiring no maid. Except for the waist, they were a decent fit, but by tightening the belt she solved that problem.

She pulled up short when she saw Desdein's valet building the fire. "Where is your master?"

"Gone."

Why did that word provoke such fear in her? "Gone where?"

"He arranged a trade with your lord father."

"Trade? What? My father shan't want a daughter who has been soiled."

He shrugged, handing her the paper. "Maybe you underestimate your father. Maybe Deshaunt ain't trading you. He figured the *Devil in Spurs* would do the trick. Sought to spare you."

Ashlyn's eyes skimmed her father's words, startled by the emotion they conveyed. In spite, she could spare little time to wonder at him. She paled when Jacob revealed Desdein's intentions. "He cannot! Yes, the blasted man would. Oh, drat. How long ago did he leave? Where did he go?"

She dashed to the door, then remembered Cyril. In a

dither, she hunted for his basket, recalled they hadn't bought it, then searched for her shoes, but could only locate one. Shaking, she was doing her best not to cry, but she feared she'd be too late. Blasted man might do something stupid, like give himself up or shoot her father and get shot himself. Of course, with her father it would be an accident since the man couldn't hit the broad side of a barn.

"Here now, you cannot go barefooted." The valet came back into the room with a pair of boots. "They were Master Jeremy's when he was but a lad. They might fit."

"Thank you." She sat down and tugged one on, pleased by how well they fit. "Where did he go?"

"The master said not to tell you, but I figure you are the only one to stop him getting himself killed. Hallowden Hill. There is a ship anchored in Hallowden Bay. The master hopes to see his brother onboard and at sea by first light."

"How long ago did he leave?"

"Not long."

"Can you fetch me a horse?" She bit her lip. "I forgot. I cannot ride."

"I have a carriage awaiting you. The marquis said I should take you and the cat to Crayford Hall. He left papers naming you as the new owner."

"How kind of him, but if he thinks he is going to get away from me that easily, the man has pudding for brains."

The sour faced valet smiled. "Sounds like, miss, you care for the Marquis."

"I hate his bloody guts." She scooped up the cat. "Come, Cyril, we have to go catch a devil."

The sun was up, for all the good it did. Fog rolled in at daybreak and was so thick Desdein could hardly see a few feet ahead of him. He'd dismounted and waited. Two loaded pistols were tucked behind his belt, against his back, another was in his hand.

Warrior's Heart murmured deep in his throat, then jerked against the reins, alerting him that the black coach slowly eased forward, inching its way through the fog. The driver, Horace, reined to halt at the top of the hill when he saw Desdein. Heart slamming against his ribs, he wasn't sure he breathed until the door to the carriage opened and Kildorne finally stepped down. The man glanced back inside the coach, then back to Desdein, surprise in his eyes.

The Viscount held up both hands to show he carried no

weapon, then started forward. "Marquis de Fournier, I...did not expect you to be here. I meet that highwayman...*Devil in Spurs* they call him." His eyes rested on the pistol in Desdein's hand.

Desdein lacked time for pleasantries. "Did you bring him?"

"Then I take it *you* are the highwayman?"

Desdein sketched a mock bow. "At your service, Viscount.

"Where is my daughter?"

"Where is my brother?" He raised the pistol and trained it on Kildorne.

The elder man lifted his lower arm and made a flick with his wrist. Horace tied off the reins, then stepped down. Going to the door, he leaned in and pulled Jeremy out, hands tied before him. He looked a little mussed, but none the worse for wear. Since hearing of his arrest, Desdein feared they might have beaten him...or worse.

As his brother took a step, Desdein heard a carriage racing up behind him, driving too fast in the fog. He figured there could only be one person foolish enough to have Jacob clattering about in this mist at breakneck speed. *Ashlyn.*

His heart swelled she cared enough to come, yet it would've been much easier if the matter were over before she'd awoken. Her father's eyes tracked the carriage as it rattled to a stop behind him. The door flew open and Ashlyn leapt out, even before it came to a full rest.

"Jacob, I shall turn you out without references for bringing her."

"Yes, your lordship. Better than her beating me with the horsewhip, as she threatened." Jacob's nonplussed tone said he hadn't really feared that. The meddling valet had brought her, hoping she'd stop him. "Of course, if you are tossed in Newgate you shan't need a valet and your references would have dubious value."

The corner of his mouth twitched, seeing Ashlyn wore his clothes. She ran to him, putting her left hand on his back, and asked breathlessly, "Desdein, what are you doing? What is this about Newgate?"

Just as he opened his mouth to explain, Cyril staggered out of the carriage and came to wind around his feet. "Ashlyn, gather Cyril before he exhausts himself and then get back into the coach. Jacob, take her to Crayford Hall as per my instructions."

"No, Desdein," she refused, placing a hand on his upper

arm.

Jacob just shrugged.

Desdein glanced at her beautiful face, pale but determined. Ashlyn hadn't batted an eyelash that he held a pistol on her father, nor had she spared his brother a glance. Her focus was on him. He smiled. It felt good to have someone worry about him. Sad it came too late in his life. Maybe had he found Ashlyn years before, he'd be comfortably settled, too wrapped up in making babes with her to let vengeance claim his whole life.

"'Tis a good thing I did not ask you to marry me. I would likely have to beat you every day just to get you to obey me."

She sighed. "Most likely, and on Sunday you might try to murder Cyril and me as well."

"Trust me?"

She swallowed her fear. "I trust you not to beat me or murder me. Or Cyril."

"Then let me do what I must without interfering. Yes, Desdein?" he prompted.

She hesitated so long he feared she'd refuse. Finally she said, "Yes, Desdein."

"Stay behind me while I handle this." He looked to her father, noticing the man intently watched the byplay between then. Rather than loathing, he saw calculation and possibly a spark of hope. That puzzled him. Did the man hope to use Ashlyn against him?

"Send Jeremy toward me." His voice rang out in the hushed fog that eddied about them.

Jeremy glanced toward Kildorne, who nodded, so his brother started forward.

As he neared, his blue eyes rested on Ashlyn, then traveled the length of her body. He arched a brow as he returned his gaze to Desdein.

"Well, it seems big brother rescues me yet again." Jeremy grinned, then noticed Cyril curled around Desdein's leg. "I suppose *that* comes with her?"

Desdein tossed Jeremy the reins of Warrior's Heart. "Get on him and ride. There is a ship waiting in the bay. It shall carry you to the Colonies. Money and clothes are in the bag." He turned to Ashlyn. "Untie his hands so he can leave."

"Damned if I shall be packed off to leave you alone—"

"I must deal with this, Jeremy, in my own way." He glared at his brother, but saw it had no effect.

This seemed so easy in the planning. In his mind he'd set

Jeremy on his way, then he'd challenge Kildorne to a duel, face the man as his father once had. Then kill Edward Find-later. Fate full circle. He figured Kildorne's man would shoot him for the effort, but what did he really have to live for? He was thirty-six, wasting his life playing games of revenge, courting death—for each time he rode out as the *Devil in Spurs*, it might be the night that cost him his life. Jeremy would soon marry, start his own family. He'd be alone.

Nevertheless, as he stood facing Kildorne, he felt that mangy cat curved around his ankle, purring in his asthmatic wheeze, Ashlyn's hand at the small of his back, her fingers flexed on the muscles of his upper arm.

Suddenly, he wasn't alone. Suddenly, he no longer had nothing to lose.

Only he couldn't back off from his vengeance. He owed his father, whom he'd loved.

"You present me with a problem, Marquis. You said you'd trade yourself for Jeremy. I kept my end of the bargain." Her father moved forward, holding his hand out for Desdein's weapon.

As Desdein passed the pistol, both Jeremy and Ashlyn pulled the guns out that he'd tucked in the belt at his back. His jaw set. Everyone was muddling his plans!

"Father, give him the gun back. Now. I cannot ride a horse, but you know I am a crack shot."

Ashlyn held the gun aimed at her father. Not shaking, the woman was resolute, determination etched in the tilt of her stubborn chin. When there was no move to comply, the reckless wench actually stepped before him as a shield.

"You defend a criminal...a highwayman?" Kildorne queried.

"Yes, Father, I would. With my life."

Desdein batted his eyes, to blink away the forming tears. Knowing if he hadn't loved Ashlyn before, her words would've stolen his heart in that instant. His lady was worth a king's ransom—worth life itself. There was a strange stillness in him, regretting he couldn't have seen her value weeks, months ago, when there was still time to turn back from the course he'd set before them.

"Ashlyn, give me the gun."

She must've noticed his odd tone, a tone of finality, for confusion flooded her eyes. "You should take the gold and board the ship, Desdein. Go free. I...I would follow you...if you would but have me. I would not care where we go as long as I was at your side."

The corner of his mouth twitched in a sad smile. "You and Cyril?"

She licked her lips nervously. "Of course Cyril comes with me."

Cyril looked up at Desdein and meowed as if saying yes, he would come. "Stupid, worthless cat. I need to shoot you."

He leaned to Ashlyn and brushed his lips against hers, a kiss so gentle, so sweet he could die for it. With his left hand he took a firm grip on her wrist, then pried her fingers from around the pistol's grip. "Jeremy," he said and then gave a faint jerk of his head, signaling his brother to take control of Ashlyn and move her out of harm's way.

His brother came around, taking hold of Ashlyn's shoulders, pulling her back. "Come, Lady Ashlyn, leave Desdein to do what he must."

She jerked away and threw her arms around him. "Please, Desdein, don't go with him. We can go anywhere. I love you."

He glowered at his brother, who tried to pull her away. Desdein caressed her cheek with the back of his hand. "I am not going with him, My Love. It ends here...now."

Her father, watching Jeremy drag Ashlyn to the coach, finally allowed the words to register. He seemed befuddled, then a trace of fear spread over his countenance.

"See here, I did as you said. Release my daughter, de Fournier." He stepped backward as Desdein moved toward him.

"My name is not de Fournier."

"I...I don't...understand..."

Desdein kept walking him back toward the other coach. "Oh, I am the Marquis de Fournier, a title through my *grandmère*, distaff side. But my family name is Deshaunt—"

"Deshaunt!" The name rattled the man, his skin turning sallow.

Desdein stopped halfway between the two vehicles. "Yes, John Deshaunt's son. The man you murdered."

"It wasn't mu...murder. It...wa...was a duel."

"Just like the one we shall have now."

"Duel..." The man shook his head vigorously. "I...I am not fighting a duel."

"Shall I shoot you where you stand?"

He saw Horace chuckle silently atop the Kildorne coach, obviously thinking back on his previous threats to shoot him and Dora, so Desdein glared at him.

"Your...fa...father was killed in a fair duel—"

Desdein shrugged. "This one will be fair. Turn your back and I turn mine. Horace, count to ten."

Horace's bald head nodded. "Aye, Sir."

"On ten we turn and fire."

"And if I refuse?" The man clutched the gun by the barrel as if he'd never held it before.

"Then the *Devil in Spurs* will shoot you where you stand, your lordship." Horace appeared to be enjoying this a tad too much.

The viscount slowly turned and put his back to Desdein. He felt the trembling as they stood shoulder to shoulder.

"One!" Horace called out.

Desdein should have faced the other direction. As the coachman called out, each step took him closer to Ashlyn. Tears streamed down her face as she silently watched him, her eyes pleading. Something brushed the side of his boot and he looked down to see Cyril tottering along beside him.

He saw her mouthing the words, *I love you. Do not do this, My Love.*

Warmth filled his heart. He wasn't alone anymore— someone loved him.

Suddenly ravens took flight passing overhead, their cacophony discordant within the fog's stillness. Ravens. Birds of death in Celtic lore. They carried souls to the otherworld.

He looked at Ashlyn's grey eyes. Should he soon draw his last breath, the last thing he wanted to see, to carry with him, would be her beautiful face. Only, he'd rather see it each morn as the sun rose. Kiss her by the flicker of firelight. Gaze upon her lovely countenance as she slumbered in the shadowed night.

Sometimes life is as simple as that.

Distantly he heard *ten* called, but he could only stare at Ashlyn. *One last look.* He sucked in a breath and turned to tell Kildorne he was calling quits to this. It served no purpose. The dead were dead. Killing Kildorne wouldn't bring his parents back. Though Ashlyn harbored little love for the man, he was her father, murdering him wasn't the way to start their life together.

Desdein dropped his arm, the gun pointing to the ground and stared at the man, trembling so hard his knees nearly knocked together. Kildorne lifted the gun and tried to point it, his arm quivering so he couldn't keep the gun still. Worse, the silly man closed his right eye tight, as if struggling to see.

Then he switched and closed the left trying to focus with the right. Finally, he closed both and pulled the trigger.

The ball whizzed past, striking a tree far to his right. Desdein wanted to throw back his head and laugh. The man wasn't just scared—he was little better than half-blind! He looked to Ashlyn in question. "He always like that?"

She nodded. "He cannot see things at a distance."

Desdein drank in her tear-stained face, thinking how he loved her. But he had to finish this before he could tell her, show her. She strained against Jeremy's hold, but his brother's grip held fast. Wicked wench, she tried to kick back with her booted foot, but his brother deftly dodged.

He lifted his finger to his lips, a gesture to hush her, then slowly walked back to the trembling man. "I believe I still have a shot to take."

The man fell to his knees, hands folded before him in prayer. Eyes skyward, he beseeched, "Oh, Lord, I am a sinner, and if it is Your will that I die for those sins, then so be it. But I will not die with the untruth still spoken."

"What untruth?" Desdein demanded, stopping before the kneeling man.

The man swallowed and looked Desdein in the eyes. "I did not fire the shot that felled your sire."

"You cannot see in the distance?"

He nodded.

"Then who?"

"The Earl Whitmore. Of course, he was not the earl then. His father was alive, threatening to disinherit him if he brought any more shame upon the Whitmore name. The old man was on his deathbed. Whitmore and your father fought. Whitmore turned on a count of eight and fired."

"And you lied," Desdein accused through gritted teeth.

He nodded. "He paid me. Half his fortune upon his father's death. I needed the money...Ashlyn's mother..."

Desdein's head jerked around to his horse, taking a step. But the man lunged, catching his arm. "No, do not think it. God has judged him. Word came, night before last he was set upon by footpads in London and was beaten senseless."

"He lives?" Desdein growled.

"Aye, the man does, likely not long. The physician says he will never have his wits again—if he recovers." Kildorne looked toward his daughter. "Ashlyn has been wronged by me. I am not wicked, just selfish. I was poor when I married Ashlyn's mother. When she grew ill, it was hard keeping

Chattam Lane so it didn't fall down around our heads. It was hard to watch the woman I loved die a little each day before my eyes. I drowned my sorrow, my worthlessness in the drink, stayed away when the pain became too much. I stayed away too often. One day, I awoke to Ashlyn's hatred and no words to heal the breach between us. I was weak. Sometimes I just wanted to die so much that I failed in my duty to my daughter. Do not fail her, as well, Desdein Deshaunt."

Ashlyn finally stomped on Jeremy's foot, causing him to release her. She ran to Desdein and threw herself into his arms, sobbing.

He chuckled, then wrapped his arms around her, holding her against him. His lady in breeches. "I have never hugged a woman in trousers before." He looked past Ashlyn to her father. "Looks like you shall get the Marquis de Fournier as a son-in-law after all."

Kildorne smiled. "If my daughter shall have you."

He pulled her arms from around his chest where she nearly squeezed the breath from him and eased her back. "Will you have me, Ashlyn?"

His bride-to-be doubled up her fist and belted him in the stomach. Not expecting it, the blow caused him to bend forward. As he gasped, he looked down at the silly cat. "I think that was a yes, Cyril."

"Perhaps we should retire to Kildorne Manor." The viscount suggested tentatively, "We have much to set right. Your brother's name to clear—surely naught more than a young man's drunken joke gone awry? After all, no one would believe such of the Marquis de Fournier's younger brother. *They wouldn't dare.* Then we must concoct the demise of a phantom called the Devil in Spurs and, I presume, a marriage to arrange? And a longer apology on the ill deeds of a time when I little cared for life. I think with your love of my daughter you might comprehend." The older man's eyes watched his daughter with a mixture of pride and pain. "She is so the image of her mother."

Ashlyn reached out and touched her father's arm. "I...I never understood you loved her."

He nodded, fighting the tears. "There are many things I never permitted you to see. Maybe now you know love, you will have an ear and compassion to hear me." Kildorne forced a smile. "See, daughter, I still know a thing or two. I said the Marquis de Fournier was my choice for your husband above all others."

She smiled at Desdein, linking fingers with his. "Aye, that you did. He might be a devil in spurs, but he's my devil and I plan to keep him. Eh, Cyril?"

The cat looked up at them and meowed.

All I Want for Christmas is a Hula-Hoop... and a Mother

Gayle Wilson Award of Excellence Finalist –
Best Novella

"Allison, it's three days to Christmas Eve. Have you written your letter to Santa?" Shaking off pre-holiday blues, Keon Challenger glanced to the passenger seat where his elfin daughter sat, busy opening a box of *Chiclets*.

He spun the wheel of the black Lexus SUV, hearing the wheels sing against the pavement from the heavy rain. Today was the first day of winter. No White Christmas in the forecast—*yet*. Unseasonably warm for Kentucky, rain poured in sheets as if Noah were having a going-out-of-business sale. Despite, weathermen were keeping a close eye on a cold front bearing down from Canada. Timing was the key. If the Arctic air barreled in before all this heavy rain left, there'd be a White Christmas all right—they'd be up to their bloody hips in the stuff!

His daughter's head, with the riot of pale blonde curls, nodded as the vivid blue eyes looked up at him. "I did, Daddy, last night. I went online and sent it to Santa's email. That way I know he got it."

He smiled at this precious being. At five, his darling daughter sounded so mature in her speech patterns; her British accent only made her seem more precocious. Rather vexing at times, the teeny terror had a penchant for being bossy and took great pleasure in running his life. To say daddy was firmly wrapped around her little finger was putting it mildly.

The smile left his face. He should've remarried, given his daughter a mother. Plenty of women wanted *him*. At forty-three, he was fit and prided himself he looked a decade younger. Rich, cultured and Brit—a big turn-on for American women—*The Lexington Herald* listed him in the top ten bachelor catches for the city since his move from London two years ago. Regardless, he feared none of the ladies he'd dated would be a good mother for Allison. He needed someone who loved his daughter as much as she did him.

"That rare beastie does not exist, I fear," he muttered under his breath.

"What's a beastie, Daddy?" Allison's huge eyes stared at him as if he were the fount of all knowledge.

"A small creature."

She blinked. "What's a creature?"

"A small animal."

"What small animal doesn't exist, Daddy?"

He sighed at the pint-size Perry Mason. Allison's first word hadn't been Papa; it'd been *why*. He'd learned long ago she could *why* him to madness, so developed the habit of derailing her cross-examinations.

"Never mind, Munchkin. Tell me what you wrote Santa you wanted."

She popped a *Chiclet* into her mouth—a purple one—and chewed, then squinched up her nose. "Daddy, is that allowed? Isn't that like a birthday wish? You blow out the candles and you aren't to tell or it won't come true?"

He slowed the SUV to permit a silly woman, with a newspaper held over her head, to dash across the parking lot. The corner of his mouth twitched as he watched the compact derrière and full breasts jiggling. *Dear Santa, what I'd like to find under my tree...*

"Silly, Yank. Should carry a brellie instead of having a mess of wet ink dripping onto her hair and hands."

Allison popped her head up above the dash to see. "That's Miz Leslie, the new ballet teacher. I like her, Daddy. She's Scottish."

"New? What happened to Mrs. Henderson?"

She paused to insert a green *Chiclet* into her mouth. "Fell. Broke her hip. She's gone to Florida to get better and may not come back. Miz Leslie is her granddaughter. She's taken over teaching. She's pretty, Daddy."

*Uh oh....*time to change the topic. "So what did you tell St. Nick you wanted?" he asked, though his divided attention was still drawn to the sexy ballet teacher until she dashed through the front doors of the dance school.

"Lots of stuff, Daddy. Santa won't give me all, though I *have* been very good."

"Opening negotiations, eh?"

"Huh? Neg-oceans? What's neg-oceans, Daddy?"

"Why don't you tell me what's on your list, too, then maybe I can get some things Santa can't carry in his sleigh."

"I told him I want a pony. A kitty. A pair of skates. And a MP3 player...but,"—time to add another *Chiclet*—"I told Santa he didn't have to bring me those things if..."

Keon was going to toss that box of *Chiclets* out the window! "If...?"

"Geesh, Daddy, you're grumpy...like Scrooge on the cartoon."

He chided with humor, "I bear absolutely *no* resemblance to a duck."

"Quack—quack—quack." Allison giggled, then added another *Chiclet* to where her cheek pooched out like a chipmunk. "Mrs. Mesham told some lady friend on the phone you need to get laid."

Keon nearly choked that his housekeeper had said such a thing, but had little time to recover as Allison plowed on with another *why* session.

"She said if you played hide the pickle you'd smile more often. What's get laid, Daddy? And what's hide the pickle? Is that like hide-n-go-seek?"

Forcing a smile, he made a mental note to interview for a new housekeeper after the first of the year. "Sort of an adult version...um...yes."

"When can I play hide the pickle, Daddy?"

Now he *did* choke. "Umm...maybe thirty or forty years from now after I unchain you from your closet."

"Silly Daddy."

"Go ahead and giggle, Munchkin. Daddy's quite serious."

He parked the car—sensibly reached for his umbrella—then came around to fetch Allison. Opening the passenger door, he waited while she stowed her precious chewing gum box in her coat pocket and gathered her pink, Retro-Barbie ballet case.

She finally looked up in seriousness. "I told Santa I really wanted a hula-hoop."

Keon grinned. "Like the old Chipmunk song?"

"Yep. A hula-hoop..."—her eyes fixed him—"and a mother."

Keon's laughter died. Well, bugger. Where did one pick up a mother? Did *K-Mart* have *Blue Light Specials—mothers aisle three, half-price for the next fifteen minutes...?* He could tell the past couple weeks Allison had been on a Mother Hunt. Mommy Mania occasionally reared its head, but now that dog had a bone between its teeth and wasn't letting go. The last two Christmases she'd done the same. This time the push was stronger. Something had set her off.

Keon sighed. He adored his small daughter, would walk through fire for her, nonetheless feared this *present* was beyond his ability. Hula-hoops had made a comeback. That much was within his power. Bloody hell, getting a pony would be easy if they had a place to keep one. Ponies, cats and dogs were just not part of life in a condo. Maybe he'd look for a place in the country, farther out, away from Lexington, a home where Allison could have her kitty and a pony. Possibly along the Palisades of the Kentucky River.

Allison suddenly dashed ahead of him on the walkway, running up the stairs and inside through the white, double-doors.

"What's with females, always dashing about without umbrellas?" He smiled, watching her, his heart full of pride in his role in creating this very special child.

Opening the door, he paused to shake the umbrella, then left it in the stand just inside. He'd been in the ballet school twice before, when he brought Allison to check it out and register, then back for her first class. Originally a one-story antebellum home, a ballet studio and small stage had been built on the rear back in the 1950s. Now the foyer and rooms of the original house served as the waiting room, offices and changing rooms for students.

One dressing room door was open and lights were on over the mirrored table. A woman bent over, switching from street shoes to ballet slippers.

"Morning, Miz Leslie," Allison called, sparkling happiness in her voice. Clearly, his daughter adored her new teacher.

"Good morn to you, Allison. You're early. Class isn't for another half-hour." She dumped the wet newspaper in the trash, then wiped her hands on a towel.

"That's okay, Daddy will keep me company 'til then."

Keon arched a brow. *What happened to, hurry, Daddy, I'm going to be late?*

"Daddy, this is Miz Leslie, my teacher. Isn't she pretty?"

The woman came out of the room and offered a warm smile. "Leslie Seaforth,"—she held out her hand to shake, then paused when her eyes locked with his—"and you're Keon Challenger, Allison's *daddy.*"

A light hazel, they reminded him of a cat. Never had he been so struck by the power, the force of a woman's gaze. Hard to draw air, it felt as though he'd absorbed a physical blow, strong enough to make him sway. Being typically male, he generally didn't begin his inspection of a woman so high up. Leslie Seaforth's eyes held him, mesmerized him, leaving him unable to think or move or breathe. All about him receded to dark grey.

He grew aware Allison had hold of his wrist and pulled him closer to the fae woman who had the magic to rock him. "Say hello to Miz Leslie, Daddy." The small child finally resorted to pushing against his knee. "You know, kiss her the way you do all the other women."

The twinkle of faery dust in the woman's luminous eyes winked out. "All?"

Reality returned and everything came into focus for Keon as he saw he dropped from the level of Prince Charming to lecherous Casanova in a sweep of the long, black lashes. He tried to laugh it off. "Out of the mouths of babes..."

Her faintly stubborn chin raised a notch as her expression hardened. "Actually, I find children rather accurate reporters of the truth. They haven't developed the proper lying skills."

Well, this is going downhill fast. He held out his hand to accept her shake, and for an instant feared she'd jerk back, loathe to touch him, but with a challenge flashing in those huge eyes she took it. Her hand wasn't small, but a strong one with beautiful fingers. A hand he could imagine running over his bare chest, or wrapped around his...Keon gave his errant imaginings a shake.

One shouldn't lust after his daughter's ballet teacher. *Bloody hell! How did he stop?*

She wore a lavender leotard; the pale, stretchy *Capezio* material did little to shield her from him noticing she had beautiful breasts. Large, firm and the size of grapefruits. He thought you had to be flat chested to be a ballerina. Gor, the situation was going from bad to worse, faster than Superman's speeding bullet.

He assured, "I fear Allison exaggerates—"

"Kiss her hello, Daddy." His daughter pushed on his leg again, quite insistent.

Seeking to distract the teeny menace on wheels, he suggested, "Why don't you share a *Chiclet* with Ms. Seaforth?"

"Okay, Daddy."

Leslie Seaforth tilted her head as she watched Allison rush into the changing room. "Points for the deft derailing. Does she always insist you kiss women, or is that solely your initiative?"

"She only insists I kiss her auburn-haired ballet teacher." He couldn't resist the taunt, nor his predator's smile as she blushed.

Heat spread up Leslie Seaforth's body to her neck, then her face. She could barely think, so flustered by the potently sexual man before her. Males like him didn't walk through a ballet studio door every day of the week. Hell, they were rarer than hen's teeth, as Aunt Morag always said. Keon Challenger was hard on a female's system, a throwback to when men were men, and not kinder and gentler, politically correct, androgynous beings.

This man exuded enough pheromones she had a hard time thinking of anything but him. And when he spoke—the sexy British accent evoked a twinge of homesickness. The emotion was quickly overridden by flashes of him whispering dark words in the hush of deep night.

Rampant sexual attraction received a cold dose of reality by sweet Allison telling that her father kissed *all* the women. Yeah, Leslie believed that. This stud in Italian loafers and the John Phillips' suit didn't have to do one thing, just stand still and women would be all over him.

The kind of man any sane woman ran from, *heartbreaker* was stamped on his forehead. The type she wanted *nothing* to do with, having been down that road once before.

Allison returned with her box of gum and offered a green one. Then she took out another and put it in her father's hand. "Daddy likes purple ones."

He leaned over and kissed the blonde curls, then winked at Leslie as he popped the square of gum into his mouth. "Absolutely my fav." Her heart warmed as his rolling eyes said just the opposite. He mouthed the words, "Too sweet."

"Daddy said he'd help tomorrow," Allison announced with a beam on her face, while patting his thigh.

By Challenger's expression, Leslie saw this was the first

he'd heard of *volunteering*. She almost laughed. This pint-size cherub had horns hidden in those pale curls and daddy firmly wrapped around her pinkie.

"Are you sure, Mr. Challenger? It'll be three to four hours for the dress rehearsal. That many ballerinas can be a bit fraying to male nerves." Leslie nearly shook, thinking of being around Keon Challenger for that length of time. Talk about hard on nerves—*hers*!

His hand touched his daughter's shoulder. "I always find time for Allison."

Leslie's heart thawed. Most fathers would ask what they were volunteering for, when it would be, how long, and then check their *Palm Pilot* to see if it could be penciled in. His putting Allison first said much about the man. His love for his beautiful little daughter was clear upon his face and in how he kept patting the child's shoulder or caressing her blonde curls.

Allison was a cutie. The precocious darling had stolen Leslie's heart the first time they'd met. The child obviously had the look of the mother, for she was angelic while her father was black-headed and had stormy grey eyes, which held a hint of green. Allison mentioned her mother was dead, but no details. It was hard to imagine the little girl with no mum to read her faerytales or kiss her booboos.

"It's kind of you to volunteer. May I offer refreshments, fortify you while you adjust to volunteering? Coffee, tea, soft drink?"

"Tea would be nice."

Struggling to keep her wits about her, Leslie found it nearly impossible to breathe when she stared into those stormy eyes. "You can relax in the salon. I shall fetch it."

"If you don't mind, Allison and I would enjoy keeping you company in the kitchen." He slid off his overcoat, handing it to Leslie.

She hung it in the closet. "Certainly. Come on through."

Allison knew the way and already had his index finger, pulling him along. She released her hold on her daddy when she spotted the pet carrier on the kitchen floor. "A kitty!" With a squeal, she was on her knees before it. "Here, kitty, kitty, kitty."

Leslie opened her mouth to caution Allison to keep her fingers back, but the minx had opened the carrier's grate door and the cat zoomed out. "Och, I was going to say don't let him out. He's a grump today. I had him at the vet's for shots."

"Poor kitty." Allison petted the fat orange tabby and he seemed happy to have an adoring audience. "What's kitty's name?"

"Alvin."

Allison giggled. "Like the chipmunk in the cartoons? I love the chipmunk song about the hula-hoop. It's Daddy's favorite song, too, isn't it, Daddy?"

"It is indeed." Putting his hands in his pockets, Challenger nodded. He lowered his voice, meant for Leslie's ears only, "You have Allison's heart with the puss. She's been begging for one for Christmas. Our condo won't permit pets. I'm considering moving to the country, getting a place where she can have a kitty, maybe a pony."

Assured cat and child were bonding, Leslie moved to the cupboard and took out the tin of *Brodie's Edinburgh Tea* and put the kettle on. "Children need space. Pets are good friends, teaches them responsibility and love. Plenty of room to burn up all that energy. I cannot wait to get away from Lexington each night and back to the river house. I fear I'm not a city girl."

"You live on the river?" Interested, Challenger took a seat on a stool by the counter. "I originally held back buying a place in the country, not sure I'd stay. Once I set up the offices for my investment firm, I'd considered going back to London. Only, I like it here. A nice safe place to raise a child. It was good Allison and I had a change of scenery—starting fresh. Now I'm thinking of staying permanently."

"The river area resembles Scotland. I don't feel homesick there. My gran wants to retire to Florida to be near her sister. I'm considering buying her home. It's a beautiful place." *Perfect for a family.*

"See, Daddy, kitties are fun!" She had Alvin's mouse-on-a-string toy and the silly, pudgy cat was jumping and showing off for her like a kitten.

"He doesn't usually take to children. He likes her. But then, how could anyone resist Allison?"

He smiled. "She's special, isn't she?"

"Very. You're lucky."

He grinned. "Being a proud papa, I'm prejudiced."

"You should be. Allison's remarkable." Getting the cups down, she glanced to the child laughing at the cat bouncing across the floor. "If you don't mind me asking, Allison mentioned her mother's dead..."

"Lemon, no sugar," he said for the tea. After a moment's

hesitation he answered. "Meredith died in a car accident when Allison was barely two."

"Did you love her?" She blushed at her crass invasion of his privacy, but it'd popped out before she could stop the words.

His stormy grey eyes met hers with a levelness that said he gave her the truth, bald and unvarnished, in the simple reply. "Yes."

She was unable to break the stare, could lose herself in those shifting green-grey eyes. Her breath caught and held as they stripped her bare, not just her body—as men tend to do—*but her very soul*. She was oddly unsettled that he'd loved his wife. By contrast, Leslie knew her husband died loving another woman. Sometimes she wished to know a man loved her with the conviction she heard in Challenger's words. Other moments, she feared she'd never open herself to the possibility of that pain again.

"I'm sorry. For your loss—and my vulgar intrusion."

Leslie lowered her eyes to the tea, mentally kicking herself for being insensitive. He was a stranger. What right did she have to pry into his life, his feelings?

It was Allison. The little girl needed a mother, but she wondered if this man would remarry or enjoyed playing the field. She gnawed on the inside of her lower lip. It was none of her business.

Only, she was attracted to him. Deeply. No man had slipped past her guards so easily since Kevin's death. She kept all males at arm's length. Problem was, the little girl had already stolen her heart.

Ah, the road to ruin. Keon Challenger was a heartbreaker of the first order. She'd be safer sticking her finger in a light socket than kiss him. *Oh, boy! Who put that silly thought into my mind?*

As she held the teacup out for him, it rattled in her hand. With a thanks, he lifted the cup and sipped. Mesmerized by the beautiful mouth closing on the Belleek China, a hot flush started at her toes, rolled up her body and came out in a blush. Overpowering arousal hit her lower belly like a fist.

And damn him—he noticed. Those eyes, the color of the North Sea in winter, moved down her body and then back up, not missing evidence of her reaction to him, hardly hidden by the lavender leotard. The black brows lifted in a taunt as the corner of his mouth tugged into an arrogant, sexy smile.

Perversely, she wanted to slap that expression off his

smug face. Bloody bastard, she was sure small herds of women stampeded to make goo-goo faces before him. A woman would never feel safe, secure with Keon Challenger, always fearing aggressive females who'd stop at nothing to get in his bed, in his life.

"Do you need any help today?" he asked, glancing at his watch. "I've meetings later this morning, but I could cancel."

"I can always use an extra set of hands. I'm setting up chairs and tables, checking to see if any light bulbs are burnt out in the footlights and such." She smiled, taking in his expensive suit. "You aren't dressed for that sort of thing. Thanks for the offer."

Allison dashed about with Alvin chasing the streamer of red ribbon from where Leslie had wrapped packages for a display for the recital. Silly—and cruel—her mind summoned a vision of Christmas morn, Allison opening presents and playing with Alvin, Leslie watching on with Challenger, sharing that special joy. A beautiful tableau that solidified in her heart, made her crave for it to be real. Swallowing her tea, she let the hot liquid scald the picture from her mind.

She didn't know this man, so it was stupid to spin fantasies. Too much to risk. She'd learned, only too well, hope led to heartache.

The light from the doorway to the classroom was blocked. Leslie glanced up from tying the strings on Allison's tennis shoes. She figured Challenger would pick up his daughter. Almost breathlessly, she found herself waiting for his return, found herself dreading it. She often saw the Black Lexus sitting in the lot waiting for Allison, though sometimes his assistant fetched the child when the father was tied up. His coming back wasn't a surprise.

Her reaction to him was. She couldn't draw enough air as she stared at the sexy man in worn blue jeans and black sweater. His black hair was windblown, not the polished businessman of just an hour ago. Vividly, she envisioned him standing along the cliffs of her home, watching the winding Kentucky River below. Her heart whispered this man could easily fit into her self-contained life.

If she dared take that risk.

"Talk about delusions," she muttered under her breath.

Challenger looked down, feeling Alvin rubbing around his legs. "I'm dressed properly now. Put me to work, Teacher."

He and Alvin dodged as a dozen pint-size ballerinas

shoved by him. The only one in the class who was five, Allison was so small compared to the girls who were two-to-three years older. Her face brightened when she looked up to see her father on the end of those long legs. She wrapped her arms about his thigh and hugged him.

"Love you, Daddy."

"Love you, too, Munchkin. Where are you and the herd of marauding midgets heading in such a rush?"

She grinned. "Cookies!"

"Only one. After we finish up here I'll take you to lunch."

"McDonalds!" she squealed.

"We'll see."

He turned, his eyes following the small girl until she disappeared into the kitchen. His love for Allison was apparent to Leslie. A few fathers picked up their daughters from classes. Some looked bored, others appeared rushed. She couldn't recall any watching their daughter with such pride, such true devotion.

"Thanks for the helping hands. The weathermen issued a warning the rain might turn to snow suddenly, so a couple other volunteers called and cancelled. I won't turn you down again."

It was foolish she knew, but her heart stuttered as he neared. Oh, being around Challenger wasn't wise. Then why was she so pleased he'd returned to help? He was here for Allison, not because of her. She needed a strong dose of reality. Taking a deep breath to steady herself was a waste. She drew in air laced with potent pheromones from this super attractive male.

"What's first?" He invaded her space, deliberately pushing her buttons. A flash in the stormy eyes said he was very aware of her reaction to him, liked that she was aware of him.

As sophisticated as a teen—an idiotic way to feel at age thirty-three—she blushed and quickly looked away, motioning to the chairs stacked in the corner. "Ah...we need to set them up in rows in two sections. Tables at the back for refreshments."

He leaned close and whispered with a grin, "Then I'm your man."

Mercy! *If only*...Leslie sighed.

She watched Challenger unfold the chairs and place them in double sections—twenty across with fifteen rows, which would easily hold the parents, grandparents, aunts and uncles. Balanced atop the tall stepladder, she struggled to change light bulbs in the overhead spotlights. And tried *not* to watch him. She suffered from mild vertigo, so she didn't need to keep switching focus points between the bulbs overhead and the sexy man working methodically on the floor below the stage.

He moved well. Confident. Muscular, though not in a bulky body-builder style. He was lean, hard. The man had beautiful thighs and one super arse!

Challenger made it damn hard to keep her eyes off him.

Which proved dangerous! Her vertigo kicked up as her eyes were constantly pulled toward him. Feeling a total dolt, she stared at Challenger, desire searing every fiber in her being. It was pathetic to want what you couldn't have, however she hadn't been attracted to a man like this in...well... *never*.

Oddly, it was true. She couldn't recall Kevin ever making her this breathless. Her whole life she'd instinctively shied away from men like Challenger, played in the shallows and fallen for a man who was safe. Or at least she'd thought he'd been safe. Boy had she been blindsided!

Allison was running up and down the aisles dragging a ribbon with Alvin trailing after her. Poor Alvin hadn't had that much exercise in years. For a cat disdainful of children, the feline certainly had taken to the angelic girl.

The ladder wobbled and she grabbed the sides to steady herself. Vertigo spiraled and everything seemed to bend in on itself. Leslie closed her eyes, willing it away, but the whirling wouldn't stop, making it impossible to focus on heights and see them in their real relation. Instead, everything undulated about her as if she were on a rollercoaster.

"People pay for this cheap high," she muttered, trying to make light of her weakness.

Leslie shuddered, truly terrified as the ladder rattled and everything about her turned to a whirl of colors, fearful she'd lost her balance. She had. For a breathless instant she fell backward, floating free in space and desperately arching like a cat—frantically clutching at anything to keep from falling to the stage.

Then her back slammed into something solid. "Shhhhh... I've got you."

It took a panicked breath to realize Keon's right arm was around her waist; his left had hold of the ladder, securing them. He remained that way, letting her regain her balance.

As the vertigo subsided, she became aware of other

things, like the deceptive power of the man. He was strong, much stronger than the John Phillip's suit of the high-powered businessman had revealed. He obviously exercised regularly, for the arms felt like bands of steel, protecting her from falling. The strong pounding of his heart against her back. His radiant heat poured through her, calming her fear. It was so tempting to turn and bury her face against his neck, inhale the super-charged pheromones exuded by the sexy man. Let arousal drive the fear away.

"You all right?" he asked, his head against hers.

Leslie managed a faint nod. "Just a spot of dizziness."

"Spot, my arse." He growled. "I'm stepping down a rung and I want you to do the same. I won't let go. Just step when I say. We won't move until you have your footing."

Leslie did as Keon said and felt an utter fool for the whole episode. She was sweating by the time her feet touched the stage floor. Trembling, the worst of her fear ebbing, she allowed Keon to wrap his arms about her and just let her shaking fade. She welcomed that high body heat. Felt she could stay there for an hour. She liked standing in Challenger's embrace too much.

Keon finally stepped back, put his hands on his hips and fixed her with those stormy eyes. "You suffer vertigo?"

She nodded.

"Then why the bloody hell were you up on a ten-foot ladder? Of all the stupid, moronic, imbecilic..."

Allison came over with Alvin twining around her legs. She patted Challenger's thigh. "That's okay, Miz Leslie. Daddy's a Scrooge grouch with me, too. He just needs to play hide the pickle and get laid, then he'll smile more."

Leslie sniggered as she placed the cat carrier down and turned to lock the studio doors. "Hide the pickle, indeed."

Challenger explained his housekeeper had given that *medical diagnosis* to a friend over the phone and Allison overheard. Leslie had bit her lip to keep from asking all sorts of loaded questions that could've quickly spiraled out of control. Gherkin or Polish Dill, being one.

Bracing against the bitter wind, she shivered. She'd worn a light blazer to work, too light now the temperatures were dropping fast. Picking up Alvin's carrier, she hurried down the steps, only to have the Black SUV coast to a stop before her.

The tinted window of the passenger side rolled down and

Allison's elfin face appeared. "Hi, Miz Leslie." She was on her knees to see out the window.

"Hello, Allison. I thought you already left."

"Daddy and I want you to come Christmas shopping with us."

"If I have to suffer the Merry Ho Ho throngs, I thought you could come along and hold my hand. Men in such situations are apt to break out in a rash." He flashed that to-die-for-smile. "Please come."

Shopping with Challenger and his beautiful child. For a woman looking toward Christmas with only Alvin, it'd be a way to capture the missing, childlike magic of a holiday that promised to be lonely. Swallowing regret, she lifted the carrier higher. "Sorry, it's turned frigid. I have to get Alvin home."

Determination flashed in the grey eyes. "Then how about lunch?"

"Yea! McDonalds!" Allison bounced in the seat.

Challenger chuckled. "How about Burger King instead?"

"Scrooge McDaddy...quack–quack–quack." Allison wiggled her head back and forth as she quacked.

Seeing her hesitation, he added, "Alvin can come. I'm sure he'd love a burger."

"Yea! Alvin wants a Big Mac!"

Challenger shook his head. "If this child of mine could just get enthusiastic about things..."

Not giving Leslie a chance to say no, he hopped out of the car and came around. Opening the passenger door, he scooped out his daughter and spun with her in the air, then opened the backseat door and pretended to toss her in. She squealed delight and laughed, but scampered over to the far side, then buckled her seat belt.

He turned to Leslie. "Next, the moggie." When she still held back, he pressed, "Oh, come, come. How can you resist a Big Mac, the best fries around and my scintillating company?"

"I'm sizzalating, too!" Allison added, "Pleeeeeeeese."

Leslie *wanted* to go with them, however her protective mode kicked in. It'd be too easy to fall for both father and daughter, her heart already too close to weaving castles in the air. Only a fool would set herself up for that. Yet, as she met those eyes, the color of the North Sea, reason died a quick death and she threw caution to the wind. *Call me fool.*

With a resigned sigh, she handed him Alvin's tote, earning another of those sexy smiles, capable of melting her heart. He placed it on the seat next to Allison, who instantly complained.

"Daddy, can't see Allllllllllvvvvvvvvvvvvvvin! Daddy!"

"Ok-ay!!!" Imitating the cartoon chipmunk, he flipped the carrier's door to face his very insistent daughter. "There, you can see Allllllllllvvvvvvvvvvvvvvin."

Cat secured, he held the door for Leslie. As she slid onto the leather seat, she smiled up at him. He was good with Allison, not just there and seeing to her needs, but he interacted well with the child, their strong rapport clear in the banter.

She wondered if he'd been that openly loving with his wife. A slight twinge of jealousy shot through her, envying the woman. Did he have it in him to love again? As her eyes followed him striding around the car, she swallowed, forcing back the longing that had no right to live.

He climbed in and reversed the SUV. Pausing to wait for traffic before pulling out, he said, "I still think we should go to Burger King." He winked at Leslie to show he teased.

"McDonalds!" Allison piped on cue.

"She's a very good child, except she's a bit one-tracked when she wants something. Is McDonalds fine with you? I don't take her there often, so she's putting me on the spot in front of you." Challenger's eyes sought his daughter's reflection in the rear view mirror. "She's playing innocent like she cannot hear me, but she does."

"Quack—quack—quack," the voice from the backseat commented.

Leslie chuckled. "Sorry, Challenger, I think you're outmatched. Big Macs are fine."

"Daddy needs—"

"Munchkin, if you want a Happy Meal, you'd better stop telling Miz Leslie what I need."

"Quack—quack—quack." Switching gears, Allison cried out, "Oh, look, Miz Leslie! Flakes!"

Leslie took her eyes off the handsome man to watch the huge, fluffy flurries. "Wow, perhaps we'll have a White Christmas after all."

"I want snow! Santa likes snow!" Allison kicked her legs in excitement. "Scrooge McDaddy likes snow! Miz Mesham said Daddy needs to do more with his pickle—"

"Allison Anne..." Challenger growled a warning.

"—than write his name in the snow. How do you write your name in the snow with a pickle, Daddy?"

Leslie tried to contain the laughter, only when Challenger's eyes met hers they both lost it. She enjoyed watching father and daughter fussing, the sort of chatter rising from their deep love. A pang of wanting a family twisted within her. She could see baking cookies, Allison playing nearby with Alvin, Challenger carrying in wood for the fireplace. Images of a quiet family life she hadn't let herself think about for the past five years. She pushed the yearning back into its shoebox.

"I haven't had a White Christmas in...well, I don't recall the last one." Leslie pondered wistfully. She watched the beautiful snow swirling thicker as it changed over from the rain. "Sadly, it won't stick. All the rain and the warm ground will keep it melting. Still, it's beautiful while it lasts."

Challenger coasted into the drive-in lane of Mickey-Ds. "Happy Meal for the quacking brat. A burger for Alvin. What will you have?"

"Big Mac meal, super-size me, please. I missed breakfast."

Challenger tilted his head, the grey eyes heatedly raking over her body. A cocky grin spread across his sensual mouth. "I love a lass with a good appetite."

Wanting to fan her face, the temperature soared in her skin as she caught he meant for more than food. Clearly he was flirting, nevertheless she feared Keon Challenger flirted as he breathed. What was done carelessly, second nature to him, could have a lass' heart going pitter-patter.

He gave the order to the voice on the speaker, then pulled around. As he waited in line, he turned on the radio, pushing buttons until he found one reporting weather.

"It's looking nasty out there, folks. The rain didn't move out and the Arctic air came in faster than predicted. It's overrun the warm front and prevents the rain from leaving. Temperatures are dropping fast, nearly twenty degrees in the last hour. Rain's shifting to snow all over the state. The National Weather Service has issued a winter storm advisory. Get where you're going. Make sure you're stocked up with everything you need...food, flashlight, batteries. Those of you far away from the cities might see you have plenty of wood in or crank up those kerosene heaters in case your power fails. Expect six inches of snow by nightfall and more on the way...could be one for the record books."

"Yea, Santa got my email!" Allison unbuckled the seatbelt and stood on the floorboard to see the thickening flurries. "Daddy, Santa sent us snow! Bet Santa will give me the other things I asked him for, too."

Leslie turned to watch Allison marvel at the snowstorm. "What else did you ask Santa for?"

The child grinned. "A hula-hoop and a mo—"

Accepting the sack of food, Challenger quickly shoved the box at his daughter even before he parked. "Here, Munchkin, Happy Meal."

"Hey, where's Alvin's? He wants a Happy Meal."

Challenger parked the SUV, but left the car on battery, the wipers running. At this rate, the snow was so heavy they'd be covered before they finished eating. He handed back a hamburger wrapped in paper. "Chow for the cat. Don't let him—"

Allison opened the carrier's door and Alvin hopped on top of it, ready for din din.

"—out." Challenger rolled his eyes. "He doesn't panic in a car, does he?"

"It takes a lot to ruffle Alvin."

He watched her munch french fries. "I love their fries, too." Stuffing a couple in his mouth, he looked at the snow sticking to the side windows. "You seem wrong about the snow not sticking."

"I hope so. It'd be lovely to have a White Christmas."

Leslie concentrated on eating her meal. Being in the car with Challenger and his potent male pheromones swamped her senses. With the snow covering the side windows, they were cocooned. It was too close. She had to remind herself to eat her burger and not stare at the handsome man.

"That cute little Beetle convertible of yours is great for gas mileage, but you'll face problems getting to the river with this coming down."

Leslie saw the wipers moving the snow, falling faster than the blades could swipe the glass clean. "Alvin and I'll be fine," she said without much conviction.

"If it keeps coming down like this, there won't be a ballet recital."

"That will disappoint the students. They've worked so hard. We won't be able to reschedule it until after the first of the year."

"Alvin ate his burger. He wants more." Allison poked her head between the seats, then her small hand held out a slice of pickle from her burger and waggled it in the air. "Here, Daddy, you can play hide the pickle with Miz Leslie now."

Leslie nearly strangled on her coke.

"I think I'll leave Alvin out and stick *you* in the cat carrier." He snatched the pickle slice and ate it before Allison could carry on with her train of thought.

"Silly Daddy. You're supposed to hide the pickle, not eat it."

This time Leslie did strangle. "Here...feed Alvin part of my burger." She tried to keep a straight face, but the chuckle slipped out.

Challenger started to laugh, too. Wiping his mouth, he shook a finger at her. "Not—one—word."

"I wouldn't touch it with a ten-foot pole."

Finishing the last slurp of his soda, he formed his face to seriousness and arched a brow. "The topic...or my *pickle*?"

By the time Keon neared the ballet studio, he'd reached a decision.

The snow fell heavier with each passing minute. So far the highway was just slushy with sporadic patches of ice, only he fretted about what Leslie would face the closer she got to the river house. The roads along the Palisades were steep and winding, often treacherous in spots. Under normal conditions, she said she had a forty-minute drive during rush hour. This was far from normal.

The day darkened due to the storm, with decreased visibility seeing traffic at a crawl. Everyone puttered along at 20 mph, forced to use headlights. It was still a couple hours until the evening rush. Even so, his anxiety increased. This being Friday, every mother's son would be leaving work early in hopes of avoiding the twilight snarl as conditions worsened. Instead of evading the mess, Lexington would have the weekend exodus sooner. Leslie would be right in the middle of that.

"People go nuts with the first snowfall. They forget how to drive, none have snow tires on their cars," Keon commented, setting the stage to asking Leslie to come home with them. "The police will be tied up with wrecks."

"The officers stop responding," she agreed. "You get to the point if it's a fender bender, just exchange insurance info and get out of the way." Leslie glanced over her shoulder to see Alvin rested quietly on Allison's lap.

"Garages will be swamped with emergency runs due to people skidding off the roads. Like that eegit there." He nodded toward a red Lumina off in a ditch.

Two more cars were off on the opposite side up ahead.

That did it! He wasn't about to let Leslie out in that mess alone. Only how do you ask your daughter's ballet teacher to come home for the weekend, yet convince her he wasn't trying to corner her to play hide the pickle?

Actually, he really would like to get cozy with Miz Leslie. The lady had a body that was hard to get off his mind. *But it was more.* A warmth about her drew him. He loved watching her eyes as she looked at Allison, saw the hunger there. Oh, Leslie was attracted to him. He spotted the pulse in her neck jump when his shoulder brushed hers. Her auburn hair was neatly coiled, ballerina perfect, at the back of her head. His groin throbbed as he contemplated uncoiling the long braid and letting it play over his fingers. Oh yes, Leslie Seaforth was quickly becoming an obsession, and not only with him, but Allison. This woman was already half in love with his daughter.

Suppressing a smug grin, he lowly sang, "*It's beginning to look a lot like Christmas...*"

Maybe Santa did read emails after all.

Clearing his throat, he tried to sound casual. "Leslie, perhaps you should come home with Allison and me. Everyone's leaving Lexington, heading toward Nicholasville and Danville to beat the evening rush. No one wants to get stuck in this mess. A killer drive in that Beetle of yours." Keon presented it as nothing more than simple logic.

He wanted her to come home with them and it had nothing to do with the bad weather. Allison did a "Yippie!" from the back seat, but then he didn't have concerns from how the *peanut gallery* would take the invite. He had a feeling Leslie Seaforth was the reason Allison was on her Mommy Hunt kick.

Leslie smiled sadly. "It's kind of you to offer, but I have to get home."

"I'll smuggle Alvin in under my jacket. The super won't know he's there," he teased.

"It's not Alvin. I can't leave Edward alone."

Edward? Who the bloody hell is Edward? Husband? Why did images of men battling with claymores arise to mind?

"Edward?" He patted himself on the back for the laid-back tone. Jealousy burned within him like a brand, the emotion knotting his stomach with an intensity he couldn't ever recall experiencing.

"The pony."

"Pony?"

Allison squealed and her head popped between the seats, her eyes alight. "A pony, Daddy! See Santa read my email—"

"Allison Anne, back in the seat belt." He pulled his *official daddy voice*—obey or you shall be sorry. He didn't think Leslie was ready to hear Allison's updated rendition of *Christmas Don't Be Late.*

Hell, *his* mind was forced to shift gears. A few hours ago, he'd gone to drop his daughter off for dance class. Now his whole world had turned upside-down. He had to deal with the suspicion Santa not only read emails, he read minds!

"I can't leave him alone. His water might freeze up. If it does, I'll have to carry it from the house. He'll need extra bedding and plenty of food so he has fuel to keep warm during the storm.

"Want to see Edward, Daddy!" Allison bounced up and down infected with pony-mania.

He cocked an eyebrow. "*Edward* the Pony? I thought ponies had pony names, like Trigger or Buttermilk."

She laughed softly. The musical sound, similar to wind chimes in a summer breeze, sent a shiver up his spine. It summoned images of that muffled laughter in a darkened bedroom. Such flashes fired his hunger to take, to claim, a warrior's need to possess her rising in his blood, despite his mind warning they were moving too fast. He was deeply attracted to Leslie, appreciated her fondness for Allison. There was a sense of belonging, a comfortable feeling of them ...*fitting.*

The disc jockey broke into the cozy daydream with a dose of reality. "*Repeating, we have a Winter Storm Advisory. The roads are turning to mush. If you don't have to be out, stay home. If you're at work, leave early. The police ask you stay home once you get there. Salt and sand crews will be out; make their job easier by giving them less traffic. AAA is already reporting fender-benders. The temperature is dropping fast, people. Weathermen predict a foot of the white stuff by morning. Get home, prop your feet up by the fire and relax. Here's a song to lend seasonal cheer.*"

Dean Martin crooned, *let it snow, let it snow.*

Keon smirked at the radio. "Sing it, Dean."

Leslie's neck whipped around as he passed the turn off for the studio. "Och, my car's back there."

"You won't need it. Since you won't come home with us because of Edward, then Allison and I shall go with you."

Keon pushed the buggy down the grocery aisle of Wal-mart, gathering food for three people—and a cat—like he played *Beat the Clock*. Not sure what ponies ate, he grabbed big bags of carrots and apples, just in case. Fortunately, the Superstore was on the way, off Nicholasville Pike. Even with the weather situation worsening, his SUV and its four-wheel traction would see they reached the river house easily. Once there, they'd have to stay put until road crews salted, sanded and plowed. Leslie said she was several miles off the main road, so it could be days until they cleared secondary lanes.

"Ah, sacrifices." A smile spread over his lips, saying he fancied spending the weekend getting to know Leslie Sea-forth.

Christmas was always special because of Allison, only for the first time since Meredith's death he was in high spirits. Everything was magical again, filling his heart with a child's joy. The anticipation for the holiday had always been to see his daughter at her happiest. Her merriment was his. This time, he relished the sudden rush of Christmas cheer zinging through him.

"Dear St. Nick, let it snow, let it snow, let it snow."

He'd left Allison and Leslie in the car. They'd keep it running and warm for Alvin, while he dashed in to pick up emergency supplies. If he knew his daughter, she immediately launched into her wish list for St. Nick. A Kodak moment. He would've loved to see Leslie's reaction. He just hoped it hadn't put her off. Somehow, he had an idea the lass took it in stride.

Always leaving shopping to his housekeeper, he'd never been in a Superstore before. Deftly wheeling his cart up and down aisles, dodging other frantic shoppers, he was getting into the groove of collecting stuff. "The male reverts to his caveman food-gatherer and provider. Me, Keon. You, Jane... hmm...Leslie." While visions of Leslie in one of those Maureen O'Sullivan outfits played through his horny brain, he paused by the meat case, eyeing the fresh turkeys. "Bet even Alvin likes white meat."

Selecting one, he added it to his growing stack of purchases. With the same relentless pace, he snatched up a couple pair of jeans for himself, two sweaters and underwear.

"Ah, the bare necessities!"

Thoroughly enjoying himself, he zoomed through the kids' department and snagged items for Allison. Happening upon the pet section, he found *recreational drugs* for the cat.

So intent on evading other customers, who dashed about in the same frenzied manner, he almost missed the colorful hula-hoops sitting on the end of the aisle.

"Thanks, Santa." He blushed sheepishly when a passing lady glared at him as if he'd lost his marbles.

Taking the final turn to the registers, he stopped abruptly as he spotted the glass cases. He suddenly knew he had one more purchase to make.

Back at the car, he quietly slipped the hula-hoop in the back and then hid it with the groceries, not wanting Allison to see it.

Leslie got out and came around to help him load. She rolled her eyes. "You sure you got enough?"

"Depends..." He bumped shoulders with her deliberately.

"Upon what?"

"Upon whether Alvin likes white meat or dark." Flashing her a wicked grin, he leaned close, invading her space to inhale her light, lemony scent. "Personally, being a breast-man myself, I like white meat."

Leslie chuckled. "Challenger, you should be outlawed."

Traffic exiting Lexington had been worse than Keon anticipated. Multiple vehicles were off the sides of the road; he'd stopped counting all the fender benders. It seemed flashing lights of cop cars and wreckers were around nearly every turn. Even after they passed through the small town of Nicholasville, about fifteen miles southwest of Lexington, they still had to fight the flow of people rushing home to Wilmore and beyond to Danville. Pleased that he'd insisted on bringing Leslie home, he was glad the Lexus had four-wheel drive. Without it, it would've been a nightmare.

As the car pulled down the winding drive, the pony heard it and came running from the barn. Allison zeroed in on the small black beast like a heat-seeking missile.

"Look, Daddy, Edward!" Even before they parked, she was unbuckling the seatbelt and opening the door.

"Don't let the..."—he frowned as she flung the door open and nearly leapt out—"...cat out." Alvin was right on her heels. "I hope he's good with being outside."

"Alvin loves to chase snowflakes." Leslie chuckled as the feline started doing just that. "Thank you."

He paused, caught up in those mesmerizing eyes. "For what?"

"Bringing me home. I appreciate it. You were right. I'd

never have gotten through in the Beetle. I'm rattled as it is. Alvin and I would've ended up in the ditch somewhere."

His hand lifted and he dragged the outside of his index finger along her soft cheek. "You're most welcome, Leslie Seaforth. Hope your unexpected guests don't put a damper on your holiday plans."

Nervous, she started to glance away, but her amber gaze came back to him. "I'm happy to have Allison and you."

"And we're glad to be here." Catching himself before he kissed her, he opened the car door.

The landscape hit Keon with a deep yearning. This was the place his mind conjured when he dreamt of a property away from the city. Hunger and admiration filled him as he studied the sloping hillside and clever layout of the home and stable. The barn's rear was nestled against the bend in the steep hillside, while the house front sat on stilts and looked out over the river below. A view that would endlessly fascinate him, each passing season would render it another portrait of the Palisades' breathtaking splendor.

Right now, it was a winter wonderland. Nearly six inches of snow blanketed the landscape, lending a hush to the wooded terrain.

Keon loved the house, coveted it. He couldn't imagine one designed that could suit him better. A huge deck ran around three sides with an A-frame front, all glass, creek stone and redwood. The two-story structure was perfect. Nestled in the woods, the acreage was so isolated.

Ideal place for a child to have a pony and a kitty.

Leslie climbed out and came around the Lexus, watching him study the grounds. "Magnificent, eh? I love it. Plenty of privacy with the hills surrounding three sides, yet lots of open room for—"

"Edward! Look, Daddy, isn't he cool?" Allison came dashing up. She'd already turned the pony loose and had him in tow.

Keon laughed out loud. "*That* is Edward? That isn't a pony, that's a shaggy dog."

"Don't insult Edward," Leslie teased. The animal's head was barely above her waist as she patted the tiny horse's forehead. "He may be what they call a 'miniature pony', but he's a big horsie in his heart. My gran rescued him from a petting zoo outside of Lexington. She didn't like how he was treated so bought him for a ridiculously high price."

"He's just right!" Allison bounced, half climbing up his

leg. "Daddy, I want to ride him. PLEASE!"

He looked to Leslie, who nodded. "I need to put him back in the barn. She can ride to there." He lifted Allison upon the fat pony's back, the child grabbing a handful of mane to hold on."

"I want him to run!"

"NO!" He made a grab for Allison, but the pony was already bouncing toward the stable. "I need to put a chain on this wild child of mine."

"Don't fret. Edward only has two speeds—slow and stop. He's very good with kids. Adores them."

She turned and smiled at him, her eyes shining with love for his daughter. As their stares locked, the smile slowly faded, awareness of him clearly spreading through her. Yes, she adored Allison, but her hunger for him had a raw edge. For the longest moment their connection held, neither able to break it. Barely breathing. Then he saw a flash of pain, of the child standing before the candy store with her nose pressed to the window. Wanting, but knowing she couldn't have.

His heart did a slow roll. He was in love with Leslie Seaforth. Had been since he first looked in her amber eyes.

Sorting out the mounds of sacks Challenger carried in, Leslie glanced over the kitchen counter and into the living room. Allison sat wrapped up in a cozy tartan, Alvin sleeping on her lap. The child rocked in the rocking chair, content as she watched the weather report.

"More snow, Leslie," she called. The little girl was way too happy with the repeated pronouncements of additional snow and warnings everyone should stay home.

Obviously, Allison had decided she was no longer *Miz* Leslie.

Challenger came inside with another load of plastic sacks. Dropping them on the counter, he met her eyes and smiled sheepishly. He'd bought a lot of stuff, more than what three people would need for the weekend.

She raised her brows. "That turkey would feed a family of ten."

"Alvin and I have big appetites." The silly man grinned.

Inventorying the purchases, she had a feeling Challenger had an eye on Christmas, rather than just toughing it out until the plows came through. Her heart warmed at that notion.

She'd planned a quiet holiday with Alvin. Her sisters called and begged her to come home to England for the holiday. Oddly, she resisted. She didn't have the heart to watch other people planning a future of Christmases, when she was at loose ends...waiting.

No real reason to decorate when she was spending it alone, she hadn't even put up a tree.

With her husband's death behind her, she wasn't sure what she wanted to do with her life. Why she'd jumped at the chance to come to the States and take over the dance school after her gran's accident. A new start, a new direction. This season would be a quiet time of reflection, soul-searching hoping to find her way.

She glanced around the lovely home, at the wood panel walls, the massive creek stone fireplace and the high-beamed ceiling. The room cried out for a Christmas tree. A huge one, in the corner, loaded with decorations and knee-deep with presents underneath. The scent of baking gingerbread cookies filtered through her imaginings.

Returning to sort the groceries, she pushed the silly dream-building away. She'd learnt long ago that was the road to disappointment. If she permitted herself to construct a beautiful Christmas—the holiday in the heart—then the weather front would shift and Challenger, with his drop-dead sexy smile, and his darling little girl would be gone, off to the Christmas already planned.

Stomping his feet to shake off the snow, Challenger came inside, this time with a load of wood in his arms. "Another hour and you won't be able to see our tire tracks on the drive."

He stacked the wood in the built in bin, then went out for more. Two more trips saw them with plenty of wood for the night. As he squatted to his knees to build the fire, Leslie watched the man and child in the living room, pain twisting her heart. This was almost too cruel.

They fit so well...as if they belonged.

Fearful Leslie wouldn't eat proper meals, her grandmother had left her tubs of frozen soup stock. She started one to simmer while she chopped veggies to add to it. With a smile, she glanced at Challenger making a cocoa for Allison. Unlike most men, he seemed at home with such chores. Puttering in the kitchen with him again brought those longings for a family to her heart.

She couldn't help but ask, "Ovaltine? Don't most kids want Nestles?"

He glanced at Allison, now watching the *Cartoon Net-*

work. Vintage Toons of *Auggie Doggie and Doggie Daddy* had her giggling. "Allison has a deep affinity for anything Retro. I think she must be reincarnated from someone who lived in the 1950s."

As a commercial came on, she wandered into the kitchen ready for her hot chocolate. "I want five marshmallows, Daddy." Grasping the countertop, she pulled up on tiptoes to watch.

"One." He shook his head.

She waved her fingers to say five.

"Don't be greedy, Munchkin. You had a pony ride, played with Alvin for hours and went to McDonalds." He handed her the small cup with *one* marshmallow.

"'Kay," she grumbled and took it. Sipping, her eyes roved over the pile of sacks containing clothes, still to be put away. Something caught her interest. She picked up an aqua-colored box and held it upside-down. "What's this, Daddy?"

Challenger, pouring another cup, tipped the mug over. Quick reflexes, he caught it before the chocolate spilled more than a tablespoonful. He stopped, looked to the ceiling and then closed his eyes as if praying for the floor to open up beneath his feet.

"Daddy's got a headache," Allison said.

"Yeah, Daddy has a headache." He laughed and grabbed for the box where Allison was waving it in the air. After three misses, he caught her wrist and tugged it from her hand. "And its name is Allison Anne."

Snatching up the plastic sack, he shoved the box into it, only to have the bottom rip. His package of underwear, can of shave cream and the box of condoms tumbled to the floor at Leslie's feet.

Suppressing a smile, she bent to pick it up. Challenger blushed. She wondered when was the last time this dynamic man *blushed.* She tried to arrange her face to appear serious, but the smirk slipped out. "I believe you dropped this."

He shrugged, trying to be nonchalant. "You know, the bare necessities."

"*Bare* necessities?" Leslie nearly lost it.

Challenger snatched the box from her and shoved it under the packages of briefs and the pump bottle of *Kiss My Face* shavecream.

"*Kiss my Face* shavecream?" She steepled her fingers over her nose and mouth trying to keep in the laughter.

"They didn't have my regular brand."

Leslie's laughter was cleansing, chasing away the cobwebs of the past. Opening her fragile heart.

The chuckle died as she stared into those stormy grey eyes. *She was in love with Keon Challenger.* Wanted him with a passion that left her breathless. Wanted him and his darling daughter in her life.

And that terrified her.

Allison yawned, nearly falling asleep in the dining room chair.

"You've had a busy day, Munchkin." Challenger suggested, "Why don't you go sit in the rocker until I'm done. Then I'll tuck you up in bed."

"'Kay." Allison slid from the chair and came to Leslie. Leaning against her arm, she looked up with big blue eyes. "Will you rock me?"

Leslie's heart squeezed. Touching her napkin to her mouth, she glanced at Challenger. He'd stopped eating and intently watched them, a banked question in his eyes. Scooting the chair back, she took Allison's hand and led her to the rocker. She helped the little girl into her lap and set the chair in motion.

"Can I ride Edward tomorrow?" Allison yawned.

"Depends upon the snow. Even if you can't ride him, you can help me brush him and feed him an apple."

"'Kay."

Leslie enjoyed cradling the small body, feeling her delicate muscles relax against her. It was both soothing and heartrending holding Allison. So easily, she could imagine doing this for more than just a few nights.

"I don't have a mommy to rock me." Allison's sad whisper spoke how important this moment was to her, too. "I asked Santa for a mother. Sometimes he doesn't give me what I ask for. Mrs. Mesham said I have to be very good to get what I want from Santa. I've been very good this year, Leslie. Long time ago, I asked Santa to bring my mommy back. He didn't. Last Christmas I just asked for a mother. He didn't listen then either. Maybe he'll listen this year."

Maybe. Leslie patted the child's back. She glanced up to see Challenger standing by the wall of windows, watching her hold his daughter. His expression was guarded, concerned. Fearful of what she saw there, she quickly looked away to the fire.

Challenger was aware of Allison's needs. Would he ask a

woman to be the little girl's mother when he didn't love her? She ached to hold Allison, rock her, play with her, watch her grow. And she wanted Keon. Only she didn't want to be just a candidate for Allison's mother in his eyes.

She wanted Keon to fall in love with her, just as she was in love with him.

Giggling, Allison held up her arms for Challenger to grasp. When he did, she did a complete 'Ferris wheel' turn. "Do me again, Daddy." Rolling his eyes, he helped the little girl summersault in the air. Of course, the laughing child instantly demanded, "Do me again, Daddy."

"No, you greedy child. Three spins is enough. Hop in bed." Challenger tried to sound gruff, but Allison ignored him and started to spin on her own. Instead of flipping her over, he just held her upside-down. "Oh, look, the naughty child is stuck."

Leslie smiled at their antics, clear the two often played like this. Challenger didn't just take his responsibilities of being a single parent seriously, he enjoyed being a father to Allison. Fearing she made a fool of herself by staring at him, she turned down the covers on the bottom bunk bed for the child.

When Keon finally set her down, Allison was laughing so hard she could barely breathe. Leslie feared the child would have trouble settling down to sleep, but she let out a giggly yawn and said, "Do me again. Do me again."

"No and that's final. You used up your spins for one night."

She pushed on his leg. "Then do Leslie. Do her, Daddy."

Challenger's flashing eyes met hers with a power that rocked Leslie to her toes. "Well, do you want me to *do you*, Leslie?"

Oh, man, what a loaded question!

"Mmm...well...uh..."

"I think the cat's got Leslie's tongue," Challenger goaded.

Allison crawled up on the bed and stuck her foot up for Leslie to pull off her sock. "Why does Alvin have your tongue?"

"Your daddy's teasing."

"Daddy's silly." She stretched and yawned again. "Do piggies."

The phone rang in the kitchen, causing Challenger to look at her. "Go ahead, answer it while I go on piggy patrol."

Leslie hated to leave the family moment, but knew it was likely her gran. She'd worry if Leslie didn't answer. With a last glance at father and daughter, she went to the phone in the kitchen.

Sure enough, it was Gran. "Leslie! I was beginning to worry. Are you all right? They say you're getting hit with a blizzard." Maggie Henderson's worry came through the wire.

Leslie carried the phone to the patio doors. Flipping out the overhead lights, she left the room illuminated by only the firelight. She stared out into the winter wonderland, the night landscape a world of magical blue-white. "Don't fash, Gran. Yes, it's coming down at the rate of a couple inches an hour. It's rather beautiful."

"I'm worried about you there. What if the electricity goes out? What if the phone goes?"

"I'm all tucked up. Plenty of food, heating oil and wood," she assured. "I have the cell phone."

"Yes, but you're alone, all the way out there. What if something happens?"

Leslie hated to admit Keon and his daughter were staying the weekend, fearful her grandmother would start planning a spring wedding. Since Kevin's death five years ago, the family fretted over her not 'getting on with her life', but none as worrisome as her grandmother. Still, it'd ease her gran's heart to know.

"Actually, I'm not alone..."

"Alvin and Edward don't count, my dear. I'm talking about two legged animals, six-foot tall, muscles, preferably in a kilt."

"Not kilted, but I have one who fits that description under the roof now."

The bubbly laughter conveyed Maggie Henderson didn't believe her. "You were never a good liar, Leslie."

"And I'm not lying now."

"If you say. Anyone I know?"

"In fact, you've met him. Keon Challenger and his daughter, Allison."

"Och, you move fast, lass. You can't see me, but I'm bowing in your honor. How did you snag that big fish? Half the women in the state have been hot on his trail since he came from London a couple years ago."

"He invited me to lunch with his daughter and we were caught in the snowstorm. He wouldn't let me drive the Beetle back, but fetched me home in his four-wheel-drive vehicle. It was clear we're going to be stuck for the weekend, so he stopped for supplies. Please don't worry."

"Worry? I might be sixty-something,"—she cleared her throat—"but being snowbound with that man is every woman's fantasy. I won't keep you since you need to entertain your guests. And in case your phone goes down and I don't get to speak with you again, Merry Christmas, darling. Have fun unwrapping *things*."

"Merry Christmas, Gran." Leslie didn't bother to remind her grandmother cell phones didn't *go down*. The elderly woman just didn't get today's *newfangled things*, as she called them.

She paused, wanting to go back to Challenger and Allison, but in another mind feared the family intimacy she'd intrude upon. They belonged together. Bedtime was a special time. She had no right to impose just because Challenger had been kind enough to see her safely home.

A lie. She hesitated because, like rocking Allison, she hungered for these things, the quiet nighttime ritual, the gentle sharing of family life that was beyond her hope.

Treading silently down the hall, she intended to fetch extra blankets. Only the orange glow of the bedside lamp on low pulled her, just like that silly moth attracted to the dangerous flame.

Challenger sat holding the little hand of his daughter. "I'll leave the lamp on in case you wake up." He glanced at the cat stretched out by Allison's far side, clearly determined to stay. "And Alvin is here to keep you company."

"'Kay, Daddy." She patted Alvin. "See, kitties are nice. He'll protect me from monsters."

"He will most certainly." Challenger kissed her tiny finger.

Allison gave a big yawn. "Daddy, Leslie won't fit in Santa's sleigh. Neither will Edward."

He leaned over and kissed Allison's forehead. "Close your eyes. We'll worry about St. Nick tomorrow."

"'Kay, Daddy. Will Leslie kiss me goodnight?"

His back to the door, until he spoke Leslie hadn't realized he was aware of her presence, hovering at the door's edge.

"Come, Leslie, Allison Anne requests a goodnight kiss." His head turned and he offered a gentle smile.

A smile that turned her heart upside down. Leslie walked to the bed and leaned over to kiss the angelic child on the forehead. "Night, night, Allison. Pretty dreams."

"Night..."—another yawn came out—"I like it here, Leslie."

She rolled over and her small arm loosely embraced Alvin.

With a last look at the precious girl, she followed Challenger to the living room. He added another log to the fire while she turned on the news to watch the weather update.

"The Kentucky State Police ask everyone to stay off the roads. If you have a medical emergency, contact your local police or the State Police Station nearest you." The weatherman turned to the digital map to show what was happening. *"This cold front is straight out of Canada with frigid air. It overran the rain, so now we have snow. Oh, boy do we have snow! Close to a foot. At this point we could have six-to-ten inches of additional snow before daybreak..."*

Leslie noticed Challenger smiled as he lowly sang, *"Let it snow, let it snow, let it snow..."*

"Are you a snow freak?"

He closed the chain mail spark guard and then came to sit beside her on the sofa. "I suddenly have a fondness for the stuff. Do you mind—being stuck with Allison and me through Christmas? I'm actually rather handy to have about. Moderately tidy, not averse to doing chores around the house, and I can tote water for Edward if need. This snow is giving me a wonderful opportunity to get to know you, a crash course on who Leslie Seaforth is."

"You might be bored to death." She suppressed the tight laugh wanting to pop out.

Challenger's presence was too intense, too unsettling. Even so, she forced herself not to look away from him, but watched his fascinating grey eyes. There was such warmth there. A complex man, a strong man, his love for Allison revealed how special he was.

"Not bored...never bored." Putting his elbow on the back of the couch, he inclined toward her. "I know we just met today, so things are moving a bit fast in some fashion. In others,"—he leaned forward and faintly brushed his lips against hers—"not fast enough. However, I'm a patient man. I can wait."

Leslie savored that kiss, the promise it held, yet she steeled herself not to read too much into it.

"Shall we get the baggage out of the way? Then we won't have to deal with it again. I said I loved my wife. I did. However, I didn't idolize her, saw her faults as well as her goodness. Had she lived, I'm not sure she would've been the mother Allison needs. A rising reporter for telly, she was very career oriented. She was, I fear, living for the chase of the next breaking news story. I'd hoped that would change. She was killed in a multi-car pile up on the M-1, rushing to yet another scoop, so we'll never know. I'd like to think she'd come to see Allison was the most important thing in our lives. Deep down, I have doubts. Deep down, I worry if our marriage would've survived that."

Leslie's hands fidgeted, not caring to talk about Kevin, for while there were possible problems ahead in the Challenger marriage, he'd loved his wife. "You loved her. She loved you. Anything is possible with love." How could any woman not walk through fire for this man?

"Sometimes." He picked up her hand and linked pinkies. "She loved me, but I think the career, the jazz of being a television reporter was a bit more important. In the final year of our marriage, this drive had strengthened, not lessened. I did more and more for Allison, to make up for Meredith not always being there. I wanted something more than the job—I wanted a family. My investment firm was doing well. I was in position to work less so I'd be able to give more to Allison."

She met the question in his eyes. "My turn?" When he nodded, she sighed. "I don't talk about my marriage...the failure. Not sure what went wrong. Not meant to be, perhaps. Kevin was a sweet guy. Everyone liked him. He felt safe to me, someone I could trust with my future. I think what upset me the most—I never saw it coming. Everything was going along the same, rather happy—I thought. I go in one day to put away the wash and I find a small packet of letters at the back of his sock drawer. I admit it. I'm nosy. Your husband hiding letters in his sock drawer—what woman would put them back without reading?"

Leslie got up, nervous, and paced to the glass doors. She hated this—that the emotions could still provoke after all this time. "So dreadfully predictable...as you can guess, I found he was in love with another woman. They'd meet when he was out of town for business. She pursued him; he was flattered. She was exciting, sexy, thrilling. I was dull, boring. Things fell into place, small things. How he suggested I cut my hair...lose a few pounds...start wearing sexy dresses. I'm a jeans sort of lass. What? Was I supposed to look like a Frederick's of Hollywood version of June Cleaver? I told him to get out. He said, thank you; I just made it easy. He'd wanted to leave for some time, but felt guilty. They were heading to a vacation in Spain when they were hit head-on by a drunk driver."

He followed her to the doors to watch the beautiful peace

of the falling snow. "Early today, you asked me if I loved Meredith and I answered you."

"Instead of telling me to mind my own beeswax?" She chuckled, feeling the memories, the feelings of betrayal, of pain, fading.

Challenger asked softly, "Did you love him?"

Leslie stared into the grey eyes, knowing she owed him the truth. Nothing less. "No."

"But you were deeply hurt. He betrayed you, took a marriage you worked hard to make good and just tossed it and you aside."

"I thought I loved him. And I guess in a way I really did. But I wasn't *in love* with him. I didn't understand the difference." She turned away to look out to the snowy night-scape, unable to watch Keon's eyes any longer, afraid to see the pity in them for a woman who'd deluded herself into marrying a man who wasn't *the one*. She put her hand to the glass feeling the cool of the winter night. "I wanted a home, a family, that anchor they provide. I needed the security of belonging to another."

"You weren't wrong, Leslie. Those are good things to want. Meredith's and Kevin's deaths demonstrate how easily life can slip through our fingers. You need to reach out and find what you want, what can make you happy." Challenger moved so he could slowly place his larger hand over hers, matching the finger spread.

She tried to chuckle, but it came out self-derisive. "I'm not a competitive person. I chose a man I felt safe with. Instead, he taught me there's no safety. I fear if I sought love again I'd be this green-eyed monster. Every time a woman might look at him or he glanced her way, I'd twist inside with doubt. I'm not sure I could survive that pain again."

"Or maybe you'd get lucky and find the right man, the man who'd make you so secure, doubt would never come your way."

His head started to dip toward her as if he meant to kiss her, but a hard gust of wind hit the side of the house, rattling the glass. An intense chill seemed to come straight through the well-insulated walls.

Being a coward, she used the drop in temperature to end the emotional tell-all. "I better get some extra blankets. Little children don't have the body heat adults do."

Challenger's eyes said he saw she was running from him, but he let it pass, recognizing the intensity of what was rising still too new. He picked up his purchases and followed her. "If you'll show me where I am to..."

"Put your *bare* necessities?" She paused by the door to the huge walk in closet and flipped on the light. "Ordinarily, I'd put you up in one of the upstairs rooms, let you enjoy the view in the morn, but they get a bit chilly when the wind is up. "We'll be warmer down here and can hear Allison if she calls."

He arched a brow. "We?"

She crossed the hall and turned on a light in the largest bedroom downstairs. "Not the breathtaking view from upstairs, but it overlooks the river." She opened the curtains so he could see.

He moved to the bed, placing his purchases on top of the spread, then joined her by the window. The moody grey eyes assessed the huge deck and then cliffs of the river on the other side. A faint smile tugged at the corner of his sensual mouth.

"I find it hard to believe anyone can improve on this." His gaze encompassed her. "Or what is before them."

With a magician's pass, he reached up and pulled the pins from her bun one by one. They clattered to the floor with a deliberateness that sent a frisson up her spine. What would it be like to make love to a man so focused, with so much recoiled power within him? Leslie wasn't sure she was strong enough to face the demand it'd require of her, knew she was helpless to resist.

He allowed the silken mass to slide through his fingers, a fire flaring within the grey depths. Slowly they traced over her face, assessing. "Your husband was a bloody fool."

Leslie fought the tears threatening to cloud her eyes, and swallowed the knot in her throat, almost swaying to the pull of his hypnotic power. The wind buffeting the house pulled her back from making a big mistake. A coward, she grabbed at the feeble excuse.

"I better get the blankets. I wouldn't want Allison to be chilled." She rushed from the room before her will—and commonsense—weakened.

The soothing scent of the cedar walls greeted Leslie as she entered the windowless room. Turning on the low-watt light, she allowed sensations to rush over her. As children, her sister, Dara, and she would come and sit in here on hot summer days, spinning tales of handsome knights who came to claim them.

The huge room was lined with racks of clothes on one

side, floor to ceiling built-in drawers and cabinets on the opposite. In the far corner, boxes labeled *Christmas Decorations* caught her eye. Drawn to them, she pulled off one of the lids to reveal glittering silver and gold garland. She examined the ornaments her gran had collected over the years. Old fashioned, there was a beauty about them not found in the fancy ornaments of today.

Leslie picked up a tiny wooden rocking horse, painted with red enamel and with white string for the mane and tail. She wondered if Allison would like it. Challenger said she loved stuff that was Retro.

"I was in love with the house before, but this cinched it." Challenger sauntered in, checking out the room-size closet. "Most houses don't have good storage space. Someone really designed this well. And wow...the scent's heady."

Leslie smiled, pleased he liked it. "My sister, Dara, and I used to sneak in here with our blankets and pillows and sleep. Once we hid in here when a tornado passed over. Since it's at the heart of the A-frame, steel beams are in the walls and ceilings for bearing weight. Excellent protection."

"What wonderful decorations. My Retro Baby would love them." He moved closer. "Beautiful treasures like these should be handled carefully, protected."

Leslie found it hard to breathe as Challenger stared at her, not the box containing all the makings of a beautiful Christmas. What she saw in those grey eyes felt like a physical blow to her heart. He watched her as if she was something rare, something precious, watched her with a banked hunger that both compelled him, yet scared him.

Unable to maintain the stare, she turned away, fearing it was a trick of the shadows within the cedar closet. Scared she was seeing what she wanted to see.

Going to the far shelf, she pulled out two tartan blankets and two thirteen-togs duvets, pretending absorption in removing them from their plastic cases.

"You're running from me, Leslie." He blocked her way.

"Don't think to use Allison against me," she whispered her fear.

It was clear Allison wanted a mother, needed a mother. He was aware of his daughter's Christmas wish. Oh, he was attracted to her. More so, he knew she was drawn to him and his child. She didn't want him to paint anything between them with the faery dust of love merely to lure her into being a mother for a lonely little girl. Oh, she wanted to be a mother to Allison, but her heart clamored for Keon to want her. *Just her.*

"Meaning?" A stillness about him unsettled her, similar to a wolf or a big cat watching prey. So focused, so intent.

She swallowed, summoning courage. "I've been hurt—"

"I'm aware. What happened before has nothing to do with us. I'm not the fool your husband was."

"I adore Allison. She's special to me. She wants a mother and I have a feeling you'll move heaven and earth to see her happy. I think you capable of using my physical attraction to you against me, using my growing love for Allison against me."

Keon moved so fast she barely had time to blink. She sucked in a hard breath as he knocked away the covers she held and then caught her in his arms. One hand on the small of her spine, the other at the back of her head, he kissed her. Oh, did he kiss her. Not a gentle first kiss, not one of seduction. This was a warrior home from battle, taking what he wanted, no holds barred, demanding all and would settle for nothing less.

He arched her body against his, let her feel the length of his arousal. Her blood vibrated until she felt dizzy. So close, the enthralling scent of male hit her brain full force, flooding her senses to the point it was painful. Her heart slammed against her ribcage and she tried not to take a breath, to inhale that heady, drugging scent of Keon Challenger. It wasn't the faint woodsy cologne or the clear whiff of soap with the hint of lemon. What clouded her brain was the scent of *him.* She wanted to bury her nose against the heat of his skin and just inhale that fragrance. Challenger smelled...*right.* Oddly, her mind registered she'd never sensed that off Kevin's skin. No female animalistic sense of finding *the one.*

Only Challenger.

Crippled by the fears and insecurities, she tried to hold back. It was too much. *He* was too much. Challenger wouldn't let her, issuing the silent demand, *open to him.* Open her heart, her soul.

She almost cried out when he stepped back. The stormy eyes flashing in triumph, he watched her for a moment, then bent and picked up the quilts and blankets.

Leslie stood stunned, unable to move or think. Everything was too fast, too soon, yet she knew there was no turning back. Trembling, she put a hand to her heart to will it to slow.

Challenger paused at the door. "Don't *you* use me to get Allison either. Don't you think I see how you adore her, how you want to be a mother to her? Don't use me to reach that goal, Leslie. Yes, I want someone to look at my daughter the way you do, want her to have that comfort of being rocked and kissed good night. Just remember, I'm not the means to Allison. When you want me—and only me—come to me. When you come to my bed be damn sure it's only for *me*." He tilted his head with a sexy half-smile that spelled checkmate. "Good night, luv. Pleasant dreams."

Shaken, Leslie watched Challenger stroll from the cedar closet with an arrogance that made her want to kick him in the arse. "Mercy. What am I to do?"

"Kiss me. I need something to warm me up—fast."

Leslie realized she was being kissed—by a pair of icy lips. She tasted tea and Krispy Kreme donuts—and Challenger. What a way to wake up. Sliding her arms around his neck, she enjoyed the gentle kiss.

What would it be like to wake up this way every morn?

"Daddy's kissing Leslie!"

Challenger chuckled and then pulled back. "Nothing gets past this child of mine."

Not hesitating, Allison crawled up on the bed. "Daddy got us a tree!"

Leslie yawned as Allison used the bed as a trampo-line, nearly bouncing poor Alvin off. "So the city lad went out and hunted down a tree and dragged it back? I'm impressed, Challenger."

"I did indeed. A very beautiful one, too."

"How's the weather?"

"White. Very white. The weatherman said seventeen inches already. The whole state is snowbound. I'm sure the retailers are bitchin' and moanin'. Last three days before Christmas to shop and no one is going anywhere. The police are warning everyone stay put. Seems you're stuck with Allison and me—likely Christmas and beyond." She thought she heard him mutter, "W*ay beyond*."

Reaching for her robe, Leslie paused. "It won't be a hard-ship."

"Good, get dressed while I change into some dry clothes. Then we can take the Munchkin to feed and water Edward."

"Edward! Yea!" Allison clapped.

"And then we can prepare for a very wonderful Christmas."

Leslie rocked the sleeping Allison. The little girl had worn herself out playing with Edward and Alvin. She glanced to the cat passed out in front of the fireplace. Poor kitty was exhausted, too. Partners-in-crime, Allison and he had been into every phase of decorating, 'helping'.

She smiled. "The tree is beautiful."

Kneeling in front of the fireplace, Challenger used the poker to make room for another log. "I don't think I've seen any to compare. Picture perfect. Told you the old-time ornaments would fascinate Retro Baby."

"It'd be a delight to see Allison ripping through the ribbons and paper. Shame we cannot load the tree with gifts for her."

He came and gently stroked Allison's head. "I have her hula-hoop. One of the four things on her *Dear Santa* list."

She looked up at him. "Four?"

"She requested a pony and a kitty, but I think she realized we didn't have the room. She was willing to settle on the two things most important to her—a hula-hoop and a mother." He squatted down so his eyes were on the same level with hers, his thumb gently stroking her hand that cradled Allison's shoulder. "We're a package, she and I. Not that big of a risk, Leslie. If you'd just open your eyes and your heart."

With such gentle care, Challenger lifted the sleeping child and then carried her to the bunk bed. A yawning and stretching Alvin followed.

Clearly the cat had done what she was too scared to do— claim the child and man as hers.

She stood watching the twinkling lights of the tree that reached eight-feet tall. So perfect. Only she wanted Allison to have something under it, more than just a hula-hoop.

Images of the cedar closet popped to mind. She rushed there and rummaged around, until she finally found the old toy chest at the back, hidden under a pile of boxes. So intent in uncovering it, she didn't hear Challenger's footsteps before he partially blocked the light.

"She's asking for you to kiss her goodnight." He glanced over her shoulder as she unwrapped the contents of the wooden box.

Unfolding the tissue paper, she revealed the vintage Bubblecut Barbie. "It's a collector's item since they only put out a small number with raven hair. She's still in her original black and white swimsuit, open-toe shoes and holding her sunglasses. I took such care of her. Gran said she put her away because some day I would have a little girl to share her with. And here are my sock monkey and a stuffed Snoopy. Do you think Allison would like these? I know they aren't new, but they were special to me."

Challenger picked up the silly monkey and smiled. "I had one of these when I was a boy."

Leslie felt unsure. Maybe Challenger felt she was insulting his daughter by offering her second-hand toys. "I'm sorry. I didn't think..." She snatched the monkey from his hand and pushed it back in the box, barely seeing what she was doing because tears flooded her eyes.

Challenger's hands took her arms and swung her around to face him. "Whoa, what's this about?"

"I know you can buy her anything she wants, I didn't mean..." She stopped talking, knowing if she opened her mouth a sob would escape.

"Leslie Seaforth, these treasures will mean more to Allison than a dump truck full of Harrods's best. My Retro Baby will be in toy heaven with these precious gifts from you. You could give my little girl a stick and I'm sure it would be the best stick in the whole world. She loves you, you know." He paused as if fearful of speaking the words. "And so do I."

Leslie's heart leapt, wanting to believe he meant them. Only a man once said that before and proved the vow to be made of nothing stronger than the tissue paper wrapped around the doll. She hated that scarred her, left her in such doubt—but loving Challenger and losing him would be so much worse. She knew she wasn't strong enough to survive that.

She was in love with this man with the stormy grey eyes. Nothing had ever felt so right. Nothing had ever been so terrifying.

"Come, lass, let's say nite nite to the Munchkin." He took the toys and set them carefully in the box. "Then we can talk while we wrap presents."

Too stunned for words, too fearful to even hope his love could be real, she allowed him to lead her from the closet and down the hall to Allison's room.

Allison was half-asleep, but she clearly waited for Leslie to come kiss her goodnight. Alvin was already curled up at her side, purring.

"Leslie, can I ride Edward outside tomorrow?" Allison

asked, fighting a yawn.

She pressed her lips to Allison's forehead. "Probably not. The snow is too deep for him. You can take him some treats and brush him again though."

"'Kay." The little girl reached up, putting her arms around Leslie's neck and hugged her tightly. "Love you, Leslie."

Tears instantly filled her eyes as she squeezed back. "I love you, Allison."

Challenger's hand gently cupped the back of her neck, but then the fingers flexed harder, rubbing, the gesture conveying how deeply the scene affected him.

Allison whispered against her ear, "Shhh...it's a secret. I asked Santa if you could be my mommy and that Daddy and I can live here with you, Edward and Alvin. I'd like that very much. The bestest Christmas present ever."

Leslie was unsure how to answer the child. She'd love to assure her Christmas wishes did come true. Wanted them to come true. Still too scared to believe, she hesitated to give pledges she might not be able to keep. "Maybe if we both wish very hard."

Keon saw Leslie ran from him. After Allison had fallen asleep, Leslie used the excuse of visiting the bathroom and had hidden in there—likely crying—for the last half hour. Fine. Not that he wanted her to cry, but he figured she needed a little space and it provided him with the opportunity to set the stage.

He turned out all the lights in the kitchen and living room, leaving only the glow of the fireplace and the twinkling tree as illumination. As he rummaged through Leslie's CDs, he found they had similar tastes in music, so was delighted to locate precisely the song he was searching for—*Save Room* by John Legend. Finally, he moved the coffee table before the sofa out of the way.

Setting up the player, he picked up the remote and waited for her to come out. As moments passed, he figured enough with the water works, and went and rapped on the bathroom door.

"Come, Leslie. Stop hiding from me."

"I'm not hiding," came the muffled reply.

He rattled the knob. "Open up or the big bad wolf will huff and puff."

Just as he assumed she wasn't coming out, the lock rattled and she cracked open the door. She'd washed her face and brushed her teeth, the scent of cinnamon *Crest* lingering on her breath.

"What? You thought I'd give up and go to bed? Do you really think I'm so dull and predictable? Sorry, lass. My Retro Baby is sound asleep. The night is young. All sorts of magic and Christmas wishes lay ahead." When she just stood, blinking up at him with those huge brown eyes, he took her wrist and tugged her from her bolthole.

As they entered the living room, he hit the remote to start Legend crooning the seductive song. Leslie took in his preparations, that glint of hunger banked by fear flickered in her luminous eyes. "What's this?"

He handed her the on-the-rocks-glass with a scotch and water. "My baby girl is resting in Sugarplum land, riding Edward with Alvin in her arms. It's time for us. Just us."

He didn't give her a chance to protest, but pulled her into dancing, rocking to the provocative beat. The corner of his mouth lifted as they fell into an easy rhythm, her dancer's skill overriding her reluctance.

Spinning her out and then pulling her back, he sang along with Legend, "*Let down your guard, just a little...I'll keep you safe in these arms of mine...*"

He saw recognition flash on her countenance, with that kissable doe-in-the-headlights expression. And kiss her is just what he wanted to do, but if he did he wouldn't stop. He still had a few aces up his sleeve to win her heart.

"*Hold on to me, pretty baby...You'll see I can be all you need.*" When he sang that portion of the lyrics, she stumbled, then stopped dancing completely. "Okay, I don't have the sexy voice Legend has, but it doesn't mean the words are any less felt. I can be all you need, Leslie, if you give me the chance. I'd love to make love to you before the fireplace, but I figure you're too skittish for that right now, so I arranged something else."

"Challenger..." She moaned weakening resistance.

Ignoring her feeble protest, he led her down the hall to the cedar closet and pushed open the door, showing the candles he'd lit atop the toy chest. On the floor were the fluffy duvets and pillows. "I recalled how your sister, Dara, and you had slumber parties in here. Thought we might have a *slumber party*. We can talk and laugh all night, get to know each other to where you learn to trust me. You *can* trust me, Leslie. I'll never hurt you. Save room in your heart for me."

Leslie felt the lightbulb go on in her head, and with it all fears vanished. This man's heart was so open, so full of love for Allison. He didn't just see she was properly cared for, he adored being a father to her. His banter and play with the child showed he put her first, held nothing back. He'd love a woman in the same way, in a way Kevin had never loved her. A man that full of giving had no dark shadows in his ego.

Now she felt a total idiot for letting the past hold so much sway, keeping her from reaching out for what she wanted so desperately.

Challenger lifted the back of his hand to the side of her face and stroked it in near reverence. In his eyes she saw all she needed.

"Seriously, I won't touch you or kiss you...we can—"

She grabbed the front of his shirt and yanked him to her. "Shut up and kiss me, or you'll make me think you don't want me."

His brows lifted, as the grey eyes telegraphed his mind quickly switched gears. A playful smile spread over those sensual lips. "And what if I'd rather talk than smooch you, you demandsome wench?"

Leslie slowly undid the buttons, grinning when she saw he didn't have on a t-shirt. All the better to have my wicked way with him. "You're telling me to take a chance. I'm convinced you're candidate for Father of the Year. Now convince me you're up to being Husband of the Year."

"*Up?*" His chuckle rumbled in his chest as she pushed his shirt aside, then kissed his neck. Wickedly, she thumbed his flat male nipple. When she tweaked it, he inhaled sharply and his body went taut. "I...I wanted to give you candlelight and romance."

"Scratch plan A." Leslie chained kisses up his neck, then nipped his jaw with her sharp teeth. His muscles jerked as if he were a marionette and someone just pulled his strings.

"Oooo-kay. With the remaining vestige of my sanity, my poor, bloodless male brain is trying to catch up to your wicked ways. Playing conquering warrior claiming the fair maid has possibilities, however I rather fancy being the abused sex slave, too." When she ran her hand up his pant zipper, he groaned. "Ever hear the term *playing with fire*, lass?"

"Walk in fire with me, Challenger. Kiss me."

"Burn, baby, burn," he whispered, then his mouth took hers in a kiss that held back nothing.

Using those mobile lips, teeth and tongue, he kissed her

like she'd never been kissed before, yanking her body against his. She didn't feel like *boring old Leslie.* She felt like a woman in love, real love, the stuff poets wrote about, singers sang odes to, the thrill-you-down-to-your-toes sort of love that goes beyond the physical wanting something so pure and rare it could only be magic. *Yeah, burn, baby, burn.*

Her hands trembled as she tugged the shirt from his pants, then pushed it off his beautiful shoulders. Urgency clawing at her, she wanted to savor the sensations, the power, but the need was too compelling. She skimmed her arms up his, reveled in their strength, over the muscular shoulders and finally to weave her fingers in his thick black hair. Arching her body against him, she sighed at their perfect fit. A deep inner sense said that in his arms is where she belonged.

The passion, the need, the love he summoned within her was overwhelming. It was *agonizing.* It was too much...it was not nearly enough.

Keon wanted so many things, and like the greedy kid in the candy store, he wanted everything all at once. He wanted to worship her like a princess, to bind this wonderful lady to him so she'd say yes to being his wife. It was hard to imagine how little time they'd known each other; she seemed to be a part of him, to belong in his life. Short time aside, he didn't have a moment of doubt. This feeling of perfection, of the final pieces of the puzzle making the picture complete, had never been there with Meredith.

With Leslie everything was so right.

Only that awe took a backseat to his clamoring libido. He'd barely slept the night before, thinking of her just down the hall. Burning to go to her, yet wanting to give her time to adjust to the idea of Allison and him as part of her life. At war with his honorable side, the primeval male in him wanted to conquer her, claim her, bind her to him in the age-old fashion.

As he undid the pearl buttons on her sweater, his hands trembled. He wanted her so badly. "Lass, I'd like this to be special, but I'm fast losing my mind."

She tugged on his belt buckle to loosen it, then unsnapped his jeans. "Actually, fast has its appeal."

"You want fast?" He captured her other wrist and backed her to the wall, pinning her with his unyielding body. Holding her hands at the side of her head, he ground his pelvis against hers, as he kissed her with all the ravenous hunger clawing at him. She arched like a cat against him, seeking even more. "Wrap your legs around my waist."

When he released her wrists, she clung to him, her fingers clawing into his biceps. Hands sliding over her body to that firm derrière, he skimmed her jeans down. She stepped out of them. His right hand fumbled with his own jeans; the left pushed aside her pale pink bra. He drew a sigh from her when he palmed her breast and squeezed, then brushed his thumb back and forth over the pebbled nipple. Leaning to her, he took the tip of her tight breast into his mouth, sucking hard. He'd mark her. Leslie's sharp claws flexed in response. She'd mark him.

Keon smiled, drawing in the scent of her arousal, the female fragrance clouding his brain. Unable to hold back, he jerked her up and impaled her on his hard length of flesh. Ecstasy rolling over his sense and slamming into his brain, he paused to savor the delicious marvel of being inside Leslie's tight body.

Of belonging to her.

"Sure you want fast?" He withdrew partially and then flexed his hips, going deeper in a slow, sure movement. "I can do slow, too." Repeating the action, he delighted in watching her passion play across her beautiful face. "Very...slow."

"Slow...ah...has...ahhhhhhhh...possibilities."

Keon wanted to prolong this madness, this beauty, but her body tightened as she climaxed with a force that surprised her. Surprised him, too, for she let out with the start of a loud moan. He promptly closed his mouth over hers, swallowing the keen. Holding the leash of control for a minute more, he slammed into her pushing her into a second climax even before the first ended. Her internal muscles clenched around him, dragging him with her into the swirling maelstrom. He could no more hold back than not draw his next breath. His body exploded, pounding in his blood to where he nearly lost consciousness.

"Challenger," she gasped as he let her slide to her feet, "you sure do play hide the pickle well, but can we take this to the bed? I'm not sure I can stand after that."

He scooped her up and placed her on the quilts on the floor. "Oh, we'll get there...eventually."

"Leslie..." There was a small shake to Leslie's hand. "May I give Edward an apple?"

Allison.

She struggled to awaken, but it was damn hard. It hurt to move. There wasn't a spot in her whole body where she didn't ache. She moaned and tried to blink, but her eyes were crusted from sleep and tears. Glued-shut, they didn't want to open. Challenger and she had made love, talked, laughed and cried. *Best damn slumber party I've ever had.*

"I gave him a carrot and ten lumps of sugar. I wasn't sure if ponies ate apples, so I thought I'd ask if it was okay." Allison jabbered away.

Pony? Sugar? Carrots? Another sigh and she rubbed her eyes and yawned. "We can take Edward an apple when we go see him later."

"Oh, that's okay. He's hungry now. I can give it to him." A soft knicker followed Allison's words.

Leslie wanted to burrow down under the heavy duvet with that male body heat keeping the covers snug. Challenger was the best bed warmer. She smiled, thinking of many such morns to come, waking in his arms.

Now?

Her eyes flew open as she jerked to sit up. Only she recalled she had nothing on so tried to clutch the covers to her chest. Challenger's heavy arm had her and the blankets pinned. Her movements caused him to wake up. Giving a sleepy yawn, he raised up on his elbow to see his daughter.

"Allison Anne *why* is Edward in the bedroom? Ponies belong in the barn." Challenger rubbed his face, trying to wake up.

She grinned and then threw her arms around the teeny pony's neck and hugged him. "Edward was cold and lonely, so I brought him in to be near the fire. Then he said he was hungry."

"Did he? Did he also tell you little girls who sneak outside when they know better and bring ponies into the house get a spanking?" Challenger leaned over and made a half-hearted swipe at her, but giggling Allison danced out of reach.

"Daddy's smiling! Did you play hide the pickle with him Leslie? Is she my mommy now? Did Santa give me Alvin, Edward...and Leslie?"

Leslie shivered when he leaned close and kissed her bare shoulder.

"This isn't how a woman might want to hear a proposal, but the kid asked a question. If you don't answer the pint-size Perry Mason she'll just keep gnawing on your ankle with why...why...why." When she hesitated, he said, "Maybe the question should be did St. Nick give Allison and me to you for Christmas. You going to keep us? We need you."

Leslie couldn't speak, her throat was so tight with emotion, so she just nodded. Allison gave a squeal of delight, which scared Alvin and set the pony to fussing.

Challenger laughed. "Allison, take Edward and give him his apple. I shall kiss Leslie good morning and then get dressed and we'll return Edward where he belongs, and you and I shall have a long discussion on little girls leaving the house without permission."

"Quack—quack—quack," was her departing shot as she led Edward from the room.

Leslie looked down at the sleeping child, tuckered out after opening all the presents on Christmas Day. She was curled up with Alvin, her sock monkey, the 1964 edition Bubblehead Barbie and the *Creative Logic* Mp3 player in the midst of all the discarded wrapping paper. She smiled at their little Christmas Angel.

"Told you Retro Baby would love Barbie and Sock Monkey." Challenger lifted the sleeping child to carry her to bed. "In case you haven't noticed, when she goes to sleep for the night, she's out. She wakes up at the crack of dawn, but never during the night, wanting a drink-a-water, or fearful there's a monster-in-the-closet."

Leslie stroked the pale curls, where Challenger held her draped against his shoulder. "She did love them."

"Thank you for making all her Christmas wishes come true. She got everything on her list—a kitty, a pony, your MP3 player—thank you, again." He leaned to her and kissed her softly. "A hula-hoop and a mother."

"What about you? I didn't have anything for you."

"My unspoken Christmas wish would've been for someone to bring the magic to my life, to fill my heart until Christmas morn was as special for me as it was for Allison. You're the answer to everything I'd want."

Leslie followed him to the bedroom to help tuck up Allison. The little girl was so exhausted from opening all the gifts, the turkey dinner and several trips to feed Edward peppermint candy canes, that she never woke and asked for a goodnight kiss. Leslie gave her new daughter one anyway, then patted Alvin, Allison's self-appointed protector.

Back in the living room, Challenger scooped up the hula-hoop and began using it. "You know, sexy lady, I have this feeling we could keep the hula-hoop going while we make love. Want to find out?"

Laughing, she allowed him to pull her inside the hoop's circle with him. They tried several times to set it into motion, but ended up laughing so hard her side hurt.

Challenger looked down, his love clear in his eyes. "Marry me, Leslie. As soon as the snow melts, we can get a license. Call your grandmother in the morn and tell her we want to buy the house. I'll pay whatever she wants, no haggling. I'd like to start New Year's with you being Leslie Challenger."

She smiled. "It has a certain ring to it."

"Ring to it...which reminds me." His right hand reached into his jeans pocket. "I was saving this to last. Okay, not everyone gets an engagement ring from Wally World, but I was in a bit of a rush. It's not a diamond, just a citrine. Since the band is gold, she said it can be resized if it doesn't fit."

Leslie opened the box and stared at the yellow, oval stone, lovely against the black velvet of the box, barely able to speak. "It's beautiful. You're beautiful. But...why?"

"I saw it as I passed the case. I almost walked on by. But then a little voice warned me I'd need it. I never believed in love at first sight, but I fell hard for you the instant I looked into your amber eyes." When she continued to stare at it, he took it from her and slipped it onto her ring finger, the band going on easily. "I'll get you a more expensive ring once the snows melt."

"Touch my ring, Challenger, I'll break your fingers. This one is perfect."

He laughed, kissing her forehead and pulling her body against hers. "Hmm...up to a game of hide the pickle?"

"Ah, you sweet talker." Leslie hugged his chest tightly. "Always, Challenger. Always."

Blue Christmas Cat

P.E.A.R.L. Award Nominee 2006 –
Best Short Story from an Anthology

Dara Seaforth hung the receiver in the phone cradle, then groaned. Amplifying her irritation, the television played Elvis singing *Blue Christmas* to advertise a re-release of the King's *If Every Day Was Like Christmas* album for the holiday season.

"Blue Christmas? Yeah, is it ever! This promises to be the worst Christmas Eve in my entire life, Dext–" She glanced down at her feet. *No cat.*

Depressed by the prospect, she sighed. It was hard adjusting to the empty space now Dexter had passed over the *Rainbow Bridge*. It'd been six weeks, yet she still missed the silly cat so. Her first Christmas in eighteen years without him. It didn't feel strange nattering aloud to a cat. Talking to thin air had her pondering if she'd lost her marbles.

She glared at her laptop on the kitchen table, her *Deadwood* screensaver reminding she needed to be writing not complaining to an 'invisible cat'. The January deadline loomed, and with time ticking away, she wasn't anywhere near typing *The End*.

"How can I write a hot sexy romance when life is so dreadfully dull?"

Her sister Leslie's call had been to wish her a Merry Christmas. She wouldn't be coming home for Christmas this year. Her younger sister was in love and spending the holiday with *Mr. Tall, Dark and Sexy* and his small daughter. Oh, Leslie hadn't admitted it, but the emotion was clear in her voice when she spoke about Keon Challenger.

"Bloody hell, with a name like that I'd fall for him, too," she muttered. Naturally, she was happy for Leslie, yet admitted in the same breath that she was envious. "I'm the last Seaforth sister not coupled with some sexy stud. Leslie's a year younger than I. Least she could've done was wait her turn. In olden days, the younger sister couldn't marry until the older one found a lad. Of course, it isn't as if I had any prospects. And like some blethering eegit, I can't stop talking to a cat who's not there. Am I pitiable or what?"

Dara glanced out the window at the swirling snow. A snowstorm dumped a meter of the white stuff over everything the night before, blocking her from reaching the airport to catch her flight to her grandfather's home in Colchester, England.

"Bloody airport is probably closed anyway," she grumbled.

Going home for the Hols had lost its appeal when Leslie broke the news a couple days ago that she wouldn't be there. Past dinners were a gauntlet of *are you seeing anyone special?, why didn't you bring a young man to dinner?*—or the guaranteed to make her teeth grind, *you're so pretty, I can't understand why you haven't landed a husband.* Her aunts, great aunts and grandfather, bless their souls, could make life a virtual hell with their old-fashioned way of still viewing anyone over twenty-five as an *Old Maid.* Without Leslie's presence, all that would be focused on her. Worse, when they heard Leslie was in love it'd be even more, *tsk... tsk...poor Dara.*

She caught herself starting to tell Dexter she'd love to see Great Aunt Janet's face if she wickedly replied the reason she was minus a husband was she couldn't find a tall, sexy, elegant man that gave her hot sex three times a day—and had a name like Keon Challenger. She sniggered.

The chuckle died as an image of a man with pale eyes, a light hazel that bordered on yellow, shimmered before her mind. *Welsh eyes.* Strange after all this time his image remained so clear in her mind. Over the years, at odd moments such as this, she'd wondered about Rhys St. John and gleefully tried to picture him as bald and potbellied. No such luck. She'd seen him several times over the past weeks since his return. If anything, he was as lean and hard as ever, age only sharpening his male beauty.

"As if I care, the bloody bastard." She tossed another brick of peat on the fire, ignoring the tightness around her heart. *But she did care. Always had. Always would.* "Oh, Dexter, up in Kitty Heaven, if you hear me, send me a friend. Please. I'm not picky. He doesn't have to look like you, he doesn't even have to be a *he*, just a feline friend to make this cottage less empty. Someone I can talk to and not feel a loon."

As she replaced the fireplace poker in the stand, a cat yowled. She paused, feeling twenty kinds of a fool for hearing it. *"The mind is a terrible thing to waste—*especially on a cat who doesn't exist anymore."

"Meeeeeeeeeeeeooooooooooooooooooow!"

The howl persisted, louder.

"Och, I give up. I *am* losing it. Next thing, Sci-Fi Channel will be investigating me—*see the woman who talks to a ghost cat."*

Strong winds buffeted the house, rattling the windows. Shivering, she reached for her oversized jumper and slid her arms into the warm, fisherman's knit. The lights flickered, causing her to glance to the chandelier, fearful power would go out. After a few tense seconds, the electricity returned to steady.

"Meeeeeeeeeeeeooooooooooooooooooow!"

Dara sighed. "Next time I'm facing a deadline, I'm going to Aruba where the temps are hot and sexy cabaña boys are hotter and will wait on me hand and foot. That way, if I lose my marbles there'd be someone to call the men in the white coats to come and take me away...haha."

Instead of visions of cabaña boys dancing through her head, the image of Rhys St. John roared back into her consciousness. "Where's a voodoo doll when I need one?"

She couldn't recall a time when she hadn't loved Rhys. The memory of when she first knew she loved him was clear. She'd been eleven-years-old, out riding bikes with her sisters, Leslie and Jenna. Rhys had zoomed past in his white MGB and swung into Castle MacNeill's long driveway. Top down, wavy black hair rippling in the wind, he was everything her pre-teen heart could want in a hero. From there, as she'd grown and changed, so had her love for Rhys, though she doubted he ever paid her more than fleeting attention. Nine years older, he was always too busy to notice the adoration she found hard to hide.

She'd spent a large portion of her life just watching Rhys St. John. Wishing. Knowing it could never be. Ruining her life, she was ashamed to admit. How could she ever commit to any man, knowing she'd never love him as she loved Rhys?

"Gor, how utterly pathetic is that?"

The sexy half-Welshman had finally come home and taken possession of Castle MacNeill, the medieval fortress down the road. She hated absentee owners, especially owners who weren't Scot...well, full Scot. Scotland's heritage should be treasured, protected. Rhys had inherited the castle from his grandfather nearly three years ago, but this was the first visit he'd deigned to pay since becoming owner. The arrogant man obviously had been too busy with his jetsetter life to return to the wee village where his father had been born. Keeping to himself, few had seen him since his arrival. Oddly enough, she'd spotted him frequently from a distance on horseback, riding in the woods. Other times zooming about in the midnight black Ferrari Testarossa.

"Och, silly man won't get very far in the 'rari tonight." She chuckled, thinking how the sleek black car wasn't built for the thigh-deep snowdrifts of the Highlands.

It seemed she couldn't set foot outside her cottage that Rhys wasn't about somewhere, lurking. Last week, when she'd peddled her bike to the village to pick up a few things, she saw him pull up at the end of the castle's long drive. He looked over at her, making contact with those pale, amber eyes, almost a gold seen only in those with ancient Welsh blood.

Curse his black head! She'd felt the power of the man's gaze so strongly, the force ripping into her soul, as if he could strip her mind of every thought. No secret would be safe from him. The strength of her reaction made her vulnerable, reminded she'd always loved this man too deeply, always would. While he was married he was safely out of reach, no possibility for her dreams to ever come true. Now he was divorced, it was harder to remind her Cinderella heart of the realities that Rhys would never want her. Fear, fear of pain, fear of opening herself to a heartache that wouldn't die, pushed her to run from him, to get as far away from him as possible.

Rhys was trouble with a capital T. Even so, she couldn't do anything but stand flatfooted and want him with every fiber of her being. Then the warlock eyes moved away, and with a flick of those long black lashes dismissed her as not worthy of his note. She'd blushed, ashamed of her reaction to this arrogant man. Hurt seared through her.

Rhys hadn't remembered her.

Why did that pain so much? That he'd forgotten her was a lance to her heart. He hadn't recalled the dance under the moonlight on Halloween fifteen years ago. Hadn't remembered the kiss. That magical kiss.

The pain was a familiar one. By eighteen her love had matured from that of hero worship to that of a woman's. She couldn't sleep or eat and found the old expression *living on love* had been rather accurate. Despite that, Rhys and everyone else had thought it nothing more than puppy love. They refused to see she was nearly nineteen and no longer a child.

In her first blush of womanhood, she believed all things were possible. A future shimmered in her mind of Rhys continuing to live at the castle with his grandfather and over time come to see her there, waiting, and so much in love with him that it hurt to breathe.

At night, her heart spun castles in the air, so vivid, she was convinced they'd one day come true, that their love was fated. Instead, she'd watched him move away, marry. Thought she'd die from the agony of knowing her dreams were shattered forever. Rhys belonged to another. Not for one day had that pain lessened or gone away. Eventually, she'd learned to get on with her life. Even so, she still loved Rhys. Never stopped loving Rhys.

"Why did he have to come back, start the ache all over again?" She hated him all the more for carelessly dismissing from his memory something so special to her. A night when those dreams took on reality, if only for a moment.

"Meeeeeeeeeeoooooooooooooooooooow!"

Dara closed her eyes and counted to ten. "I'm *not* hearing a cat. It's bad enough I talk to a cat who's not here anymore. If he's answering, I'm in trouble. Next, I'll start talking to a head in a box like Al Swearengen. Geesh, that's what I get for opening and watching the *Deadwood* DVDs Leslie sent me for a Christmas present."

"Meeeeeeeeeeoooooooooooooooooooow!"

"Bugger. I refuse to converse with a Jacob Marley cat."

"Meeeeeeeeeeoooooooooooooooooooow!"

The last one sounded so insistent, so poignant, she gave up and believed. However unlikely, there had to be a cat outside in the snowstorm. Going to the door, she opened it a crack, braced herself against the gusting wind that nearly jerked the door out of her grip. She finally looked down to the stoop.

Sitting, nearly white from the snow, was a British Blue cat, the blue-grey so dark it was almost blackish. The poor, pudgy thing was hunched, shivering. "You pitiful darling. Would you like to come inside?"

She glanced toward Kitty Heaven and mouthed, "Thank you." to Angel Dexter.

This kitty looked at her with amber eyes. Odd, for some

reason they reminded her of Rhys St. John's. Since the man wasn't welcome in her mind, she tried to blink away the illusion, thinking it a trick of light. The peculiar impression lingered, stayed to the point where she half-expected to see the cat shake off the snow and suddenly morph into the sexy, conceited man.

"A werekitty!" Dara giggled. "Cat, I've spent too many weeks in this isolated cottage with no one to talk to but my characters now Dexter's gone. Come on through—but no shapeshifting." She wagged her finger at him. "Rhys St. John is the *last* person I want to see tonight. Life is simply too sucky to put up with his arrogance on Christmas Eve."

As if he understood the instructions, he shook off the heavy snow and dashed inside and straight to the fireplace. Sitting next to the metal-mesh spark guard, he proceeded to tongue bathe his wet fur.

Figuring kitty would be hungry, she went to the kitchen cabinet and took out a tin of cat food left from Dexter. As she started to set the saucer on the bricks before the preening cat, she noticed he wasn't solid British Blue after all. He had a little white 'moustache' rather like he'd been drinking milk. Strange, this cat was dark where Dexter had been white and white where Dexter had been dark grey. They could be the positive-negative of each other. Noticing he wore a collar, she looked at it, spotting a nameplate.

"Elvis the Cat." Dara laughed. "Move over, Alice, I'm late for a very important date."

"It's getting late."

Frustrated that night put in an appearance in early afternoon in Scotland this time of year, Rhys St. John glanced at his watch and muttered about 101 uses for a dead cat, thinking of the black humor paperback out a few years ago. At the time of its release nearly all cat owners were outraged by the premise.

"Given the circumstances of the moment, I could easily pen suggestions 102 and 103. Maybe even a 104. Damn creature. Why pick Christmas Eve to go walkabout—as Paul Hogan would say? My mood's crappy enough without having to chase down a cat that shouldn't be outside. That fat puss couldn't outrun a snail if his life depended upon it."

After following the tracks across Castle MacNeill's grounds, he stopped and glanced back. It was weird. The cat wasn't wandering about. He seemed intent on heading somewhere. Silly feline didn't know the terrain, so it was almost as if someone guided him. The heavy snow coming down had already half-filled in the path of his paw prints. Fearful they'd soon be covered entirely and he'd be unable to track Elvis, he broke into a jog.

In the distance he spotted a faint orange glow. As he paused to get his bearing, the corner of his mouth tugged up. He was nearing the cottage where Dara Seaforth stayed, a small hunting box on the edge of the Seaforth estate, which bordered Castle MacNeill. A romance writer, the villagers said. Somehow, it didn't surprise him Dara wrote romances. His mind cast back to fifteen years ago to a night under the autumn full moon and to a lass with stars in her eyes.

Too bad you couldn't hit the *Restore* option like on your computer and turn back your life to a time where it carried the sheen of hope. All futures were possible. If he had the choice to make all over again, he'd go back to that night, fix in his mind he had a couple years before he could claim Miz Dara Seaforth. He was a patient man. He would've waited. The instant she'd turned twenty-one, he would've married her so fast it'd make her pretty head spin. Instead, he'd allowed his mother and grandfather to push him into a loveless marriage just to save the family's fortune.

He swallowed regret. Had he chosen another path on that Halloween night, they'd have children by now and would be spending this Christmas Eve preparing to play St. Nick and watch their eager faces come alive.

"Well, I was stupid once. No more."

His mind conjured the image of Dara, her soft brown hair, long and about her shoulders.

The penetrating grey eyes are what he carried with him the most. Forever burned into his soul. Long into the night, those eyes haunted his dreams. Being a fool, it'd taken him several years to admit he was in love with Dara, never stopped loving her. Then it had been too late.

Since his return, he'd seen her here and there, watched her. Stalked her, if truth be told. He couldn't seem to stay away from her, though she was unaware of his new diversion. She'd grown into a sexy woman. One he wanted. One who could hold the key to the future—if she chose to give him a second chance.

For the past two weeks, he'd debated how to break the ice, scared spitless on messing this up. He'd almost made up his mind to approach her last Friday when he happened upon her at the end of his drive. She'd stopped her bike and just stood staring up at the castle. As he got up his nerve to speak, she'd looked at him with a strange mix of hunger and intense loathing. That'd thrown him.

Puzzling. Maybe not the initial reaction he'd hoped to see from her, but it gave him room to work. For the first time in years, he felt alive again, determined.

He'd returned to Dunnagal trying to find a new direction in life. Strange, the direction he now took in following the errant cat was straight to Dara's cottage.

"Maybe that cat isn't so stupid, after all." He smiled, blood of the predator rising within him. "Here, kitty, kitty, kitty. Ah, Fate moves in wonderful and mysterious ways."

Elvis finished his meal and stretched out as close as he could get to the screen guard, then proceeded to purr.

Dara wasn't sure where Elvis the Cat had come from, but she was glad for his presence.

"I don't have to spend Christmas Eve alone now, Elvis. Thank you."

He yawned a 'you're welcome' and then stared at the undecorated tree, a curious expression on his intelligent face. He almost seemed to ask the question of why? It was a bit unnerving, this cat being the negative to Dexter's positive. Only he didn't have Dexter's eyes. He had human eyes. Rhys St. John's eyes. It was spooky.

"Remember, you promised—no shapeshifting. I haven't bothered decorating, Elvis. It's just me. It didn't seem worth the effort."

The cat snapped his tail angrily. *That's no excuse*, was in the eerie eyes.

A rap on the door startled her. *"By the pricking of my thumbs...something wicked this way comes.* I don't know anyone with sense who would be out on a night light this."

She opened the door and her heart stopped. Looking so sexy he should be outlawed, Rhys St. John hunched his shoulders against the snow. Stupid man was in a lightweight coat not suitable for this wet snow. No cap on the black hair that was damp and mostly covered with white stuff.

She stiffened as if she received a blow to her chest, nearly reeling. *Oh, Rhys.* Why the bloody hell turn up on her doorstep tonight? On Christmas Eve when she was alone except for a cat named Elvis, when she was so low, she wanted to curl up and cry. She had no defenses against a man she'd loved for over fifteen years.

She drew upon her last ounce of pride and asked frostily, "May I help you?"

Rhys smiled, but it was a mask. So that was how she planned to play it—as if they were strangers. Fine. He'd give her plenty of rope before he gave a good swift yank on it.

"I'm looking for a cat. A British Blue, yellow eyes with a white mustache, answers to the name of Elvis."

She tried to block his view into the room. "A cat? You're out on a night like this in search of a cat? Sorry, I'm afraid I can't help you."

"You were never a good liar when you were growing up, Dara." He arched a brow at her audacity.

"I don't know what you're talking about." She huffed and stiffened her spine.

Rhys glanced past her shoulder at the cat on the fireplace, and pointed. "That cat— Elvis. Or did you fail to notice him?"

"Oh, *him*."

"Oh, him?" He echoed softly. "Going to jail for *cat-napping*?"

"Actually, I did forget about him. I was busy writing. I don't take notice of things sometimes."

A chuckle vibrated through him. "Good thing Elvis can open cabinets and use a can opener then, eh? He might've starved waiting for you to pay attention."

She had the grace to blush and shrug. "Well, cats are intelligent creatures."

"Dara, while I'd love to stand here and natter, I'm bloody wet and cold and you're letting all the heat out of the house." Not waiting for her to graciously step back and ask him in, he pushed past her, moving to the fire to warm up.

She turned, her mouth hanging open, though finally closed the door after another gust of wind blasted the side of the house. "I'm not sure I should let you in. How do I know you aren't a deranged killer?"

"Deranged? Not yet, lass." He unbuttoned his coat, but didn't stop there. He tugged off the pullover sweater, tossed it down by his coat and started to undo the buttons on the flannel shirt.

Dara backed up a step. "Maybe I should call Hamish Macduff..."

Rhys laughed. "Oh aye, do that. By the time the snow

stops and he pumps up the tire on his bicycle, it'll be New Years."

When the shirt came off, she was momentarily distracted by the expanse of his naked chest. He liked her wide-eyed expression. Only it changed to shock as he reached for his belt and began to unbuckle it.

"Rhys St. John, what are you doing?"

"Ah, you remember me now. You're a writer, Dara lass—of sexy romances—you figure it out. I just walked miles in the snow, am soaking wet from trying to catch that stupid cat before he fell into the burn and drowned or got lost and died in the storm. Now I'm doing what any intelligent man would do—getting out of the wet clothes before I take pneumonia."

"But...ah..."

"It's dark out. I'm not walking home in this storm, Dara. Once you get over drooling at my chest, you'll come to grips with you have Elvis and me as Christmas guests now. Get me a blanket to wrap up in, lass. Next stop is *what waits below—*and I'm so cold I can't recall if I bothered with underwear today. Or is it your wish to drool over more than just my braw chest?"

"Rhys St. John, you're a candidate for Bedlam!"

Rhys smiled as he noticed she kept the couch between them as if that was any sort of protection. Ah, thanks to Elvis, Christmas Eve suddenly was looking up. He made a mental note to get Elvis a truckload of *Armitage Good Girl Catnip Drops*, enough to last through the coming year. This silly beastie had played matchmaker! Here was the opening he wanted and he planned to press every advantage. He was staying today, tomorrow...and beyond.

"Determination is my middle name," he said under his breath.

"Damn you, Rhys, you've been back to Dunnagal for weeks and not even said hello. Now you think you can barge in here, strip to your skivvies without a by-your-leave—"

"I'm not stopping at my skivvies, lass. I warned you. I'm wet. I need to get dry and warmed up. So stop standing there ogling me and fetch a blanket and a dram of Whisky."

When he acted as if he was unzipping his pants, she let out with a squawk and rushed from the room. He laughed at her skittishness. Well, she'd just have to get over that. Sitting down on the footstool, he undid the Wellies and tugged them off, then the socks.

He leaned over and patted Elvis. "Thanks, lad. I appreciate it. You got me in and I'm not leaving."

He stood as she came back carrying a fluffy blanket and unfolding it. Winking at the cat, he started to unzip his fly. She gasped and held up the blanket like a screen to the middle of his chest.

"Ah, Dara lass, don't tell me you're modest."

She blinked, trying to keep her eyes off his chest and on his face. "Don't try to call me a prude, St. John. You come shoving your way in here, accusing me of stealing your cat and now play at being a candidate for Chippendales—"

"Playing at?" He leaned close to her, inhaling her soft perfume with a hint of tuberose and the woman underneath. His body went from frozen popsicle to a slow burn faster than he could count one, two, three. "Lass, hang onto that blanket because that's all that is separating us right now."

Her fist tightened on the soft covers, just as he intended. Dara was so focused on preserving his modesty that she was an easy target. His hands seized her waist and yanked her hard against him, his mouth closing over hers. This was no gentle wooing, this was picking up that kiss where it was left off fifteen years ago. This was him silently staking his claim.

A kiss with a promise of endless tomorrows.

Their lives had come full circle.

For the first time since that night fifteen years ago, he actually felt in control of his life again. Dara and he could be so happy, if only he could convince her of his love, of the future they could build. Her shock translated in her remaining stiff as he plundered that sweet mouth, took the heat from her and let it warm his body, his soul.

She leaned back, trying to break his hold on her. Though he didn't want to let her go.

She started to step back, then recalled her hold on the blanket. Trembling, she said, "Here," tossed it at him and fled.

"Oh, Dara lass, it's a night to believe in magic," he said to her retreating back.

"Way to go, St. John." Rhys' tone was chiding. "You're twelve kinds of a bloody fool."

Disgusted, he tossed another peat brick on the fire and closed the glass spark-guard.

Poor Dara was hiding in her room, door locked against the madman stalking back and forth in the hallway. A grimace etched his mouth when he conjured the image of her in there, crying. At one point, his impatience had driven him to pound on the door, even considered breaking it down. His last shard of common sense warned she wouldn't appreciate his caveman routine. It severely taxed him to wait. He was anxious to see Dara, kiss away the tears staining her cheeks, then explain why he'd been such an eegit.

Hold her through the night.

He lay on the comfortable sofa, staring into the flickering blue flames while he made up his mind how to put things right. By coming on too strongly he feared he'd botched everything.

The peat in the fireplace was warm, heady, the scent making him crave a cigarette. Last year he'd given up smoking because it caused Elvis to sneeze. Rarely did he miss the habit, but right now he really could use a nicotine buzz.

Over the past couple of weeks, he'd watched Dara puttering around the village. The small notions store on the village green had Dara's Romance novels prominently displayed in the front window—proud of the local lass now a bestselling author. He'd bought them all. Outside of fetching supplies or taking his stallion out for exercise, he'd been holed up reading her books—all thirteen of them. She had range, with the mix being half Historicals and half zany Contemporary Romances. After the first three, he got over the shock of seeing himself portrayed as the hero in each of them. Oh, there were variances in her characters, slightly taller, maybe just a bit prettier, but it was clear to him he'd been the seed for her inspiration.

Fifteen years ago she'd been eighteen years old, a breathtakingly beautiful eighteen. And she'd been in love with him. He had to have been blind not to see. Of course, at twenty-seven, he feigned ignorance of her adoring eyes when she came with her grandfather every Sunday when he played chess with his grandfather.

It'd been a good time in his life. *Salad Days.* He'd been preparing to follow his dream of being a historian. Then grandfather explained the realities of the family's financial situation—or lack of it. Suddenly, he had to put his whole life's work away and learn big business fast. St. John's Ltd. was a department store chain throughout Britain, Canada and US. Through his father's mismanagement, it was in near collapse. Now it fell to him to save it, even if it meant giving up on his passion for history.

Each time she was around, Dara's grey eyes had followed

his every move, worshipped him. The pretty lass with the incisive mind intrigued him, challenged him, too much so, thus when she began turning up in his dreams he'd thought it best to keep his distance. Of another mind, Dara had taken to following him around. Oh, not blatantly. She just *happened* to be wherever he was. Had she been three years older, things might have been different. So he assumed the role of big brother, much to her disappointment.

Except that one night...

That Halloween night saw him restless, edgy. Bags already packed, in the morning he'd take a plane to New York, where he'd assume command as the new head of St. Johns Ltd. His task was to save the seventy-five stores that were in imminent danger of going under. Like a horse chaffing at the bit, he hadn't wanted to leave Scotland. Making matters worse, there was *something* holding him here, an indefinable pull.

The answer to that riddle remained illusive and just out of reach.

Seeking diversion from the itchy feeling clawing under his skin, he'd gone to the *cèilidh* to forget he no longer had choices in his life. He'd spotted Dara in the corner, watching the dancers. Oddly, he saw she kept turning down offers from the local lads to dance. She hadn't noticed him lurking in the shadows. In a pensive mood, he, too, hadn't felt like joining in with the merrymakers. When she excused herself and stepped outside, he followed.

Big mistake. There under the full moon, he saw she was no longer a kid, but was nineteen in three weeks, a woman.

A woman he wanted.

He'd approached her and asked if she'd like to dance. Her poleaxed expression was so enchanting. He'd taken her wrist and pulled her into his arms to slow dance to an old Gene Pitney tune, *Something's Gotten Hold of My Heart*. He guessed something had a hold of his heart, too, for halfway through the song, he stopped and stared down on the beautiful woman Dara had grown into. Unable to resist, he kissed her. Lightly at first. Then with the full passion rising within him. It was only with the last shred of sanity that he ended that kiss.

Ended with despair and regret, because he finally had the answer to that riddle. And it was too bloody late.

"Sometimes, I think the only thing right I did in my bloody whole life was kiss her that night," he confided to

Elvis, sitting on the couch beside him.

"Why do you say that?" She spoke from the shadows, tears choking her words.

He hadn't realized she'd been standing in the shadows, watching him. "Because it's the truth, the whole truth and nothing but the truth."

"Oh, Rhys..."

"I'm sorry, Dara. I didn't mean to scare you by coming on like a steamroller. It's just this is Christmas Eve and I am here with you—"

"Only because you followed the cat." She put a hand to her neck massaging it, obviously tense from emotions.

"Fate. Tonight's Christmas Eve, maybe the first one I've looked forward to in fifteen years. I think St. Nick granted me a wish—with a little prod from Elvis. Come sit." He noticed her hesitation. "I promise not to jump your bones. We can just talk."

Skittish, she came forward, but instead of sitting on the couch, she sat on the floor, crossing her legs. "Why did you come back to Dunnagal?"

"For you. Oh, I belong here, want to see the Castle is taken care of, find where I need to go with my life. I'd finally like to do what I always wanted, restore the family records, preserve the past. I can afford to follow that dream now. Only, it's you that pulled me here."

"I didn't think you recalled the kiss."

He smiled, "Oh, I recalled it...deep in the night...in my dreams." His hand reached out and touched her cheek. "I love you, Dara. Took a while to fully under-stand that. Then life was too bloody complicated. I feared you'd moved on. I've read your books you know."

"My books?" Her cheeks burned red. "You really read them?"

"All of them. I guess that's why I feel so close to you. I see of lot of your heart in the books, a lot of your dreams." When she looked down, his crooked finger lifted her chin forcing her to meet his gaze. "I see a lot of me in those books, too."

"Rhys...please don't play games. I couldn't take it. I'd die."

"No games, Dara. I want my life back. *My life.* Not what my grandfather decided was best, or what my mother shamed me into through guilt. I now have things back on track—but I need you. I lived too long in a cold, loveless marriage that I never wanted. I want magic, I want to know someone loves me, that I count."

"What happened? I heard you left the business, gave it up after the divorce."

"Gave up? Yes, I guess I did. There was a hostile takeover of the company I helped build, to take into the 21st Century. When the blood bath was over, I lost the company, but was very rich because my stock tripled nearly overnight. The new owners wanted a new CEO, so they offered me a golden parachute, which I took without looking back."

"I'd think they'd have wanted you to stay on, since you built the company, knew it better than anyone."

"The new owners figured I wouldn't work well with them and their vision for my company. You see, my ex-wife and her lover were heading the takeover consortium."

"Ohhhhhhhhh."

He grinned. "Yes, ohhhhhhhhh. I started to stay and make their life a living hell. Then I didn't see anything to hang onto, a reason to go on. When they offered the golden parachute, with a bonus to get hell and gone, I jumped at it. I was tired, had no personal life. The business took too much from me, I lived for it. St. Johns Ltd. is a cold mistress, love. I kept my stock so I can be a thorn in their sides come stock voting, only I wanted to go some place and find myself. *Me*. Not Rhys St. John, CEO of St. Johns. I went for a long walk, thinking. Stopped before this pub and looked in the window, reflecting like a mirror. I didn't know who I was, what I liked in life, where I wanted to be five years from now. That's how I ended up with Elvis. While I stood, trying to figure out who I really was, he waddled up. Thin, hungry, shaking from the cold. He seemed about as lost as I."

"Why Elvis?"

"Why else? Elvis the King...uh hun. The bloody beast went from grateful for shelter, food and a few pets, to running my life. Also, because the pub was playing *Blue Christmas* on the juke box when I found him." He reached out and petted the smug cat. "I've been wanting to approach you the last couple of weeks, but I was still finding myself. Your glaring at me like I crawled out from under a rock wasn't encouraging either, lass."

Dara leaned against the couch to be closer. "I thought you didn't remember me. My heart was breaking. How did you expect me to look?" She choked on a sob, trying to keep the tears in.

He cupped the side of her face, his thumb stroking her eyebrow. "If I died tonight, the last thought I'd have would be your eyes. I've found it's never too late, Dara Seaforth. Life, fate, people pushed us away from each other. Those nine years between us that seemed too wide to bridge fifteen years ago doesn't matter anymore. Strange isn't it? Oh, sweet lass, what better way to start Christmas Eve than with each other?"

The cat pushed between them and meowed. They both chuckled and petted him.

"And with Elvis." He took her hand and kissed the finger where he'd place a wedding ring. "Marry me on Valentine's Day in a big wedding at the castle. We can invite the whole village, all your family. Until then, come live with Elvis and me and be my love, my life. You can write sexy romances while I translate obscure Gaelic poetry. We can be so happy."

A smile finally cracked at the corner of her mouth. "Are you really naked under that blanket?"

"Unwrap me and find out. I'm your very own personal Christmas present."

After pouring an eggnog, Rhys tiptoed into the living room to add a couple bricks of peat to the fire. The only light in the room came from the twinkling Christmas tree. He paused to admire the decorations. They had made love, frantically, tenderly, crying, laughing. Then they'd gotten up, ate supper and decorated the tree. He smiled thinking of making love on the couch by its twinkling glow. He had a feeling he would be sore from head to toe tomorrow, but wow! Did that lass of his make love! He smiled at the grey puss sleeping before the fire, a smug expression of contentment upon his face.

"The wench is greedy, Elvis. But then, I think I can keep her satisfied." Elvis lifted his head and yawned a sleepy smile. "Proud of yourself are you? I didn't know cupids wore fur and had long tails."

"Meeeoooooooow," he rumbled.

Rhys took a sip of the eggnog and then poured some out on the saucer. Elvis stretched and lazily dragged himself over to lap at the thick liquid. "So horribly bright of you to come here. Still, it's so odd how you knew to come straight to Dara's cottage...like someone guided you."

"Hmm...thankyouverymuch...."

Rhys froze upon hearing the male voice. He knew there wasn't anyone in the cottage but Dara, the cat and him. So who was speaking? The cat stopped drinking the nog and looked past Rhys to the tree, staring at something.

"Either you're suddenly a ventriloquist, Cat, or I'm barmy. Neither possibility is comforting." He shook a finger at Elvis. "Stop staring at the tree like that. I'm not going to look only to have you go *gotcha hahahaha, fooled the silly person again.*"

Dara, dressed in only socks and his flannel shirt, rushed out, put her arms around his waist from behind and squeezed. "You took all that wonderful male heat away. The bed's cold without you, Rhys."

He turned so he could pull her into his arms. "Warming up a bed with you is my idea of a way to spend Christmas Morn." He kissed her, feeling her renewing energy pouring through every fiber of his being, making him whole, making him alive again. Breaking the kiss, he turned to follow Dara back to bed, only to see the cat was staring at the tree again.

Unable to resist, he followed the line of the cat's vision to see what drew his attention.

He fought the instinct to reel from the shock. For in the shadows stood a man dressed in black leather. As Rhys stood, mouth slightly agape, the black-headed man winked as he made his finger and thumb into a gun. So startled, Rhys blinked once, but then the vision was gone.

"Rhys what is it?" Dara's concern was etched in her voice.

Rhys chuckled and hugged her. "Just a guardian angel that helped Elvis find his way here in the snowstorm."

"Rhys, I love you so. Always have, always will."

"Dara, my love, my heart, it took me a bit longer to reach that understanding, but it makes me recognize how precious that love is. I have loved you and always will love you."

As he kissed her, letting her feel all the joy within him, the DVD player came on in the living room behind them. The soft crooning of Elvis Presley filled the air, *"I'll have a blue, blue blue blue Christmas..."*

Chicken What Du Hell?

or

Bubba the Cat Plays Matchmaker

Outside of New Orleans, Louisiana

"Hoo lo', dat purdy gurl sure do have a mad on, and I'd say, Cuz, she's got you in her sights." Jack Roboleau playfully ladled on the Cajun accent thick as gumbo, then laughed, warming to the coming confrontation.

Ignoring Jack's teasing, Royce Torqhill Remington Kinross, the thirteenth Marquis of Dunmoor and Seafeld, stared out the huge picture window at the woman who'd just hopped out of the red Jeep Cherokee. She slammed the door and headed his way with a singular determination that set his blood to buzzing. Yep, she sure *was* mad, and she was heading his way.

The corner of his mouth quirked up. "Am I lucky or what?"

Something bumped his arm, distracting him. Royce glanced to his side at the giant economy-size tabby cat who watched the woman intently.

Bubba was in love.

Taking the nails out of his shirt pocket, he nudged the feline with his hammer. Bubba only spared a quick, non-interested look at the man prodding him. The cat's attention remained focused on the sexy redhead, with breasts that made a man's mouth water. She jiggled her way across his front lawn—if you could call that plot of land overgrown with wild rose briar, honeysuckle and cudzoo a *lawn*.

"Hey, pal, did you get me in hot water again?" he asked the feline.

Bubba licked his cat chomps and smiled. *The damn cat*

smiled.

Long ago, Royce reached the conclusion that his cat actually had once been a man, some Casanova who'd royally pissed off a witch or a faery queen a couple centuries back, and for spite she'd turned him into a cat. While Bubba thoroughly enjoyed his *catitudeness,* that male libido trapped in the feline brain remembered his past satyrical glories and went on hormonal alert when Catonia Flemyn was around.

"I've seen you butting your head against her boobs, pretending you only want pats—like you don't know what you're doing. You're a sly one, Bubba Kinross." He scratched the cat's head.

Royce didn't blame the feline. The feisty, auburn-haired lass also had a witchy effect on his blood. Fortunately, he was a bit more adapt at hiding it than Bubba was.

The door flung open, slamming against the wall with a crash, and Catonia marched in, toting a burlap sack. "Ooooh." She made a sour face and glared in his direction, as though she faced Ted Kazenski in his orange prison jumpsuit.

"Yeah, she wants to pounce on my bod and can hardly contain herself. So watch your jealousy, Bubba. It's *me* she wants." He laughed under his breath, fighting the urge to do a little pouncing of his own.

"Hey, purdy gurl," Jack called to her, as he climbed the ladder to varnish the rail on the staircase. "I sure am glad for you to see me," he said in a typical Cajun greeting.

Good manners taking hold, she glanced up to Royce's second cousin and gave him a smile. *Lucky Jack*—that smile could melt a man's heart. "Morning, Jack. Tell your mama thank you for the mustard greens she sent over. They were delicious...really brightened up my garden salad."

"Salad? Hooo-lo, gurgle, you're in *Nawlins* now, not some place where they serve Beef Wellington," Jack flirted. Of course, if it had two legs and wore a skirt—even occasionally —Jack Roboleau flirted. "You're supposed to serve them with chopped green onions, blanched with hot bacon grease. Fry up a mess of *andouille. Umm...umm...good.*"

Royce almost laughed at Ms. Calorie Watcher's suppressed shudder, but then she turned that hazel gaze on him and his laughter died. Not that he was scared of that *teacher-catching-a-student-writing-dirty-words-on-the-blackboard* glare. Nope, not him. *Fools and Royce Kinross rush in.* It was the fact when he looked into those whisky-colored eyes he lost all sense of self. Dark images of silk sheets and candle wax suddenly arose in his mind, and he envisioned himself staring into those bewitching eyes illuminated by moonlight, as his body pumped hard into hers. Or more frustrating, he just gazed into them like some lovesick puppy.

Either way his eyeglasses always steamed up.

Mindful of this, Royce reached up and snagged his glasses off his nose. Laying them on the counter, he tried to blank his face. This was going to be fun. "Morning, Catonia. What brings you to *Belle Trelonge?*"

He almost snorted. *As if he didn't know.* The sack was a dead give away. Third time in two weeks she'd sashayed in here with one.

She swung the feed sack atop the oak bar with a thud. "This." The penetrating eyes flashed daggers at Bubba. The cat didn't even look sheepish, but stuck his chest out proudly, and then immediately head-butted her right breast.

Royce opened the sack and let the contents roll out of the burlap and onto the counter. "Why it's a snake, *cher,*" he announced redundantly, merely to tweak her temper.

She pursed her mouth and put her hands on her hips. Damn fine hips, too, he might add. Forcing his vision back to her lovely face, he had a hard time keeping his expression deadpan.

"*Yes,* a snake," she snapped, as if he were a total idiot.

Royce watched her temper rise another notch as he said, "It's dead, *cher.*"

"Of course it's dead! You think I'd touch that thing otherwise!"

He arched a brow and with a straight face summoned up his *Ragin' Cajun* accent. "You killed dat poor thang, *cher?*"

She about lost it. Her eyes narrowed on him. "Have you been drinking Billy-Ray's joy juice?" she said, speaking of the local moonshiner.

Baiting her was dead easy, but he sure enjoyed doing it. She'd recently moved into the cottage on the border of *Belle Trelonge's* land. Both properties had been hard hit by Hurricane Katrina, but like New Orleans, they were survivors. Her home was put back into working order within a few weeks after she'd bought it, not hard to do since it was a one-story, three-bedroom dwelling. She'd purchased it from her great aunt, who swore she wasn't returning after the 'big blow'. Repairs completed, she'd moved in last week.

Not a native to the area, Catonia had been born in England, then ended up as a model in New York, bathing suits and lingerie mostly for catalogues. At five-seven, she wasn't tall enough for runway work, he judged. The first time he saw her face he knew it was familiar, but days passed before he recalled from where. Cleaning out old magazines from the pantry where his gran kept them for a coon's age—as Jack would say, though Royce was never *quite* sure what they meant—he found an old copy of *My Lady's Fashion—swimsuit issue.* Seeing her in a one-piece black suit, with French cut legs, and low on those magnificent breasts, made his temperature rise just staring at it. Needless to say when he chucked the magazines out, the picture stayed. He'd gone down to the local library to check for back issues, hoping to spot more advertisements with her as a model. He'd found two. One for a perfume ad with her dressed as a Medieval lady and another for eye makeup. The last one was mostly of her face with the focus upon her haunting amber eyes. He couldn't breathe as he stared at them. For the first time in his thirty-nine years on this green earth he'd resorted to a life of crime; when he left the library the ripped out advertisements had been neatly rolled up in his coat pocket.

Halo firmly in place, he graced her with a quizzical smile. "Joy juice? Now, do I look like I've had a wee dram?"

From on high, Jack cleared his throat warning his cousin Cajuns didn't say things like *wee dram.* And damned if she didn't catch it.

"Wee dram?" she echoed in puzzlement, her eyes targeting him.

Mercy. A sexy woman who had a brain. His body bucked. Fortunately, the oak counter was between them.

How in the bloody hell her jackass of an ex-husband ever let her go, he couldn't begin to fathom. Insanity? The moron had traded Catonia in on a 'newer year model', some blonde bimbo actress, and presently they were on the Riviera, Paparazzi in tow, pictures of their honeymoon splashed all over every tabloid magazine around the world.

"Catonia, I presume you brought me this snake for a reason. Very neighborly. Perhaps you wish me to use it to cook up some *Chicken What Du Hell, cher?*" His stomach muscles flexed, tightening as he held in the laughter.

Bubba meowed, then butted her breast again, silly creature wanting praise for his 'gift'. She glowered at the cat, pushing him back from her 'pointed anatomy.' "This *thing* you call a cat is the reason I brought that serpent. *Again.* This is the third time in seven days, Kinross."

Bubba upped the decibel of his yowl as he proudly admitted his deeds.

"Ah, *cher*, Bubba was playing Welcome Wagon. He wanted to make sure you're well cared for." Royce almost cringed at his pathetic Cajun accent. He had the *cher* part down, but he feared that too much of his Scots burr slipped through.

Not that he was trying to deceive her specifically. He was tired of golddigging women wanting to marry him just to get a title and a fat bank account. *Remy* Kinross was a good way to filter out all the users and abusers in his life. So fed up with it all, he'd come to *Belle Trelonge* a year ago and assumed the *Remy* just to find himself again.

"Cared for? He keeps bringing me snakes!" She pushed Bubba back again as he was moving in for another boob-bump. "Now stop that." She shook her finger at Bubba. The undaunted feline purred loud enough to rival a diesel engine, and rubbed his chin against the long, graceful finger.

The cat sure had a one-tracked mind! Oh, Royce envied that silly beast. He'd like to rub against her as well. Maybe he should try meowing, then she'd let him near enough to do a boob-bump. Oh, boy did he want to do that!

"Stop what, *cher*?" Royce asked, miming confusion.

She huffed. "Not *you*, this ridiculous feline. He keeps bumping my...my..." Turning bright red, her eyes flashed wide and that kissable mouth formed an 'O'.

"Breasts, I believe they're called. Well, *cher*, they do tend to poke out, hum? Bubba takes that as an open invitation to do a little chin rubbing." He bit the inside of his mouth to keep the chuckle from escaping.

Jack dropped the putty knife and about fell off the ladder, writhing in silent guffaws. Royce flashed him a warning that he'd kill him if he didn't stop. "Hey, Cuz, why don't you go on back and see what Mama Lou is going to fix for supper, eh?"

Jack nodded, climbing down. "Sure thing, Remy. See you later, Catonia."

Catonia's pinched expression increased as her gaze returned to the counter. "Back to the snake—"

"*Cher*, even if it were alive, that's a harmless garter—"

"No snake is harmless when it gives me a heart attack. I took a shower, came out and started to lie down and..."—she pointed as if the poor creature would rise from the dead like some King Cobra and start spitting—"that was in my bed! I'm not kidding, Kinross. Do something about that...that...*cat* or I shall call the sheriff."

Royce was relieved he wasn't wearing his glasses. Visions of Catonia straight from a shower, her body dewy with dampness, maybe glistening with body oil, sent his temperature spiraling. "Um...I'm sure Jefferson Parrish's finest will be more than willing to discuss your concerns, *cher*." Yeah, he could imagine them licking their lips while she complained. They'd probably crave to bump her boobs, too, like Bubba did. "Cats take care of their people. It's their nature. Bubba doesn't want you to go hungry. You should praise the lad for such diligent behavior."

Her brow crinkled at the *lad* slip, but then let it pass. She had more important things on her agenda. "But he's *not* my cat. I'm not kidding, Kinross. I *hate* snakes." She glared pointedly at him. "The kind that slither through the grass and the two-legged ones. Sometimes, I'm not sure which the bigger menace is. However, I do know I don't like coming in and finding that the *Monster of Trelonge* has left me a present. That scared me out of ten years of my life!"

"Ah, *cher*, Bubba is in love. He's only trying to see you have plenty of food. Let me make it up to you. Stay, I'll cook supper for you. Something special. We could dine in the gazebo. There's a full moon tonight."

She flashed him the same look she did the dead snake. "While I *am* impressed with a man who can actually cook, I want nothing to do with you—or that stupid cat."

Bubba's head snapped back and he blinked.

"Now you've done it, *cher*. Gone and hurt Bubba's feelings."

"I mean it, Kinross. Stay away from me—and keep that snake killing Grendel away as well." She stared at him for a minute, confusion flittering through her haunting eyes, then she stormed out of the old plantation house, screen door slamming in her wake.

The cat bounced on his paws then leaned over against Royce's shoulder with a thud, Bubba's heart on his kitty sleeve. "Sorry, Bubba. I don't care if you take that pretty lady snakes twice a week. Won't do you any good. She's mine, all mine. I'd hike my tail and spray her leg to mark my property, but I don't think she'd get the point in the fashion it was offered."

He watched her speed down his gravel driveway, driving like a bat out of hell.

Smiling, he wondered if she made love the same way.

Catonia Flemyn slowed as she swung out of Remy Kinross's drive, then floored it, sending gravel and dust flying. *Remy Kinross?* Why was that so discordant? Obviously, there was Scot on his father's side. Maybe first generation? That would account for the hint of a burr that slipped through every now and again. He'd taken over restoring *Belle Trelonge*, inherited it from his grandmother who died after Katrina hit New Orleans. The *Remy* was explained by the mother's Louisiana side. So daddy was a Scot and Mama a Cajun.

Who was responsible for those damnable lavender eyes?

Just thinking about them gave her hot flashes. Something about Remy Kinross hit her low in the pit of her stomach, in some strange manner as no man had. It unnerved her. Every night for the past two weeks those lilac eyes had invaded her dreams...*erotic* dreams with such a vivid clairvoyant feel to them. Never in her whole life had she experienced such sensual fantasies. Come morning, she didn't want to awaken. Her body pulsed, ached, so aroused from the realness of the visions of Remy making love to her. She held little doubt if she ever let down her guard he'd be in her bed before she could blink.

"Better him than a dead snake," she spoke for her reflection in the rearview mirror. Playing rebuttal to her image, she reminded, "Ah, but you've already had one snake there. You don't want to risk another."

Damn David Sinclair! What a pathetic fool she'd been. Temporary insanity was the only answer for why she ever trusted that worm. Maybe she'd been lonely for too long and simply blinded herself against the things she hadn't wanted to see. She wasn't cut out to be single. Many women elected to live alone nowadays, fed up with the men that waltzed through their lives. Not her. She'd wanted to quit modeling, actually eat a full meal again without worrying about putting on a pound, and was old-fashioned enough to want a home, a husband...children. Well, she'd mistakenly married an international playboy, heir to a cruise line, believing...well, she *had* been a fool. And paid for that self-deceit, very publicly.

She never suspected David viewed her as a *trophy wife*, the beautiful model on his arm that complemented the décor. When she'd announced she was quitting modeling, stopping the frantic jetsetter life they'd lived for nearly three years, that she wanted a *real* home not an apartment, suddenly everything fell apart. He did a 'wife upgrade 2.0' so fast her head didn't even have time to spin. She hungered for a special home; some place where she belonged, nothing too big, just a house with a heritage attached to it, and in a nice neighborhood where kids could play, maybe even have a cat.

Cat. That brought Bubba the Menace and his lavender-eyed owner to her mind again. Kinross scared the hell out of her, yet she was drawn to him. Oh, how she wanted to say yes to him cooking dinner for her. She huffed a small chuckle. She could just imagine David in the kitchen; he'd be more at home in an alien spacecraft. A man who actually cooked—now *that* had possibilities. Visions arose in her thoughts of them quietly preparing a meal together, the tension just under the surface, their minds filled with images of what would happen after supper.

"Silly female." She glared at the woman in the mirror. "Didn't being burned by David Sinclair teach you a lesson?"

She spun the wheel on the Jeep, then parked in front of the dilapidated garage. Poor thing leaned about ten degrees, courtesy of Katrina. She'd have to replace it, just not yet. Again, she'd been a fool. When it was clear David was divorcing her and remarrying faster than you could say Mickey Rooney, she simply wanted the hell away from him, to erase him from her life. That included alimony. She wanted none of David's money. Prideful, she wasn't some damn charity case. She quit modeling seven months ago, put on seventeen much-needed pounds and used her savings to buy this house. Now she was trying desperately to peddle her first romance novel. She gave herself two years to sell. With careful living, she had enough money for that long. After that...well, she wouldn't think of *after that.*

Just like she wouldn't think of a man with haunting lilac eyes.

She stomped up the wooden stairs to the small cottage, muttering to herself, then opened the door. *To silence.* Not even a cat to talk to, to keep her company. She could be sharing supper with Bubba and Remy tonight in the big kitchen at *Belle Trelonge,* watching the sexy man—a woman's fantasy come to life—cook.

"*Remy.* Strange, he simply doesn't strike me as a Remy," she muttered to herself. She wasn't quite sure what he should be named, but she supposed Remy was short for something. Remington? That suited him better

She went into the kitchen and put the kettle on. "Stupid

woman, instant noodle soup and a cheese sandwich for supper. You could have had *Chicken What Du Hell*—whatever the hell that is."

She laughed. Then she sat down at the kitchen table and cried.

At the front door of the small cottage, Royce took a deep breath. He stared at his reflection in the glass pane, straightened his jacket and ran a hand through his wavy black hair. Damn stuff had a mind of its own to the point where combing it was a waste of time. Usually he little cared, just let the thick mass do what it wanted. Only, he hadn't been this nervous on a date since he was seventeen.

"Of course, Bubba, this isn't really a date. I may get the door slammed in our faces, but I can't stay home alone tonight, thinking about her." He looked down at the long-haired tabby cat with big green eyes, who was dancing from foot-to-foot in eagerness. Poor Bubba wanted in there, too. "Hey, Pal, best behavior if she lets us in the door, *please*. No unrolling the toilet tissue in a pile in the bathroom, no shredding couch cushions, and especially no spraying to mark things as yours. Understood? If we're mannered enough maybe she'll let us come again...maybe will come visit us at *Belle Trelonge*."

The images of his four-poster bed with curtained tester arose in his mind. He'd bought it last month at an estate auction, but had yet to sleep in it. When he thought of that bed, he saw Catonia there; wanted her in it, though he had a feeling he wanted her there for more than just sex, and for longer than just one night.

Maybe forever.

Why he was so damn anxious. He'd given up believing in love at first sight. Oh, he was a romantic enough to dream that it could happen to him, but bloody hell, he'd be forty-years-old next month. Not once had that 'real thing' ever appeared on the horizon. Then, he looked into Catonia's eyes and felt the earth shift under his feet.

"That was just before my glasses steamed up, Bubba."

He frowned at his reflection in the glass door, hoping he wouldn't look as nervous to her as he did to himself. Holding a loaded picnic basket, and with Bubba in tow, how could he not melt her heart? Surely, she felt that special connection between them?

He'd cooked dinner, carefully packed it to keep the dishes

warm and the wine chilled. If Catonia refused to come dine with him, then he was invading her space. "I've taken my first steps to being a stalker. We're going to wear her down, Pal."

Growing impatient, he pressed the buzzer again, wondering if she were in there hiding and simply ignoring him. Maybe he should've left Bubba at home. After all, gift snakes obviously weren't winning her heart as the feline intended. Of course, if he had a man-to-man natter with Bubba, and asked him not to fetch her any more snakes, the idiot might take her something worse. If Catonia thought finding a dead snake in her bed was a horror, she'd have a cow if she found a mangled swamp rat.

"Love me, love my kitty..." He sighed. "Bubba, you're a trial."

The silly feline grinned. Bubba wasn't your ordinary tabby cat. He was part Scottish Wildcat, closer to a Lynx than a housecat. Oh, he looked like a pretty tabby puss, just a little on the 'large' side. He was more muscular, stronger, feral, and keeping him inside was a no go. Bubba *had* to go out and hunt, his untamed feral side still calling to his nature. Bubba could whip all the dogs in a twenty-mile radius, including Bobby-Ray Judd's pit-bull. The damn dog, once the terror of the whole area, took one look at Bubba and ran. The ridiculous cat grinned when he saw the pit-bull now. Bubba was forty-pounds of solid muscle and one mean hunter.

His cousin, Katlyn Mackenzie St. Giles, had given him Bubba as a Christmas present two years earlier. Her kitty, Auggie Moggie—also part Scottish Wildcat—tended to knock up the neighborhood females, and disgruntled owners brought the kitty spawn to her to find homes for. Smart people. A whole herd of Auggies was a scary thought. That Christmas she'd come bearing Bubba with a big green and gold ribbon. His first reaction was to send both her and the cat packing, but Bubba jumped out of the basket and into his lap, then declared his immediate and unconditional love.

It was just after his divorce, when he learned people could love you for your money, love you for the title of Marquis of Dunmoor and Seafeld, but not really love *you*. Bubba loved him. It had touched his heart in a way he hadn't been able to put into words through the whole messy divorce. So Bubba stayed. The cat was the best thing that had happened in his life in the last few years.

Until Catonia waltzed through the door of *Belle Trelonge* two weeks ago.

They say your pets look a lot like you. It struck him— Bubba and he were wearing the same starry-eyed expression of anticipation as they waited for the door to open. He reached out to push the doorbell a third time, but then stopped.

"Maybe she doesn't want a candlelight dinner with us, Bubba." He exhaled his disappointment, but almost laughed when the cat shot him a dirty look like *well, do something*.

"What, Bubba, kick down the door? I don't think so. Come on, pal. Just not our night."

Dejection sat heavy on his heart. He didn't want to wait for another time. He wanted to be with Catonia *tonight*. In any way she wanted him. She could call the shots if she just let him in. He was lonely and knew this special lady could bring magic to his world, make life new again.

Swallowing regret, he turned on his heels and started down the short set of stairs, then noticed Bubba wasn't following. Turning to call the cat, he heard the lock rattling and then the knob rotated. He smiled as he saw Catonia slowly open the door. Bubba didn't hesitate, but barreled inside, nearly knocking her off her feet. *Got to love that cat*, he thought.

"There's an old Scots proverb that says it's better to keep the cat out, than try to put him out." The corner of his mouth curved up as he slowly mounted the stairs. He realized perhaps that a Cajun might not be well versed in Gaelic proverbs, so he qualified his use of it. "My Kinross blood rearing its head." Which *was* the truth.

When she just gave a small nod, instead of jumping all over his little slip, his eyes studied her. His heart squeezed, seeing her struggle to appear normal. Her eyes were red; she'd been crying. It made him want to hit something— *hard* —like that louse David Sinclair. He'd take great pleasure in mopping the floor with that pretty boy face. Those haunting eyes should never cry, unless they were tears of joy.

Stopping before her, Royce lifted his hand to her cheek, his thumb catching the unwanted tear she couldn't stop from falling. Catonia jerked back and quickly swiped her face; too late, he held the precious droplet, examining the crystalline bead in the orange shadows of evening, trying to decide what the right step to take with her was. She stood like a fawn; one wrong move, she'd bolt back inside and slam the door in his face. His eyes watched hers for a moment, assessing. Poor lass, she kept glancing away, unable to meet his direct stare, and realizing he was aware she'd been crying.

The side of his mouth lifted in a small tick; probably, she couldn't even see it, but he *felt* it. He stuck his thumb in his mouth and tasted her salty tear. In surprise, her head snapped up, those intense eyes finally meeting his, watching as his lips closed around it. "I thank you for the special gift, but *he* wasn't worth it, *cher*."

The beautiful face paled, then two spots of red flamed her cheeks. He done just the right thing, but he and Bubba weren't out of the woods yet. Maybe he should just barrel into the house Bubba-style.

"I...I don't know what you mean," she stammered out. Catonia wasted her breath, knew it, but seemed trapped into going through the motions. "Why did you come, Kinross?"

"*Cher*, didn't your mama send her purdy gurl to school?" He nearly winced at the heavy dose of *pardy on down* Cajun accent. It was a fun sound, too easy to get carried away with, especially when trying to tease a smile from a sexy woman. "Me and Bubba fetched you supper. Now, you can stand there pretending you weren't crying, get huffy, try to evict my cat, and then spend the rest of the evening alone. Or you can invite me in—seeing Bubba is already making himself at home—and I can finish fixing a meal for us."

Her eyes finally glanced to the wicker hamper he carried. "You fixed me supper?"

"It needs heating up and me to chop up a nice garden salad—with some mustard greens, eh?" He offered her one of his best grins.

"What did you fix?"

He chuckled. Damn, but she was a hard sell. "Why I cooked up dat snake you brung me."

"Drop the Doug Kershaw accent, Kinross. You don't talk like that normally."

"You know who Doug Kershaw is? I'm impressed. Normally I'm not diggy-diggy-lo with the accent, but I'm playing court jester, trying to get you to smile."

She swallowed back the remaining tears as one side of her mouth—her luscious mouth—twitched. "You didn't really cook that horrid snake, did you?"

"Ah, *cher*, it tastes just like chicken, especially with a little Louisiana Hot Sauce on it." He enjoyed teasing Catonia. "Ah, come on, let me in and I'll prove what a good cook I am. I even made some fresh sourdough rolls. Not a good enough bribe? I have lemon meringue pie. I confess, I make the filling a little on the tart side. Nice balance to the too sweet egg whites."

"Kinross, I might buy you can cook, but baking a lemon meringue pie?"

He smiled, not in a winning fashion, just happy to be with her. He raised his hand and *drew* on his chest. "Cross my heart, *cher*. I didn't make the crust. Sorry, there are limits. And the lemon came from Jell-O pudding mix; though I adjust the sugar a bit to make it tarter. But I did beat the poor egg whites until they are nearly four inches high. So, you really going to turn away sourdough rolls, Bubba, lemon meringue pie and me?"

She stepped back and pulled the door wide to let him enter. Yes! If he had a football he would have spiked the damn thing and done one of those end zone dances.

Her little cottage was warm, cozy, and instantly put him at ease. The walls were dark teal, with oak trim and planked flooring; the wood gleamed and the hint of lemon oil filled the air. A needlepoint French Aubusson rug was the focal point of the large room, and a matching runner graced the long hall. Royce glanced around. This was the look he wanted for *Belle Trelonge* when he'd finish the restoration, the feel of the old turn of the century parlor. He smiled a secret smile, delighted their tastes ran in the same vein.

Bubba was already on her expensive rug 'killing' a throw pillow. "Hey, Bubba, see you're making yourself at home."

"Oh, that cat!" she exclaimed, the two red spots on her cheeks deepened to ones of anger.

Catonia started toward Bubba to retrieve her cushion, only to be stopped by Royce. He practically jumped several steps to snag her wrist before she made the mistake of trying to take the pillow from Bubba. One simply didn't interrupt Bubba the Mighty Hunter when he was delivering the Vulcan Death Pinch to anything he considered his 'kill'.

"I wouldn't do that. Bubba doesn't take well to someone stealing his prey—"

"Prey? That's my cushion, *not* something to eat."

"You'd rather he bring you another snake?" Royce almost laughed at her flummoxed expression. "I'll buy you another... buy you a dozen. Let him have his pillow to mangle and he'll leave everything else alone, and won't feel the need to drag in some poor snake. And *never* interrupt Bubba when he's taking his kill down for the death throes. You're apt to get slapped. He's not mean, but has a paw span that's lethal."

She glared at the feline. "Why would you want a beast like that? He's a menace."

"He was my Christmas gift from my cousin, Katlyn. Spawn of her darling Auggie Moggie. He's half-Scottish wildcat. I guess that makes Bubba one-quarter, but I think he received an overload of the feral genes." He smiled down at the zany Bubba gnawing on the pillow. "It was just after my divorce. Not a high point in my life. The marriage hadn't been what I wanted by that time, but I worked very hard at it, tried to make it work. I hate to fail at anything. Failing at something as important as a marriage, and for all the wrong reasons, left me rather low. Bubba came along when I needed him. Kat knew, I guess. She gave me a basket with this cute little fuzzy kitten with a big green ribbon. And he loved me. Instantly, unconditionally. I needed very badly for someone to love me at that point. So I'll be eternally grateful to Bubba."

She stared at him, reserved yet curious. "You're divorced?"

"Nearly three years ago. Water under the bridge now, as they say." He held up the hamper as a hint, not really wanting to get maudlin about ex-wives and ex-husbands. He wanted this evening to be special. About them.

"Oh, sorry." She started to turn, but then paused. "You're sure he'll only destroy the cushion? I've put a lot of work into this place."

"Promise. The pillow will keep him happy. It's his now. Just leave it out so he finds it when he comes to visit and everything else is safe."

She finally relaxed a tad and gave him a soft smile. "Small price for insurance? The kitchen's this way. I have a formal dining room,"—she pushed through the swinging door and held it open for him—"but we can eat in the breakfast alcove if you'd rather. It's very cozy."

The kitchen was done in more of the same warm oak, with exposed ceiling beams. The modern, steel appliances were woven into the old-time feel. His eyes took in how beautiful, how much love she had expended putting the small house back into mint condition. If he hadn't already set his sights on Catonia from the first moment he laid eyes on her, the care with which she'd made the house a home would steal his heart. This nurturing and reverence is what he envisioned for *Belle Trelonge*. Someone to love it. To love him.

He set the hamper on the cabinet and started to take out the warming dishes. He lifted the lid on the *Chicken What Du*

Hell and waved it under her nose. "See, aren't you glad you let Bubba and me in?"

She inhaled deeply, closing her eyes to savor the delicious aromas. Her expression was a punch to his gut, his groin instantly throbbing to life. He was glad he'd left his glasses off! So easily, he could imagine that dreamy look, with the Mona Lisa smile on her kissable face as he woke her in the soft pink rays of dawn by making love to her.

"That smells wonderful. What's in it?"

"A little this and that." He offered her a smile and placed the pan on the burner of the stove to set it to warming.

"Ah, a man with secrets." She took down two wine glasses as he pulled out the bottle snug in the chiller-carrier. "That can be dangerous."

He used the corkscrew, and then poured some into each glass. Handing one to Catonia, he clicked it against hers. "A wee dram of danger can also be very good."

She started to take a sip, but her eyes locked with his. And held. The power between them arced, with the sizzle and pop of heat lightning in summer. There was something very special weaving between them, and it made him a little crazy. He wanted to take that glass from her hand, yank that lush body against his, and teach her just how dangerous he was, just how delicious it could be. Taking a deep breath, he lifted his goblet and slowly drank, reminding himself that moving too fast could scare her.

Her hand trembled as she lifted the crystal glass, barely taking a sip of the red wine. "So...what is in the delicious looking dish?"

Easing back on his sexual predator's impulse pushing him to toss her to the floor, and take her then and there, Royce stirred the chicken in the pan on the stove. He set the rice to warm on another burner. "Why, *cher*, I told you. I cooked that snake Bubba brung you."

"Cut the Cajun. I'm not eating snake."

"Actually, the recipe calls for gator's tail, but snake will do in a pinch. On the bayou you learn to eat what nature offers you." He teased, "Snake, gator, possum, swamp rat—"

"That's enough. I don't believe you cooked the snake. And you have *never* eaten possum or swamp rat. So stop pulling my leg, Remy."

He flashed a winning smile and gave her his most innocent look of *who me?* "*Cher*, that ain't all I want to do to your leg."

A slight frown flickered in her beautiful whisky-brown eyes. "You don't look like a Remy."

"Oh?" He made pretence of stirring the rice, caught off guard by her perception. "And what do I look like, *cher*?"

She studied him, those hazel colored eyes really taking in every detail. "I'm unsure, but not a Remy. Maybe a Rhys. Something with one syllable, old, Celtic."

He nearly strangled by how close her guess came. "My father was Scot; mother was half-Welsh and half-Cajun. What's a name but a label?"

"You don't care for labels?"

"Not especially. It's a way to pigeonhole people. Labels can be misleading. I'd rather you love me for me."

The moment lengthened as their eyes locked; his telling he meant precisely what he'd said. Hers, on the other hand, bespoke how she ached for that dream to be true. Even so, she was too damn scared even to risk that small hope.

Reining back on the wild impulses surging in his blood, Royce suppressed his smile. He studied the bewitching eyes, the brilliant, incisive intelligence behind them. The lady had a sharp mind and saw too bloody much. Oh, what a gem he had discovered! A precious treasure to capture and keep, protect, cherish.

To distract the pounding need within him to claim her as his mate, he speared a chunk of the chicken, blew on it and then offered it to her. So caught up in the magic weaving around them, she blinked surprise, then clearly hesitated, as if taking that bite was a commitment. This time he couldn't stop the corner of his mouth from lifting. It sure was a commitment—one bite of his Chicken What Du Hell and Catonia was his—though he wouldn't let her in on that secret *...just yet.*

"Go ahead, *cher*. It can't bite you now..." He couldn't resist the little taunt.

The long black eyelashes flicked as she switched her focus from the chicken piece to him. "You really didn't cook that snake, did you, Kinross?"

"Ah, come on, be adventuresome. Try it, you might like it." He watched until she took the bite, then added, "Might like me, too, if you try me."

Catonia nearly choked.

The dinner was delicious, Catonia had to admit—whether the mystery meat was chicken or not! More delicious was the company of this unusual man. Now that she was around him for longer spells, it was clear the heavy Cajun accent came and went. When he was being playful, he was *Remy*. The rest of the time...well, she wasn't sure about the rest of the time. His accent modulated to Brit, with a strong hint of a Scots burr.

Though, while the accent didn't ring true, his love for that ridiculous cat did. He and Bubba were pals, a package deal; if she wanted the man, then she'd better be prepared to accept the cat. As they finished the meal, and were carrying dishes to the sink, Bubba came in dragging his 'dead pillow' and offered it as a present. She conceded it *was* an improvement over a dead snake. To that aim, one murdered throw cushion seemed a wise investment. The way Kinross and the cat interacted touched her heart. She liked cats, wanted one; David hadn't liked cat hair, and repeatedly pointed out a cat wasn't suited to the jetsetter lifestyle they'd lived. The question if Bubba was really a cat was still debatable in her mind. Bubba was like no housecat she'd ever seen.

But then, it was becoming fast apparent that his owner was like no man she'd ever seen, too.

Oh, this black-headed charmer was quickly getting past all her defenses, breaking down the barriers she'd erected to ensure no one got close, denying them the power to hurt her. She'd spent two weeks trying to keep a distance from him. Despite her best efforts, Remy Kinross, with his discordant name, fakey Cajun accent and Bubba the Wonder-Beast, was quickly crawling under her skin and burrowing deep.

Taking a steadying breath, she concentrated on carefully placing the plates into the soapy water. She'd hoped doing the dishes would give her space from Kinross's lethal magnetism. It had—for all of five seconds. He surprised her by helping clear the table. Ah, a man who cooked *and* cleaned!

"Be still my heart," she laughed under her breath.

And had violet eyes that seemed to reach inside her, straight to her soul, to her heart.

That heart had done a flip earlier over him saying, *I'd rather you love me for me.* As she stared into the hypnotic eyes, she almost believed he meant it, *wanted* to believe he meant it. Her foolish, foolish heart knew how easy it would be to love him, really love him. Only was that what he truly wanted? She wasn't the kind for a little slap and tickle, until something better came along for him. Catonia knew the pain that came from making imprudent choices, and wasn't sure she could face it again. Deep inside, she knew loving Remy

Kinross would be the real thing. Losing him would destroy her.

She almost wanted to cry at how wonderful it felt, just them sharing the clean up chores. A simple act. Gentle smiles, laughing over Bubba dragging around that half-shredded cushion. This was what she so wanted in her life, what was missing. To experience this quiet splendor and not have it for nights to come seemed too cruel.

Before, she was beginning to wonder if maybe she was being a bit unrealistic, a Goldilocks wanting things *just right*, especially after David's continual snide remarks about her wanting the '*Old Lady in the Shoe* life.' Her former husband had accused her of tossing away something good with both hands as she chased after a chimera. Now she saw her dreams could be reality, it was a knife to her heart. The hungry looks Kinross flashed her as he wiped down the stove nearly brought a tear to her eye for it was just as she'd envisioned, craved.

He came over and slid the serving dish into the water. His incisive gaze traced over her face taking in every detail, judging her mood, her thoughts. Catonia nearly cringed knowing how open she was, aware he could read the fathomless hunger reflected in her eyes. That ravenous need as a rule sent most men running. She gave him credit. Kinross wasn't running.

"What's wrong, *cher*? You didn't like my snake, after all? I thought it tasted like chicken," he teased.

"Save the *Remy* routine. That wasn't snake. It *was* chicken." She smiled as he picked up the dishtowel and dried the plates as she rinsed each.

His head rocked to the song softly playing on CD system. "Cool tunes? Who's the artist?"

"Mike Duncan. Absolutely my fav. Writes a lot of his stuff."

He grinned, took her soapy hand and pulled her into his arms, then started slow dancing and singing along with the catchy lyrics. "*'I can see I've lost this game...I'm in love with the most beautiful girl, and I know that she's gonna rule my world...I'm in love, babe, with you...'*"

"Please don't..." Catonia swallowed hard.

His head tilted, puzzled by her reaction. Instead of backing off, he invaded her space. Reaching out, he caught her upper arms as she took a step back. "Don't what, Catonia? Say things like love? That I'm in love? That I'm in love with you?"

"Don't say things you don't mean." She swallowed hard forcing the words out of her tightening throat. "You don't even know me."

"I know enough. I like how you made this house a home, the care you put into it, how special you fashioned it. You'd give the same care to a family...a husband."

"Please...maybe...you better leave." Catonia put out a hand to stop him from stepping closer. Only it landed over his heart. It beat strong, steady, though a little rapid. She stared at where they were joined, feeling each beat, each thud under her palm. Almost fused to him, she was unable to pull away.

His grip clamped about her wrist holding her hand to his heart; refused to let her remove it. "Things are moving a little fast for you. You want to erect barriers between us, simply to protect yourself. I promise, Catonia...I won't hurt you. Ever. I'm the one who can be hurt here. Something rare, something special is happening between us. We both failed before because of other people. This time, it will be different."

Catonia tried to jerk back, but he held her firm. Not forceful or hurting, just not letting her run from him.

"Please don't cry," he entreated. "I see the tears forming in your beautiful eyes. We can go slowly, but it's a dance, Catonia. We both know where we are going."

She trembled as he pulled her into his arms. "It's like being on a rollercoaster as it crests over that first big drop. Your stomach slams up into your throat; you just want to close your eyes and hang on."

"Then hang on to me, *cher*." He chuckled, playing at his Remy the Cajun again, hoping to tease her into a less panicky mood. "Perhaps Fate dealt a bad hand, gave us a raw deal the first time around just so we'd appreciate how extraordinary it is when the real thing walks into our world. I could tell you what I want for tonight...*for all the coming nights,* but think that's too soon for you to accept my words, accept me. So, I'll settle for a goodnight kiss."

The will to fight against the very thing she wanted burned out, gone was all her careful resistance. As his lips closed over hers, and she leaned into him, her soul found sanctuary in his strong arms. She relished the solid feel of his body, how his height was perfect for her, inhaled his intoxicating male scent that clouded her brain, made her crazy. Sliding her arms around his strong, sexy neck, she kissed him back, savored the soft lips, tasting him.

He smelled right. He tasted right.

The kiss began to take over, feeding their passion. Almost regretfully, he lifted his head, then cleared his throat. Filled with awe, the lavender eyes traced the lines of her face. "I said a *goodnight* kiss, *cher. That* was not a goodnight kiss."

Catonia ran her thumb across his lower lip. "That's the problem, Kinross. I don't want a goodnight kiss."

His eyebrows lifted. "You have no idea how happy that makes Bubba and me." Then his smile faded. "You do understand we're a two-for-one deal?"

"Yeah, I think that was the last straw. I saw how you loved that worthless cat."

"Worthless?" He laughed as he tilted to scoop her into his arms, spinning around with her until she was dizzy. Catonia clung to him.

She might be making the biggest mistake in her life, but she wanted this man, wanted to share his heat through the night, hold him as the soft rays of dawn flooded her bedroom. Oh, how she wanted him! "You think maybe I could bribe you to stay with me tonight, Kinross, and defend me from Bubba's gifts?"

"Just tonight?" He seemed saddened by her offer.

She reached up and stroked his cheek. "I'm not a one night stand, Kinross."

He nodded. "I know."

"Let's take it slow as you promised. Tonight. Then tomorrow will take care of tomorrows."

"Deal. Bubba and I are the understanding sort," he teased.

Instead of releasing her, he carried her down the short hall to her shadowy bedroom. Setting her on her feet, he speared his hands into her long hair, flexed his fingers to savor the thickness, the silkiness. Then cradling the back of her head, he pulled her closer and kissed her. Softly at first, then deeper. It made her want to close her eyes and revel in the sensations he brought to her, but she so loved looking into those violet eyes. Loved what she saw reflected there.

Those eyes made her believe this was real, and not folly.

She saw something dark flicker in those pale eyes, glimmering in the dimness broken only by the hall light, but then he spun her around to face the large Victorian Cheval mirror. She blinked, confused, until his hands moved on her. He put them around her waist, then slid them up and over her breasts, finally to the buttons of her blouse, releasing them one-by-one.

"Don't move. Just stand and watch while I worship you," he whispered against her hair.

Placing his hand on her shoulders, he gradually pulled the soft cotton blouse down her arms. Each shift of the material, every touch of his warlock hands, sent shivers over her sensitive skin and up her spine to slam into her brain with a force she'd never known. Leaving her bra on, he nuzzled her hair below her ear. His shaking fingers undid the snap on her jeans, then peeled the denim away from her hips. Agonizingly slow, to the point where her teeth ached, he pushed them down her thighs and then allowed her to kick out of them.

He dragged his hands up her outer thighs, slightly scoring his nails against her over sensitized flesh, sending waves of hot hunger skittering across her skin. She shivered, but not from cold. His reflection in the mirror smiled at her, the penetrating eyes glowing at her complete surrender. Magician's hands snaked over the curve of her hips, lingered to give a small squeeze, then continued on their leisurely journey across her belly and over the dip of her waist. They moved too slowly. Unbearable. Excruciating. And it wasn't enough.

Not nearly enough.

Swallowing back consuming desire, Catonia fought the urge to turn in his strong embrace, press her body against his. Only, the vexing man still had all his clothes on. She wanted to feel flesh-against-flesh; it was hard to rein in the overpowering, grinding need he set loose inside her.

His gentle grasp conformed to her ribcage, sliding upward at a snail's pace. Catonia quivered, craving those maddening hands upon her breasts. As if she couldn't get enough air, her breathing was raspy. She almost stopped, as his fingers skimmed over the soft satin bra; her sharp inhale sounded ragged, edgy with need, as he finally reached the clasp and released it. She smiled, seeing Kinross tremble. He let her slip into his cupped palms, squeezed the aching flesh, hard, swollen from her deep arousal, and for several breaths that was enough. Then she wanted more. *Much more.* Her body jerked as his thumbs brushed across her jutting nipples, her gasp harsh as he tweaked them, sending lightning arcing through her body and slamming into her womb.

Unable to stand, she turned in his arms. The side of his mouth lifted, smug from his power over her, what it did to her, how he affected her.

"I said don't move," he teased.

She began to unbutton his shirt. "You will find, Kinross,

I'm not good at following orders."

"Oh, pity that." He kissed her chin, then the corner of her mouth. "I might have to tie you down to get compliance, hmm?"

Catonia pushed the shirt off his strong shoulders. "Or I might tie *you* up. I have this marvelous bunch of peacock feathers downstairs. Could be a journey to discover where Kinross is the most ticklish."

He laughed and scooped her into his arms so fast she gasped. "Kiss me, you wicked woman. Kiss me slow. Kiss me long. Kiss me all night long."

She nipped his chin instead. "Told you, I'm not too swift on orders. But...this...one...time..."

Catonia drank in his handsome face, as she lifted her mouth to his and kissed him. Soft butterfly kisses that quickly deepened as she savored the sheer pleasure of kissing this man. Breaking the contact, she looked into the violet eyes, searching for answers and finding them, finding so much more. She wanted to speak the words he made her feel, but it was still too early. This dizzy, spinning madness was just too new. That didn't mean they weren't in her heart. She was falling in love, loved this man with a humbling power that whispered this was the real thing. Not gash, not something you convince yourself is love, but a pure shining reality, something rare and precious to be treasured.

He slowly placed her on the bed on her knees. With an impish grin, she helped him unbuckle his belt, and in short order, he skimmed both the jeans and his boxers down. Putting a knee on the bed, his body forced hers back on the mattress. There was something so elemental in that act, her surrender so empowering.

"Oops...forgot something," he said, playfully slipping her panties off.

Bubba jumped up on the end of the bed and laid down on all fours. The silly beast had this odd look to his face as he watched them.

"Kinross, we have an audience."

"Long ago, I reached the conclusion that Bubba once had been a man, some Casanova, and centuries ago he royally pissed off a witch or a faery queen. For spite she'd turned him into a cat. That male libido trapped in Bubba's brain remembers his past satyrical glories. He goes on hormonal alert when you're around."

"So, I'm to be leered at by a cat?" She laughed.

"You bet. Get used to it."

She wrapped her arms around his neck as his thigh pushed between hers. "Maybe we can get Bubba a girlfriend."

"Yeah, maybe one the color of your hair."

Kinross entered her with a sharp thrust, but she was more than ready for him. Her body rapidly re-conformed to his invading male flesh, relishing the tightness, the delicious pressure. He gently brushed a kiss against her lips. Then he looked over at the lecherously grinning cat. "Eat your heart out, Bubba. She's mine. All mine."

He proved it all night long. In a dozen different ways. And he was right...she was his...*all his.*

On her way to a supper at *Belle Trelonge*, Catonia pulled into Wal-Mart to pick up a few things first. Happy, ecstatically happy, she hummed to herself as she zipped along the aisles. Three days of pure bliss and she couldn't ever recall being this content with herself, the world...the man she loved. She wasn't even hungry. *Living on love*, they say. Well, they were telling the truth. Oh, she ate. Lunchtime she would visit *Belle Trelonge* and share the meal with Bubba and Kinross. On the second day, he took her upstairs and made love to her in the beautiful old-fashioned bed. Laughing, he said they were christening it. She loved the bed, with its intricate carvings and wooden tester. Loved the old house.

Loved Kinross.

She still had a hard time calling him Remy. She supposed she'd get used to it. Still, it just didn't seem to fit him. "His mama named him wrong," she said to the stuffed gorilla she was holding. Poor thing didn't know he was soon to be Bubba prey. With a giggle, she dropped it into her cart.

She was glad the football stadium size store had everything under the sun. In case Harry the Hairy Ape didn't please Kinross's beastie, she selected an oversized Bubba cushion, top on her list. She picked one in heavy material, a bit more Bubba-resistant than the feeble watermark silk one that didn't survive the first night. This fabric was upholstery tough, so might go a few more rounds with the cat that had tiny switchblades for claws. With a grin of mission accomplished, she dumped it into the cart beside the gorilla, hesitated, and added a second. With Kinross's cat the best defense was definitely an offence! Three packets of catnip— maybe a little bribery of feline recreational drugs would chill the feisty pussycat out now and again. Next, she hit the grocery and found Sunkissed Tuna in spring water, the kind in packets. She knew it tasted better than the ones in cans; maybe if Bubba was well fed, he'd forgo the snake hunts. Swinging through the health and beauty section, she found her shampoo, bubble bath and toothpaste. Then, it was a straight beeline to the registers.

Since she had more than the number permitted for the express checkout, she got in the only lane open, behind a husband and wife and their four kids and their two carts piled high. The little monsters...uh, little darlings...were a handful, driving rather pregnant mommy to distraction with their climbing all over the buggy and the checkout counter. The clerk made eye contact with Catonia, rolled her eyes, and then looked longingly toward the sporting goods area, clearly wondering if they stocked Tazers. After suffering five minutes of mom's ineffective warnings of dire punishment against the spawn of the Evil Empire, Catonia was more than willing to go halfsies on the stun gun.

Trying her best to tune out Mother Hubbard and her menacing munchkins, her eyes wandered to the rag newspapers. Not fond of celeb stalking or manufactured news, she generally eschewed them from her reading preference. However, she could only stare at the bubblegum, lighter fluid and phone cards so long before getting bored; unwillingly, she ended up reading about the shocking revelation by the latest media darling, Hollywood tell-all divorces, and the woman having a Martian baby. Sniggering, she was about to pass over the nonsense when one headline and picture caught her attention.

Thinking it funny the black & white picture looked like Kinross, she snagged it up, intending to buy it and tease him. *Fifty-thousand dollar reward offered for the whereabouts of the Missing Marquis.* She flipped inside, wanting a good chuckle, but her blood turned to ice. She had to read it three times before it really sank in.

> *Royce Torqhill Remington Kinross, the thirteenth Marquis of Dunmoor and Seafeld has been missing for six months. His distraught wife fears he is dead. A reward has been posted for anyone providing concrete proof of the whereabouts or information pertaining to the death of the Marquis..."*

Rage—*murderous rage*—flooded through her blood, warming her with a furious wrath, the likes she'd never known. Not even through the long months of her divorce and dealing with the pod-husband, had she been this nearly blind with anger. *Wife? Marquis of Dunmoor and Seafeld?* Her hands held onto the basket to keep from fainting.

"*Royce?* Bloody bastard, I knew he wasn't a *Remy!*" She closed her eyes, silently counting to ten, the whole floor seeming to shift under her feet.

"Oooooooh, *what* she said!" monster child number three —the one about six-years-old—said loudly, hanging off the side of the shopping cart, with a finger half up his nose.

Catonia opened her eyes, and narrowed on the poor unsuspecting child, the immediate surrogate for her black temper. "Get down off that cart before you tump it over with your sister in it, and take your finger out of your nose. It's bad manners to pick your nose in public."

The mother and father stared at her as if she had two heads. The child did, too. But, surprisingly, the little boy stepped off the cart, hid his hand behind his back and uttered a, "Yes, ma'am." The parents' heads snapped around to their son, then back to her.

Catonia feared the mother was opening her mouth to give her a piece of her mind; instead she asked, "How *did* you do that?"

"Madam, a good dose of anger does wonders for a woman. You should try it."

Catonia wasn't sure how she got through the checkout line, or how she'd paid for the merchandise. She didn't recall any of it. Only the pictures of Royce Kinross—and Royce and his wife. It seemed like a nightmare, but getting through that was nothing compared to what she'd have to face in the next few hours. Royce expected her to come to *Belle Trelonge*. He was cooking supper for her, and wanted her opinion on some of the aspects of the old plantation house's restoration.

Royce.

She liked that name. *Royce Kinross*. It suited him. Too bad she hated his bloody guts. "And too bad there's a *Mrs. Royce Kinross*, the lying two-faced bastard," she told the pale woman staring back from her review mirror. "If something is too good to be true, then it generally is. Oh, why did he have to be?"

Hurt and disappointed beyond all words that he was

merely another rich boy who used people and then tossed them aside—what he'd do when he tired of her—she just wanted to go home. There she'd pull out the bottle of *The Macallan* she was saving for a toast when she sold her first book, and drink the whole damn thing. Get rip-roaring drunk, then cry herself to sleep.

Instead of taking the cut off going to her cottage, she found herself zooming down the wandering drive of *Belle Trelonge*. Jack Roboleau was just coming out the front door as she cut the engine and climbed out. Reaching in the back, she pulled out the sack, which contained all the stuff for Bubba, and clutched it to her chest as if a shield. She hesitated, even took a step back toward the car, cowardly thinking of running until Jack spoke.

"Hey, *cher*, our boy's out back. Been all excited today, running around, wanting everything to be perfect. I think something *special* might be in the wind." He grinned, but then question lit his gray eyes as they skimmed over her, taking in her rigid stance. "Go on back and surprise him that you're here early. He'll be tickled."

She gave a tight little nod. "Yeah, I have a big surprise for him."

"He's good people, *cher*. He's really hung up on you, done nothing but talk about you for three weeks, ever since you danced in here with that burlap sack. He and Bubba both have it bad. So you treat him right, you hear?"

She nodded, confused by Jack's words, unable to say anything as he climbed into his Ford pickup and pulled away.

Her eyes took in the old planter's house. It was coming alive under the work Royce was doing. It would make a beautiful home for someone. A home like the one she dreamed about, so like the one she hoped for with all her heart. The perfect place for a family.

Not the home for a Marquis.

Clutching her sack tighter, she slowly walked around the beautiful old home. Each step took all her strength. It seemed as if she'd walked miles as she finally turned the corner of the house. The pain increased as she looked at the love with which Royce had restored the hexagon-shaped, antebellum gazebo, far back at the edge of the property. The green-gabled roof was supported by posts painted a pale blush, and each side was closed in with black screen, lending it a secretive feel as if someone inside could see out, but the privacy of the small structure was maintained. It was perfectly landscaped with deep rose azalea bushes on either side of the walkway; everything so faultless it was as thought she'd walked into a painter's vision.

She stopped several paces away and stood, pathetically clasping the things she'd purchased for Bubba. The cat saw her and came bounding across the yard. The purring feline grinned as she squatted down, opened the bag and pulled out the silly gorilla. "Thought you might like this, Bubba."

He snatched the stuffed toy and proceeded to drag it all over the enclosed backyard in serious pursuit of killing that dangerous animal before it escaped and reeked havoc upon the world.

The screen door squeaked as Royce came out. He smiled softly, and then took in Bubba mauling the stuff toy. "Catonia, what a sweet thing to do for my feline. I don't know how long Morilla the Gorilla will last at that rate, but you sure made Bubba happy."

Catonia struggled for something to say. Nothing came to mind. Actually, *too much* was coming all at once. She wanted to rail at him for being a married man, to scream he was nothing but another pretty playboy who used people without ever caring about them. Wanted to break down and cry. She did none of those things. Her pride was about all she had left. Somehow, that would see her through the next few minutes. The edge of her fury was wearing off and shock was creeping in. She'd made a big mistake in coming to *Belle Trelonge*. She should've gone home. Now, Catonia wasn't sure she'd make it.

"These are for Bubba." Trembling she held out the sack to him. As Royce took it, she reached in and pulled out the rag magazine. "And this, *Marquis*, is for you." She flung it against his chest.

His expression switching to confusion, he picked it up and glanced at the headlines. She couldn't stand to stay and hear the lies, so she spun on her heels and fled.

Royce called, "Catonia, wait! This is a bunch of nonsense!" and started after her.

However, Bubba saw she was leaving and came bounding in her wake. He dashed in front of Royce's path, his solid body mass knocking the feet out from under his master. Royce crashed to the ground.

Catonia didn't slow, but rushed to her Jeep, and sped away from *Belle Trelonge*.

Leaving her heart behind.

Royce set the bottle of Scotch on the floor at his feet. Half empty. He wondered when that had happened. Self-pity was a bastard and accomplished nothing. He needed to pull out of this stupor. Well, he knew for certain Catonia loved him for himself, not that he was a very rich man and a titled one. Unfortunately, in finding out how she truly felt about *him*, he hadn't foreseen her reaction when she discovered that he was as rich as her ex-husband. She now blindly lumped him under the playboy-jetsetter banner and wouldn't trust him. Worse, she was punishing him for all her pent up anger toward the jerk she'd married.

"Stop wallowing in self-pity and do something, *Remy*." His words echoed in the large house, empty without Catonia. And Bubba. "Bloody cat's probably taken up residence with his ladylove. Damn sight smarter than me. I need to march over there, and drag her back to *Belle Trelonge,* caveman style."

Royce scratched the day's growth of beard, then realized he'd slept in his clothes. Glancing in the mirror across the room, he took in his decrepit state. What love can do to a man! Maybe a shower and a shave were in order first. Catonia might not like his currently gamey state. Then again, maybe if she saw how pathetic he appeared, she'd take pity on him and let him into her heart.

In the bathroom, Royce undressed and stepped under the cold spray of the shower, flinching at the sting. Catonia needed to know he loved her, *really* loved her, and find security in that love. She would, if not for how she'd been treated before. He simply needed to get past all those thorns Catonia wrapped about her, hold her until her heart felt safe with him. His mind spun out several scenarios, little movies in his brain, of him groveling on his feet when she opened the door, or singing her a moonlight serenade of Mike Duncan's *'I'm in Love'*—too bad he didn't sound as good as Duncan! The one that played strongest in his mind—waiting outside her cottage, tossing a bag over her head and carrying her off to *Belle Trelonge,* maybe tying her to the bed until she dropped all her resistance to him.

Then he hit on the best one: giving her the engagement ring he'd bought three days ago, the one he planned to give her before all this mess came down on their heads. It wasn't worth a fortune. He could easily afford to buy one that would have Liz Taylor sitting up and taking notice. Something whispered that wouldn't suit Catonia. He'd found a beautiful peridot ring, an oval of three carats, flanked by a half-carat diamond on either side. Something told him it was the perfect ring for his lady. He had a sense when she saw he selected an engagement ring that truly represented their love, then she'd understand he meant forever.

As he stepped out of the shower and reached for a towel, he saw Bubba sitting there. His chest huffed with a chuckle as he spied the dead snake in the middle of the floor.

"Yeah, Bubba. I get the message."

Royce cut the engine and headlights of his black Viper, then coasted into Catornia's driveway, parking behind her jeep. Bubba sat patiently in the passenger seat, the burlap sack on the floorboard before him. Eyes bright, he was ready for Mission Not-Impossible. Royce smiled and patted the feline.

The windows in Catonia's cottage were dark, save for the dim lights toward the rear. Her bedroom and bathroom.

"Yeah, Bubba, we're a team. She doesn't stand a chance against us."

Climbing out of the low-slung car, Royce pocketed the keys; his eyes lingered on the cottage scoping the situation, as he moved to the back of the car. Catonia had paid Jack to put in new storm windows. That stopped Bubba's impromptu visits. Being thrifty Catonia, they were the cheapest sort so he doubted they'd prove a problem, though.

He fetched a small screwdriver from the trunk, then set Bubba loose. The cat didn't even miss a beat, but went straight to the rear of the house. "Smart Bubba." Royce snatched up the sack and followed, staying in the cover of the shadows as he approached.

Turning the corner, he heard the shower running, grinned when he spotted the bedroom window cracked for air. Reaching around to his back pocket, he whipped out the screwdriver. "Riddle me, riddle me, ree, Catonia's about to find something she doesn't want to see," he said lowly to Bubba.

Keeping silent, he slid the flat head between the screen and the frame, levered it until he heard the satisfying snap of the catch breaking free on one side, then pushed the screen all the way up. Taking the poor dead snake out of the sack he handed it to Bubba. The cat immediately clamped onto his valuable prey.

"Don't muff this, Pal." He pushed the window up so

Bubba had plenty of clearance. "Our future depends upon you."

Lifting the cat, he barely got him halfway to the window frame before Bubba was already vaulting through. The cat pushed off against his chest, shoving Royce back a step. He watched Bubba dash to Catonia's antique bed, hop onto the spread, and then deposit his heartfelt gift for his beloved.

Royce adjusted the curtains so he could see through the narrow gap of the drapes, yet Catonia wouldn't immediately spot him. He chuckled as Bubba jumped down on the far side of the bed, where he was hidden from view. Bloody cat. Too human by half! Bubba and he didn't have long to wait. The shower fell silent; then Catonia was moving about in the other room. He nearly held his breath, waiting to hear that door creak open.

Barefooted and clad in a big bath towel, Catonia padded to the built-in wardrobe and disappeared within. *Be still my beating heart,* Royce heaved a sigh. He couldn't see directly into the closet due to the angle of the door, but that big arse mirror was at the perfect tilt to provide him a clear view of her dropping the towel. It revealed that perfect body, slick with beaded moisture from the steamy shower.

Royce blinked thrice as his view was suddenly blocked. Ready to growl, he recalled he was wearing his glasses, reached up, snagged them off his nose and stuck them in his shirt pocket. By damn, he missed the show as the light in the closet flicked off and Catonia came shuffling out. Shuffling, because she wore a pair of footed Bunny PJs, the kind little kids wear. A stark contrast—sexy Catonia in such virginal nightwear—that his body nearly cramped from the punch of blood that hit his groin. So wrapped up in watching those footies—and all his blood having gone south—he totally forgot about the damn snake until she screamed.

He jerked in response, his head slamming upward against the window frame. She whipped around at the noise he'd made, then right back to the bed as Bubba hopped up on the bed and began meowing for praise and pats.

"You!" She hurled the one word accusation, though Royce wasn't sure if she addressed Bubba or him.

While Catonia spluttered for words, Royce took the opportunity to hoist himself inside through the window. He managed the maneuver rather deftly, but at the last second, his boot buckle became tangled with the curtains. Too busy trying not to land on his face, he ended up wrapped in the stupid drapes and lying on his back at Catonia's feet–her bunny feet.

"You look like a pig in a blanket," she said.

He sighed, looked up the long legs encased in pink flannel, to the hands on her hips, forced himself to get past bunny boobs, and finally reached her glaring face. Her kissable mouth was pursed into a sour expression.

"This...isn't working out quite how I planned it." Royce offered her a winning grin. From the bed Bubba meowed.

Her face darkened. *Storm warnings on the horizon.* "You *planned* it? I'd never guess you had a plan. It seemed more on par with fools rush in–"

"Fools and Royce Kinross." He should get up, but suddenly he was too tired. No sleep for three days and too much Scotch had taken their toll. Pathetically, he stayed where he was, looking up at the woman he loved more than life. "I love you, Catonia."

She huffed. "What about your wife?"

"There's *no* wife. I told the truth. I divorced her nearly three years ago. My guess, she came around for money, and when she couldn't find me, saw a new way to get attention and finances. She received cash for the stories, used them to flush me out of hiding, and likely assumes I'll pay her to go away again. If you hadn't been intent on punishing me for David's mistakes, you'd have given me a chance to tell you, and neither of us would've spent three days in Hell."

He tried to move; groaned when his leg didn't appreciate being bent at the odd angle.

Instantly, Catonia was on her knees beside him, her face filled with worry. Bubba padded over and sniffed Royce's cheek, but he reached up to push the silly feline back.

"Royce, are you all right?" Her voice quivered with concern.

Okay, he wasn't above using a little empathy to a higher purpose. "My leg's numb. If you'll let me rest for a moment." She ran her hands over his body, as if to make certain nothing was broken. Being a male he just lay there and took the 'punishment'. *Oh, yeah, punish me, baby!*

"Oh dear, you have a knot on your leg." Catonia's eyes reflected puzzlement as she felt the ring box in his pant's pocket. Ferreting it out, her brows raised as she lifted the velvet lid.

"Marry me, Catonia?" He shoved Bubba back and levered up on his arms to sit. "Make Bubba and me happy."

Her hand shook as she stared at the ring that seemed so perfect for her. "This is how you propose? Breaking and entering? Crawling through my window, having that demon kitty spawn stick a snake in my bed?"

"I was supposed to make a heroic entrance and rescue you." Royce reached up and brushed the tear from her cheek. "Think of the wonderful tales we will have for the grand-children."

She gnawed on the corner of her lip for a heartbeat. "But I don't want to marry a marquis."

"Get over it. Bubba and I aren't taking no for an answer.

A shadow of a smile played over her sexy mouth. "You won't, hmm?"

"Absolutely, positively, we shan't accept a no. Bubba and I might have to hogtie you—as Jack so colorfully puts it—and feed you snake until you give in and say you'll marry us."

A chuckle shuddered through her, but she managed to keep it suppressed. Just barely. "Us?"

He hung his arm around the cat. "Bubba and I are a package deal."

She reached out to brush a stray curl off his forehead, her eyes so full of love. "Since you two leave me no choice..." Her hand moved to his cheek and cupped it. "I love you and that silly beast, so I guess I better marry you."

Bubba stuck out his chest and meowed proudly. Mission accomplished!

***

Chicken What Du Hell is a sequel to the award-winning
Bad Cat from No Law Against Love.
Reviewers International Award of Excellence – 2006 –
Best Short Story
PEARL Award Nominee for Best Short Story 2006

Chicken What Du Hell

Ingredients

1/2 cup chopped green onions
1-tablespoon dried parsley
1-teaspoon garlic powder
3-cups water or chicken stock
3-tablespoons steak sauce
1 to 2-teaspoons Louisiana hot sauce (to taste)
4-cups peeled tomatoes
4-cups boneless boiled chicken pieces, from a chicken boiled in water to cover
1 cup of white wine

Directions

Mix the green onions, parsley and garlic powder with 2 cups of the water and set aside. Let this mixture soak for about 1 hour.

Meanwhile, combine the remaining 2 cups water, the wine, tomatoes, steak sauce, hot sauce and peeled tomatoes in a large pot and cook for about 30 minutes over a low fire.

Add the vegetables and liquid to the pot of cooked chicken and simmer for 30 minutes over a low fire.

Serve on a bed of rice.

A Very Special Man

Simon leaned close to the woman—*his woman*—his nose pressing to her softly fragrant skin, drowning, almost drunk on her female essence. His mind hummed with possession. She *belonged* to him. *Only him.* He could lie here for hours, his brain absorbing her womanly scent, the heady phero-mones weaving into the magic that formed her 'signature'. Blindfold him and put her in a room with a thousand other women and he'd go straight to her unerringly. His skin burned, on fire with the drive to claim her, brand her as *his* in the most primitive, elemental way, bond with her until she admitted his possession, his ownership. Welcomed it. There was only *one* woman in the whole world that could spin this primeval enchantment, hold him spellbound. Enthralled.

Desdemona.

Desdemona Vashon was the light in his universe. His sole purpose for drawing each and every breath. *His life.* No matter how depressed he became at his current situation, she'd run those magic fingers over his back, sending a shiver through his muscles; suddenly, he cared for nothing but those gentle strokes, of lying with her at night, his head pillowed against her breast. Then, and only then, all his problems seemed to vanish.

There was only Desdemona.

She was pure magic, and he loved her with every fiber of his being. He would die for her, his Desdemona.

Of course, he didn't call her that. For nearly a year they had lived together, and during all that time, to him she was Dezzy. That suited her better. She was absentminded, loving and loyal. He had a feeling, silly female, she would die for him, too. Dezzy was special in ways he couldn't began to speak...*for more reasons than one.*

Simon yawned and stretched. Nothing like a lazy nap on a snowy night in Dezzy's bed. He rolled over to be closer to her, absorb her radiant warmth. Very carefully, so not to awaken her, he reached out and hooked the soft silk of her ice blue chemise, then slowly dragged it down the slope of her breast, the pink nipple pebbling in reaction to the drag of the material. Finally, he exposed that soft crest. By damn, Dezzy had the most beautiful breasts! His reaction to her near naked perfection hit him dead center in his chest—*and lower*—to where he found it hard to draw air. He wanted her so much, worshipped her as a man would worship *the woman* who was above all others.

Loved her so much it hurt.

With a slight murmur, she shifted in her sleep. Just a small adjustment. He grinned when her pale breast was exposed further. The fire in the fireplace had died down, letting the cool night air caress her skin with a chill, and in response her areola tightened, puckered, causing that berry of a nipple to jut out even more. Oh, he wanted to close his mouth around it, suckle it slowly while she slept, allow the sensations to filter into her dreams. Then gradually, he'd bring her awake with a burning hunger. As her eyes would flutter open, he'd draw hard, causing her to come. She was so responsive he knew that would be all it'd take.

Breathing shallow, his heart pounding, he watched her beautiful face, judging how deeply she was napping after the small stirrings. As sleep's serenity smoothed her countenance, he smiled. Lifting his head, he leaned close and gently rasped his tongue against the nubbin of flesh. He wanted to close his mouth around that soft breast, however, that would disturb his Sleeping Beauty.

For now, he needed her to slumber, to dream. *Dream of me wanting you, Dezzy. Me tasting you...taking you, Dezzy. See the real me as I make you come, deep and hard.*

Love me. Only me.

A small shudder of sexual awareness rippled through her body, finally reaching her lips in one of those half-sexy, half-agony expressions as desire rose within her. Simon smiled, satisfied. He knew when she slept her mind was open to him, heard him just as clearly as if he spoke. It told him so much about the *rightness* of their bond. Everything would be perfect for them; he'd make her so happy...just as soon as they handled a *certain problem* or two resulting from it.

It couldn't be soon enough for him. If only he could figure out the key. The riddle's answer just remained out of reach.

With a wicked grin, he lowered his head and closed his hot mouth around her cool breast, sucked on it in a slow fashion to feed her dreams about him, yet not enough to awaken her. He savored watching her when she dreamed of him, of their being together, of him taking her in a hundred different ways. In her dreams, he touched her mind as well as her body, causing him to relish this telepathic connection they shared. Drawing on her nipple, he watched as her breathing grew faster, shallow, as she started to ride the crest of passion, of needing him.

Craving only him.

Desdemona didn't want to waken. The dream was too delicious. *Utterly delicious.* Her body tensed, driving to a hot pinnacle, the pulsating blindness thrumming from the need, such intense responses to her dream lover. His coming to her in dreams was more frequent of late. He was beautiful, long of body, lean, but with those recoiled muscles you would find in a big cat, a tiger or a panther. *Yeah, a panther*—that's what he reminded her of. His hair was blue-black and wavy, so sleek to the touch. She wanted to fist her fingers in the thick mass, as she wrapped her legs around his narrow waist—

"Oh, Simon," she sighed breathlessly.

Simon? That shattered the realness of her dream! *What the hell?* Why was she calling *his* name?

An annoying buzz shattered her wonderful vision. She squinted at the clock—couldn't see it since she'd removed her contacts last night. Reaching out blindly, she swatted in the general direction and finally tagged the snooze button on the third try. She shivered. With an unladylike grump, she felt around for the duvet to pull over her head, cuddle for those fifteen more minutes, only there was no quilt to snuggle under.

"Well, bugger." She sat up and searched for the blasted thing. On the floor. Again. For some reason, despite usually hugging her 15-tog duvet the way Linus did his blanket, she'd kicked it off every night this week. So unlike her.

Nothing was on the bed, but the large—*very large*—black cat with pale amber eyes. Staring at her. The beast lay on the bed, smiling. Sometimes, her cat wore eerily human expressions. She noticed her gown had slipped down so she pulled it up. As she did, the cat leered at her. His eyes flashed with... well, it *was*...a leer! When she blushed and finished tugging the gown back into place, the silly feline smiled.

"Simon, you're spooky."

She glanced over at the calendar hanging on the wall

seeing it was the 23rd of December. Today she planned to decorate her Christmas tree. To reinforce that dour determination, she announced, "I shall absolutely positively trim the tree tonight." Simon murred in his throat, so she patted his head. "Very well, *we* shall trim the tree."

She eyed the sprig of mistletoe sealed in plastic, sitting on her dresser. On impulse she'd bought it when she was going through the checkout line at the drugstore. A waste of money, she sighed. For the past week, she kept saying, *today is the day*. She'd even gotten as far as getting the trunk with the decorations down from the attic and putting up the Christmas tree last night—lovely though artificial. Even so, she couldn't find the heart to trim it. It sat in the corner by the fireplace, undecorated and—

"Unloved. Just like me," she said glumly.

Purring loudly, Simon pushed to his feet and came to bump his head against her chest. He did that a lot. The silly cat was bizarre. He had the strangest habit of sticking his nose in her cleavage—or worse, her crotch! Odd times, he even stole her panties and lay on them. Still, Simon loved her. That she didn't doubt. Sadly, she couldn't think of anyone else who did, thus she tended to ignore the eccentricities of her feline.

She scratched his ear and then lifted his huge head, putting a kiss on the tip of his nose. "Yeah, big boy. I know you love me." The rumble of his purr deepened as he crawled into her lap and wanted to cuddle. Forty pounds of cat was a lot to cuddle, but when Simon wanted to cuddle *you cuddled!*

"I'm not a fortunate person, Simon. However, Lady Luck smiled the day I opened the door and found you sitting in the rain on the welcome mat." She hugged his warm, vibrating body, glad of his companionship. "Okay, today we decorate, pal. I keep putting it off since it seems rather impractical to go through all the trouble just for you and me. But, hey, we're special, eh? I'm blessed to have my gran's house, my health and you. Maybe soon I'll sell a book—get that call, as they say. In any case, the to-do list for today: breakfast, then trim the tree, maybe we'll even tie big plaid bows around the lampposts at the end of the drive. And after lunch I shall start a new book. How about a paranormal...a woman visited by a ghostly lover, and I'll name the hero after you. Would you like that?"

"Meeeeeeeeee-ow!" He stuck his chest out proudly.

The doorbell buzzed, disturbing their scratch session.

Simon went into instant attack mode. The blasted beast was as big as a medium-size dog. In fact,

Mavis Beaumont's pit bull—the terror of the neighborhood—actually ran when the stupid dog spotted Simon.

"Aw crud. I forgot the DirecTV guy was coming this morning." She snatched up her jeans and shimmied into them. Yanking off her teddy, she tugged on a red pullover sweater.

The bell sounded again as she hurried to the front door. "Coming!" she called loudly, hoping he wouldn't give up and go away. A movie addict, she was looking forward to getting the satellite dish—her Christmas present to herself.

Desdemona opened the door and was surprised to find an attractive man, with a jacket that said *Kelvin Electronics* on a patch on the left side of his chest, and the name Jordon embroidered above the company's logo. Around her age, he was a few inches taller than she, and he had a pleasant smile.

"Thought you'd forgotten I was coming. My name is Jordon Gleason; I'm the DirecTV rep for this area. I came to install your dish." He glanced at the work order on his clipboard. "You wanted receivers in the bedroom and living room, and a *Tivo*?"

She swung the door open. "Yes, that's right. Thanks for coming."

Simon jumped upon the back of the couch to glare and growl at the repairman. Desdemona sighed. She feared this would happen when she'd made the appointment. Anytime there was a man between twenty-five and forty-five in the house, the silly beast went into attack mode.

"Geez, Louise. What are you doing with a panther in the house, lady?" The man stopped just inside the door, watching the cat with a cautious air.

Desdemona shook her head at Simon doing his usual once over of any male that *dared* put a foot over the threshold of the front door. "Ignore him. That's Simon. He's just a house cat—well, a very large house cat. He tends to vet any male that comes into the house."

"Looks more like a small panther to me. Are you sure it's safe to keep him? Isn't it illegal to keep exotic animals or something?"

"Seriously, he's just a housecat. Nothing more," she assured him, moving to intercept Simon as he closed in for an inspection of Gleason. She was used to Simon's protective mode, but realized to someone unfamiliar with him, the cat would appear formidable. She took hold of his fancy collar and gave it a small shake to redirect his attention. "Feed... the...kitty?"

"I don't mean to argue with you, lady, but that cat is more. *A whole lot more.* You're smart to keep him fed. I don't cotton to a panther taking a chomp out of my rear." The poor man looked uncomfortably at Simon, still she gave him credit as he reached out and gingerly petted the cat's forehead. "Nice, kitty, kitty."

Simon's eyelids lowered and he gave the man a grin. Of course, with Simon a grin was closer to a smirk, like he'd sized up his next meal. He loved doing that to people. It was uncannily human how he interacted with people, as if he fully understood everything they thought and said. Sometimes, it proved damn unnerving. Simon refused to budge until he'd given the man a thorough once-over.

"Simon the mighty watch-cat," she chuckled under her breath, tugging him back.

Satisfied the workman was no imminent threat, Simon hopped down and followed her into the kitchen while the man went outside to collect the boxes that contained her satellite dish, receivers and *Tivo* from his van. Still keeping an eye on the living room, Simon ambled to the kitchen chair at the table and sat, patiently waiting while she fixed him some fresh prawns and halibut. Simon refused to eat if she put food in a bowl on the floor; his plate had to be in a chair. Oddly, she wasted money if she tried to offer him canned cat food. He loved good ground chuck, raw or cooked, enjoyed seafood, but none of the cheap stuff. How the cat survived before finding his way to her door she couldn't begin to guess.

She placed the sliced seafood before Simon, then went to pour a glass of milk for her and some in a bowl for him. When she glanced over at the feline, he grinned at her. "Silly cat." She chuckled.

Life had been pretty crappy the last three years, but now Simon was here. She was never alone as long as he was with her. As if he read her thoughts, he arched up on his huge paws, so he could lean against her as she sat his milk down. Desdemona reached out and stroked his midnight fur. Simon had this unusual patch of hair between his ears. The rest of his body was sleek, so glossy it had a sheen. But on top of his head, between his ears, it was thicker, wavier.

She smiled, then petted him. "My life changed for the better when you came to my door that snowy night."

Simon bumped against her thigh and then rubbed, going, "Meeeeee...um."

Almost sounded like me, too.

"My wishful imagination."

Same old, same old. Every night the identical routine, Simon sighed: feed the kitty, nuke—her word, for he had *no idea* what it meant—a Stouffers' dinner for herself, then Dezzy goes to the box on her desk and works her fingers on that things she calls a keyboard and fiddles to no point he could see with that bloody thing she said was a mouse, which really wasn't a mouse. *Poor delusional woman.* While he refused to eat *any* mouse—for various reasons—he, at least, did know they were different from that hard-shell turtle she scooted around on the tabletop.

Simon's tail twitched.

Well, he liked the *feed the kitty* part. He soon had trained Dezzy that he wouldn't eat just any old thing, though she still insisted on giving him catnip toys.

He'd merely eyed her with disdain. He'd been in this condition for so long, *the why* he was the way he was, and how he got in this state in the first place, was beyond him. As time had gone on, he lost more of himself—the man—and adapted into his role of the cat. Peculiar, after so many years he'd seemed to have given up and just accepted his condition.

It wasn't until he'd come to Dezzy's door that he recalled he was actually something other than a cat. What that *other* was still remained elusive for the moment. But the more he was with Dezzy, the more he wanted her, the stronger the male in him became, and the less he liked living—for the want of a better term—in a cat suit.

I am not a cat. I am not a cat. The more he repeated that sentence like a mantra, the closer he came to grasping the mystery of this bizarre situation. Once he did, he was sure Dezzy and he could unravel...whatever it was he needed to unravel.

While *The Man* had been here, Simon had stretched out on the back of the sofa to keep an eye on the stranger, not trusting the interloper. He'd looked Dezzy over and licked his chops. Oh, he'd been sly about it. Only another male would recognize the telltale signs. Why Dezzy needed him—*Simon Attack Cat Extraordinaire*. His size and feral nature tended to see men back off instead of coming on to her. That was worth a chuckle, but every time he attempted to laugh poor

Dezzy thought he was trying to cough up a hairball and got in a dither.

Dezzy split the tray of Chicken Alfredo between her plate and his. He grinned. He loved Chicken Alfredo. The Stouffers' person always put big chunks of chicken in the cheese and noodles. He wasn't sure who that guy Alfredo was—maybe one of the Stouffers' cooks?—but he liked it when Dezzy fixed this for him. Since he'd come to live with her, she had begun to eat better. When he'd first arrived, she often skipped meals, or forgot them entirely, busy clicking keyboard keys and scooting that fake mouse around. He soon fixed that. Once she saw he refused to eat something called *9-Lives*—shudder—and wanted what she'd termed as 'people food', she'd shopped for stuff they both could enjoy. She said it was fun to have someone else to cook for. If only he could get her to give him some wine instead of that *Nestles'* water in a bottle. He was not sure why people this day and time felt the need to stick water in a bottle.

"I shouldn't give you the biggest portion of the chicken chunks, Simon. You really were a spaz while the satellite guy was here," she fussed.

Spaz? What the bloody hell is a spaz, pray tell? It didn't sound like something he wanted to be. Maybe it was worse than being a cat. Possibly a dog! Simon glared at her, barely hearing her words. Dezzy tended to prattle to him. He had an idea she was lonely. *Dezzy needs a man.*

"...he might even have asked me out if you hadn't been stalking him." She put the plate down before him, but he was too busy frowning at her to pay attention.

I said she needed a man. I didn't mean any man. The idea of Mr. Jerk with the big grin putting his arm around *his* Dezzy didn't set well on his stomach.

I might be getting a megrim. Did cats get a megrim? Oh, well, perhaps it was indigestion. Human frailties often confuse me of late.

He closed his eyes in frustration. *I am not a cat. I am not a cat. Say it ten times, Simon, and click your ruby slippers...*

"Come on, eat up. Then, we'll set about decorating the tree." She pushed the plate toward him in encouragement. "I got you some neat presents," she nattered on.

Simon sniffed. *Better not be any more catnip mousies, I am running out of places to stash them. Silly woman thinks it's a game—me hiding them everywhere, says it's similar to Hide & Go Seek. Yeah, I hide and she goes and seeks.*

Dezzy sat down in her chair and then took a bite of chicken. Waving her fork, she said, "You know what I wish?"

Wish? That triggers something in my brain. The male brain, not the cat brain. Something about a wish. Only what?

Simon watched intently. He knew what *he* wished. He could imagine taking her wrist, and pulling her to stand. Dezzy would get that confused look on her beautiful face—her kissable, adorable face. He would nuzzle that soft spot on her throat, where her pulse pounded. Then, he'd back her against the table, bending her onto its surface, and teach her that his tongue had other talents...*hmm*...besides washing his fur.

Sometimes, being a feline domesticus really is the pits.

"Simon, are you ignoring me?" Dezzy asked. "You're looking at me very strangely. You aren't eating. You love Chicken Alfredo." She reached out and touched his nose. "It's cold. I guess you're not sick." Suddenly, big tears welled in her brown eyes. "Don't you go and get sick on me, Simon. It'd be the last straw. I need you."

Frustration rose in him. He wanted Dezzy. Wanted to make love to her in a hundred ways. But he wanted more, *so much more.* He wanted to laugh with her, hold her while she cried. He wanted to topple kingdoms and give her the moon and stars. Teach her there was still magic in the world. He loved Dezzy so. It was maddening to have to sit here and pretend to be a cat. If he could only have Dezzy in this manner, then so be it. He'd do anything to stay with her. Maybe that was his punishment.

Punishment. That caused his skin to ripple. There was something about the word which caused a reaction in him, same as the word *wish.* He sighed. Whatever the meaning, it was too illusive for him to snatch from the fog of his brain.

"Simon, do hurry and clean your plate so I won't worry about you. Then we can trim the tree and watch our new two-hundred plus channels." Dezzy touched her napkin to her mouth. The action made Simon yearn to kiss her so much. Dezzy's Chicken Alfredo kisses would be heaven!

He knew kissing Dezzy would be sublime; one of those things he wasn't sure *how* he knew—he just did. He'd kiss her softly, slowly, bringing a sigh to her lips. He wanted Dezzy to be happy. Sometimes, he had the feeling she was very sad, and that brought pain to his chest.

If eating his meal reassured Dezzy, then he could scarf the dinner down. Scarf was a new word he'd gotten from watching that Bart Simpson person, one of the people in that other bizarre box Dezzy called tell-a-vision. Strange little person, all yellow. *But then, who am I to quibble? I'm a cat.* He nearly groaned. *I am not a cat. I am not a cat. I am not a bloody cat!*

Making short work of the chicken and noodles, he licked the last bit off his nose. *Nose?* Simon nearly went cross-eyed staring down at it. The action of his tongue was one of those now automatic to him—the cat side asserting itself. He simply found it outlandish he performed personal hygiene mainly with his tongue! Until he found Dezzy nearly a year ago, he'd forgotten all these *man thoughts*. He was merely a cat, content to be a cat. Dezzy made him yearn for something more...if he could only recall how he got this way. There had to be a key to fulfilling Dezzy's wishes.

Wishes...the word skittered along his skin again.

"Simon you're so silly like that. I didn't know cats could look cross-eyed." She leaned forward and cupped his chin, then kissed his nose. "I love you, pal. I wish..." She sighed. "Well, never mind. Gran said if wishes were horses beggars would say giddy up."

Simon barely heard her. The words *I wish* hit his brain like a witch's charm—*three-times-three, let it be*—and caused a mild explosion within him. *That was it! Dezzy has to make a wish then kiss my nose. So bloody simple I feel stupid for not recalling it before. Only, how do I convey that to her?*

"Come on, pal, I'm suddenly in the mood to decorate," she said, setting the plates in the sink.

Simon couldn't recall anything about horses or beggars, but he understood if Dezzy would only believe and make the wish, everything would come true, and it would, indeed, be a Christmas to remember.

Well, now that she had DirecTV, Desdemona was swamped with too many choices. *HBO, Showtime, Starz, Cinemax*...and several of each of them. Movies, movies and more movies! Unable to choose, she put on the nature channel, thinking Simon might enjoy the segment they were airing on big cats. He twitched his long tail and shot her a disgusted look.

"Okay, what about *How The Grinch Stole Christmas?*" Switching over to the beloved Christmas cartoon, she tossed up her hands when Simon was instantly enthralled. "*Now* he's interested. Cat, you're a puzzle. Of course, you love the

Simpsons. Maybe you're a toon addict."

Simon tossed one of his human smiles over his shoulder to show he really liked *the Grinch*. Going to the hall closet, she dragged out the trunk where her gran had stored all the old ornaments. It'd been stowed in the attic, but she brought it down two weeks ago, though couldn't find the heart to face the memories that'd come with handling the treasured bulbs and ornaments. Most were old even when she was a kid.

In various ways, this was a sad holiday. She didn't have family, no sisters or brothers. Either all the aunts and uncles were dead, or she had no idea where they lived, losing touch decades ago. This was the first Christmas she'd lived in the house that had been her grandmother's. A beautiful turn of the century—the *other* century—Victorian 'gingerbread house', it was painted with the quaint shade similar to orange sherbet. Unhappily, she'd closed off the seven bedrooms upstairs, saving heating costs. It seemed a wasteful extravagance just for one person.

She was glad of the move here, yet though the house now belonged to her it hadn't fully sunk in that it was hers. As she was growing up, she'd spent a month in the summer visiting, and generally came at Thanksgiving and Christmas time. Still, despite changes she'd made to the house's space since settling in, she couldn't shake the sense that her stay here was merely another visit in a long line, as though she was in a state of waiting for *something* to happen. She didn't know what, but it was as though some wonderful incident would occur and change everything; until it did, life for her was in a strange suspension. The downstairs had a formal living room, a sitting room, dining room, a breakfast cozy, parlor, music room and drawing room. That was simply too many *rooms* used for sitting. She'd taken the music room and turned it into her bedroom, then converted the drawing room into her study where she labored to be a romance writer.

It was strange she'd chosen to write romances. Gran always thought her granddaughter would be a writer some day, but likely Cozy Mysteries or the next *To Kill a Mocking Bird* is what Madeline Vashon envisioned. No matter what Desdemona wrote, the romance always took over; she gave up and was going for the throat, so to speak. In spite, it seemed odd that she could write romances when she was such a failure in that department. Somewhere deep inside was still a little girl who believed in kissing a frog and getting a prince, had never stopped wishing for love and happily ever after, despite all the bad cards life had dealt her.

She glanced in the long mirror behind the console piano in the corner, catching sight of herself. It wasn't vain to say she was pretty. She had long, dark blond hair and big brown eyes. Men were always whistling at her when she jogged in the mornings. Only, few ever bothered to ask her out.

Going through a divorce was bad enough. Living in a small town had only made matters worse. Everyone whispered about her husband leaving her for another woman, pitied her. Then to compound the unpleasant situation, her soon to be ex-husband and the other woman were killed in a head-on car crash with a drunk driver. She reigned as topic of choice from the gossips for months.

Barely dealing with the fall out of that mess, the sad news came her grandmother had died in her sleep. Losing Gran was hard. She was surprised when the lawyer said Madeline willed her this marvelous old house and enough money to get by for a couple years. It was as if her grandmother were saying, *go for your dream,* and giving her the means to do so as a final gift.

Desdemona packed up her few cherished belongings, had a three-day yard sale with the rest—more money to live on while she worked to sell to some lucky publisher in New York. With hope riding in her heart, she'd moved in to her new home high on a hill at the edge of town. Started fresh. The only problem with moving into an older settled area, while she had lovely neighbors, most were married with kids or elderly. Not the best dating prospects.

But then, she didn't want to *date.* Dating was a lot of bother. She just wanted someone special to love, who loved her, someone to share her days.

"Not a lot to ask," she muttered. Simon came over and rubbed against her leg, clearly sympathizing with her dilemma. "Ah, Simon, I wish there was a man just like you, who loved me the way you do."

Well, bloody hell, the fool woman could've had her wish if she'd kissed me on the nose as she usually does. Last time she kissed me, then made her wish. The ritual was reversed so didn't work. A certain protocol to these things has to be observed. First the wish, then the kiss. Afterward, everything is possible. What is so ruddy hard in that?

Simon snapped his tail. His head whipped around and glared at it. He had to admit that for expressing your displeasure a snapping tail was a pretty nifty thing to have. Then he frowned. He knew he frowned because he could feel the space between his ears flex, but wasn't sure if real cats frowned. It'd been so long, it was hard to remember some things. *I am not a cat. I am not a cat. I am not a stupid, delusional cat!* Did he have a tail when he was in his other form? And precisely *what* was his other form? That there *was* another form he was growing surer of with every passing minute, merely some details still eluded his thoughts. It had been so long. *However, if Dezzy would simply make her wish and kiss my nose, then we could get down to Ho Ho time.*

Simon watched her lovingly handle the old Christmas ornaments. Since coming, he gathered that Dezzy hadn't always lived here, but it was the home of her *grand-mère.* Through one of Dezzy's constant prattles, he'd learnt she'd been married once. Obviously, the guy didn't deserve her. Simon sniffed. Actually, no mere mortal deserved his Dezzy. His lady needed magic in her life, and he fully intended to give it to her...just as soon as she made the bloody wish and gave him a kiss! *Hmm*, he communicated with Dezzy's mind when she was asleep. Perhaps, if she couldn't get her act together and make her wish soon, he'd reach her on that level and plant the suggestion of what she needed to do to release him from the dark spell.

Dezzy dangled the glittering garland before him, enticing him to chase it. Oh, well, until he got her to do her thing with the magic words and the kiss, why not be a cat? He might as well enjoy catdom for a little while longer.

Simon jumped down and ran around the living room, chasing the garland and making an utter fool of himself.

Ah, what a man won't do for the woman he loves.

Desdemona couldn't believe how gorgeous the tree was. Now she was sorry she'd put off decorating it for the past two weeks. Simon and she had a blast trimming it. They'd shared eggnog laced with rum. Ridiculous cat had gotten drunk, and was a sight staggering around. Now, he lay on the leather sofa on his back, totally blatzed, the stones of his collar reflecting the firelight.

Simon had been wearing that strange collar when she found him at her front door, just after she moved in last January. Late one night, as the clock had chimed twelve times for midnight, she'd heard a scratching at the front door. Opening it, she found him sitting there, his fur wet from the near freezing rain. Poor thing was tired, cold and hungry. After he'd been with her a few weeks, he'd started to put on weight. Fearing the collar was growing too tight for him, she'd tried to loosen it, only she couldn't find any way to release the catch. There was a small metal closure that almost looked like the head of a signet ring. However, there must be some trick to releasing it, and for the life of her, she'd failed to figure it out. Resorting to a quicker solution: she'd attempted to cut it off with a pair of sheers, only Simon grew very agitated. Afraid she'd accidentally injure him, she'd let it ride a few days. The next time she checked, it was oddly loose on his neck. An expensive collar, the glittering stones of yellow, green and red looked real. She was surprised a foundling ran around with such a high-priced choker about his neck.

Ready to call it a night, she went to check the front door was locked and the security chain in place. Absently peeking out the panes that ran up the side of the door, she stared down the long drive. It was snowing heavily, and obviously had been for some time. The heavy blanket of white made the whole hillside appear like a scene from some Victorian Christmas card.

"Oh, Simon, come look," she called in her excitement.

The cat gave a disgusted sigh at having to move from his comfy position, but finally padded over to her. She bent down and picked him up, hefting him into her arms so he could look out the panes, too.

"Isn't it beautiful? We're going to have a White Christmas. It's been years since I've had one. It's magical. Like something special is going to happen."

The cat shifted in her arms and put his front legs, one on either shoulder, and then looked at her nose-to-nose. It scared the bloody hell out of her! For a long minute, they stood staring into each other's eyes; suddenly she wasn't staring into the amber cat eyes, but the eyes of a man. She mentally tried to shake the notion, but the impression lingered.

The bloody cat smiled slyly, only she had a hard time remembering he was a cat. "Simon, I think I am losing it." She hastily put him down, eager to be rid of the bizarre impression. Peculiarly, it left her aching for the nearness of a man. "Let's turn out the lights in the house. Enjoy the tree and the falling snow, and see what my magic dish has on for us to watch. Surely with all these channels there'll be something good." Using the new remote she flipped through the menu.

"Ah, *A Christmas Story* in letterbox. Ralphie and his Red Rider bb gun is the perfect prescription to welcome Christmas Eve. I'll fetch us eggnog, poke the fire, and we can enjoy. Are we lucky or what, Simon?"

Lucky is watching Dezzy's cute derrière in her tight stretch jeans. Simon leered. *Ah, what a delightful sight.* But then Dezzy was a treasure from any angle. It was still surprising some man hadn't long ago seen Dezzy for the gem she is. He'd seen that repairman drooling. Jealousy rising, he'd been afraid he'd need to go into that scary attack-cat mode to set the man running. Dezzy was *his.*
Maybe tonight I shall get to show her that.
Dezzy came back and set the crystal cups of eggnog on the coffee table, then turned out the lights. Humming *Greensleeves*, she opened the glass doors on the fireplace and added a log, then poked several times with the poker to stir up the embers. Simon liked it when she hummed. It meant Dezzy was happy, and nothing was more important to him than that.
She settled down on the comfortable sofa, and put up her feet, then stretched out partially on her side. Seeking her nearness, Simon curled up next to her stomach. Dezzy stroked the length of his back, her touch soothing. His skin rippled, responding to the sheer sensuality. It made him crave that hand on his bare flesh. How long had it been since he felt that sensation? It hardly mattered. Nothing mattered but Dezzy. Everything would be new again with her.
As she watched the movie, the rum went to work. Dezzy was not a drinker, too much into fruit drinks and colas. She had, however, bought a bottle of *The Macallans* and kept it on a special shelf in her office. The wench planned to toast herself when she finally sold one of her romance books. Dezzy would sell. She had the soul, the heart of a romantic. It was just a matter of time until someone spotted that. Perhaps, she might want to toast another event: the return of Simon Glashiel Ravensdale, the seventh Viscount Moordon.
Wouldn't Dezzy be surprised? He wondered how she felt about being a Viscountess. Of course, he would be an earl now. His father would be long dead, naturally, but then they had never been close. Thus, he would be the eleventh Earl. Now that memories were returning to him, they came in a flood. His father had sent him away to France, which is what landed him into this mess. Creighton Ravensdale could not

accept his son's true nature, that his wife had been one of the *Cait Sidhe*, a race of witches originating from the Picts of Scotland. People of his blood had the ability to change into a cat nine times in their lifetime. His father had come upon Simon when he'd just turned seventeen, in the midst of undergoing the first transformation. Revolted, and perhaps a little scared by his son's 'unnatural abilities', his father had banished him to Paris, hoping...well, Simon couldn't remember what had been his father's intent. It hardly mattered now.

Simon was thrilled his memories were becoming clearer. It seemed the more he thought like a man, the more vividly he recalled his past, and now understood what happened to him. After his father turned his back on him, he had landed in a small village on the edge of Paris. Unfortunately—or in light of him ultimately finding Dezzy, fortunately—his path had crossed that of a woman, Tamina Wybranda. She was of Friesian blood, an ancient enemy of the Picts, though he failed to recall that fact upon their first meeting. From the start she'd targeted him for her lover, but Simon refused. Race memory, possibly, caused an immediate distrust of her and her motives. He learnt she was a witch, of modest talent she thought, who understood his powers only too well. She saw the chance to increase her abilities through controlling him.

When he refused her continual advances, she put him under a dark enchantment—come the seven nights of the next full moon he'd be unable to resist the change. Once transformed, he would stay in his cat shape until he found true love. Only a woman who loved him with her whole heart could break the spell. What he didn't know—Tamina fed him a potion that slowly triggered the change in him, and also dictated the type of cat he became. He tried to fight the curse, but each night the moon rose his resistance waned. As he understood what was happening to him, he'd set up a peculiar trust fund for the 'heirs' of the Viscount. All properties and funds would be held in trust until the new Viscount showed up with the seal of Moordon to prove he was the true heir to the line. In the end, his shapeshift was into that of a mere cat, not the panther form he usually took. Poor Tamina never understood just how powerful a witch she really had been.

It had been three centuries, three *long* centuries, so long, he began to forget who he was and give over to the cat side. Then, he found Dezzy. He could barely recall the various journeys that brought him from France, back to Scotland and then eventually to the Colonies. It'd been a slow path to Dezzy. That night, nearly a year ago, he felt so lost, and didn't know where his feet carried him. The rain was icy; he was tired and hungry. He just wanted a home and someone to love him. Suddenly, at the end of the long winding road, he saw the large house sitting up on the hill. The gates at the bottom of the drive had lampposts glowing softly. It seemed a welcome beacon.

And Dezzy had opened the door to him.

He stared at her now, drinking in her quiet beauty. Dezzy drifted toward dreamland unaware that he watched every breath, treasured every sigh. He opened his mind and allowed it to brush hers, judging how deeply she slept. It was imperative she'd reach a certain level, the stage when the subconscious is still awake while the consciousness slumbers. Lucid dreaming, some call it. When she reached that plane, her mind would hear him as clearly as if he spoke. He hoped to reach her and plant the suggestion of what she needed to do.

The clock on the mantle softly chimed the first of twelve times. *The Witching Hour.*

Simon smiled. When all things were possible.

Desdemona drifted. In the background, she heard Bugs Bunny wishing everyone a *Merry Christmas.* Distantly, she realized the shows must've switched, but she couldn't find the strength to get up and go to bed. She was resting peacefully, Simon's warm body lending his heat to make her cozy. On the fireplace mantle, the clock chimed.

Desdemona....

The sexy voice filtered through her light dream state. A voice of culture, British, with a hint of Scottish burr. Her dream lover. It was almost as if her body recognized him just by his nearness. Oh, why couldn't she find a man in real life like him? A very special man...someone who would love her, cherish her, hold her at night?

Desdemona...I am here. I love you. I cherish you above all others. Above my own life. I want to hold you...but first, you must make a wish.

A wish? Could it be that simple? She thought back on the past few years and all that had occurred to her. Surely, she'd made hundreds of wishes.

For a wish to work, you have to do it properly, lass. Different wishes require you to do different things and per-

*form them in a set order. You think you just say I wish and
abracadabra it would happen? This is magic, my love. You
have to assemble the right ingredients, work the ritual.*

What ritual? Desdemona thought this a strange dream.
Her night lover had never spoken of such things before.

*I have not spoken thusly because I had to know you are
the one. Trust is earned, Dezzy. I trust you because I love you
and know you love me. The clock is striking twelve. Now is
the moment. All you have to do is speak the words and kiss
the nose of your cat.*

She chuckled, stirring. That brought her awake more. Kiss
Simon? Dreams were silly things. *Garbage in-garbage out,*
they say. Yet, a dream also bespoke of your hidden desires.
Your guards were down and you were dealing with the
emotions and yearnings you couldn't hide from. She wanted
someone to share her life with, a man to laugh with...to have
him love her. Oh, she didn't expect anything extraordinary
like marrying Prince Charming. In fact, she doubted Prince
Baby really existed. But just to have that very special man,
one you would die for without a moment's hesitation, now
that would be a Christmas wish come true, indeed.

Simon stood on her chest and bumped his head against
hers. She chuckled. "Silly cat. You're not a small puss."

*All you have to do is speak the words and kiss the nose of
your cat and all you yearn for will be made real.*

What the hell? It was a lovely Christmas Eve dream.
Yawning, she struggled to open her eyes. The cat purred
loudly, rubbing his face against her cheek. Pushing him back
she tried to sit up. However, with Simon the baby leopard
standing on her chest, she couldn't muster enough strength.

"Oh, Simon. My dream told me to make a wish and kiss
your nose. My magical puttytat, eh?"

"Merrrrrrrrrrrrrrrrrrrrrrrrrr." He rumbled even louder.

She exhaled deeply. "Let's see if I can stay awake long
enough to do the ritual. Some ritual, kissing a cat on the nose.
Well, nothing ventured, nothing gained—here goes. I wish I
had a very special man who loved me, let me love him, and
that we could be so happy together."

She smiled at the whimsy. It wouldn't happen. There was
no Christmas Eve magic. No enchanted pussycat. Still...she
put her hands around Simon's large head. He had stopped
purring and seemed to be holding his breath, as if he waited
for her to finish the ritual.

"Simon, I love you. I don't know what I would do without

you." She pulled his big boy face down and kissed his nose. "There. I made my wish and kissed you. You're supposed to give me Mr. Tall, Dark and Handsome with a biffity boffity."

Hearing the clock tick on the mantle, she waited, holding her breath like Simon did, as though she truly expected something wondrous to happen.

Then it did. *The clock stopped ticking.* She could hear Burl Ives singing *Frosty the Snowman*, as another cartoon came on the screen, but the world held its breath. Slowly, her sleepy vision wavered. Simon got off her chest, but he still oddly hovered just above her. He became less distinct as if she looked at him through a fog. Then slowly, the smiling cat faded away, the swirling mists growing so thick they screened him. With a swirl the fog parted, Simon's face was no longer there.

She stared at the face of a man. A handsome man. A *beautiful* man. He had longish hair, which lay in waves around his face and brushed the back of his neck. Black hair. Not that dark brown that appeared black; this was true blueback. His eyes struck her, a pale amber that twinkled with a sexy smile.

Maybe wishes did come true.

Maybe she'd had too much eggnog.

Simon watched Dezzy's eyelids close. As he looked at her, his hands shook from wanting her so badly. *His Dezzy.* The woman he loved more than life. By damn, she'd done it—her love had broken his curse! *After all these years.* It had taken him traveling halfway around the world to find this one very special woman.

Only, it had been too long for him being in his *Cait Sidhe* form. He hardly knew how to stand or act as a man again. He wanted to share so many things with his Dezzy, but he had to rein in, control his eagerness, his ravenous hunger for her. She would need time to adjust to him being a man. *He* needed time to adjust to being a man.

Simon reached out and smoothed her hair away from her face, then with his index finger devotedly traced its contours. Loving that he could now touch her as a man. She wrinkled her nose as he kissed it. *His Dezzy.* What a precious gem she was!

Simon gently picked her up and carried her to the bedroom. His first steps were wobbly, but he quickly recalled the motions of walking upright on two legs instead of all fours. Ever so slowly, he placed her down on the bed, then reverently knelt down on his knees on the floor, his hands on the bed's edge, as he just watched her. With a near kitten mew, she stirred then settled on her side. Satisfied that she was resting, he slid off her jeans and left her in the soft sweater and her red thong. He smiled. His Dezzy had a secret passion for sexy underwear.

There was so much love inside his Dezzy just waiting for the right man to help her release it. And he was that man. Her very special man.

Right now, he wanted just to hold her. In the living room, *Rudolph the Red Nose Reindeer* played on the box. He liked cartoons. There was an innocence about them that appealed to him. The perfect backdrop to cuddle chastely with his Dezzy. He pulled the comforter over her, then lifted it so he could slide down beside her.

Holding Dezzy was pure heaven. And when daylight came and she opened her eyes, she'd see that wishes do come true.

For them both.

In the hours before dawn, Desdemona sighed deeply, a sound that nearly resembled a purr of contentment. She was so warm; the hot flesh curled against her and half over her was delicious. So nice to have a man to hold her.

A man?

Her eyelids flew open and she blinked, trying to see. Her vision was hazy; it took several heartbeats before she could actually focus. When she did, she stared into the smiling face of a handsome man. No, handsome failed to describe this beautiful male. She raised the cover and peeked under the duvet—the beautiful *naked* male!

"Holy Moly," she told herself. "I'm dreaming."

"Morning, Dezzy." The stranger reached up to stroke her cheek, then finally inclined to her and brushed a light kiss to her shocked mouth.

The kiss felt real. Oh boy it felt real! Dezzy? That's what her dream lover called her. He smiled slyly, then started to lean in to her for another kiss. She wanted that kiss, but this was simply *too much* for her mind to absorb. At the last second, she put a finger to his lips to stop him. The amber eyes flashed in devilment as his tongue stroked out and laved two fingers. In response, her toes started a slow burn—*she* started a slow burn.

"Kiss me, Dezzy, I've been waiting all night for you to

awaken." His eyes roved over her face as if she were the most rare and precious object he'd ever seen. "Waiting for you a very long time."

Bloody hell, how was a woman to resist that? If this was a dream it was a wonderful one. "So let me dream," she whispered to herself more than him.

"No, Dezzy. This *is* real."

Her brain barely registering his words, her hand reached out to touch him. So warm, so vital, his heart pounded under her palm as she placed it against his chest. Like a hungry child pressing its nose to the bakery window, she wanted this to be reality, only she knew the disappointment that could come in believing was too much to pay. Life had hurt her so many times before. She didn't think she could stand another disappointment. Unable to let go and trust, she stared into his pale eyes, mesmerized by the myriad of emotions reflected in them—everything she could hope to see in the man she loved —aching inside because, despite logic telling her otherwise, she so wanted this magic to be genuine.

A spark of hope ignited in her heart, only the fragile acceptance was instantly shattered, when her hand reached up to caress the side of his neck. It took a heartbeat for her mind to shift gears; when it did, she jerked straight up about six inches. This was beyond acceptance! She stood up in the bed, wobbling backward until her hips hit the headboard, and her head cracked against the wall.

"Ow..." Rubbing it, she stammered out, "Who...ar...are you? Wha...what are you?" She dragged the duvet up before her like a shield. "Tha...that's Simon's collar." *But Simon's collar would be too small for a man.* Feeling the onslaught of shock hitting her, she gazed at the devastatingly sexy man sitting on her bed, wearing nothing but a duplicate of her cat's choker.

"Who am I?" He smiled, rolled his eyes, then turned his hand to his chest and tapped it. "I am Simon."

"You are *not* my bloody cat." A note of hysteria crept into her voice.

One side of his mouth quirked up in a confused half-frown. "Actually, I am."

"Don't try to tell me that. *Don't even start.*" Desdemona skirted around the edge of the bed, dragging the comforter with her.

"Oh, but I must. I *am* Simon. To be specific, I am Simon Glashiel Ravensdale, Viscount Moordon, Earl Glendour, and I am most pleased to finally be able to converse with you, Dezzy." He reached out and stroked her calf muscle. "Touch you."

"Don't say that! You *cannot* be Viscount somebody or other and a cat, too." She waved her free hand to add impact to her sentence.

"You spoke the words, '*I wish I had a very special man who loved me, let me love him, and that we could be so happy together.*' Then you kissed me on the nose. You broke the spell and set me free." He tilted his head in challenge, daring her to refute it.

Desdemona felt the blood drain from her brain. Words she'd spoken to Simon before kissing him on the nose. No one else was in the house. *There was only one way he could know...*

He just grinned when her mouth worked trying to find logical words and came up empty. And oddly enough, there was something about the eyes...a glittering, light shade of amber that reminded her of—*Simon!* Where was he? He rarely left her side. Where was her cat? Warily, she eased off the bed, stepping down, doing her best not to fall while still holding the quilt up between them. The man didn't move, merely watched her intently. *Just like Simon does.*

"Simon? Here, kitty kitty." Keeping a half eye on the stranger in her bed, she whistled, lifting the dust ruffle to peek under the bed. "Simon. Here, kitty kitty. Please come here. *Please...*"

With a panther's power, he lunged crosswise over the bed's plane and snatched the quilt. She didn't even have time to blink, though she gave a small squeal. With one jerk, he spun her like a top until she landed across the bed, her legs half-dangling over the edge. Before she could draw a breath, he was over her, his hands on the bed beside her shoulders, and his knees planted on either side of her thighs. He was still smiling, but there was a predator's gleam of triumph of having cornered his prey.

"No, *here*, kitty kitty," he smirked. The penetrating gaze bore into hers, almost seeming to read her mind. "Yes, to some degree I read your thoughts and emotions. It tells me how perfect we are together. I have never experienced that until I came to you, Dezzy." He frowned down at the duvet as if it were a snake. "I don't like this thing between us." He snatched it away and tossed it to the floor, landing in the same spot where she'd found her quilt every morning this past week.

A frission shuddered through her, but one of sexual awareness not fear. Odd, here she was pinned under a very virile man—*a very virile naked man in a cat collar*—and yet, she didn't fear him. Logic said she should be screaming, or trying to bash him over the head with the lamp on the nightstand—things a person usually did when they awakened to a naked stranger in their bed. Instead, as she stared into the mesmerizing eyes, the hungry side of her, lonely too long, roared to life.

She shut her eyelids tightly trying to focus her thoughts. "Things like this just do not happen."

"They do and did. I understand the change is jarring—"

"Jarring? *Jarring?*" Her voice rose. "I go to sleep cuddled up with my cat—"

He countered, "You went to sleep very lonely, aching for someone to love you."

With those simple words he disarmed her in a fashion she couldn't fight.

He saw into her, understood her need to love and be loved. She swallowed hard struggling against the tears.

"Accept me. I am your very special man. Oh, Dezzy, for so long I have watched you, hungered for you, wanted you. It was maddening." The emotions were clear in his eyes, and threaded in the reed of his voice. "You are the light in my life. My reason for going on. Without you there would be no meaning to my existence."

His softly spoken words cut straight to her womb, it contracting and cramping with the need to believe him, then the power slammed into her heart. She wanted him with a soul deep craving that went beyond the physical, beyond simple emotions. In that simple breath, she didn't know how or why, she just understood magic *did* exist.

"Simon..." The name came on a whisper of awe, of her yielding.

He smiled relief, victory, and perhaps even a little vindication in her acceptance...her surrender. "I love you, Dezzy. I have never felt what you bring to me, never felt as if I belonged to another human being. Never wanted to possess one as I want to possess you, own you, brand you. Love me, Dezzy."

He lowered his soft lips to hers, gently tasting her, coaxing her to open to him. Despite the overwhelming circumstances, the implausibility, she did believe him, did want him. Kissing Simon was magic, pure and simple. Anything else failed to say what he made her feel.

Heat filled the pit of her belly, making her nearly cramp with intense yearning, then it ricocheted, sped like wildfire to scorch her heart. She was dizzy, aching with a primeval need to belong to this very unusual man. To be one with him. The scent off his skin was an aphrodisiac, filling her mind until nothing else mattered but Simon. All the worries and the questions would have to wait. Nothing was more important than this moment, than touching him, having him touch her.

He pulled back, watching, waiting. He wanted her to offer her surrender, not to take it.

Simon...her mind whispered; it felt like coming home. In some ways in her heart, she'd never grown up, always believing in faerytales and wishes that come true. Here was her chance...if only she were brave enough. Life had often tried to beat her down, to take away her hopes, teaching her to dream was to open herself up to disappointment and pain. It felt like stepping off a cliff, but as she stared up into the amber eyes she knew Simon would 'catch her'.

"Kiss me, Simon. Fill this empty ache inside me I've lived with for too long. My heart has so much love to give."

"As you wish, my lady." Simon smiled. "Touch me... *please*. I loved how you stroked me before; it made me yearn for those soft hands to touch the *real* me. I used to lie here in this bed at night and watch you and dream, yearn, crave. You are so beautiful, and I wanted you so much."

She reached up and stroked his face, his planes and shadows merging to form a countenance that enthralled her with its perfection. The long eyelashes, the intensely focused eyes, the aristocratic nose, and high cheekbones all saw Simon Ravensdale everything a woman could dream of. Resisting her deepest dream a woman would have to be foolish. And while she was scared of being hurt, she was *never* foolish.

She put her arms around his neck, letting her fingers twine in this thick waves of the blue-black curls. "Want me, Simon. I need to be wanted very badly, I need to be loved."

"I shall cherish you, worship you, adore you." Simon nuzzled her cheek, then chained kisses along her jawline.

Her heart pounded, erratic, as his soft lips traveled down the column of her neck where he paused to suck on the pulse point where her blood throbbed strongest. Her flesh stung, as she felt the graze of his teeth. She had a feeling Simon's teeth were a wee bit sharper than an ordinary male.

He raised up, conquest glittering in his pale amber eyes. "I marked you, my love—my first sign of possession. I shall mark you many more times before I am through. Understand, my dearest Dezzy, I am feral in many ways. I mate for life... same as a wolf. Does that alarm you?"

Soft laughter bubbled in her throat. "Alarm me? It *terrifies* me, Simon. But I think it's a trait a woman would kill to experience." Laughter died as her lower lip quivered with emotion. All shields down, she admitted, "It's what I need."

"I can give you that and more, lass," he promised.

Her smile was weak, still afraid to dare accept. "Show me, Simon."

"It would be my intense pleasure." He brushed a soft kiss over her lips, so light like the flutter of butterfly wings. Relishing every tiny touch, his eyes studied her small reactions.

Desdemona couldn't think, could hardly draw air. She turned into a being of sensations, lost to the power of overwhelming emotions, of the sensual response to his nearness, his heat. His potent pheromones washed over her, through her, priming her body for her surrender...*his possession.* There was only Simon and this breath-stealing shard of time, a space where for once magic ruled.

The light kisses weren't enough; she wanted more. Using the leverage of her arms around his neck, she tried to pull him to her. Only, Simon's strength was amazing and he literally raised her off the bed to sit, teasing her, pleased by her demonstration of hunger.

"Kiss me, Simon," she whispered against his mouth. "Really kiss me."

He hesitated for a heartbeat, his eyes dancing from merriment. "Well, if you insist."

His mouth took her savagely, devouring, demanding, sending her insides to twist into a knot of need. Feeling heavy, her breasts pressed against his chest. She gasped surprise then pleasure as his hands grabbed the hem on the red sweater, and with a quick twist skimmed it up her body and over her head, leaving her bare for his inspection. He just stared at her, his thoughts unreadable. A moment of fear flashed through her almost making her want to cover her breasts with her arms. But then he moved, those big hands with long elegant fingers gently cupping their weight, then finally, his thumbs lightly brushing her stiffened nipples.

"Ahhhh." The sound escaped from her throat. She swallowed hard, relishing the sensations he brought to her body. She burned, aching as never before, yet knew this was only the beginning.

"I used to watch you sleeping...it nearly drove me insane not being able to touch you how I wanted. He suddenly grabbed her by the waist and spun her around, pushing her down the canopied bed to the footboard. His lips spread into a slow smile; he leaned her back against the cross rail, then stretched her arms out along its length. "Grab the railing and don't let go."

The wood was hard at her back, but she paid little attention. The half-inclined position left her large breasts displayed up high. There was no hiding from him. Not moving, Simon looked at her. Savoring the moment? Allowing the anticipation to build? She couldn't tell what he was doing, just knew she was ready to scream.

Then he finally touched her, putting those strong hands on her waist, then squeezing. He worked them slowly up her ribcage until his thumbs were under her breasts. They brushed back and forth in a soft fashion, nearly touching the tips of her nipples, yet just as she sucked in a breath in expectancy, they'd retreat to start the maddening sweep again. As his palms finally covered her breasts, he leaned forward and nuzzled her neck and gave her a stinging nip.

She sighed pleasure as he squeezed her rounded flesh. "Simon, my what sharp teeth you have."

Lifting his head, he wiggled his eyebrows. "What did that Red Riding Hood person say, *'My, what a big tongue you have?'*"

"Simon, I don't recall grannie's tongue ever being mentioned." Desdemona laughed, feeling all the sorrows she'd carried for the past three years fade away. With Simon love was new, it was special. A gift. A treasure.

He joined her laugh. "Pity that." He dragged his tongue down her neck to the tip of her breast, then lifted his head. "Tongues...are...such...*useful*...things. It shall be my pleasure to enlighten you just how *useful*."

He swirled it around the crest of her breast, making her arch as his hot mouth sent desire to knife through her womb; the agony of yearning blotted out all thoughts. She could only accept the pleasure he wielded. Suddenly, he stopped drawing circles around her nipple with his tongue and took it into his mouth sucking hard, rhythmically. A deep keen rose in her throat as her body arched against him, seeking that hard body, needing more...so much more. Then suddenly, that shimmering grandeur was there. The climax slammed into her, pushing her to that shining hot pinnacle. Hardly able to hold her head up, she moaned.

His mouth released her breast as he rocked back on his haunches to watch the emotions play out across her face. "I knew it," he pronounced smugly. "I knew you'd come just like that. You're so responsive, my Dezzy."

Words and responses were beyond her. The force of the climax still rippled within her body. It wasn't enough. She wanted him inside her, wanted to be one with him. She wrapped her legs about his waist and her arms around his strong neck, nearly sitting on his rock hard thighs.

"Simon the Smug." She kissed his smiling mouth.

His hand splayed across the middle of her back, easily providing the balance to keep her upright. "Hmm...*Simon says* you didn't ask *may I* for permission to release your hold on the rail."

With a sharp thrust of his hips, he was inside her, filling her. She had to take several breaths to adjust to his hot, pulsing flesh. Then they were one. Never had she felt as if she truly belonged to another, but to this very special man, the bond was of the flesh, but also of the heart. This was a mating of two souls, fusing them into a single existence.

"Simon, may I—"

"*Simon says* Dezzy is mine," he teased. Then seriousness flooded his face. "Thank you for saving me, giving my life back again. Thank you for giving me the most wonderful gift." Then the wicked grin was back as he lowered her to the bed's plane. "*On the first day of Christmas, my true love gave to me...*"

His body slammed inside of hers and didn't let up. He gave. And kept giving.

Wrapping the towel around his waist, Simon stepped from the shower, then leaned close to Desdemona, kissing her softly. He liked kissing Dezzy. "You smell clean, my love. Like lemons. I liked that about you when I first came. You did not wear fussy a perfume that would make me sneeze." His lips moved over hers again, then his hand grabbed her hips and yanked her close. "I also like the scent of *me* on you."

Desdemona pushed at his chest, nearly growling her frustration. "Stop that, Simon. We *have* to eat. It's nearly midnight."

He chuckled. "Feed the kitty?"

"Let me adjust to you, *please*. The image you were—"

"Are..." he corrected.

With a deep sigh of coming to grips with the enormity, Desdemona nodded. "Okay, are...will be you changing...a lot? You have been with me for most of this year and you never changed into a man before."

"I couldn't. You broke the spell with your wish and the kiss. I don't change at the full moon, Dezzy. In fact, I don't have to change at all. The *Cait Sidhe* shift the first time when they turn seventeen. After that, there are only eight more changes left within our lifetime. Generally, you never change the last time, because you will remain in cat form until you die." He shrugged. "So lore says. I have never known any like me besides my mother. Legend says the *Cait Sidhe* stopped taking cat form for fear of being hunted down and burnt at the stake during *the Burning Times*."

"That's sad. The world needs more magic. Instead, it would be destroyed from fear or exploited." She reached out and touched his cheek, feeling her regret that humankind was often less than worthy of the gifts life bestows upon them. "Let's get dressed. I'll be able to concentrate better on the situation, and try to figure out what we're going to do, with you in clothes and food in my stomach." She pulled out a baggy sweater and sweat pants from the chest that would work for Simon and tossed them at his midsection. "Make do with these. I'll order some things online after we eat, since there won't be getting anywhere near the shopping mall tomorrow. I'll get second day delivery."

"Wal-Mart opens at 6 a.m." Simon slid on her black jog pants and her oversized sweater. When she just stared at him, he asked, "What bothers you, my love?"

She chuckled. "How do you know about Wal-Mart?"

"I watched the vision box. Very informative. I like cartoons best." He looked down at the clothes as if finding it strange to be wearing them. "These shall do for now, though I shall need to be concerned with finding a proper tailor. I am especially delighted I shan't have to take tongue baths any longer." He leaned close pressing her back against the bedpost, his tongue tracing a path up the side of her neck. "Delicious Dezzy. I wouldn't mind teaching you just how good I am with my tongue."

"Simon, please...we have to talk." She somehow got the words out. "This is all very well that you're back to being a human, but I have concerns...about us. You don't have papers that are needed in this world today. Birth certificates..."

"That can be gotten around, I would assume. People with money can arrange anything." He shrugged.

"Simon, while I do own this house and have a little money Gran left me, I'm not rich, not the sort of money it'd take to fix your situation."

"Not to worry. Still afraid to truly believe in magic, Dezzy? Everything will be fine." His large hands smoothed across her hips and then jerked her hard against his strong body, letting her feel his erection. "What concerns you, my love?"

"Well, there's the matter of how we will live—"

"We shall live together as man and wife—"

"Simon, hmm, you're over three hundred years old. I mean...are you immortal? If you are, then what about me? I will grow old—"

His chest vibrated with what could be a purr. "You worry too much, Dezzy. Just accept. You wanted a very special man. I don't think you can get more special than I am."

Her laughter popped out. "Ah, yeah, you're very special. Simon, could we have a conversation without you ending up trying to seduce me?"

"No. I like seducing you. I think I shall spend my life seducing you, my countess."

"Whoa, I'm not a countess—"

"You soon will be." His pale eyes suddenly softened with concern, maybe fear. "Will you not?"

She huffed her exasperation, her pain. "That's just it. Life isn't a dream, Simon. There's the question of papers. We cannot get married without them. You don't have a birth certificate, for all purposes you don't really exist; possibly you are in this country illegally. The government tends to frown on someone who materializes from thin air—

"Actually, it was very thick fog," he kidded drolly.

"Simon, fixing stuff like that will take more money than I have," she argued, fretting over a hundred imagined scenarios —all bad.

Simon shrugged. "I am not troubled. Things will sort themselves out in due time."

"Then there is the problem of us..."

"Us? I love you, and already you are coming to grips with loving me. Everything else will be fine. What I do not already know about this world from watching the box, you can teach me. Maybe we can hire that guy—Thomas Magnum to fix things," he suggested in earnest.

"Simon, not all the people on the box are real. Thomas Magnum is an old detective show—a play." She chuckled, hugging him. "Just actors—like on a stage. But that isn't the biggest obstacle," she exhaled in worry. "If you're immortal, you shall stay young and beautiful, while my hair turns grey."

"Better than it falling out," he teased, flashing an unrepentant grin.

She hit him in the chest, but not hard. There was no force behind her punch, only fear and pain. Suddenly, she broke into tears, crumbling against him and crying. His strong arms closed about her.

"Hush, my love. You fret about things that will be sorted out in the course of our lives. Money fixes things. Though the world has changed a very great deal since I last walked as Simon the Man, that is a constant, is it not? We just need to concentrate on each other, and all else matters little." When she kept crying he lifted her chin with the crook of his index finger. "Ah, Dezzy, please don't cry. It breaks my heart. Tell me why you shed tears? Is it for certificates of birth, bills and grey hairs? *Mon dieu!* I was a bloody cat for the last three centuries. If I can prevail over all the obstacles in my path to come halfway around the world to find my way to you, do you think grey hair and bills can be but a trifling?"

"To find me?" she asked in awe, yet still too scared to let go and just believe Simon was here and was hers.

"You and only you, with your loving heart could've broken my enchantment. Allow me to walk as a man once more. Without your pure love, your belief in dreams, the magic would never have happened. Do you love me, Desdemona?" he asked, serious.

So strange, they'd only known each other in this fashion for one day, yet she sensed she belonged to Simon. Desperately, she wanted everything he promised to be real. Yet, she was too petrified to risk letting herself love him the way she wanted, the way she yearned to.

"Dezzy, you fear I shall stay young while you grow old? If I remove that barrier, will you trust we can solve anything else that arises?" he asked.

She frowned. "How can you remove that? You've lived for over three centuries."

He kissed the tip of her nose. "Ah, Dezzy, I can work magic. I cannot make you as I am. Only, if you truly love me, want me, then you have the power to change me to be like you. Just press the seal on my collar."

Desdemona brushed her thumb pad across the crest. "If I do what happens?"

"The collar falls off."

"That's it, the collar falls off? How does that change you?" She ran her index finger over the seal showing a cat rampant with wings.

"Once you push that crest and the collar is released, I no longer will be able to shift. I become human, and shall age just as you do," Simon explained.

Glancing up into his beautiful eyes, Desdemona searched his face. Reaching up she traced the perfection of how he was created. To think of him changing and growing old simply so he could share a few years with her seemed too much to ask of him. She couldn't do that to Simon.

She shook her head. "I can't ask that of you. You're very, very special, it's not my right to change you into something other than you are. You gave me companionship when my life was so depressing. You showed me real magic does exist. I can't take something very rare from you like that."

"Take?" His large hand wrapped around her wrist and raised it to his neck.

When she understood what he was doing, she tried to fight him, but his strength was simply too much. She had suspicion the power in his muscles was more than the average well toned man. "No! Don't, Simon. You can't."

"I don't take...*I give.*" With that, he forced her finger against the seal. For a breath nothing happened, then he leaned close and brushed his lips softly against hers. She felt the latch release. "Love me, Dezzy. I need you more than air. Without you there is no meaning to life."

The kiss was so poignant, it made her heart ache for the growing love she felt for this very special man. Only, as she pulled back and saw the collar separate and fall from his neck, did she feel as if that heart broke. It wasn't right! He shouldn't have to change to share her life. Shaking her head in denial, she backed up a couple steps, regret lancing through her at what he'd done, humbled by the sacrifice he'd made for her.

Turning on her heels, she tossed herself onto the bed, sobbing. No one had ever loved her. Oh, her parents had when she was growing up, but they were killed in a car accident when she was nineteen. Gran had loved her. But she had never found that one true love, a special man willing to give up everything just to be with her. She figured there was something wrong with her, yearning for a love found only in faerytales, that she couldn't accept that sort of love just didn't exist...at least, not for her. What Simon had just done was a demonstration of his love. Only in doing that, he'd chosen a road that'd see him die in a short span of years, when he could've lived on.

The bed shifted under Simon's weight as he stretched out alongside her.

"Silly woman, she wishes for the man of her dreams. She gets him and she's crying because I don't come with papers of pedigree." His tone was joking, as he ran a hand down her back to soothe.

Lifting her head, she stared at the handsome man. He inclined on his side, his knee cocked, the collar held in one hand. His wavy hair spilled about his face, framing his beautiful countenance. Simon was everything she could ever wish for in a man, and she couldn't doubt the depth of his love despite its newness. He'd gifted her with proof beyond challenge.

"If you put the collar back on," she asked hopefully, swallowing the tears, "will you go back to being as you were?"

He gave her a half smile and shook his head. "No, I am mortal now." Absently, he began loosening the stones from the choker, until they dropped to the bed between them. "They are real, you know. Rubies, emeralds...the yellow ones are flawless canary diamonds."

"Real?" she asked incredulously.

He nodded, then asked with a slight tone of arrogance, "You think one of the *Cait Sidhe* would run around in paste?" Finished, he scooped them into his hand. "A small fortune in stones. I think they shall finance me getting papers. Once that is done, I shall set about to claim my lands and money from my estate that has been held in trust for my return. I should imagine my assets are rather vast. So, my love, I don't think money shall be a worry. We will be able to pay the bills, as you so put it. As I told you, everything shall be sorted out if you only trust in me. You do trust me, don't you, Dezzy?"

She nodded. "Strangely, I can't explain it. I do."

Simon leaned forward and brushed his lips against hers, almost as if they were sealing a bargain. She sighed and started to slide her hands around his neck when the phone rang.

Simon leaned back and picked up the receiver. "I've seen you do this. Here starts Simon's big adventure in the world of humans." With a confident grin he said, "Hello, Simon here."

Desdemona chuckled. "You have it upside-down, Simon."

His brows lifted in confusion; he flipped it around so the receiver was to his ear. "Sorry, about that. Hello, Simon speaking." He listened for a moment, and then held the phone away from his head to stare at the phone. Shrugging, he put it back to his ear. "Yes, yes. She is here. This is her fiancé, Simon Ravensdale. Yes, very well." To her he said, "Someone from Kensington books...about your manuscript, Dezzy."

Several hours later, Desdemona sat at her desk ordering clothes for Simon off the Internet. She'd gone overboard, getting him shirts, sweaters, jeans, socks, underwear, a robe and a good winter coat, but it'd been a while since she'd someone to shop for. Pausing from the buying giddy spree, she glanced over at Simon who was stretched out on the couch, absorbed in watching *Mr. Magoo's Christmas Carol*. Smiling, she clicked the mouse over to the DVD section at Amazon and ordered sets of *Rocky and Bullwinkle*, *The Tic* and *The Muppets Show*. *On the second day of Christmas my true love gave to me, a Tic, a Frog, a Moose and Rocky...*

"My toon addict needs some high class toons," she said to *herself.* "Enough, Dezzy. Come watch this with me." He patted the couch in front of him.

She could just imagine him snapping his tail if he still had one. "Coming." Shutting down the computer, she went to the sofa.

Simon scooted back to make room for her. "I want to lay here with the lights out, and watch cartoons and hold you, Dezzy."

Desdemona snapped out the light, plunging the room into shadows, lit now only by the warm glow from the fireplace and the twinkling of Christmas tree lights. She slid down on the sofa, resting on her back so she could watch Simon watching his cartoons. *That* was the real show!

With a grin he raised his arm, and between his thumb and index fingers was a sprig of mistletoe that he'd swiped from her dresser. He held it over her head. "I think this tradition is still valid? Yes?"

Desdemona smiled into the face of the man who loved her. The very special man she loved. "Yes, I do believe it is, though I've never been kissed under the mistletoe before."

His grin widened. "Good. You belong to me my soon-to-be author, soon-to-be-countess. Merry Christmas, my love."

He leaned forward and kissed her. A kiss that held the

promise of things to come. A kiss that was magic.

Deborah MacGillivray is the author of —
A RESTLESS KNIGHT, IN HER BED, INVASION OF
FALGANNON ISLE, and RIDING THE THUNDER.

Be sure to visit Deborah's website
www.deborahmacgillivray.co.uk

Author Information

An award-winning author for *Kensington Books -*
(*A Restless Knight*, 2006; *In Her Bed*, 2007;
One Snowy Knight, 2008;
Yield to the Knight, TBA)
and
Dorchester Publishing's Love Spell -
(*The Invasion of Falgannon Isle*, 2006;
Riding the Thunder, 2007);
and *Highland Press Publishing*, Deborah is known
for sharing her home with a long line of foundling
kitties. She loves ancient history, dancing, old
horror movies, horseback riding, walking in
the rain, web design and doing book videos. She
loves to hear from readers - you may email her at

contact@deborahmacgillivray.co.uk

website: http://deborahmacgillivray.co.uk

Be Sure to Look for Deborah's Books

Praise for *A Restless Knight*

Deborah magically takes you to stand amidst the heather & mist of another time...breathtaking beautiful, award-caliber writing." ~ Lynsay Sands, *NY Times Bestselling Author*

MacGillivray writes with a style and grace befitting noble Knights and Clans of Yore...I all but inhaled this novel... Highly recommended! ~ *Detra Fitch, Huntress Reviews*

An accomplished wordsmith MacGillivray's inspired prose will move you from laughter to tears...unforgettable characters to remain forever in your hearts. ~ *Marilyn Rondeau, Romance Designs*

This IS historical romance. If any among us need a poster child for the genre. A RESTLESS KNIGHT is IT! ~ Dawn Thompson, *award-winning author of Lord of the Deep; The Ravening*

Praise for *In Her Bed*

Mccgillivray continuing the story she began in *A Reckless Knight* with passion and humor; presents a sexy captive/ captor romance that hearkens back to the classic themes of the genre. It's so well done. ~ *Romantic Times, a K.I.S.S Award for August 2007*

IN HER BED to my mind is nothing short of brilliant for this fast rising star of historical romance. ~ *Marilyn Rondeau, Paranormal Romance Reviews*

In Her Bed has risen to the top of my favorite historical novels... ~ *Tammie King, Night Owl Reviews*

Praise for *The Invasion of Falgannon Isle*

What makes MacGillivray's romance so special are the eccentric characters, right down to the cat, and Desmond and B.A.'s growing relationship. ~ *Maria Hatton, Booklist*

"Mesmerizing and magical. You won't want to leave..." ~ *Nationally Bestselling Author, Tori Carrington*

The characters' emotions are what make this book a brilliant read...will delight and captivate from beginning to end. ~ *Charissa, Coffee Time Romance*

Praise for **Riding the Thunder**

With "Riding the Thunder," Deborah Macgillivray does what she does best, putting well-developed characters into extraordinary situations and letting their actions speak for themselves. This one was a page-turner that was hard to put down. ~ *Amy Wolff Sorter, author of Soul Obsession*

MacGillivray's storylines do more than give you an escape from reality, they allow you to dream of a world where happily-ever-afters are possible and love conquers all. Beautifully done! ~ *Chrissy Dionne, Romance Junkies*

This second story about the Mershan brothers is as interesting, fast moving, suspenseful and fun as the first one. ~ *Susan Mobley, Romantic Times*

Also Available from Highland Press

Leanne Burroughs
Highland Wishes
Leanne Burroughs
Her Highland Rogue
Jannine Corti Petska
Rebel Heart
Cynthia Owens
In Sunshine or In Shadow
Isabel Mere
Almost Taken
Ashley Kath-Bilsky
The Sense of Honor
R.R. Smythe
Into the Woods
(A Young Adult Fantasy)
Phyllis Campbell
Pretend I'm Yours
Jacquie Rogers
Faery Special Romances
(A Young Adult Romance)
Katherine Deauxville
The Crystal Heart
Rebecca Andrews
The Millennium Phrase Book
Chris Holmes
Blood on the Tartan
Jean Harrington
The Barefoot Queen

Holiday Romance Anthology
Christmas Wishes
Holiday Romance Anthology
Holiday in the Heart
Romance Anthology
No Law Against Love
Romance Anthology
Blue Moon Magic
Romance Anthology
Blue Moon Enchantment
Romance Anthology
Recipe for Love

Upcoming

Holiday Romance Anthology
Romance Upon A Midnight Clear
Holiday Romance Anthology
Love Under the Mistletoe
Anne Kimberly
Dark Well of Decision
John Nieman & Karen Laurence
The Amazing Rabbitini
(Children's Illustrated)
Isabel Mere
Almost Guilty
Chai/Ivey/Porter/Young
Mail Order Brides
Candace Gold
A Heated Romance
Romance Anthology
No Law Against Love 2

Eric Fullilove .
The Zero Day Event
Jannine Corti Petska
The Lily and the Falcon
Romance Anthology
The Way to a Man's Heart
Romance Anthology
Love on a Harley
*MacGillivray/Burroughs/Bowen/
Ahlers/Houseman*
Dance en L'Aire
Lance Martin
The Little Hermit
(Children's Illustrated)
Brynn Chapman
Bride of Blackbeard
Sorter/MacGillivray/Burroughs
Faith, Hope and Redemption
Anne Holman
The Master of Strathgian
Romance Anthology
Second Time Around
Jannine Corti Petska
Surrender to Honor
Romance Anthology
Love and Glory
Sandra Cox
Sundial
Ginger Simpson
Sparta Rose
Freddie Currie
Changing Wind
Molly Zenk
Chasing Byron

Cleora Comer
Just DeEtta
Don Brookes
With Silence and Tears
Linda Bilodeau
The Wine Seekers
Jeanmarie Hamilton
Seduction
Diane Davis White
Moon of Falling Leaves
Katherine Shaw
Love Thy Neighbor
Jo Webnar
Saving Tampa
Jean Harrington
In the Lion's Mouth
Inspirational Romance Anthology
The Miracle of Love
Katherine Deauxville
The Amethyst Crown
Katherine Deauxville
Enraptured
Katherine Deauxville
Eyes of Love

Check our website frequently for future
Highland Press releases.

www.highlandpress.org

Cover by DeborahAnne MacGillivray

Printed in the United States
95675LV00001B/125/A

9 780978 713904